RELENTLESS

AN OPTION ZERO NOVEL

CHRISTY REECE

Relentless
An Option Zero Novel
Published by Christy Reece
Cover Art by Kelly A. Martin of KAM Design
Copyright 2020 by Christy Reece
ISBN: 978-1-7337257-5-0

To obtain permission to excerpt portions of the text, please contact the author at *Christy@christyreece.com*.

RELENTLESS

They met in darkness. Each one going through their own personal hell, they gave each other hope and a reason to live. Their connection was real and true, but fate had a different plan.

OZ operative Liam Stryker is known for his bravery, his wit, and his ability to find an escape when there's no way out. He's also a man on a mission. He needs to find *her*. She's out there somewhere. He refuses to believe she's gone. Someday, somehow, he will find the woman he's never seen but loves with all his heart. And if it's the last thing he does, he'll find the people responsible for causing her pain.

Aubrey Starr once had a plan for her future, but when her life is derailed and upended, she's motivated to create a new one. As an award-winning documentary filmmaker, she's known for digging deep to uncover and expose evil. Few know about the past that drives her or the man who inspires her. She never knew his real name, never got to see his face, but without him, she wouldn't have survived. Even though she doubts that he's still alive, she dreams that one day she'll see him.

Evil takes many avenues and insinuates itself into every aspect of life, causing havoc and pain. Some are born to fight against it with every fiber of their being. Others are thrown into its path and have no choice but to stand up to it or die. Liam and Aubrey have been on parallel paths for years. When their paths finally converge, it's as if life has given them another chance, and everything has fallen into place.

But there are enemies out there who will do everything they can to make sure Liam and Aubrey never find the happiness they seek. When events take a tragic turn, they're faced with the knowledge that fate has thrown them a new, cruel twist.

And this time, there's no way out.

"The purpose of life is a life of purpose." –Robert Byrne

CHAPTER ONE

Twelve Years Ago
Damascus, Syria

L iam Stryker winced at the sound of fists slamming into flesh. It happened again, then again. Jaw rigid with fury, teeth clinched, Liam stayed quiet. He'd learned that shouting, saying anything at all, only spurred the bastards on. He listened in silence, suffering along with his friend. And knowing they would be coming for him next.

Dying was easy. It was living that Liam was struggling with. What made a man give up? How did he decide he'd just had enough? A part of him wanted to know, another part thought it'd be best not to have an answer. That might make it easy…might make their job more fun. They wanted him to give up, to reveal all his secrets and then just die. Damned if he'd make it easy for them.

A cell door opened and then clanged shut. The interrogation was over for the time being. A groan came from Xavier, and the agony in the sound sent a new surge of rage gushing through Liam's bloodstream. Even though he would be next up, he was glad Xavier's beating was over. Liam had suffered with every blow, every grunt, and every curse. That was part of their torture, too. Their captors hoped that hearing each other's pain took a little more of their strength each time. Little did they know that such things only made them more determined to live. These people would pay…they would pay with everything.

"Hey, you okay?"

There was no answer and Liam closed his eyes in fear. Had they finally defeated one of the strongest men he knew? Xavier had been shot when they'd been taken. Liam had been conscious, but his hands had been tied and a bag had covered his head. He hadn't been able to see the injury for himself. Xavier had told him it wasn't bad, only a flesh wound, but how long before infection set in? How long had they been here? Felt like a year, but he figured it hadn't been more than a week. Still, who the hell knew when your every waking hour was spent in agony?

"Hey? You hear me over there? Hang in there. We're going to get out of here."

"That you?"

Relief flooded Liam. The bastards hadn't won yet. "Yeah. Still here. How you doing?"

"Been better." He snorted out a dry, very Xavier-like chuckle. "Been worse, too."

"You about ready to get out of this place?"

"Yeah, I am."

"Good. Been thinking…"

And with that, Liam began to tap on the wall. He'd devised the secret code when he'd first started deep-cover missions. He and Xavier had communicated with it on numerous ops. Liam hadn't used it in a while, but Xavier would have no trouble following. Communicating wasn't the problem. The plan was. Even as he tapped, a part of Liam knew it would likely get them killed. But if they didn't try, they wouldn't survive anyway. It was as simple as that.

"We can do that," Xavier tapped. "I can—"

Liam sat up, his ears straining. "Shh. Hold that thought. Somebody's coming."

Laughter, followed by curses, came closer and closer. What had gotten the monsters riled up this time? Were they already coming back for him?

"Get off me!"

No. Apparently they had a new prisoner to torture. Another American, from the sound of his accent. An extremely pissed one. Which was good. Anger kept hopelessness at bay.

The next few moments were painful as Liam listened to their questions and the brutal aftermath when the man refused to answer with anything other than curses.

Having been on the receiving end of their interrogation tactics more than once, Liam knew what the guy was feeling. Anger, pain, and a pit-deep feeling that the agony would never end.

For what seemed like an hour or more, they worked the guy over. When they finally got tired of not getting any answers, they issued a few guttural warnings that the next time they wouldn't be so easy on him. The cell door clanged shut, and the assholes stomped away.

Liam waited a couple of minutes and then called out, "Hey, you still with us?"

When there was no answer, Liam figured they'd gone too far. "Guess they got the worst of the poor bastard," he said to Xavier.

Before Xavier could respond, a deep voice growled, "Don't count this poor bastard out yet."

Relieved, Liam said, "How bad are you hurt?"

"Been better...been worse."

Liam smiled at the similar answer Xavier had given earlier.

"What's your name, man?"

"How do I know you're not a plant to get something out of me?"

Reasonable question, considering the circumstances.

"You don't."

"Then I guess I'll remain nameless."

A chuckle came from Xavier's cell. "You'll have to forgive him. He's only had me to talk to for weeks."

"You two came in together?"

"Something like that."

"Who are these bozos?" the stranger asked.

"Not sure yet," Xavier said. "They're not much on sharing."

"I've heard English, French, Arabic, and German," Liam added.

"Nice to know I was sold to such a diverse group."

"You were sold?"

"That's my guess. I was in Colombia, got attacked by some kind of cartel. Things got bloody and bad. Next time I woke up, my surroundings looked nothing like Colombia."

"Hate to be the one to break the news to you, man, but you're in Syria," Liam said.

"Ah, hell."

There was a wealth of meaning in that statement. One that Liam could identify with. There were so many factions and groups here, it was hard to know who was responsible and what they wanted.

Not that he and Xavier didn't know what these goons wanted from them. That had been made clear the first day they arrived. And they would die before they gave it up.

"How long you two been here?" the newcomer asked.

"Hard to say," Liam said. "What do you think, Bear?"

"Bear?" the man said.

"Since we're not saying names, I thought we'd just give each other nicknames. The guy in the other cell is Bear. I'm—"

"Let me guess. Lion?"

"That'll work. You can be Tiger."

"So tell me, Bear, does Lion always talk incessantly, or do I just bring it out in him?"

For the first time in days, both Xavier and Liam laughed. It felt good, real good. Liam was liking this guy more and more.

"Yep. My mama used to tell me that I—" Liam cut off when heavy footsteps headed their way. The footsteps stopped at his cell. His body tense, he waited. He knew what was coming.

The cell door opened, and Liam didn't even bother to look. He refused to give them even that much respect.

Grabbing him under his armpits, they picked him up and carried him toward the door. They were taking him away? That had never happened. They'd always interrogated him inside his cell. What was going on?

"Hey! Where're you taking me?"

Refusing to go without a fight, Liam put all his energy into kicking and throwing punches. Using his bound hands, he swung with all his might, making contact with a hard jaw. He had less than a second to feel triumph before a fist slammed into his head, and he went limp. The last thing he heard was Xavier shouting.

CHAPTER TWO

A strange, unfamiliar noise jogged him awake. Blinking open heavy, swollen eyes, he looked blearily around. This wasn't his regular cell. He'd figured after the questions and the subsequent beating, they would've returned him to his old one. This one was cleaner, in better condition. Not only was there a toilet, as opposed to a bucket, he was lying on a narrow cot, and a small, high window blew a cold breeze through the openings in the bars. Liam inhaled the first fresh air he'd felt in days. Icy air went through him, waking him further. The beating hadn't been as bad this time. Just a few good punches, three or four kicks, and then a solid head thunk. So what was the point of moving him here?

In the midst of wondering, he heard a sound again. Someone was in the cell next to him. Before he could speak, a harsh cough followed by a moan of misery had him on alert. The moan had been distinctly female.

Oh hell, they'd taken a woman hostage?

"Hello?" he said.

Like a faucet being switched off, the noise ended abruptly.

"Sorry," he said, "didn't mean to scare you."

"Hello?" The voice was tentative, most definitely female, and painfully hoarse. From the hacking cough he'd heard earlier, he imagined she'd been ill for a while.

"Are you okay?" Stupid question. Of course she wasn't okay, but for the first time in years, he was stumped for the right words.

"No." Another harsh cough, and then she continued, "Not really."

"How long have you been here?"

"I don't know. A few days...maybe a week?"

"Have they given you any medical treatment?"

"No." She sighed and then coughed again. "I don't think making me well is in their plan."

"You're American?"

"Yes."

"You were abducted?"

"Yes. One minute I was in the market looking at a scarf, and the next minute I had a hood over my head, and I was in some kind of vehicle."

"Have they hurt you?"

There was a long pause, much too long for the answer to be favorable. "Yes," she finally said softly.

There was no need for her to elaborate. And since she wasn't dead, they weren't through with her yet. The chances of her getting out of this hellhole without being hurt again, or killed, were almost zero.

"Were you with friends, relatives?"

"No. I came to Paris to do some research for—"

"Paris?"

"Yes."

Telling her that she was no longer in Paris without freaking her out was probably not going to happen. But she deserved to know.

7

"You're not in Paris. You're in Syria."

There was a long pause and then the shocked words, "That's not possible."

"I wish it wasn't, but it is."

"But how…why?"

"Were you knocked out?"

"Yes…wait…no. Not knocked out. I think maybe they gave me an injection of something. My brain was all fuzzy for a while."

Being drugged would account for the confusion. What was less apparent was why she'd been taken in the first place. He knew almost nothing about their captors, but kidnapping a woman in Paris and bringing her here to brutalize her seemed like an awful lot of trouble. There had to be something they wanted from her.

"You were in Paris alone?"

"Yes. My cousin was supposed to come, too, but she got sick at the last minute. I decided to come alone. I'm up for a part in a play. My character is French. I can read and understand French, but I can't speak it as well as I need to. I thought a few days in Paris would help."

"You're an actress?"

"Yes…well, that and a college student."

Liam's heart hurt for her. She was young and naïve…an innocent. Even if she survived and returned home, that innocence would be gone.

"You have any family that would pay your ransom?"

"You think that's why they took me? To ransom me?"

That would be a best-case scenario for her. And the one that made the most sense. Didn't mean they wouldn't abuse her while they had her, but if someone was willing to pay for her release, there was a chance she could survive.

Ransom wasn't the reason for his and Xavier's abductions. Even if it had been, they were SOL. No one was going to pay a ransom for them. Being on a black ops mission didn't always mean you were on your own, but in this case it most definitely did. Five people had known about their op. The question of which one of those five had betrayed them would have to be answered after they got out of here. For now, he had enough on his plate.

Their captors apparently had prisoners here for a variety of reasons. What was this place? Some kind of eclectic prison clearinghouse?

"Are you still there?"

Liam shook his head to clear it. "Yeah…sorry. What questions have they asked you?"

"None, really. And they haven't answered any of mine. My parents aren't wealthy…I'm not wealthy. I don't know why they would think I am." She paused and then added, "Do you…are you here for ransom, too?"

For the first time, it occurred to him that she could be a plant. The delay in wondering about such a thing showed just how screwed up his head was. She could be a sister or wife to one of these assholes. Soften him up, charm him, and make him spill his secrets.

That wouldn't happen. He knew how to keep secrets. But if she was legit, then he needed to figure out a way to help her.

"Do you think that's why the other women are here, too? They're going to ransom them?"

His heart sank. "Other women?"

"Yes. I was thrown in with them for a while, but when I couldn't stop coughing, I think they decided I might be contagious. That's when they put me in here by myself."

It was clearer and much more dire than he'd feared. If they had other women here, ransoming her was not the likely reason she'd been taken. Things had just gotten a lot

9

more serious and complicated. Human trafficking was rampant everywhere.

"Did you talk with any of the other women?"

"No. Not really. I was kind of out of it, but I saw them… heard them."

"How many?"

"I don't know. Maybe a half dozen or so."

This changed things. He was going to have to scrap the escape plan he'd come up with before. No way in hell was he leaving this woman, or any of the others, behind.

She coughed again, the sound torturous. She wasn't going to last long without medical care.

In a raspy voice, she asked tentatively, "Do you…can you tell me your name?"

He delayed in answering and her next words told him she understood immediately. "I'm sorry…you don't know me. I could be an enemy for all you know. I'm not, but you don't know that."

If she was a plant, she was a good one because Liam suddenly wanted to tell her everything. If that wasn't a dangerous thought, he didn't know what was.

Before he could say anything, she hurriedly added, "Could you just talk to me? Even if it's not the truth, it would help so much to know that I'm not alone."

That he could do. His mother often said that Liam had started talking at three months old and hadn't stopped since.

"My name is Lion."

"Oh…okay." He thought he heard a smile in her voice as she said, "Then you can call me…" She paused for a moment and then sighed. "I think my creativity is on hiatus. The only thing I can come up with is Cat."

"Nothing wrong with Cat."

"Okay, Cat it is. So, Lion, tell me something about yourself."

He hesitated again, wanting the impossible. He wished they were just two people who'd met under very different circumstances, found each other interesting, and wanted to spend time together.

"Remember," she said softly, "it doesn't have to be true."

Liam shook his head at his stupid thoughts. The way things were going, neither of them would get out of here alive. Wishing that they could really get to know each other was an idiotic hope.

"I grew up on Mars."

"I...what?"

He grinned at the surprise in her voice. "Yep. Just came down here last week for a look-see, and these bastards grabbed me faster than we Martians can say jackrabbit."

She giggled and Liam thought it was the sweetest sound he'd ever heard. A harsh cough followed, and he winced at how painful it sounded.

Finally recovering, she asked hoarsely, "Why were you visiting Earth?"

"Things have been boring on Mars lately."

"Tell me about Mars. What does it look like? Do you have family there?"

Settling into a dirty corner, Liam stretched out his long legs and began to talk. Weaving a story of his childhood on Mars, he created scenarios of daring adventures on the Red Planet. He talked about his family, his sisters, nieces and nephews. He even told her about his orange cat named Toby. The wilder and sillier he got, the happier she seemed.

His dad had been the storyteller in the family. Family story hour right before bedtime was one of Liam's favorite memories. He and his sisters would sit wide-eyed while Hugh Stryker entertained them. The more unbelievable the tale, the more they liked it.

After his dad passed, years went by without their unique

family tradition. When Robin, his oldest sister, had her first child, Liam took it upon himself to carry on for his dad. In the years since, he had regaled his many nieces and nephews with all sorts of wild stories. Some he made up, but many of them were the ones his dad had told.

He missed those days. Wasn't even sure he'd ever see his family again.

"Lion, why did you stop?"

"Sorry, got stuck in the memories. You want to try it?"

"You mean I should tell you a story?"

"Yeah. Unless your throat's too sore."

"No. It doesn't hurt that much."

"Good. Tell me a story. And remember, it doesn't have to be real."

"All right…let's see. I grew up in Caldoria."

"And where is that?"

"It's a magical, invisible kingdom. Only people with names that start with C can live there or even see it."

"What happens in the magical, invisible kingdom of Caldoria?"

She started slowly, haltingly, but finally got into the story of how an unassuming little Caldorian like herself became the ruler of the entire kingdom. It was sweet, funny, and touching.

When she trailed off, he knew she'd likely worn herself out. Seconds later, he heard shallow breaths and figured she'd fallen asleep. That was good. She needed all the rest she could get.

He pushed to his feet and walked around the small area, testing his strength and injuries. Not too bad. Nothing broken. Just bruises and a few cuts. Even though he hadn't had a decent meal in a while, he was young, healthy, and strong. His stamina would hold for a while.

He'd been right about the cell. It was newer and in better

condition than the other one. Something else he noticed was the camera. There had been an obvious microphone in his other cell, but this one had both a mic and a camera in the corner. They could see and hear everything.

The reason they'd brought him to this one was easy to figure out. At that realization, his gut twisted. They wanted him to make a connection with Cat. Once he had, they would use her to make him talk. There was no other reason to bring them together. And he'd fallen right in with their plan.

He had taken an oath to protect and defend his country. He would do that to his last breath. The secrets he held were substantial and deadly serious. A lot of people would die if he spilled his guts. Weighing that against what would happen to Cat wasn't easy, but he knew one irrefutable truth. No matter if he spilled his secrets—told every single thing he knew—Cat would not be spared. Yeah, they'd use her to get to him, but once they were through with her, then what? There was another reason she'd been grabbed from a Paris marketplace and brought here to Syria. The fact that there were other women here, too, was a good indicator of what would happen once they'd finished with her.

He was going to have to do some quick thinking if he and Cat were going to survive what lay ahead for them.

CHAPTER THREE

The sound of harsh coughing jerked Liam awake. Cat's breathing sounded more labored than it had earlier. If she didn't get medical care soon, she wasn't going to survive. The infection had set up in her lungs and sounded like severe bronchitis. If left untreated, she'd develop pneumonia, if she hadn't already.

"Cat?"

"Lion?" She hacked another cough and then added, "Are you awake?"

"Yeah, I'm awake. How you doing?"

"Okay, I guess."

He didn't believe it for a moment. She sounded awful, but one of the many things he'd learned in their long conversations with each other—Cat was not a complainer.

"You get any sleep?"

"A little. It's awfully quiet. I'm used to city noises."

"Caldoria has big cities?"

"Cal...?" She gave a little laugh and then coughed again. After several seconds of coughing, she finally caught her breath and answered, "Yes, we have several large cities."

"Bet it gets confusing to keep naming children with names that start with a C."

"It does. In fact, I have decided to make a change. Upon a royal decree, we are going to allow another letter into our kingdom."

"Oh really. What is it?"

"L."

Liam grinned. "Then I'll just have to come for a visit."

"When we get out of here, I'll send you an official invitation." She paused for a second and then added, all humor gone, "Will we get out of here?"

"Yes, we will. I promise you, Cat."

"How can you be sure?"

"Because we're still alive. If they'd wanted us dead, they would have killed us already."

"I'm not sure that's much of a comfort."

Probably not, but the fairy tales could last only so long. One eventually had to face the harsh reality of life. And this was about as harsh as it could get.

"Can I ask you something...something personal?"

"You can ask me anything, Cat."

"Okay, thanks. Umm. What do you look like?"

The question didn't surprise him. With only brief interruptions from their jailers for their one measly meal, they'd talked continuously. Cold canned beans and stale bread could take you only so far. Talking had staved off the hunger pangs as well as the loneliness.

During that time, they'd shared more than a few personal stories. Nothing that could be used against them, but he and Cat were beginning to know each other very well. The more he learned, the more he wanted to know. She was fascinating and sweet, wise but still so very innocent. And he'd been wondering about her, too. Was she as pretty as she sounded?

"You don't have to tell me if you don't want to."

"I don't mind. Let's see. I'm six-foot-three, weigh around two-ten or so. I've got brown hair. Brown eyes."

"Dark brown or light brown hair?"

"Umm. Dark."

"Short or long?"

"Longish…for a guy."

"And your eyes? Light brown, dark?"

"Kind of medium dark."

"Pointed, round, or square jaw?"

"Not pointed or round, so I guess kind of square."

Each question became more and more specific. He'd never had to describe himself. If anyone asked, he'd probably just say he was average looking. Though a few former girlfriends had told him that he was handsome, it wasn't something he gave a lot of thought to. He was who he was.

For Cat, though, he did his best to give her an image she could carry in her head. If picturing him helped her deal with what was happening, then he'd give her whatever detail she needed.

Once he finished answering her last question, she was silent for several long seconds. He could imagine her sitting in her own corner, her eyes closed as she created an image in her mind.

When she spoke at last, there was a smile in her voice. "You sound very handsome."

"I do?"

"Yes."

"Okay…well, good." Liam didn't know why, but he could feel himself blushing. "Now it's your turn. Describe yourself."

"Okay. Let's see… Blond hair—with some gold and light brown tones. Not exactly curly…kind of wavy. It just touches my shoulders. I have slightly high cheekbones, my chin's a little pointed. I'm about five-five, and if you think I'm going to tell you my weight, think again."

"Not a problem. My sisters are—" Liam snapped his mouth shut. What the hell was he doing?

As if he hadn't just revealed a secret, she continued, "I have gray eyes, but they sometimes turn a light blue, depending on what I'm wearing. My skin is kind of pale…I burn easily in the sun."

As she continued to describe herself, Liam closed his eyes. She was very good at description, and in that moment there was nothing he wanted more than to see her. She sounded as pretty as he'd thought she would be.

"Lion?"

"Yeah?"

"They'll try to use us against each other, won't they?"

She was wise beyond her years. These bastards weren't leaving them alone out of the kindness of their hearts, or because they'd forgotten about them. They were allowing them to create a connection. When their captors felt it was strong enough, they would strike.

"Yeah, they will."

"I don't have any secrets to tell them."

No, but he did.

He wanted to tell her she would be fine. That they wouldn't hurt her again. But the fairy tales were over. The time to face the music was coming.

"Listen, Cat. You're right, they will try to use us against each other. And when they do, I'll do everything I can to keep you safe."

"But what can you do?"

"You let me worry about that. I just want you to fight as hard as you can and know that we'll figure a way out of this for you. Okay?"

"But what about you? How are you going to get out?"

"Don't you worry about me. Can you come closer?"

"Yes."

He heard some soft shuffling and knew she'd scooted as close to his side of the wall as she could get.

"Put your ear against the wall."

"Okay. I'm here." She sounded both breathless and nervous.

"Here's what I want you to do."

He kept his voice low. They might be able to pick up a word here or there, but the mic shouldn't be strong enough to detect every word. The things he shared were a blend of moves he'd told his sisters to help them protect themselves and some other methods he'd learned in the military.

"But what…"

"Hold on. There's more. If they ask what I've told you, tell them I haven't told you anything yet, but you're sure you can get what they want from me."

"I don't understand," she whispered.

"I know you don't, but tell them you know you can make me talk. Tell them you've created a bond with me and to give you a chance to find out what they want to know."

"To buy us some time."

She was catching on.

"Yes."

"Will they believe me?"

"You're an actress. You can make people believe anything you want. Hey," he added with a smile in his voice, "you've got a part of me believing there really is a Caldoria."

She didn't laugh as he had hoped she would. Instead, she said something that broke his heart. "I'm scared, Lion."

"I know you are, but there's no shame in being afraid. Fear gives you the edge you need to survive. And you will survive this. I promise you."

"How can you be so sure of that?"

"Because you're strong, Cat. Stronger than you give yourself credit for."

"You don't know me."

"Yes, I do. When people tell stories, they give a little of themselves in each one. I've been sitting here day and night learning the real you. You're an incredibly brave and strong woman. You've got a light inside you that no one can extinguish. You were meant for greater things than this, Cat. You were created for a purpose, and it isn't to die in a cold, filthy prison in Syria. You've got a long life ahead of you. Trust me on this."

"You're not afraid?"

Yeah, he was, but mostly for her. He'd faced death more times than he could count. And he'd known fear lots of times, but letting it stop him from doing his job had never been an option.

"Just make sure you tell them that you can get whatever information they want from me by letting you come back here."

"Okay…I can do that." She took a breath and said with more resolve, "I can do that."

"Yes, you can…and you will."

"Do you think we'll ever meet…I mean see each other face-to-face?"

"I hope so…I'd like that."

"Me, too."

"How about we make a date?"

"When and where?"

"I'll choose the time, you choose the place. How about two months from today?"

"What's today?"

Using his best guess, he said, "February 27, I think."

"So April 27? That's a long while away."

"I have some things I need to take care of after I get out of here."

She didn't ask any questions, but her silence was full of them.

"Okay, I set the date. Now, where do you want to meet?"

He heard a long, shaky breath and then, "I'll be in the middle of the play. Can we meet in New York?"

Her comment lifted his heart. Not only was she determined to get out of here, she had decided she would win the role.

"Not a problem." His voice held a smile as he added, "Top of the Empire State Building? Even though Valentine's Day will be long past."

She laughed softly. "You know that movie?"

With three sisters, he'd been schooled on romantic movies at an early age. That had been one of their favorites.

"Oh yeah, I know it."

"Let's do something a little less traditional, then."

"Just name the place."

"New York Public Library." There was a smile in her voice when she added, "In front of the lions."

"Which lion? Patience or Fortitude?"

"You choose."

"Definitely Fortitude."

"Fortitude it is, then.

"What time?"

"One o'clock."

"Might be crowded. How will we recognize each other?"

"I'll be wearing a navy blue dress with white and yellow daisies. And you…how will I know it's you?"

"What's your favorite flower?"

"Pink roses."

"I'll be carrying a bouquet of pink roses."

She breathed out a little laugh. "You've got yourself a date."

Doors creaked, heavy footsteps came closer. It wasn't

time for their one measly meal, which meant their time was up. What happened next was all that mattered.

"Remember what I said, Cat," Liam whispered. "Stay strong. You are an amazing person and can survive anything these bastards throw at you. You can do this."

Her cell door squealed as it opened. Liam could picture it in his mind. Soulless men with grim faces and conscienceless hearts stomped inside her cell.

"What are you doing?"

Liam knew Cat had meant the words to sound demanding and angry, but the shaking in her voice ripped out his heart. She was terrified but trying her best to sound brave.

"Leave her alone, asshole," Liam growled. "It's me you want, not her. She doesn't know anything."

"Oh, I beg to differ. She knows much more than you give her credit for."

What did that mean? And who was this new guy? He had a British accent, sounded older than the other men, and was most definitely the one in charge.

"I'll tell you whatever you want," Liam said. "Just leave her alone."

"You mean you'll tell me whatever you want me to hear. Believe me, when we're through with your little Cat, you'll tell me everything down to your shoe size."

"Lion!" Cat screamed.

"I'm here, Cat. Fight them. Fight them for all you're worth."

Unable to do anything else, Liam gripped the bars of his cell door and tried to angle his head so he could see what was happening. They were out of his line of vision. All he could do was listen to Cat's terror-filled voice pleading with them to leave her alone.

Liam yelled obscenities, expletives, insults—every

derogatory word he knew and some he just made up. Every word he screamed was from his heart. And he would keep his promise, every one of them would pay for what they were about to put her through.

Cat screamed and fought. Liam heard every gasp, every cry. They didn't say anything, but he had a clear image in his mind of the horror she was experiencing. The screams grew fainter and fainter as they carried her out the door.

The screams cut off abruptly, leaving him with only a stark silence and the gut-sick knowledge that he was responsible for what Cat was going through. He shouldn't have talked to her, shouldn't have tried to comfort her. They'd seen that, and now Cat was paying the price.

The quiet, dead and still, permeated his surroundings. Gripping the bars of his cell, Liam felt tears fill his eyes. He hadn't cried in a long time. It'd been longer since he'd prayed. He did both now.

How long he stood there he would never know. Every nightmare, every ounce of fear he'd ever felt were wrapped up in what Cat was enduring. His heart ripped to shreds, and his soul screamed at the cruel injustice for the innocent and the wickedness of monsters.

When he heard the doors creak open again, he braced himself for the worst. Footsteps sounded, belonging to only one person—a heavy, booted male.

Liam gripped the steel bars, waiting and dreading. Was Cat being carried back to her cell? Was she unconscious? Was she dead?

The door to the cell next to his opened, and someone entered. Something dropped on the ground. Liam heard a low curse, but the sound was so soft it was indistinguishable, unrecognizable.

"Where is she, asshole?" Liam growled.

No answer. Just some heavy breathing as if someone was

frustrated and then he heard a grunt of satisfaction, a couple of clicks. Sounds filled the air, loud and full of anguish.

"No, please don't do this. Please don't!"

Cat's voice, full of fear, of tears, soared around him. They had recorded her assault…brought it in to torture him.

Liam shouted over Cat's screams, "Where is she? Dammit, what have you done to her?"

"Your little Cat isn't holding up too well."

The Brit again.

"What have you—"

"We're not through with her yet, but I wanted to bring you her greatest hits. Enjoy them."

The volume increased, and Cat's screams and pleas for mercy echoed through the hollow prison. She screamed his name multiple times, pleading for his help. Help he could not give her.

This was his punishment for not talking, his incentive to finally give them what they wanted.

Dropping to his knees, Liam crouched in a corner and, having no choice, listened to Cat being tortured. The recording lasted only a couple of minutes and then repeated, again and again.

At first he could concentrate only on Cat's anguish, pain, and obvious fear. After a while, Liam forced himself to listen to other things. Three distinct voices—one with a French accent, one German, and the British one—engraved themselves into his mind. And as he listened, as he died a little inside with every scream and cry that Cat uttered, he swore vengeance on the men who tortured her. Someway, somehow, he would get out of here, and he would make each of them pay. This he swore. They would pay with their lives.

CHAPTER FOUR

Liam lay facedown on his cot. It had been three days since they'd taken Cat away. Three days of hell. Seventy-two hours of torture. Four thousand, three hundred and twenty agonizing minutes of not knowing if she was still alive. Still being brutalized, beaten.

There had been times in his life when he'd felt helpless, even hopeless. Nothing compared to this.

The recording of her assault had played for two days straight. Finally, in the middle of the second night, the batteries had gone dead. Didn't matter. The words, the pain, the terror and degradation in her voice were ingrained in his brain, etched in his soul. He would never forget them for as long as he lived.

Despite his shouts and demands to talk to someone, no one had spoken to him. In silence, his daily meal was slid into his cell. He'd like to tell them to shove it up their asses, but starving to death would not save Cat. He had to be strong enough to rescue her. For that to take place, he had to get out of here.

He had a plan. Knew it likely wouldn't work, but waiting

for the perfect opportunity was not going to happen. He had to make it happen. If he died, then he'd damn well die fighting for something he believed in. Rotting in a cell was not the way he intended to go out of this life.

Next time his meal was delivered, he would strike. One way or the other, he would not be spending another night in this hellhole.

He closed his eyes, envisioning how he would escape, find Cat, and save her. There was no other option.

The ground shook violently, bringing him upright from his cot. What the… Earthquake? No. That had been no rumble, but a loud blast of sound. Two more blasts followed. Liam sprang to his feet, ready to go. Didn't matter if this was friend or foe, he was damn well going to get out of this shithole and find Cat.

Was she still alive? Had they killed her? Was that the reason they hadn't tried to question him again? What about Xavier? Was he still alive?

He didn't have answers to any of his questions, but he was going to get out of here and find out.

Another blast sounded, this one even closer. Then the unmistakable noise of submachine guns. Whoever was here had come armed to win.

A door squealed open and Liam crouched in a corner. When the cell opened, he'd be ready to pounce

"Stryker!"

Xavier Quinn's gruff shout was one of the best sounds he'd ever heard. Springing to his feet, Liam leaped to the cell door and yelled, "In here!"

Seconds later, Xavier appeared at his cell, AK-47 in one hand, a set of keys in the other. Dirty, bloodied, and disheveled, his friend was a sight for sore eyes.

"You okay?" Xavier asked.

"I am now. Who's here?"

"Me and a couple of friends."

As Xavier worked on getting his cell opened, Liam peered out and saw one of the men he'd been hoping to see since this shitstorm had started—Nicholas Hawthorne—and he was armed to the teeth. Liam wasn't surprised. The man had been in charge of this op and would make it his personal responsibility to oversee the rescue.

"Good to see you, Hawke."

"Back at you, Stryker."

The lock finally gave way and the door squeaked open. Liam took his first step outside his cell and felt a freedom like no other.

"We've got a chopper waiting."

Before Liam could speak, a voice shouted from the hallway, "Let's haul ass. These pricks could come back anytime."

"We can't go yet," Liam said. "There's someone else here."

Xavier shook his head. "If you're talking about the guy we met that you nicknamed Tiger, he's already on the chopper."

"No, there's a woman. She was in the cell next to mine. They took her away a few days ago. I've got to find her."

"Sorry, man," Xavier said. "There's no one else here. We've been everywhere."

No, he couldn't accept that. Liam took a step forward. "She's got to be here."

A tall, light-haired man walked up behind Xavier. "We've checked all the rooms and cells. Only people we've seen were the three guys we took out when we first arrived."

Refusing to believe Cat was gone, Liam accepted the nine millimeter Xavier held out to him and took off. "I've got to find her."

Ignoring the cursing of the men, Liam ran through the dark, dingy hallways, peering into each cell he passed. All were empty. Some showed signs that they'd been occupied recently. Discarded clothing, the stench of human waste, blood, rotting food, but there were no people.

"Cat!" he shouted. An increasing panic seized him. Where was she? What had they done to her?

The small prison was a maze of hallways. Anxiety increased with each empty cell he passed. The guys were right. There was no one else here but Liam refused to give up. There had to be something. Some shred of evidence of what had happened to her.

A hand landed on his arm. "Come on, man," Xavier said. "We've got to get out of here."

No. He refused to accept this. She had to be somewhere. She had to be. Shaking off Xavier's hand, Liam ran through the prison, yelling, "Cat! Where are you? Cat!"

"We've gotta leave, Stryker," Hawke shouted. "There's no one else here."

Liam halted midstride, his gut twisting, his heart aching. They were right. She was gone.

Xavier threw an arm around his shoulders. "Let's go."

Hopelessness and rage tearing his insides to pieces, Liam gave a grim nod.

In silence, they walked out of the prison toward the helicopter waiting in the distance. Though his body welcomed the fresh air and sunshine, his mind and heart were preoccupied with questions about Cat. Where had they taken her? Had they killed her and buried her somewhere? Had they sold her and the other women she'd told him about?

Without a word, Liam climbed into the chopper. A man he didn't recognize sat across from him. His eyes opened the minute Liam sat down. Dirty blond hair, bruises and cuts on his face. This must be the guy they'd brought in several days ago.

"Lion, I'm assuming?" the man asked.

"Liam Stryker. Glad to see you made it."

The man nodded. "You, too. The name's Asher Drake."

His body was weak from lack of water and food and Liam told himself to close his eyes and rest. His mind refused to do the same. Voices surrounded him, oddly distant and surreal. He couldn't stop thinking of Cat. What had happened to her? What had they done to her?

He opened his eyes when the helicopter lifted from the ground. A huge part of him wanted to jump out and go back to the prison. There had to be some evidence of where they'd taken her. But he couldn't do that. Not only would he be putting everyone in more danger, he was on the last of his reserves. But he would come back here, and he wouldn't rest until he found her.

"Let's take a look at you, buddy."

He turned his head and stared blearily at a blond stranger with icy blue eyes. "Who are you?"

"Gideon Wright. A friend of Hawke's."

That was good enough for Liam. Leaning his head back against the wall, he gave monosyllabic answers to the questions Wright asked. Even though there wasn't a place on his body that wasn't either bruised or cut, he felt numb. A heaviness had settled around his heart and emptiness flooded through his being. Although he was sure she hadn't been there, he still felt as if he was leaving her behind.

"Here." Wright handed him a bottle of water and a protein bar. "Chew slowly."

Liam nodded and took a bite and then another. His first sip of cold, clean water went down easy and tasted like nectar. He took another swallow.

"Dammit!" somebody shouted. "We've got incoming!"

With barely enough time to comprehend what was happening, Liam grabbed on to the hanging belt behind him just as an explosion rocked the chopper. Another blast followed. Beeps and alarms blared through the cabin. As the helicopter whirled in circles like an out-of-control spinning top, Liam fought to hang on. The chopper took a sudden nose dive, speeding toward the ground. They were going to crash.

The pilot shouted, "Brace for impact!"

Liam's thoughts spun. If he died today, he'd never be able to find Cat. He had to survive this. He couldn't let her down.

A loud roar rushed throughout the chopper. He caught a glimpse of Xavier's grim face a second before they slammed to the ground. Metal squealed, the world shook.

Agony seared through Liam's entire body. And then there was darkness.

CHAPTER FIVE

Two months later
New York
NYC Public Library

Katarina Aubrey Starr stood on the steps in front of the lion statue known as Fortitude, just as she had promised. She wore a navy blue dress with white and yellow daisies, just as she had promised. When she'd described the dress to Lion, it had been hanging in her closet at home. She'd put it on this morning and had been appalled at the fit. That couldn't be helped. This was the dress he expected her to be wearing. She had cinched the waist with a belt, used pins in strategic places to keep the dress from falling from her shoulders, and called a cab. Nothing was going to stop her from making this date.

People went up and down the steps, all strangers. Everyone seemed to have important errands to run or serious business to handle. None of them was her Lion. She might not have ever seen him, but she knew exactly what he looked like. She had envisioned him a million times. Besides that, how many men would be carrying a bouquet of pink roses up the library steps? So yes, she would definitely know him.

She told herself he would be here. Having no idea what his real name was or what had happened to him after she'd been rescued had not deterred her from making this meeting. He had to be here. There was no other option.

The sun beat down on her unprotected head and a small voice of caution told her to sit down. She'd been released from the hospital only two weeks ago and was still recovering. The last thing she needed was a setback. But she feared that if she moved, she would miss him.

A clock chimed in the distance, clanging twice. He was an hour late. She used the excuse that he might have arrived in the city from a different time zone. Yes, it was lame, and yes, it was a stupid hope, but still she stood, waiting.

She thought about what she would say to him. A thousand times, she'd reviewed in her mind the first thing she would do. Would it be too forward to throw herself into his arms? Probably, but that's what she wanted to do. He had given her hope when there had been none. Without him, she was sure she would have given up.

When the clock chimed three times, she dropped down to the steps and sat. She could still see everyone. She wouldn't miss him. Her limbs, especially her legs, were still a bit weak.

What exactly did Lion do? The authoritative way he'd talked, the advice he'd given her about protecting herself, had sounded very knowledgeable. She assumed he was military trained. Had he still been in the military? Was that why he'd been a prisoner? If so, had he been able to escape?

The prison they'd been held in was gone—decimated. She'd seen the aerial photos. All that remained was a barbwire fence that had surrounded the structure. Everything else had been flattened. No one could give her any answers

31

of what had happened. She'd been told only that there were no known survivors.

She refused to believe that Lion hadn't survived. He had to be alive—she would accept no other option.

At four o'clock, she opened the small picnic basket she'd brought for them. Taking out the plastic container holding the apple slices she'd cut up this morning, she forced herself to eat a few pieces. Even though she wasn't hungry, she needed to keep her energy up.

He was now three hours late. She pushed that knowledge aside. So what? Where did she have to go? Lion was worth waiting for. She refused to give up on him.

The call came just a little after five. Not surprisingly her mother sounded both concerned and angry. "Kat, where are you?"

"I'm in New York. At the library."

"Oh, Kat…" Now she just sounded sad.

"Mom, you know I had to try."

"Sweetie, he's dead."

"You don't know that. It was never confirmed."

She tried to be relieved that at least her mother was acknowledging that Lion actually existed. She and other well-meaning people had tried to tell her that Lion had been a figment of her imagination. A hallucination brought on by fear and pain. A mystery man her mind had created to keep hope alive. She knew that wasn't the truth. He was real and he was alive. She knew it!

Her mother gave that sad, pitying sigh that she'd adopted ever since her daughter had returned home. "Come home, darling, where we can take care of you."

"Mom…" She tried, she really tried, to keep the irritation from her voice. "I can take care of myself."

"Yes, as you proved so well."

Though it hurt, she couldn't argue with the statement.

She had gone alone to Paris, filled with youthful arrogance, massive naïveté, and the complete certainty that nothing bad could happen to her. She had returned home a gravely injured, damaged, and fearful woman.

The blood loss had been horrific, but it had been the pneumonia that had almost taken her life. Every breath had been a struggle. The doctors had worked tirelessly to save her.

She was finally getting herself back together. She had been determined to get well so she could make this meeting.

An abrupt wave of desolation swept through her, and sadness dropped like a boulder onto her shoulders. Her mother was right. He wasn't coming. Lion was dead. The most wonderful, giving man she'd ever known was no longer alive.

A gust of warm air swept over her, bringing with it the scent of roses. Her head popped up, her eyes searched. She saw no one with pink roses. Spotted no one who looked remotely like Lion. It didn't matter. Something like optimism washed through her. She refused to accept her mother's grim assessment. There was no visual proof he was dead. There was still hope.

"Kat." Her mom's voice softened. "Come home, darling."

"I can't, Mom, I'm sorry. I learned a hard lesson, but I got through it. I'm a grown woman and don't need to be babied or taken care of."

"But—"

"You and Dad need to go on that cruise you planned, before all this happened."

"Don't be silly. We're not leaving until you're completely on your feet."

That was just more incentive for her to get a hundred percent well. She'd always been an independent person, but since her return she'd become a weak-kneed, jump-at-any-loud-noise, blubbering wimp. That was over. From now on, her family would see the Katarina they'd seen before.

Knowing she wouldn't convince her mother without full proof that she was fully recovered, she did the only thing she could do—she lied. "I've got to go. I've got a phone consultation with Dr. Jenkins at six."

"Good. I know she'll help you confront your denial about that young man."

Refusing to get back into an argument she wouldn't win, she hurriedly said, "I love you, Mom. Bye."

As she pocketed her cell, a new wave of desolation rushed through her like a raging river. It was four hours and seventeen minutes past their meeting time. Even if he had been delayed in traffic, had a flat tire, or a flight delay, he would have been here by now.

She returned the sliced apples to her picnic basket. Standing, she gave one more searching glance around without an ounce of hope. He wasn't coming. Wherever he was…whatever had kept him away must have been important. But what she absolutely, positively refused to accept was that he was dead. Someway, somehow she would find him. And when she did, she would thank him for saving her life.

She didn't care how long she had to wait for him, she would never give up on Lion. And in her heart she knew that Lion would never give up on her.

CHAPTER SIX

Eight Years Later
Prizren, Kosovo

Bullets whipped by, pinging into the metal door beside him. Liam waited half a second, peered around the door edge and fired three shots toward the guy hiding behind a stack of wood. At this rate, they'd both soon run out of bullets and would have to go hand-to-hand. That'd be just fine with him. He had enough adrenaline built up inside him to take on three of these creeps without breaking a sweat.

There had to be a better way to earn a living, but ever since he'd rescued his first baby rabbit from the jaws of Toby, their old house cat, he'd been obsessed with protecting the innocent.

Another bullet zipped by his head. Cursing, Liam jerked his head back. That had been a little too close for comfort.

Yeah, there was probably a better way to earn a living, but he couldn't think of one.

"Hey, Stryker, you copy?"

Glad to hear OZ leader Asher Drake's voice in his ear,

Liam answered, "Yeah, I'm over by the side door. Glad you could make it. Where are you?"

Ash answered, a definite sound of irritation in his tone, "Sorry I'm late. Got caught in a nest of hornets."

He knew exactly what that meant. Liam had zero tolerance for politics or diplomacy. Asher Drake, on the other hand, was a diplomat extraordinaire, seemingly able to untangle a spider web with intricate ease.

"Don't tell me we've got trouble on that end, too."

"Not anymore. We're good. I'm pinned down behind the bulldozer. I spotted Gideon on the other side of the motel. Where are Sean and Xavier stationed?"

"They're to the left of you, behind the silver semi."

"Serena and Jazz make it inside okay?"

"They got in there, but I don't know what's going on. Comms are down in the building, so we'll be going in blind."

"How many men have you counted?"

"I've seen five."

"They've got some impressive firepower."

"Yeah, but they're beginning to piss me off."

"I hear that. You got a plan?"

"Yeah. I'm coming to you. Cover me."

Liam took off. When he'd been on the track team in college, he'd run a 4:40 and thought that was a damn fine accomplishment. Outrunning bullets might not be possible but he was doing his dead-level best. Thankfully his boss, as usual, had his back and was rapid-firing to clear his path.

He dove behind the bulldozer and joined Ash. With no time to spare, Liam took aim at the man he'd been exchanging fire with for the last ten minutes. Having a better vantage point, he fired twice, heard a squeal and then silence. Dead or just winged, he didn't know. Either way, it'd bought him some time to put his plan into action.

Clicking his earbud, he said, "Xavier, you copy?"

"Yeah," his friend growled. "What's the plan?"

"Ash and I are going to hit them head on. You and Sean come at them on both sides.

Xavier responded, "Roger that."

Sean echoed Xavier's words.

"Eve and Gideon, you copy?"

OZ operatives Eve Wells and Gideon Wright were a quarter mile away at the top of a hill. Gideon answered in his usual quiet tone, "Right here."

"Either of you got a good line of sight?"

"I do," Eve answered.

"Mine's crap," Gideon said.

"Okay, Eve, take out the stragglers or any surprises. Gideon, head our way."

"Roger that," Gideon answered.

"I'm on it," Eve said.

"Okay, on my count, let's go. Three, two, one!"

They were shooting before they left cover. Hearing the gunfire from either side he knew Gideon and Xavier were doing the same. Reaching the door to the motel lobby, Liam went on one side, Ash landed on the other. Giving him a nod, Ash fired three shots through the door, and then Liam made a mad dash inside. Two men lay near the entrance. Keeping his gun at the ready, he kicked their guns out of the way and kept going. Ash would make sure they were out of commission, one way or the other.

"Serena, you copy?"

"Yes! Good to hear your voice. We're secure."

"Where are you?"

"Last room on the left, south side of the building."

"How many do you have?"

"Nine women, three children, two young men."

"Good work. Keep them there until I give the all clear."

"Roger that."

"Xavier, you guys make out okay?"

"We're good. Took care of two of them."

"Excellent. Let's clear this dump of any remaining vermin."

It took all his discipline not to hurry through the process. Ensuring the motel had indeed been cleared of all traffickers was the priority. When he was sure, then he'd take the opportunity to check on the victims.

Still on alert, he took a step through a door. He spotted the trip wire a half second too late. His ears barely registered a boom before rancid smoke filled the room. Liam jumped back, hacking and coughing. Dammit, somebody had booby-trapped the door. His nose and lungs burning like fire, he ran outside.

Coughing like he was hacking up a lung, Liam fought for every breath. What the hell had that been?

A hand slapped him on the back. He looked up to see Ash holding out a bottle of water. Grabbing it, Liam took a long gulp and then poured the rest over his face. The relief was instantaneous.

"You okay?"

His voice raspy from coughing, he said, "I will be. Stupid mistake. Hit a trip wire."

"Yeah. We found three more. Nothing dangerous. Just a smoke bomb. Probably set to keep anyone from escaping. Didn't think to look for them until you tripped over one. So thanks for that."

In between coughs, he threw Ash a crooked grin. "Any-thing—" cough, cough—

"to help the cause."

"Building's clear. Relief workers are here to transport the victims. They're gathered at the back. You'll want to see them first."

"Have you seen them?"

"Not yet."

Accepting another water bottle from Ash, Liam took several more swallows and felt halfway human again. Although his eyes were still swimming with tears and his throat felt as though he'd smoked a carton of cigarettes in one sitting, he knew he was lucky that was all the damage he'd incurred. Stupid of him, because it could've been a lot worse.

"Serena and Jazz, we're coming your way."

"Good," Jazz answered, her relief evident. "They're about to load them onto the bus."

As he headed around to the back of the building where the victims were being helped, he couldn't help but appreciate his OZ partners. Not one of them believed he'd ever find who he was looking for, but they were always willing to go the extra mile for him.

With every step he took, he felt as if this time…this time would be different. This time he would finally find her.

He rounded a corner and took in the scene. Two large vans, doors open, were parked parallel to the motel. Several aid workers milled around. The victims were easy to spot. Not because of their lack of clothing or anything materialistic. It was the expressions on their faces. The desolation in their eyes. Yes, they had been rescued and life could begin again for them, but it would take years, even a lifetime, to overcome what they'd been through.

Liam entered the area slowly, not wanting to alarm anyone. The aid workers were easy to spot, too—calmness in the midst of chaos, compassion in their eyes.

As relieved as he was that this had been another successful rescue, he couldn't deny the normal disappointment. He should be used to it by now. She wasn't here. None of the women fit Cat's description. And in the deepest, darkest part of his soul, he knew none of them ever would.

How many times had this very same scenario occurred? How many times would he experience the same crushing disappointment before he finally accepted the truth?

He didn't know—he knew only that he couldn't give up. Not yet.

The scene one he'd seen all too often, he turned to leave. He'd done his job. People were rescued, lives were saved. The traffickers would be picked up by local authorities and hopefully never released. He would have to be happy with that.

Out of the corner of his eye, he spotted one anomaly. A young woman stood several yards away from everyone. Instead of offering aid to the victims, she was speaking into what looked like a handheld recorder. Every minute or so, she'd jot something on a notepad and then would occasionally wipe her eyes of what he assumed were tears.

He didn't know how long he stood there, watching. As if she knew she was being watched, she jerked her head up and met his gaze for a brief, electrifying moment. Her eyes, a blend of light blue and electric gray, mesmerized.

She gave him an odd, cautious look and then went back to taking notes.

He was so distracted he didn't even notice that Eve had come to stand beside him until she said, "Damn fine work and I didn't even fire a shot."

"Glad you were there to back us up."

She winced at his raspy voice. "You sound like a geriatric bullfrog. Heard you got gassed."

"Yeah, something like that. Some kind of modified smoke grenade. Burned like hell."

"You need to get that checked out. You sound awful."

"Yeah, I will." He coughed and tried to clear his throat without much success. "Stupid of me."

"We've all done the stupid."

He nodded toward the group of workers. "You've worked with this relief agency before?"

"Yes, a couple of times. They're one of the finest on the planet."

He directed his gaze to the young woman talking on her recorder. "Know who she is?"

"No. Must be new. I recognize everyone else." She sent him a speculative look. "Any particular reason you want to know?"

"Just wondering. She doesn't appear to be part of the group. She's been taking notes and talking into that recorder for a while."

"I'll find out."

Liam thought about stopping her. It wasn't as if it mattered who she was. He didn't do long-distance relationships. The aid team was based in Kosovo. He lived in the US. It would never work.

Despite telling himself that, he watched in anticipation as Eve spoke with one of the aid workers. She was back within a minute.

"She's not with the relief group. She's making a documentary about human trafficking. Want an introduction?"

Shaking his head, Liam headed toward the woman. Stopping for a moment to consider his appearance never entered his mind.

When he was about five feet from her, she jerked her head up again, like a wild animal sensing danger. Her wariness intrigued him even more.

He stopped in front of her, opened his mouth, but nothing other than a croak emerged. He cleared his throat and tried again. Nothing.

What the hell?

.   .   .

AUBREY LOOKED up at the wild-haired, red-eyed stranger. He wore fatigues and was heavily armed, so she knew he was one of the people who'd rescued the human trafficking victims. He was tall, maybe about six-two, had dark brown hair that looked both wild and dirty. His face was covered with some kind of ash or soot.

Though his demeanor wasn't threatening in the least, she couldn't help but take a step back. There was something about him that felt oddly familiar. It was both exciting and alarming.

She hadn't known what to expect when he opened his mouth to speak, but it certainly hadn't been silence. He appeared to be struggling for words.

Compassion overriding her fear, she stepped forward and touched his arm in concern. "Are you okay?"

When he shook his head and gestured to his throat, she understood that, for whatever reason, he couldn't speak.

"Do you need some help?" She glanced around for a doctor or medic who might be able to assist him.

His expression one of both exasperation and frustration, the man shook his head. He turned to look behind him, and seconds later, another man came to stand beside him.

About the same size, this man had coal-black hair and startling silver eyes that twinkled with amusement. He gave Aubrey a charming smile and said, "Forgive my friend. He's a bit shy until you get to know him."

The disheveled man gave his friend a narrow-eyed glare and the man hurriedly added, "He had an encounter with a smoke bomb and can't speak right now."

"Oh…I'm sorry about your voice." She flashed a smile at both men. "You were involved in the rescue?"

"Yes," the silver-eyed man said.

"You probably get told this all the time, but I just want to say thank you for what you do."

The dark-haired man shrugged. "Glad we can do something." He glanced at the silent man beside him. "If he could talk, he'd probably say something charming, like, 'Who are you?' And, 'Why are you here?'"

"My name is Aubrey Starr. I'm a documentary filmmaker. Human trafficking, the horror and devastation it causes, is something I became interested in years ago. I don't think people understand how virulent it is and how it encompasses every aspect of our lives. I—"

She caught her breath. She was about to go on a tirade but these men knew more about the horror of human trafficking than she ever would. They'd been in the trenches saving lives. She was just a filmmaker.

"What you do is important," the silver-eyed stranger said. "The public needs to know."

She had a ton of questions she wanted to ask. On the verge of developing a mental list of all the things she wanted to know, she shifted gears when one of the aid workers called out to her, "Aubrey, we're ready."

"That's my cue." She flashed a smile at both men. "Nice talking to you." She sent a sympathetic smile to the mute man. "I hope your voice comes back soon."

She walked toward the bus, but when she heard a loud guffaw, she turned back to see that the man who couldn't speak had given his friend a rude hand gesture and stalked away.

Smiling, Aubrey stepped up onto the bus. She wished she'd been able to spend more time with them. Not only would it be fascinating to get insight into the ins and outs of a rescue operation, the zing of attraction she'd felt had been exhilarating.

The moment she got inside, she lost her smile. This was the reason she was here, the reason she'd become obsessed with telling their stories. The faces of the lost, the forgotten.

She'd fought hard to get here, to be taken seriously. Getting distracted, no matter the reason, couldn't happen. She was on a quest. Nothing could get in her way, not even a wild-haired, red-eyed man who'd lost his voice and risked his life to save others. Someday maybe…but not yet.

CHAPTER SEVEN

Present Day
Indianapolis, Indiana

"Hey, Stryker. You see El Diablo yet?"

Liam readjusted his earwig. It was hard as hell to hear anything with all the caterwauling going on. What kind of an informant wanted to meet in a karaoke bar anyway? His, that's who.

"No," Liam growled.

"Me either." Eve snorted. "Who gave this guy his name, anyway?"

"I think he did that to himself," Gideon said dryly.

Gideon was right. El Diablo's real name was Myron Clyde Hornsby. It was easy to understand why he thought *El Diablo* sounded tougher. But he was also one of the best CIs Liam had ever had. When you're five feet nothing, weigh less than a buck twenty-five, and had the kind of face that blended into a whitewashed wall, it was easy to slide in unnoticed. Even though El Diablo liked to meet in some of the most asinine places, Liam put up with his idiosyncrasies. He was quirky, weird, and a valuable informant.

"I'd like to sing this for all my friends out there."

Recognizing the voice, Liam went on alert. Moving his head slightly he spotted his erstwhile informant on the stage, microphone in his hand. Oh hell, Myron was going to sing?

When the music from the old song *Somebody's Watching Me* started up, Liam knew they were in trouble. In typical Myron fashion, he was trying to warn them.

"We've been made," Liam said softly.

He barely got the words out before a hand grabbed his arm and tugged hard. Liam didn't even bother to struggle. Allowing himself to be pulled up, Liam smoothly swung his other arm, slamming a fist into the guy's face.

As if the entire room had been waiting for a signal, the bar exploded into a free-for-all. Tables squealed across the floor as they were shoved out of the way. A chair flew through the air barely missing Liam's head. Fists came from the left and the right, jabbed and stung.

It'd been a long time since he'd been in a bar brawl. At a more convenient time, he would've jumped right in and enjoyed throwing a few more punches. But he was here for a specific purpose. Beating the snot out of someone wasn't on today's agenda.

His eyes tracked Myron's movements as he scurried off the stage. Liam took a step forward. A meaty fist hurled toward him. Liam ducked, came back with an uppercut to a broad jaw. The guy barely moved an inch. Growling his frustration, he pressed his earwig. "Eve, our man's going out the back."

"I'm on him," Eve answered.

Liam opened his mouth, about to invite Gideon to come inside and join the party, when a body flew by him, obviously thrown by someone. That someone was Gideon who was clearing a path in his typical fashion of just hurling people out of the way. The man definitely had his own style.

"You ever think about going to a bar and not starting a fight?" Gideon asked.

Ducking to avoid a fist, Liam straightened, delivering his own fist to the stranger's jaw, then turned to answer Gideon. "Now what would be the fun in that?"

"Do you know who these bozos are?"

Liam shoved Gideon out of the way of a flying chair, caught it, and hurled it back where it came from, hitting a couple of knuckleheads along the way.

"Not yet."

"Let's get out of here before the police get here."

Liam grinned. "Sounds good to me."

With that, they strode through the bar, shoving away anyone who threatened their progress. When they got to the door, Liam turned back and assessed the scene. The fight had been staged to distract. Question was why.

Spotting a movement out of the corner of his eye, Liam turned and got the answer to his question.

"Ah hell," he growled. "Drury's here."

"What's he doing here?" Gideon asked. "I thought he was locked up."

"Guess he got out." Liam jerked his head toward the door. "He's headed toward the back exit. You go around and stop him if he gets out before I get to him."

"Roger that but watch your six. He's likely got a few more friends here."

Acknowledging the statement with a nod, Liam headed toward the back. Following the creep should be easy. A scum-sucking slug like Drury would leave a trail of slime or at the very least a stench of rotten.

One good thing about Drury being here—the only good thing as far as Liam could see—was that Myron definitely had some solid intel. Drury wouldn't be interested otherwise. Nor would he take the chance of getting caught if it wasn't worth the risk.

Pressing his earwig, Liam said, "Eve, get Myron away from here. Drury's looking for him."

"Copy that," Eve replied.

Though it sounded as if few fistfights were still going on, the din behind him had quieted to a low roar. On alert for any movement, Liam entered the darkened hallway. Drury would be out for blood. Last time they'd met, they'd had a brutal, bloody fight. Liam had come out the victor in that one, and Drury no doubt held a grudge. Especially since Liam was directly responsible for Drury's most recent prison stint.

"Long time no see, Stryker."

The voice came from the shadows in front of him. When Drury stepped into the light, Liam fought to keep a straight face. Dressed in a flowered silk shirt and white slacks, his hair pulled back into some kind of man bun, Drury definitely made a fashion statement. The black T-shirt and jeans Liam wore were downright sloppy and boring compared to Drury's slick style. The man did sleaze all too well.

"I'd hoped the 'no see' part would've lasted a lot longer. How'd you get out of prison?"

"Would you believe good behavior?"

"No."

"Yeah, me neither. Turns out I've got friends with connections."

"Wait…you have friends?"

"Your insults mean nothing to me."

As much fun as the guy was to taunt, this was as deadly

serious as it got. Lives were at stake. "Then why don't we cut to the chase? Why are you here?"

"Same reason you are. Information."

"Really? You switch sides? Decide to start saving lives instead of taking them?"

"Last time I checked, you're the killer."

"You're lying to yourself if you think what you do doesn't cost lives."

Eve's voice sounded in his ear. "I've got Myron secured. Jazz and I are on the way to the safe house."

"Copy that."

"Who are you talking to, and why do you smile? I'm the one with the gun."

"Aw, Barney, did you learn nothing in prison?"

Drury glared. "My name is Barnabas, not Barney."

A gun pressed against the back of Drury's head. "Whoever you are," Gideon said in a low, menacing voice, "drop your gun."

For such a large man, Gideon could be as quiet as a church mouse when necessary.

Cursing, Drury lowered his weapon, and Liam took it from him. He searched and removed another gun from an ankle holster, along with a switchblade from a pocket.

Pocketing the weapons, Liam allowed his smile to broaden. Drury had anger-management issues. "Now let's talk about why you're really here, Barney."

"None of your damn business."

All humor gone, Liam took a step forward and growled softly, "It's very much my business. When did you get into human trafficking?"

"I don't know what you're talking about."

"A word of advice. Don't play poker."

"You've got no reason to detain me. I've done nothing wrong."

Liam cocked his head. "You think I'm law enforcement, Barney?"

Eyes gleaming with malice, he smirked. "I know exactly what you are, Stryker. You're the man that's going to bleed."

A noise behind him was his first alert that they'd missed one of Drury's friends.

Before Liam could turn, a familiar voice said, "Put the gun down."

Liam looked over his shoulder to see Xavier holding a gun on another of Drury's accomplices.

"I guess today's not my day to bleed, Barney. You, on the other hand, I'm not so sure. Xavier and Gideon, would you take these *gentlemen* to a safe place for me? I'll want to talk with them a little later."

"Be glad to," Gideon said. "I might just have a talk with them while we're waiting."

Liam threw Drury a feigned sympathetic smile. "Sorry, Barney. Guess that bleeding's going to happen after all."

Surprising him, Drury only sneered as Gideon and Xavier led the man and his cohorts toward the exit. Would've thought he'd put up more of a fight.

Shrugging, Liam took one last look at the melee winding down in the bar. The place was a mess. Chairs and tables were askew or turned over, and several men lay on the floor. More than a few of those who were still standing were bloodied. Only a couple of small fights remained and they looked halfhearted at best. It had been a good distraction. Get a bunch of drunken guys pissed at each other, and all sorts of things could happen.

The thought had barely entered his head when the entire bar went dark. For just an instant, the place was silent as if everyone was in shock. Then a roar of furious voices exploded. Seconds later, the lights from cellphones flickered on, and the scene became a surreal blur of images.

Liam pulled his flashlight from his belt and headed toward the exit, where Xavier and Gideon had taken Drury and his friends. The blackout had been a bit too convenient for his liking. The lights came on as quickly as they'd turned off. Returning his flashlight to its holder, Liam pulled his SIG. Something wasn't right.

He pushed open the exit door and heard a groan. Turning to his left, he found both Xavier and Gideon lying in the alleyway. His heart in his throat, he ran toward them. "What the hell happened?"

Gideon sat up and leaned against the brick wall. "We got jumped. Bastard had goons waiting out here. The instant the lights went out, they tased us."

"Are you okay?"

"Yeah."

Xavier pulled himself to his feet and then stumbled. Liam grabbed hold of his shoulder. "Maybe you'd better sit down for a little longer."

"I'm fine, just pissed. Haven't been tased in a while. Forgot how much it hurts."

Relieved that his friends were okay, Liam looked out at the empty alleyway. Score one for Drury. He had underestimated the man. Apparently the bastard had found a few new sleazeball friends.

Liam shrugged off the aggravation. Yeah, he'd wanted to have some one-on-one time with the slimeball. The man was into something new, and it wasn't good. But right now, Liam had bigger fish to fry. The reason for being here was waiting in a safe house miles away. He and Drury would meet up again someday soon and he would make sure he was ready.

Getting the intel that Myron had for him was a priority. The man apparently had something good or Drury wouldn't have been so prepared. He was just glad they'd managed to spirit Myron away before Drury got to him.

Even if the info didn't lead him to his ultimate destination, if it saved someone from the hell of slavery, then he'd damn well follow through.

And one day, he would do what he'd promised himself over a decade ago. He would find Cat and bring her home.

CHAPTER EIGHT

Bakersfield, California

"Tell me what plans you had for your life, Brenda."

"Well, it certainly wasn't this!" The sharp, acidic retort came from a woman filled with so much pain, it had to spill out or she would implode.

Aubrey didn't back away from the hostility and never blinked. Her expression of compassion and empathy was authentic. She was intimately familiar with such pain.

Brenda stared at the wall behind Aubrey for several long moments and then, after releasing a long, ragged sigh, she closed her eyes. A single, lone tear rolled down her lined face. The woman was in her early thirties but looked a decade older.

Though they were only a few moments from finishing the interview, Aubrey was tempted to offer another break. It had been an excruciating conversation. What should have lasted one hour at the most had stretched into a three-hour ordeal. They'd stopped so many times, her editors were probably going to pull their hair out when they got the raw footage. Aubrey didn't see that she'd had any choice. Even though Brenda had agreed to the interview, there had been times Aubrey was sure they'd have to stop for good.

She reminded herself that if today's interview was difficult, the first one had been agonizing. Aubrey had interviewed Brenda several years ago for her film documentary, *The Lost Ones*. Brenda had still been in rehab and was, in her own words, a wreck of a human being. Seeing the woman's progress, made Aubrey glad that Brenda had contacted her for a second interview. Although Brenda still suffered, she had come so very far from the deeply ravaged individual she'd once been.

Brenda released another ragged sigh, prompting Aubrey to ask, "Do you want to take a break?"

"No. Let me get this out. Both my therapist and I feel this will be a cathartic release for me. Also, if I can help just one person with my story, then it will be worth it."

"All right. Tell me what plans you had for your life before you were taken."

"I was going to be a pianist." Brenda's mouth trembled slightly and then became a straight line again. "I'd been accepted into Juilliard on a scholarship. My whole life was ahead of me."

Instead of attending Juilliard, she'd been abducted at a shopping mall and sold into sexual slavery. She'd been rescued several years later but had to battle fiercely to get her life back. She'd become addicted to cocaine and heroin while in captivity, and it had taken her years of rehab and therapy before she achieved any normalcy. Though she was now a piano teacher and had recently become engaged, her life was a far cry from what it should have been.

This was the reason Aubrey felt compelled to do this

particular documentary. People knew the hideousness of human trafficking. A large percentage of the victims were never rescued, and many died while in captivity. The ones who were rescued were never the same. Revealing the ugliness of human trafficking wasn't a difficult task. But the aftereffects were rarely explored. After reporting the initial horror story, few journalists followed up on the victims years later.

When Brenda had been abducted, she had been a bright-eyed, intelligent seventeen-year-old with the whole world in front of her. She spent almost eight years in captivity before she was rescued. It had taken her more than three years to overcome her addictions and an additional five years to find a new path for herself. Now, at thirty-three, she was finally carving out a good life, but she still suffered. It took only one look in her eyes to see her pain.

"Brenda, you wanted to do this interview. You contacted me so you could get your story told. Is there anything you want to say to the people who will see this interview?"

She took a deep breath, and with a determination Aubrey deeply admired, Brenda faced the camera. Her eyes burned with a fierce intensity. "Live life to the fullest. Never take a day for granted. Live, love, and be happy, but also never let your guard down. Be vigilant. Be aware of your surroundings. Learn how to protect yourself. Make sure your children know how to protect themselves." She swallowed audibly and then added a heartbreaking final statement. "Don't let what happened to me happen to you or someone you love."

Aubrey waited for a few seconds, not only to allow Brenda to add more if she liked, but to give the viewer a chance to see the incredibly strong woman behind the pain.

When there were no additional words, Aubrey said, "Thank you, Brenda, for sharing your story with us again.

You've come so far and I, for one, am in awe of your strength and courage. I know you've helped a lot of people." Aubrey gave her cameraman the halt signal, and the camera light went off.

While her crew gathered their equipment, Aubrey focused on Brenda. Though she looked teary-eyed, her shoulders were much less tense than they had been when they'd first started.

"You did great."

A small smile lit up the other woman's face. "Thank you for agreeing to interview me again. I know my story isn't front-page headlines anymore."

"Doesn't mean it's not still important and timely. That's why I'm doing this new film. People need to see more than just the initial horror. They need to witness the incredible strength of a survivor.

"You said you would feel it was worth it if you could help even one person. I can promise you that you helped a lot more than that."

"Thank you. I—" Brenda stopped when someone called her name. As she looked over her shoulder, her entire demeanor changed. She held out her hand to the tall, stocky man standing a few feet away. Aubrey had met Brenda's fiancé the day before. The two were so much in love. The naked emotion on John's face when he looked at Brenda was almost too painful to watch. To be the recipient of that kind of love had to be a glorious feeling.

Brenda went into John's arms and he held her close. A heaviness lying on her chest, Aubrey stepped away. If she didn't get out of here, she'd soon be in tears. She was happy Brenda had found the love she so deserved but the emotions were too much.

Calling out a goodbye and a promise to send her a link to

the finished work, Aubrey walked out the door. She drew in a cleansing breath of air.

As her team high-fived each other and talked about where they wanted to go for dinner, Aubrey stared into the darkness and remembered a beautiful, golden voice making a promise that would never be fulfilled.

When had she stopped thinking of him every day? It had been a gradual thing. At first, she had been desperate to find out what had happened to him. When she didn't get those answers, she learned to live with the memories of their short acquaintance. The timbre of his voice, the way he'd pause while telling a story, to give her time to absorb the nuance. She loved how he could make her laugh. There had been so little to laugh about then, but somehow Lion had managed to do that.

Now she heard him only in her dreams. He seemed a million miles away, a fantasy that couldn't be real.

"Aubrey? Did you hear me?"

Jerking herself from her reverie, she smiled at Owen Waters, one of the cameramen. "Sorry, what did you say?"

"We're going for dinner at a Tex-Mex place Harry says he went to a couple of years ago. Says their margaritas are incredible."

She loved her team, but she needed some time to herself. The long drive back to LA would give her that. "I need to get back to the hotel. I've got a meeting with Lawrence Medford tomorrow and I want to be ready."

Owen grimaced. "Better you than me. Heard he was an ass the other day."

"He was, but that's to be expected. Once he realized he couldn't sway me, he got nicer. I think we're going to be able to work something out."

"That's a relief. The footage we got tonight was amazing. This story needs to be told."

She agreed. Brenda's story and so many more needed to be told.

"It's a long drive back. You want me to go with you? Keep you company?"

Owen was the newest member of her team. It wasn't the first time he had indicated he'd like to know Aubrey on something other than a professional basis. He was a nice guy, but getting personally involved with a coworker was never a good idea.

"Thanks but the alone time will do me good. I'll call you guys tomorrow after the meeting and we'll make plans then."

"Okay, well…have a safe trip back."

She waved at the rest of the team as they loaded their equipment into the vans. "Great job tonight, guys. See you soon."

Amid a loud array of goodbyes, Aubrey got into her rental car and started the engine. She waited until her team had driven away, and then turned back and looked at the house where Brenda lived. What an amazing woman she was, an incredible survivor. She had endured and won.

How many more were out there? Hundreds of thousands? Millions? She knew the estimates, but that's exactly what they were. Estimates. Only God knew how many there really were. She did what she could, but making films to inform people only went so far.

Not for the first time, she thought about the man she'd briefly met a few years ago in Kosovo. Over the years, she'd met many men she'd found attractive, but few had stayed in her memory the way this man had. Which was strange since he hadn't even said a word. She didn't know his name, where he lived…knew nothing about him other than he rescued people from horrific circumstances. Something about him had not only warmed her blood, but had also touched her heart. It had been the first time she'd felt a connection to anyone since Lion.

Shifting the gear into drive, Aubrey blew out a ragged sigh as she drove away. She must be tired, wishing for things that could never be, wanting a man she would never see again. Yearning for a man she'd never even seen. Life was reality. Dreams like that just didn't come true.

CHAPTER NINE

Montana

F eet propped on the railing, icy-cold beer in his hand, Liam took in the vista before him. When he'd moved to Montana, he'd lived in an apartment for a while before finding the perfect location to build. He had known in his mind exactly what he wanted—Cat had described it perfectly.

During those few days, when they'd had nothing but darkness and each other, they had talked about everything and nothing. Amazing the intimate details that could be shared without revealing the things that most people thought were essential. He might not know Cat's real name, where she'd lived, or even what she looked like, but he knew her. There was no doubt in his mind that he knew the real Cat.

He could still hear her voice, hoarse from her coughing, as she told him her dream. "I want to live in the mountains. We went to the Rockies for vacation one year and then once to the Smokies. There's just something about the heights, they're majestic and ancient. I remember sitting at the top of a peak and just absorbing the moment. I love going to the beach for vacation but only for a few days. The thought of coming home to my own private, secluded hideaway, surrounded by mountain mists with air so clear and fresh you can taste it, would be like heaven."

She had gone on to describe in surprising detail her dream home. A house surrounded by mountains, hidden from the rest of the world. A peaceful refuge.

When he'd found the land, he'd designed the house, using Cat's words to guide him. Okay, yeah, that was stupid. The place was way too big for him. Most times he wasn't in a location long enough to even justify renting a room on a weekly basis, yet he'd felt compelled to build a house for a woman he would likely never see again.

Again? Hell, he'd never seen her at all.

Where she'd been taken, what had happened after they'd pulled her out of that cell might be something he would never know. He knew she'd been tortured, beaten, and raped. For days, he'd heard the recording of her screams of pain, of terror. She had called out for him, and he hadn't been able to do a damn thing for her. Her cries were ingrained in his psyche and would never leave him.

But what had they done to her after that? Where had they taken her?

The helicopter crash had delayed his search for weeks. Six of them had survived the crash. Dragging his ass through the Syrian desert with multiple injuries had been nothing compared to the knowledge that if he didn't get home, Cat would never be found.

As soon as he and the other survivors had made it to civilization, he'd demanded a search be conducted. Thanks to Hawke, the request had been approved. Liam hadn't been able to go himself. Four broken ribs, a broken shoulder, and a bullet in his side had prevented him from being able to do anything other than wait for word. It hadn't been good.

The entire prison was gone—demolished. Most likely a drone strike but no one could say who was responsible or why. The incinerated remains of three bodies had been found—all male. No identifications had ever been made.

She hadn't been there when he'd left. He told himself that over and over—she hadn't been there. He had gone through the prison, searched every nook and cranny, called her name. She had been taken somewhere else. But by whom? And to where?

When he was well enough, he'd gone back. He had to see for himself that there was no hope, no sign of her. He'd found nothing but the crumbling remains of a destroyed structure and a barbed wire fence that had surrounded the building.

He'd even hired a group with cadaver dogs to search the area, and they'd come up empty.

There had been no report of an American disappearing from a market in Paris. No one had filed a missing-person report that remotely matched the description she'd given him. She had family, had mentioned a cousin. Wouldn't someone have looked for her, demanded to know what happened to her?

It was as if she'd never existed, except in his mind. He might've been weak from the beatings and little nourishment, but he'd been lucid enough to know she was not a figment of his imagination. Cat was real, and he'd spent twelve years looking for her, to no avail.

He had used what little she'd told him about herself to search. He knew she was an actress and a student. There'd been no unexplained record of a student missing from any college remotely close to New York.

He'd even researched the plays in New York but couldn't

find any that purportedly needed a French-speaking actress for a part. Had she made that up? Had that been one of her "stories" and he'd missed it somehow?

His only real lead had been the knowledge that other women had been in the prison with her. They had disappeared too. Victims of human trafficking was his best guess.

During his search for her, he and his team had saved hundreds, but he had not found her, had not been able to save Cat.

Was it time to give up? Time to admit that she wasn't alive? His gut said no. What if he gave up today and tomorrow was the day he was supposed to find her?

No. No way in hell would he ever give up looking.

The ding of his phone indicated a text. Grabbing it from the table beside him, he clicked on the text from Myron.

Call me. Got something.

Liam wasted no time. The intel Myron had given him in Indianapolis had been sketchy but valuable. He had been sure he could get more. Looked like he had.

The instant Myron picked up, Liam asked, "Hey, what've you got?"

"There's a house in Bogota. Older home. Nice area, garden district. Don't know how long they've been using it. My sources say they've got a steady business going. Have maybe ten to twelve servicing the customers, day and night. Heard it's a busy place."

"You got an address or coordinates?"

"No. That's all I have. Figure your people can pinpoint it fairly quickly."

Myron was right. Serena and her team could have the address in a matter of hours, probably less.

"That's some good intel. Why don't you go to ground for a few days? I can send you to a safe house."

"Nah. I'm good. Got a new lady I'm keeping company with. We'll hole up together until this is over."

"I can protect you both."

"I know you can, but we're just getting to know each other. Don't want to spook her. I'll be fine. I know how to take care of me and mine."

"Then be safe, and thank you for this. I'm wiring the funds in a sec."

"Good enough. Be careful. Sounds like some scummy slime this time."

Anyone who made money off the misery of another was scummy slime, in his opinion.

"Thanks again."

Liam ended the call and immediately wired the funds to Myron's account. One of the most important aspects of intel gathering was paying informants what they were worth and doing so ASAP. Which was why Myron gave him good intel. He knew Liam would pay.

After sending the funds, he texted Serena, giving her the details. He had no worries that he'd be hearing from her soon.

Standing, Liam took one last look at the panorama before him. One more time he would search for her. One more time he would likely be disappointed. But someday…just maybe… he wouldn't be.

CHAPTER TEN

Brentwood, California

Lawrence Medford skimmed through another script and tried without success to stave off a yawn. Didn't anyone write anything original anymore? This was his sixth one tonight, and he could link every one of them to a movie or book that had come out in the last ten years. Yeah, he knew there was nothing new under the sun, but that didn't mean people had to be lazy about it.

Standing, he stretched his back, twisting left and right. He wasn't due for his massage for another couple of days, but the way he was feeling, he knew he needed one sooner. He grabbed his phone and sent a quick text to his masseuse for an early-morning rubdown.

Placing the phone back on his desk, he wandered restlessly around his office. The frustration wasn't just from bad scripts. Most of it stemmed from having found the perfect one and not being able to do what he wanted with it.

The meeting with Aubrey Starr had started out on a positive note. He had expressed his admiration for a good script and praised her for her previous works. She was an extraordinarily gifted filmmaker, and her new project had all the earmarks of another award-winning hit. The flattery had been truthful.

Problem was, she hadn't been as impressed with him as he had hoped. He was an Oscar-winning producer of both feature films and documentaries. He knew how to get a story told, and he had the contacts and money to achieve both successfully. Their partnership could be ideal. She would provide the basic content. He would provide the funding and use his skills to turn her words and images into a soul-grabbing, heart-stopping, searingly raw picture of the ravages of human trafficking.

People would walk out of the theaters not only moved to tears, but also moved to action. His films changed the world. This one would be no different.

He didn't have any real investment in revealing the evils of human trafficking, but he lived to tell a good story. If his work exposed evildoers, or inspired people to do good, that was just an added benefit. He certainly wasn't on any kind of crusade. Not the way Aubrey Starr seemed to be. She definitely had her own agenda.

Instead of accepting his suggestions, she had refused to alter the script in any way. She claimed she had her own vision, and it didn't coincide with his. The meeting had gone downhill from there. He was known for his temper—the mark of a creative person was to be volatile and full of emotion.

She hadn't seemed angry but had adamantly refused to continue their meeting. Lawrence breathed out an exasperated sigh. He'd known the instant she'd walked out the door that he needed to make amends. He'd waited a couple of hours and had sent a bouquet of flowers to her hotel room, along with a note requesting another meeting. She had graciously accepted.

They would meet again tomorrow afternoon. This time, things would end differently. Once they had an agreement and began to work together, he felt sure he would be able to bring her around to his way of thinking. He'd handled things badly, but that didn't mean anything in this industry. Minds changed in an instant, given the right incentive. She needed funds. He had them. It was as simple as that.

By this time tomorrow, he would be celebrating a successful partnership.

They would be stepping on some toes with this project. Starr had been upfront that some powerful people could be exposed. He had no problem with that. Wouldn't be the first time he'd uncovered dirt on the rich and powerful. But he was Lawrence Medford. Rich and powerful in his own right. A world-renowned producer. He had angered numerous people through the years. Sometimes, you had to rattle a few nerves to reveal the underbelly of truth. He was good at that. And so was Aubrey Starr. That's why he needed to make this work.

Feeling much more optimistic, Lawrence dumped the scripts he'd reviewed into the trash bin. They were not worthy of a second glance. He would have his hands full with the new project, and as he didn't like to concentrate on more than one at a time, there was no point in searching for something more.

He took two steps away from his desk and halted when he heard an odd sound. Nothing like he'd ever heard before, at least not in his home. It couldn't be...could it?

He looked down at the hardwood floor, his breath caught in his throat, and his heart almost stopped. A mere three inches from his bare foot lay a rattlesnake, coiled and poised to strike. Lawrence froze. Cold sweat slid down his spine. If he moved even an inch, the snake would bite him.

Staring at the thing, he tried to will it to move away. He could swear the creature was staring back at him, almost taunting him to make the first move.

The longer he stood there, the more he knew he would have to move. He could survive a rattlesnake bite. He was only fifty and in good health. Lots of people survived worse. Yeah, it would hurt, but nothing he couldn't handle.

Doing the only thing that made sense to him, he hopped back one step. A stinging pain shot through the back of his ankle. Crying out, Lawrence looked down just in time to see the snake in front of him strike. But where had—out of his peripheral vision, another snake struck. This pain was worse, like a hornet's sting.

The question of how two rattlesnakes came to be inside his office was far from his mind. Knowing he had no choice, Lawrence stepped sideways and gripped his desk. Agony struck again, this time in his hand. There was a snake on his desk?

Nausea swelled in his stomach. Cold sweat drenched his body. He reached for the phone and watched in a blur of pain as it moved farther away from him. He stumbled forward, reaching for the cellphone that somehow continued to be out of his reach. How was that possible?

His mind was a mass of confusion as fear and panic took control. He reached for the phone again, and that's when he heard something else. Soft, masculine laughter filled the room.

"What…who…"

"Sorry, Medford. Not going to happen."

Lawrence tried to swing around to see who had spoken behind him. His legs refused to obey him, and he teetered forward. Catching himself on the edge of the desk, he stood there, hoping to catch his breath. He was hallucinating. Maybe he was dreaming. Maybe… Agony speared through his left leg. He glanced down to see that a snake had struck again. This was no nightmare!

Grabbing a paperweight, he dropped it onto the snake and missed. It did nothing other than slither off. As he staggered, his only thought was to get help. He needed his phone. Where had it—

"Looking for this?"

Lawrence jerked around. It hadn't been his imagination. Someone was here. Holding his phone out to him. His vision wavering, he reached for it and then swallowed a gasp when the hand jerked away.

"Please…I need to call someone."

"Yeah, I know. You're not a bad guy, Medford. In fact, I really like your films. Classy but understated. Unfortunately, you pissed somebody off. Sorry about that."

"Please…I need help."

"Oh, you'll get help, but it'll come much too late for you."

Nausea swelled, twisting and knotting. The rapid thundering of his heart roared through his head. He couldn't think…couldn't think… His mouth opened but no sound emerged. His legs collapsed, and he fell forward, landing face first on the hardwood floor. He shifted his head slightly and looked up to see a vaguely familiar face.

"The venom is taking over now. You'll be dead soon."

Lawrence lay on the floor, his mind dulled with pain. His breathing labored, his heart raced faster and faster toward a dark finish line. A line he hadn't planned on crossing for several more decades.

Who hated him so much to kill him? He thought about what could have been…what could never be.

. . .

STUDYING Lawrence Medford as he took his last breaths was a unique experience. In his line of work, one needed to absorb the experience to learn the various facets. Who knew when he might need to recall the incident to enhance a scene?

Besides, if he'd learned anything in his career, it was that the job, no matter how distasteful, had to be finished. Using his phone, he clicked a couple of photos. Proof of death was also an important part of his itinerary.

The reason behind Medford's killing was of no real importance to him. He had a job to do, and as usual he took great pride in his work. Knowing why his client wanted to off the wealthy and famous man mattered nothing to him. It was a job that paid him quite a bit of money. That was his only motivation.

With meticulous care, he gathered his weapons into a box. Nasty creatures, but quite effective. He would leave only the largest snake. To the authorities, it would appear that Medford had died from multiple bites from that one snake. They would never know the man had been attacked by a half dozen of the vipers.

He looked around once more to ensure he'd left no indication that he had been there. Satisfied with what he saw and with his night's work, he let himself out the way he'd come in, through the back door.

Scaling the brick wall in the backyard, he hopped down and jogged the quarter mile to where he'd left his car. Only slightly winded, he dropped into the driver's seat, pressed the engine button, and shifted into gear. Five miles down the road, he made the call.

"It's done."

"He's dead?"

"Should be within the next ten minutes. He'll be long dead before anyone finds him."

"Excellent. The other half of your payment is on its way."

"Good."

"Stay close. It's possible I'll have another job for you soon."

"Sounds good."

He ended the call and set his eyes on the rising sun ahead of him. If he timed it right, he might be able to get in a quick swim before he was due on the set. Staying in shape was imperative for both his professions. Acting and contract killing had several things in common. One of those things was good physical health. Another was the opportunity to role-play. He had been everything from a waiter in a fancy restaurant to a middle-management pencil pusher at a CPA firm. Killing—at least the way he liked to do it—took talent and time. One couldn't rush perfection.

Took a lot of work to be at the top of one's game. He was already at the top of one. Wouldn't be long before he was on top of the other.

CHAPTER ELEVEN

Los Angeles, California

It was the cold that woke her first. Tendrils, like icy fingers, crept through her limbs, spreading desolation, a deep, aching sadness that permeated her whole being. The pressure on her chest increased as if someone were sitting on her. She woke, gasping and wheezing for breath, shivering uncontrollably as if she were encased in ice.

Why was it always the cold and that chest-squeezing pain that came first? Why not the other horror? Not that she wanted those hideous nightmares either. The cold on its own was brutal enough…the way it slowly, insidiously slid through her whole body like a poison worm attacking inch by inch. Sometimes she wondered if perhaps she was supposed to have died, and this was Death's way of reminding her that he was still around, still hovering.

She should be dead. No real reason she wasn't, other than the sheer will to live. And that voice…that beautiful, masculine voice that called to her to stay alive. To wait for him because he would come for her.

Aubrey shook her head and snorted her disgust at her thoughts. One would think she would have given up on fairy tales and romantic nonsense. Sure she was a dreamer —that came with the territory of creativity—but that didn't belong in the real world. The real world had bad people with ulterior motives and knives and fists. The real world was where she lived. Not in some fictional land where princes rescued damsels in distress. She'd learned long ago that if she needed rescuing, she damn well had to do it herself.

But late at night, when she was extremely tired or over-wrought, the nightmare would come. The pain, the fear, the absolute agony. There was no hope, no chance of survival. And then she would hear his voice, calling her name, calming her, telling her to hold on.

It was a voice she'd lived with for twelve years. The voice of the man she loved. A man she'd never seen. A man who was long dead. Her heart didn't care. It knew to whom it belonged.

She rolled over in bed and squinted at the bedside clock. Only five thirty. She'd come back to her hotel room and thrown herself into her work. The interview with Brenda had drained her, but her mind was too wired to rest.

When she'd crawled into bed at two thirty this morning, she had promised herself she would sleep late. Three hours of sleep wouldn't cut it, but she had no choice. No way would she be able to sleep after a nightmare.

Promising herself a nap after her meeting today, she slipped from the bed. The cold still holding her in its grasp, she pulled on the thick hotel robe. Taking a deep breath to refocus, she padded into the small living room area. Her laptop sat on the table where she'd left it last night, the blinking cursor a welcoming sight. Writing was her number one way of overcoming the nightmares. She could lose herself in the story and for a time completely forget what haunted her.

Only those closest to her knew what had happened twelve years ago. She wanted neither the notoriety nor the attention that would come from publicizing her own experience. She did, however, want people to be informed. What they chose to do with that information was up to them. She had once lived in the darkness of unawareness, and her ignorance had almost gotten her killed.

This was her way of fighting evil. Some people wore a badge and carried a gun. She carried a camera and a microphone.

Her first documentary had been about human trafficking. The film had established her reputation as a hard-hitting but compassionate revealer of truth. It also won her several awards and more than a few enemies. When evil people's livelihoods were threatened, they did everything they could to stop the truth.

The documentary had revealed that human trafficking happened, in every state and in every town, no matter how small. That it was an insidious, evil disease that destroyed lives and made greedy, vile people a lot of money.

Choosing human trafficking as the topic of her first documentary had been no accident. But for the grace of God, that's exactly what would have happened to her. That was what they'd planned. She'd heard them. The British one—older and very much the leader of the group—had been talking. A lot of the conversation had been in a language she didn't even recognize, but she'd heard enough English and French to get the gist. There had been a debate going on. Sell her or accept the offered ransom.

She'd been bleeding and beaten, so weak from pain and the breath-stealing pneumonia attacking her lungs, she could barely stay conscious, but she had been determined to listen, to know what was going to happen. Some man in Austria had made an offer. A ransom had been presented as well. Thankfully, the quick ransom money had been too hard to pass up.

But there had been others who hadn't been as fortunate. She had seen them, heard them. Weeping, screaming, desolate, and hopeless. When she'd returned home, she'd told anyone who would listen that others needed saving. She'd insisted something be done about the ones left behind. Not only for them but also for the man she owed her life to. It had been weeks before she'd heard anything. She'd been unconscious much of the time, struggling to stay alive. When she had woken, finally cognizant of her surroundings, she'd asked. The news had been devastating. The prison had been decimated. Nothing remained.

But Lion had been there. He had existed, and he had kept her alive, given her the courage to survive. She had long accepted that he was dead but he still deserved justice. Who were those people who had captured them? Would she ever know the truth?

And those women had existed, too. What had happened to them? Had they been sold? To whom?

The evil that people could do to their fellow human beings no longer surprised her, and she was eons past being that innocent, naïve young woman. She had tried her best to not become hardened by that knowledge. Instead, she'd worked her butt off to try to change the world.

In that dark, filthy prison, she had prayed a thousand prayers and made a million promises. With fear, pain, and sorrow tearing and shredding her soul, she had faced dark truths and excruciating lies. At nineteen, she'd been a bit shallow and a lot vain. Not a bad person, but also not one who thought too deeply. Introspection had never been her strong suit, but when forced to deal with the possibility of her death, or worse, she'd done some major soul searching. That experience had changed her life and her focus.

She had vowed to do something of value, to make a difference. Even though acting touched a lot of lives, she'd realized she needed to do something more.

Many people had asked what inspired her, and she always gave a vague answer. The reasons she did what she did were many and varied. But in the back of her mind there was always the voice. The legacy of a man named Lion would live on through the work that she did. If she could do nothing else for him, she could at least do this.

She often wondered what might have happened if he had shown up that day at the library. Would they have gone to dinner that night? Seen each other the next day? And the day after that? Their connection had been real. She might've been naïve about many things back then, but not about this. They had connected on a level she'd never known existed. She doubted she'd ever have that kind of bond again. For the past few years, she had dated various men. Not one of them had ever given her the feeling of wholeness and completeness as her extremely short relationship with a man she'd never even seen.

In the dark of night, when demons hounded, she would often call up his voice in her mind. She wished she had told him that he had been an answer to one of her prayers. If he hadn't been there, she would have just given up. She had been that lost, that hopeless.

The thought that he'd died without ever knowing what he had done for her, what he'd meant to her, hurt deep within her soul. How she longed for just one more moment so she could give him the words.

She was so lost in the memories that it took her several seconds to notice her phone was ringing. She glanced at the display, and her heart lightened. Her cousin Becca was one of her favorite people in the world.

Aubrey answered with a smile in her voice. "Hey, you. What are you doing up so early?"

"Early? It's almost ten o'clock."

Aubrey glanced at the clock on her laptop and verified the time. She also noted that she'd written almost seventeen pages. Sometimes her muse worked without her even being aware.

"Don't tell me you worked all night again," Becca said.

"No, just woke early and lost track of time." Standing, she stretched her neck and back.

"Have you heard the news?"

"What news?"

"Lawrence Medford was found dead this morning."

Aubrey dropped back into her chair, stunned. "What happened?"

"Believe it or not, he was bitten by a snake."

"But where? We were scheduled for a meeting this afternoon. Where would he have encountered a snake?"

"Apparently, one crawled into his house."

Without conscious thought, she lifted her feet from the floor. "That's terrible."

"I know. It just hit the news, but I heard about it before that. My stylist's sister is married to his masseuse. He was the one who found him."

"That's just awful."

She refused to think about what this would do to her own project. A life had ended. From what she could remember, Medford was divorced but had several grown children and a couple of grandchildren.

He was…had been an exceptionally talented producer, and she had looked forward to ironing out their differences and working with him.

"I know that puts a crimp in your plans for your next project."

"It'll put me behind, but I'll find a backer."

"You know that Daddy would do it in a heartbeat."

"No, don't even go there, Becca. Uncle Syd has done more than enough for me."

Her cousin knew the gist of what had happened to her in Paris and Syria, but not the gory details. Becca would have blamed herself for not being there with her, and Aubrey didn't want that in her head.

Her uncle Syd had paid her ransom. Without him, there was no telling where she'd be now. She already owed him her life; she refused to take anything else from him. As an Oscar-winning film director, Syd Green commanded well-deserved respect and influence. However, having him open doors for her went against every promise she'd made to herself.

Becca released a dramatic sigh. "All right. I'll stop haranguing you about that, but I do have a small favor to ask."

"What's that?"

"Go to a party with me?"

"What kind of party?"

Becca wasn't one to live on the wild side that some Hollywood stars were known for, so Aubrey wasn't too concerned, but being around a bunch of pretty people wasn't Aubrey's idea of fun either.

"It's a preproduction party for *Feathers*."

Based on the book of the same name, by bestselling author, Maggie Rhodes, the movie was one of the most-talked-about projects in Hollywood this year. It was also Becca Green's first starring role—and one that would make her a star.

"What about Chad?" Aubrey said. "Isn't he available?"

"We decided to go our separate ways."

"Oh, Becca, I'm sorry. When did that happen?"

"Last night."

Becca and Aubrey were total opposites when it came to dating. Becca fell in and out of love every few months. After the inevitable breakup, she would be blue for a couple of weeks and then move on. Aubrey, on the other hand, was in love with a man she'd never met, who was no longer alive. Why else would he haunt her dreams?

Becca gave another long, dramatic sigh, reminding Aubrey of her responsibility as a cousin and best friend.

"Come over tonight and let's do a girl thing. I'll order takeout."

"That sounds wonderful. I'll bring the wine and dessert. We'll have an old-fashioned sleepover the way we used to, Kat."

Becca was the only person who still occasionally called her Kat. In her heart, that had been Lion's name for her. It was an intimacy she wanted to share with no one else. Besides, when she'd returned from Syria she had been a different person. A different name only made sense. Using her middle name had been an easy transition.

Her family had gone along with the name change, wanting nothing more than to let her put everything that had happened behind her.

"But what about the party? Will you go with me? Please… pretty please?"

She had hoped to return home to Florida tomorrow, but now that she would likely need to meet with other prospective investors, that would have to wait. Still, attending a glitzy party held no appeal.

"There must be tons of guys who'd love to be your date for the party. Why not ask one of them?"

"Because I'm going to need all my focus to be on this movie. I don't need the distraction of a new relationship."

Becca was right. The last thing she needed was a new romance to take her focus away from this role. "Okay, I'll go."

"Thank you. I'll bring you an outfit to wear."

Aubrey ended the call on a laugh. Another thing they didn't have in common was love of fashion. She'd always chosen comfort over style, and Becca was of the mind that if an outfit looked fabulous, it was worth a little pain.

Standing, she went to the window that overlooked the large hotel pool. Several people were already swimming or lying on the lounge chairs, soaking up the morning sun. She wished she were home so she could swim in the privacy of her own pool. When she traveled, she never bothered to bring a suit. She knew she wouldn't be swimming. The scars on her body didn't define her, and she wasn't ashamed of them, but the looks and speculation were tiresome. She had learned to ignore them and the occasional rude question, but it was just easier not to reveal them to those who didn't know her.

That last day, before her ransom had been paid, was a mind-blurring day of agonizing pain and terror. She had thought they were going to torture her, use her against Lion to get whatever information they thought he had. And it had been torturous, but what had happened to her had had nothing to do with Lion.

She'd been beaten and then left alone. That was when she'd heard that a ransom had been offered and accepted. She'd been in a near state of euphoria, knowing she would be going home soon. Then everything had changed. The man with the British accent had spoken again, and she'd barely comprehended his words before the new nightmare had begun.

He'd said, "We're to send her home with a message."

When she'd woken up in the hospital days later, she'd had multiple stab wounds all over her body. None of the wounds had been to vital organs, none intended to kill her. She still didn't know who or what that "message" had been for.

She had told the men who'd come to talk to her, both from the FBI and the State Department. Though they'd been kind, no one had offered any concrete ideas on what those words had meant. She'd been told that it had likely been part of her torture. She didn't think so, but without knowing who had taken her in the first place, she'd had to let it go. She doubted she would ever know the real reason behind it all.

The scars had healed. Some had almost disappeared, but several hadn't. She rarely thought of them any longer. They were part of who she was. And though the scars on the inside were still with her, she'd learned to let them motivate her.

Had she made a difference? Yes. Was she through? Not by a long shot.

Lawrence Medford's genius would have been invaluable and would be sorely missed. However, she was determined to get this film made. Nothing and no one would stop her from telling this story.

CHAPTER TWELVE

Beverly Hills, California

The party was in full swing, and Aubrey felt like a fifth wheel. Becca was in her element and had danced with so many men, Aubrey had lost count. Not that she minded. Seeing her cousin enjoy herself was a relief. After their get-together a few nights ago, it had become apparent that the breakup with Chad had hurt her cousin more than she'd let on. It was good to see a smile back on Becca's beautiful face.

Wearing a black silk and cotton Halston cocktail dress that fit her like a glove, Aubrey had enjoyed her share of male attention. She had even danced a couple of times, but big parties were simply not her thing. She much preferred fewer people and a quieter venue.

Not that she had much of a social life. When she wasn't working, she was sleeping. At that thought, she scrunched her nose. Her dad had always claimed she was born with an old soul. They'd had a special bond she would always treasure. Little more than a year after her ordeal in Syria, he was gone. Even though his daughter had come home alive,

Matthew Starr had never really recovered from her abduction. His heart had simply given out on him.

Since his death, she and her mother weren't as close as they'd once been. Though she never came out and said it, Elizabeth Starr blamed her daughter for her husband's death. Aubrey understood that. She blamed herself, too. If she hadn't gone to Paris, none of that horror would have happened.

Even though he was long gone, she often felt as though he was still with her, guiding her. On occasion, she would catch a scent of his cologne or just get the feeling that he was watching over her. She could almost feel him now, and she smiled at the thought.

There was another reason that her heart felt lighter, too. Just before she'd walked out the door to meet Becca in the hotel lobby, her phone had rung. It had been an out-of-area call, and she had hesitated to answer. The feelers she'd put out for a new backer would all come from a California area code. The last thing she wanted was some kind of sales call. Besides, considering the response she'd gotten from the people she'd contacted, she didn't anticipate anyone in the industry funding her project.

Something inside her told her to answer the call. She was glad she had.

"This is Aubrey."

"Hello, Aubrey, my name is Kate Walker. Lawrence Medford was a dear friend of mine."

"Hello, Ms. Walker. I'm so sorry for your loss. Lawrence's death was a blow to many of us."

"Yes, it was. He told me about you…about your project. He had high hopes that you would be able to work out your differences."

"I believe we could have. He was an incredibly talented producer and my first choice for this project."

"I wonder if you would mind taking a detour before you head back home to Florida. I may be able to help you."

Her heartbeat had increased. "Help me how?"

"By providing the funding for your documentary."

"I'm sorry, but I'm not familiar with your name. Are you in the film industry?"

"Not exactly." Ms. Walker had paused for a moment and then added, "Let's just say that funding worthwhile projects is a particular hobby of mine."

Intrigued, Aubrey had said yes. She knew nothing about Kate Walker and would definitely research her before she agreed to anything, but a small bloom of optimism had replaced her worry.

She would fly to North Carolina tomorrow morning where hopefully she would find another backer. This could be the answer to her prayers.

"Mind if an old man sits down with the prettiest girl in the room?"

Looking up at her uncle, Aubrey gave him a wry grin. "I'm not sure which of those is the bigger lie. Not by any stretch of the imagination are you old. And we both know that your daughter is most definitely the prettiest girl at the party."

Stooping down, Syd Green planted a kiss on Aubrey's cheek and then dropped heavily into a chair beside her. "I'll have to disagree with you on both those counts. You look lovely tonight. And my bones are reminding me that it's way past my bedtime."

"I didn't know you were coming."

"I couldn't miss my daughter's big party, but I had a meeting that ran long."

"You work too hard, Uncle Syd."

"Now if that isn't the pot calling the kettle black, I don't know what is."

She couldn't argue with him there. They were both workaholics. "You know we wouldn't have it any other way."

A sad, melancholy look darkened his face. "Perhaps."

"Are you okay?" She touched his hand in concern. "Did something happen?"

She felt a certain responsibility to her uncle. Her aunt Jenny, Syd's wife, had passed several years ago. The stroke had hit her at an early age, stunning everyone. Aubrey had still been in the hospital recovering when the news had come. Her mother's youngest sister had been a vibrant and beautiful woman. Though she had survived, lingering for several years, she had been mentally incapacitated. She had died in her sleep only a couple of years ago.

Syd patted her hand. "Everything's fine. Don't you worry about me."

"Then what's wrong? Are you feeling okay?"

As quickly as the sad expression had appeared, it evaporated, but his eyes were still more solemn than she'd seen them in a while.

"I'm fine, my dear. It's just been a long day."

She could definitely agree that it had been a long day. She had spent hours on the phone, talking with her contacts about funding for her project. The halfhearted promises to consider the project had been almost as disheartening as the straightforward rejections. Money was tight, and some of those toes she might step on with this film were likely friends or at least acquaintances of these people. She understood that, but this story was too important not to tell.

The call from Lawrence Medford's friend Kate Walker had been out of the blue. If a deal panned out, it would be in her opinion, a bona fide miracle.

But that was a worry for tomorrow. Refocusing, she gave her uncle a bright smile. "Do you have a new project? Can you talk about it?"

"You know me. I always have five or six simmering. Nothing that'll knock anyone's socks off, but still some solid works. Speaking of projects, I'm sorry yours has been put on hold. I know Lawrence Medford was going to be your biggest financier."

"He was, but I'll get it made."

His brows furrowed in surprise. "You have the funding?"

Since she didn't know if things would work out, she wasn't ready to tell him about her conversation with Kate Walker. "I have several investors I'm talking to."

"Why don't you concentrate on scriptwriting for a while? Maybe sell one or two of them? Then, when the purse strings loosen up, you can go back to your project."

"It's an important and timely story that needs to be told now. Human trafficking is more rampant than ever. People need to know."

"Then let me help you. We'll work on it together. I can—"

Aubrey held up her hand. "Thank you, Uncle Syd, but you've done more than enough for me."

Grabbing her hand, he squeezed gently. "You're like a daughter to me, you know that."

"I don't know what Mom and I would have done without you after Dad died. You've been my lifesaver more than once. Believe me when I tell you I love you dearly and appreciate you, but I have to do this on my own."

He sighed deeply, squeezed her hand one more time. "I understand, but you know you can always come to me."

"Can I steal this handsome man away for a dance?"

They both looked up into the laughing eyes of Becca. Dressed in an off-the-shoulder cocktail dress, she was the picture of health and happiness. The azure blue of her dress was the perfect complement to her white-blond hair, creamy skin, and ocean-blue eyes. The sparkle in them said she was having the time of her life.

She and Becca had wanted to be actors since they were both little girls playing dress up together. They used to put on plays for their families and friends, and on occasion, their efforts had been filmed. When they were teens, those old recordings had been unearthed to entertain unsuspecting guests at numerous gatherings.

Aubrey was thrilled to see her cousin's dream come true in such a big way.

Uncle Syd rose slowly to his feet. "Chatting with my lovely niece and dancing with my beautiful daughter are the reasons I came tonight." Holding out his hand to Becca, he said, "Come on, sweetheart. Let's show them how it's done."

They took a step away, and then Syd turned back to Aubrey. "Give it some thought, sweetie."

Aubrey nodded her agreement, but she already knew the answer. She had taken enough from her uncle. She would meet with her possible new benefactor and hopefully get this project off the ground. If the funding didn't come through, she would find another way.

CHAPTER THIRTEEN

Bogota, Colombia

While Xavier drove, Liam sat in the passenger seat and mentally reviewed the plan for the raid. With the intel Myron had been able to give them, along with the research Serena's team had dug up on the property, Liam knew they would be successful.

No one ever questioned why he was so focused on human trafficking. They knew the story almost as well as he did. This was his op. He was the one who'd gotten the intel. The one who'd worked the assets. He was the one with the biggest investment in a successful outcome.

A small huff came from the man driving the SUV. Xavier had been his friend long before OZ. They knew everything about each other and had no issues with speaking their minds.

"You got something to say," Liam said, "say it."

"You've been looking for her for over a decade. You know the chances that she's still alive are almost nonexistent."

Yeah, he knew the statistics. The life expectancy of a trafficking victim in captivity was around seven years. It'd been over twelve years since Cat had been sold. The odds of her still being alive weren't good. But they weren't impossible, and until he had firm confirmation that she was dead, he would not stop looking.

"You think I should just give up? Stop looking for her?"

"I think you need to get on with your life."

"And what exactly does that look like? Getting on with one's life?"

"This is all you do, man. When you're not working an OZ op, you're digging up intel on human traffickers and going on raids. You have no personal life."

Liam gave a huff of laughter. "Hate to bring this up, Xavier, but you're not exactly a walking, talking example of a balanced life. If I'm not mistaken, the last woman you dated was back when cellphones weighed about ten pounds and mullets were still the rage."

His friend snorted his amusement. "Not exactly that long, but I get your point. But at least I don't spend every free moment obsessing about a hopeless cause."

"When there's hope, it's never a hopeless cause. Besides, even if she can't be saved, others can."

"I know, brother. And it's one of the greatest feelings in the world to rescue a trafficked person." He lifted his shoulder in a shrug. "I just worry about you."

"Worry about your own sorry self. When are you going to tell Jazz what you found out?"

"In time."

Liam shook his head. "You know good and well the longer you wait, the harder it's going to be. She finds out you've held on to that intel for months, you'll be in the doghouse big-time. Besides, she deserves to know the truth."

"Yeah, she does. But she's still recovering from that fall last year. When she's one hundred percent again, I'll tell her."

Liam got that. They'd almost lost Jazz—Jasmine McAlister—last year. Some maniac on a crusade to die had tried
his best to take Jazz with him. They'd managed to rescue her,
but she'd been out of commission for months. Jazz was just
now getting her strength and endurance back.

"She's stronger than you give her credit for," Liam said.

"There's no one who knows that better than me."

"And?"

Xavier murmured softly, "It'll break her heart."

"And you'll be there to help her through it. We all will."

"Yeah, we will." He shrugged. "She's got a physical eval
coming up soon. If she passes, I'll tell her."

"She'll pass."

"I know."

Liam let it go at that. He knew Xavier would do the right
thing. Jazz was special to all of them, but Xavier had a bond
with her that went beyond mere friendship. Something
everyone just accepted.

Just as they accepted that Liam had spent over a decade
searching for a woman he'd never seen and knew only by a
name that most certainly was not her own.

The day they'd escaped from that prison had been one of
the worst days of his life. Not being able to find Cat had been
hellish. When he'd left, he'd felt as if he were abandoning her,
though there had been no reason to stay. She wasn't there.
And then the helicopter had crashed, almost killing them all.

Six of them had survived the brutal trek across the desert.
They'd formed a bond that he would've sworn couldn't be
broken. Until Hawke.

"You know Olivia came to see Ash a few months back?"
Liam asked.

Though he didn't respond, the tense set of Xavier's shoulders told him all he needed to know. Xavier wasn't ready to
forgive.

"She's working for Last Chance Rescue now."

"Yeah, I know."

Of course he would. Not much got by his friend. But the man was beyond stubborn about some things, such as forgiveness.

Olivia Gates had been an OZ operative. She'd been married to Nick Hawthorne, and they'd seemed like the perfect couple, the perfect OZ partners. When things had gone south, they'd gone all the way to the bottom. Hawke had been killed, and Olivia had been lucky to leave OZ without being shot by one of her fellow operatives. That had been one of their darkest times.

Even though he understood why Olivia had made the choice she had, it was still hard to conceive that she'd actually made it. And many on the OZ team, including Xavier, would likely never forgive her.

"I've talked to her a few times for intel on a possible lead. Last Chance Rescue focuses a lot on human trafficking. She and her boss, Noah McCall, have been a big help on a couple of leads."

Silence. Liam let it sit there. He couldn't say he agreed with what Olivia had done, but refusing her help would never be an option. Her intel had saved a life—that trumped hard feelings every single time.

"Liam, you copy?"

Putting his finger to his earbud, Liam answered Gideon. "Roger that. What's up?"

"We've got a problem. We're at the surveillance house. Our target house looks empty."

"What? How is that possible?"

"Hell if I know. We got here about half an hour ago. Everything looked fine. Lights off, everybody asleep. Night crew reported nothing unusual."

"Then what makes you think it's empty?"

"Lights are still off. The past three days they've come on promptly at six thirty. It's a quarter past seven. My gut says they're gone."

Telling Gideon that maybe they'd overslept would be ludicrous. The man's instincts were never wrong. So where were they?

Sean, Serena, and Jazz had been the night crew. Highly trained and extremely capable operatives. No way would they have missed a mass exodus of the entire household. Something was way off here.

"We're about ten minutes away. Hold tight."

"Copy that," Gideon said.

Liam shut down his comm and cut his eyes over to Xavier. "This stinks big-time."

"I agree. Sean and Serena wouldn't have missed them leaving."

His mind raced with what could have happened. Pulling up schematics of the mansion, Liam examined them again. He'd reviewed the layout numerous times over the last couple of days. Could've drawn the damn thing by heart. There were two back doors, two side doors, and one front door. They had cameras on every exit. No way a group of eleven could have left without someone noticing. Unless...

He peered closer. "There's got to be a tunnel under the house."

"But where? And why would they leave? They were there yesterday. How would they know we were coming?"

His gut twisting, Liam grabbed his phone and punched Myron's number. Getting his voice mail was no surprise. Myron rarely answered his phone. "Myron, it's me. Call me back ASAP."

He ended the call, but his mind already knew the truth. They'd somehow gotten to Myron. And even though the man was no saint, Liam knew he wouldn't have given up his secrets if he hadn't been forced to do so. Question was, had Myron survived?

The trafficking house belonged to the elusive Mafia kingpin Hector Gomez, well known in the trafficking world. Rumor had it that Gomez was a frequent visitor to the house. As much as Liam had wanted to bust down the doors and rescue the victims, nabbing Gomez would put a substantial dent in the trafficking industry in this part of the world.

With the full backing of the Colombian government, Liam and his OZ teammates had watched the house for three days and nights. Men and women arrived and left at all hours. Armed men guarded the perimeter, trying without much success to conceal their weapons beneath their jackets. None of the men fit Gomez's description.

Liam had made the decision to wait no longer. The plan was to go in tonight. Now it appeared he'd waited too long.

Inwardly cursing himself, Liam mentally reviewed the op. Their intent had been to strike a couple of hours before dawn, after the entire household had quieted down for the night. It had been a good plan and should've worked. Now they'd need to regroup and figure out what had gone wrong.

They pulled into the private drive of the mansion they'd taken over. Its three stories made it easy to keep an eye on the house across the street. Xavier drove around to the back. Both Gideon and Eve were waiting at the door for them.

"I texted Jazz, Sean, and Serena," Eve said. "They're headed back here."

Liam nodded. Probably was pointless for them to return. If the house was empty, there was no one to rescue, no one to fight, no Mafia kingpin to capture.

"Let's head over. Be on the lookout for traps. If they knew about us, they might've left a message."

They'd definitely left a message, but not one Liam had anticipated. While the rest of the team continued to look for clues in the empty house, Liam stood over the tortured and brutalized body of Myron Hornsby. The man hadn't deserved this. He'd had his flaws and had been prone to having sticky fingers when an expensive piece of artwork caught his eye, but with the intel he'd provided Liam through the years, he had saved numerous lives.

Whoever had done this had wanted to send a clear message. Liam had no problem interpreting it. Now he was even more determined. These people were going down.

"We found the tunnel."

Gideon's voice punched through Liam's fury. Getting caught up in anger would accomplish nothing.

"Let's go." Following Gideon, he glanced over his shoulder once more at Myron and felt another surge of guilt and grief. Dammit, why did people do things like this?

"Hey, man, it's not your fault."

"Oh yeah? Whose is it, then?"

"Myron was no amateur. He knew exactly who he was dealing with and what could happen. He was in the business a long time and made his choices..." Gideon held up his hand before Liam could protest. "I'm not saying he deserved this, but he played a dangerous game with a lot of dangerous people. He knew the risks."

"Maybe so, but this happened on my watch."

"And you gave him the option of protection, which he declined. You're gonna have to let the guilt go, man. Focus that energy on finding the bastards. Remember, there are at least a dozen victims needing to be rescued."

As usual, Gideon's sound reasoning was hard to argue against.

Liam jerked his head in assent. "Let's go."

While Sean, Serena, Jazz, and Xavier examined each room

for any evidence that could be used, Liam, Gideon, and Eve took off down the stairs of the hidden tunnel. Even though the group was likely long gone, finding their exit point might give them a clue to where they were headed next.

The tunnel was damp and old, almost as old as the house. It hadn't been on the original blueprints but likely had been added not too long after the house was built. Though musty smelling, the brick work had held up well. Whoever had built the tunnel had put some work into it.

Liam looked over his shoulder. "What are the odds that these pricks purchased the house without knowing about the tunnel?"

"I'd say that was the biggest selling point," Gideon answered.

"Yeah. Chances are they've been transporting their victims through here all along."

In grim silence, they continued through the tunnel. The only evidence of recent use was the cigarette butt at the entrance to the tunnel and a small scrap of fabric hanging from a protruding nail. Liam collected both items. Might not tell them anything, but he didn't plan to leave any stone unturned.

The tunnel was shorter than he'd expected. Less than a mile. A small set of stairs led to an unlocked steel door. The hardware was only a few years old.

Guns at the ready, Liam pulled back the door and walked out into a small wooded area. Hearing Gideon and Eve behind him, he turned. "Looks like the ideal spot to bring in new people and take them out, too." He made a 360 observance. "Plenty of tree cover. No houses close by. Bring them in under the cover of night, and no one's the wiser."

"Stryker, you copy?" There was a unique tension in Jazz's voice.

"Yeah. What's wrong?"

"I think we've figured out who gave them Myron. You're going to want to see this in person."

"Copy. I'll be right there." He swung his gaze over to Eve and Gideon. "You guys keep searching. Let me know if you find anything."

With that, Liam took off back down to the tunnel and ran. Since he was no longer looking for clues, he made it to the house in less than five minutes.

Jazz met him at the entrance. "We searched every room and was about to call it a bust, then we found this lying in an ashtray."

Taking the evidence bag Jazz held out, Liam didn't need any explanation. There was only one man arrogant enough to have left the calling card. The Arturo Fuente cigar was not only one of the most expensive in the world, it was also one of the rarest. And Liam knew only one man who had a strong addiction to these cigars—Barnabas Drury.

Son of a bitch.

CHAPTER FOURTEEN

.

Burnsville, North Carolina

Aubrey gasped in delight as she rounded another curve and gazed up at the majesty before her. Oh how she loved the mountains! The forty-minute drive from the Asheville airport had been both awe-inspiring and breathtaking. The trees were gloriously colored in every hue and shade known to man. It took every bit of her willpower not to stop at the various pullover sites to snap a dozen pictures and just enjoy the beauty.

When the GPS voice announced she was close to the turnoff to her destination, Aubrey frowned. Had she typed in the right address? This heavily wooded patch of road didn't look like home to anything other than forest creatures. When the voice announced her turn, she slowed to a crawl. And then she saw a sign that blended so well into the surroundings, it almost looked as though it was part of the forest. The sign simply said, *Haven*.

Intrigued, Aubrey turned onto the paved drive, following the curves for at least a mile. When she spotted the mansion, she lost her breath. It was one of the largest homes she'd ever seen in the US. That was saying a lot, since she had been to homes of some of Hollywood's most elite. But this…this was as if someone had spirited an ancient castle away from the moors of England and dropped it into a small valley in North Carolina.

She'd done some research. Kate Walker was a former FBI agent who had married tech billionaire Lars Walker. Lars had died a few years ago from complications of Alzheimer's. Kate had inherited his wealth and was apparently very much a recluse. Little was known about her current life. After she'd left the FBI, it was as if she had stopped existing. Looking at her home, Aubrey could understand why she would never leave. It was magnificent.

As she parked in front of the mansion and stepped out of the car onto the paved drive, Aubrey cautioned herself. Though Mrs. Walker could likely fund her entire project many times over, that didn't mean Aubrey would agree to take her money. How much control would the woman want?

She'd had creative differences with Lawrence Medford but had known they could have eventually worked things out. That didn't mean Kate Walker would have the same goals or vision. Either way, Aubrey would give any deal careful consideration before making a decision. She knew how she wanted to do this documentary. Having someone interfere, no matter how well meaning, wasn't something she would allow.

"Aubrey, thank you for coming."

A woman of indeterminate age came swiftly down the steps toward her. Dressed in gray slacks, white turtleneck and tweed jacket, Kate Walker was the epitome of casual elegance. Her hair was pulled back into an intricate braid, and though she wore little makeup, her pale pink lipstick emphasized full lips and a light application of mascara brought out the emerald green of her eyes. She was slender but not fashionably so and had a twinkle in her eyes that made Aubrey warm to her immediately.

Aubrey held out her hand, and Kate shook it firmly. "I was afraid you'd change your mind."

"Why's that?"

"Because some people would look at my offer and see strings attached. Creative types don't usually like to take input from those not in the same field."

"Do you plan on giving your input, Mrs. Walker?"

"Let's just say I want to see what you've got planned. Who knows? I might have suggestions that will intrigue you." Before Aubrey could ask what they were, she added, "And please, call me Kate."

"All right."

"Now, let's go have some refreshments on the terrace and talk about your project."

Aubrey followed Kate into the house, trying not to gape like an overwhelmed schoolgirl.

Apparently she wasn't very good at hiding her admiration because Kate turned to her and grinned. "It's audacious, isn't it? My husband had it built years before we met. I thought about moving, maybe donating it for a children's home or a hospital, but leaving behind all the memories isn't something I'm ready to do yet."

Kate led her to a small side terrace, which had a lovely view of the vibrant, autumn-colored trees that surrounded the estate. A table was already set with a scrumptious-looking English tea. "My late husband was British. This is one of the traditions he brought with him that I have thoroughly embraced." She paused in the act of pulling out a chair. "Would you like to freshen up before we sit down?"

"If you don't mind."

Pointing her to a door, Kate said, "Down the hallway,

third door on the right. I'll pour the tea. How do you like yours?"

"Two sugars, no cream."

Aubrey quickly washed her hands and freshened her makeup. Kate Walker was nothing like she'd expected, and the optimism she'd lost earlier was now back in full force. Just in the brief few moments they'd had together she already knew she liked this woman. Could she work with her? That was the hope.

She returned to the terrace to see Kate sitting at the table, sipping her tea, a faraway expression on her face.

"Everything okay?"

Kate gave her a wistful smile. "I get melancholy sometimes when I sit down to a full English tea."

"How long has your husband been gone?"

"He passed only a few years ago, but he was gone before that."

"Alzheimer's is a dreadful, hideous disease."

"You sound as if you have personal experience with it."

"My aunt Jenny suffered from a form of dementia before she died."

"Ah, yes. Syd's wife."

"You know my uncle?"

"By reputation only. He has an impressive track record of megahits. I'm surprised he hasn't offered to fund your project."

"Oh, he has, but I prefer to keep my personal life and my business life separate."

"That's understandable. It can make for uncomfortable Thanksgivings, can't it?"

It had been years since her family had enjoyed a traditional Thanksgiving dinner. After Aubrey's father had died, her mother had no longer wanted to do anything remotely traditional. Elizabeth Starr now spent most of her holidays in Italy with an old school friend.

Uncle Syd spent his holidays with friends, and Becca was always flitting somewhere around the world. In the last few years, holidays had become just regular days for Aubrey.

When she didn't respond to Kate's remark, they went on to talk about other things. She learned that Kate was an avid pilot and had her own plane.

When they finished eating, Kate sat back in her chair and eyed her expectantly. "Now, let's talk about your project."

"You said that you and Lawrence were friends. He told you about it?"

"Yes and no. I talked to him a few weeks ago, and he mentioned that he was meeting with you."

"His death was so tragic and bizarre. Imagine having a snake enter your home like that and strike without warning."

Something flickered on Kate's face but was gone in an instant. Aubrey waited for her to comment, but all she did was nod and say, "It was indeed tragic. Lawrence had his idiosyncrasies, but he was an incredibly talented man."

"Yes he was. I looked forward to working with him. We had our differences, but I knew we could work them out."

"Tell me about your project. Lawrence told me the basics, which had me so intrigued."

"The title is *Still Lost*. It's a follow-up to the documentary I did a few years back."

"*The Lost Ones*. Which was excellent, by the way."

"Thank you. Part of the new one will include checking in with a couple of the victims we featured in *The Lost Ones*. Where they are now. What kind of life they've been able to create. What lingering impact their experience has had on them."

"That sounds interesting. What else?"

"This time, I want to cover all aspects of human trafficking—not just focus on the victims. I want to talk to some of the incarcerated traffickers to try to find out what makes them tick. What kind of person abducts, sells, and abuses another human being? How did they become who they are? Is there remorse? If not, why not?"

"Might be difficult to obtain access to those people."

"I've received permission from two prisons for interviews, and have gotten an agreement from three traffickers already. It's just a matter of arranging a meeting time."

"Excellent. What else?"

"I want to cover the rescuers. What motivates someone to put their life on the line to save others? Is it because of a personal experience? Are they on a crusade? If so, why? What drives them?"

"I might be able to help you with that aspect."

"That would be wonderful. I have a couple of prospects, but the more I have, the better insight I can get."

"You do realize that there are people out there who don't want these stories told, don't you?"

"I dealt with that on the first film, so yes, I'm aware."

"But the kind of in-depth reporting you're talking about here is the kind that could provoke some people to do whatever is necessary to keep their secrets from being revealed."

"That's one of the reasons I'm doing this. They need to be exposed."

"You could be putting yourself and your crew in danger."

"We're taking precautions, and we also don't advertise what we're working on. My team is a hundred percent loyal, and they never discuss the details of their specific jobs. I'm the only one who knows the names of my sources."

"And you take all the risks?"

"That's only fair. My people didn't sign on to become martyrs."

"But you have no problem with putting yourself at risk?"

"Not when the price of safety is someone's life."

"Why are you so committed to this? Are you on your own personal crusade?"

Before Aubrey could answer, Kate held up her hand. "I've read your bio, so I know the public answer. But I'd like to hear the personal reason. Not many people are willing to put themselves at risk unless they've experienced something that inspires and drives their efforts."

If this woman was going to give her millions of dollars, then Aubrey owed her more than the surface answer she gave everyone else. She could tell the truth without going into the details.

"I had a close call years ago. Fortunately, my uncle paid a ransom before the sale could go through. There were others that weren't so fortunate."

"I'm so sorry that happened to you. Thank God you had a better outcome."

"It took me a while to recover, when I finally did, I knew I had to change the direction of my life. I survived for a reason."

"Yes, you did. Few get to realize their purpose while they're still young enough to accomplish it."

Aubrey got the idea that Kate truly did understand, and not just from an outsider's perspective. This woman had experienced suffering and grief. And because of that, or in spite of it, she had found her purpose.

Smiling, Kate stood. "Let's go to my office and discuss how we can get this documentary made."

CHAPTER FIFTEEN

OZ Headquarters
Montana

"You want me to do what?"

Ash had a hard time keeping a straight face. Yeah, he knew he was asking a lot from Stryker, but the expression of horror on his face was priceless. Few things fazed the man, and seeing him look so nonplussed was more than amusing.

Truth was, he'd had a similar reaction less than twelve hours ago when Kate had made the request. His response had been a quick and automatic no. They didn't take civilians into dangerous situations. Period. Since Kate Walker was a good friend and a longtime ally to OZ, he had agreed to hear her out. Once he did, he had to admit he was intrigued. When Stryker settled down, Ash suspected he'd feel the same way.

Since returning from Colombia, Ash had seen a change in Liam. The man was driven by demons—they all were—but Stryker's demeanor had a tinge of hopelessness to it. Something he'd never thought he'd see from his usually even-keeled friend.

Liam carried the guilt of Myron's death. It hadn't been his fault, but that was the problem with a conscience. Guilt didn't always have to make sense. Which was why, even after all this time, he still carried the guilt of Cat's torture and disappearance. None of it had been Liam's fault but that didn't keep him from staying awake at night. The what-ifs could drive a man crazy. Ash understood that all too well.

Not being able to locate Drury was also weighing heavily on Stryker. The sleaze had a gift of escape even Houdini might admire. Ash knew Drury's elusiveness only added to Liam's frustration. Hunting down the murdering bastard was taking time away from his main focus, which was rescuing trafficking victims.

When Ash had created OZ, his goal had been to take on the cases that were the most hopeless, to help people who had nowhere else to turn. They had done that and then some. But each team member had their own agenda as well. Liam Stryker's was one of the most noble, and Ash fully supported his efforts.

Ash repeated his statement. "I want you to let a filmmaker join your next trafficking raid."

"Uh…that would be a hard 'hell no' from me, Ash. I can't believe you'd even ask me to do something so asinine."

"Hear me out, then decide."

Settling back in his chair as if he were anticipating an interesting but unbelievable fairy tale, Stryker nodded.

"The request came from Kate." As he explained her reasons, Ash watched the other man's expression change.

"But there's no real evidence this man's... What's his name? Lawrence Medford? There's no clear evidence that his death is related to this human trafficking documentary she's making?"

"Not yet. All Kate knows is what the surveillance video showed. An unknown man entered the house with a box. He's seen going into Medford's study. About an hour later, he leaves, box in hand. A few hours after that, Medford's body is discovered."

"And you think the box was filled with snakes?"

"That's the theory. Medford had multiple bites, but only one snake was found. After one bite, he still should've been able to call for help. Instead, for whatever reason, he didn't. His phone was on the desk. He was found only a foot away from the desk."

"How many snakes do they think bit him?"

"Hard to say. Kate had a wildlife expert examine the bites. He claimed they came from at least four different snakes."

"Camera show the intruder's face?"

"No. Just the back of his head. He was wearing a baseball cap. About five foot eleven. Slender, but solidly built. That's all they've got to go on."

"Who knows about this?"

"The coroner, the homicide detective in charge of the investigation, and Kate. Jules was with me when Kate's call came. She has a theory."

"What kind of theory?"

"When she was chasing serial killers, she came across a lot of different killers. One was a hit man, professional name, Promethean. He's known for his unique manner of killing, hence the moniker. She thinks the guy in the security video might be this assassin. If so, he's a top-dollar contract killer. Somebody paid big money to take Medford out of the picture."

"Maybe the producer pissed somebody off. That's bound to happen in that line of work. Doesn't mean the two are related."

"That's true, but it's a line worth pursuing."

"Most people only have cameras at the entrances to their homes. Any reason why Medford would have one inside his house?"

"Apparently, a few months ago some things were stolen. He had the cameras installed in hopes of catching the thief. According to Kate, he never did find the culprit."

"Sounds like Kate knew Lawrence Medford well. How did they know each other?"

"I believe her late husband was a longtime friend of Medford's."

"Does this filmmaker know any of what's going on?"

"No. Kate met with her yesterday to feel her out. She's a dedicated young woman determined to reveal how prevalent human trafficking is, but Kate didn't get any sense she's aware that she's running into a potential minefield."

"What's her name?"

"Aubrey Starr."

LIAM DIDN'T KNOW whether to laugh or curse. Aubrey Starr was the woman he'd made a fool of himself in front of when they'd met several years ago in Kosovo. She probably wouldn't remember him, but he definitely remembered her.

Ash continued, "She did that documentary *The Lost Ones* a few years back."

Yeah, he'd seen it a couple of times. It was hard to believe that something that gritty and dark had come from the woman he remembered. She had looked as fresh and innocent as a rose. But in the film, she had been able to convey not only the horror of human trafficking, but also the need for every person to get involved. The documentary had been a call to action. Any viewer of the film who didn't walk away with the intense desire to help in some way wasn't human.

Keeping his face expressionless, Liam said, "She's a gifted

filmmaker, but I doubt she's prepared for the kind of action we encounter."

"I agree, but I'd like for you to talk with her, see where her head is, and then make that determination."

"Why? What's the big picture here?"

"If she's got intel, or can get intel, that would make someone nervous enough to pay high dollar to see that the film doesn't get made, then there's something worth pursuing. With that kind of money, could be there's a large trafficking ring we're not aware of yet. Be good if we could take them down."

Couldn't argue on that count. That would be a good day for everyone.

Liam frowned, still bothered by the obscurity. "Something doesn't add up. Why Medford? He was just the producer and money man. Why not eliminate the main source? Taking out the filmmaker makes more sense than killing the one who's funding it."

"I agree, and I don't know the answer to that."

"Does Ms. Starr know she could be in danger?"

"Hard to say. Kate couldn't get a good read on her. She says she's hiding something but doesn't know if it's related to this or not."

"You want me to bring an outsider into one of my ops, and you don't even know if we can completely trust her?"

"You don't have to share any of your sources or even when the raid is going to happen. We'll keep her close, learn what we can from her, and—"

"And protect her as well."

"Yes."

He wasn't much of a pessimist—took energy away from solving a problem—but if he were one he'd say this plan had disaster written all over it.

"I'm assuming we need to get in touch with her, like, yesterday."

"That would be best. If Medford's death is connected to her project, and she doesn't know about the danger, then she could be living on borrowed time."

Even though he knew nothing about Aubrey Starr other than from that one encounter, the thought of her possibly in danger bothered him.

"I'll get Serena and Jazz to work with her," Ash continued. "Jazz is scheduled for her final physical eval, and it's time for Serena's recertification. They can take her to Tri-Ops, teach her some self-defense, put her through some covert training. By the time you get a lead on where those victims in Colombia were taken, she should be trained enough to not be a hindrance."

Based in Virginia, Tri-Ops was the facility that OZ used to train and hone the skills of their operatives. For someone with no training at all, it'd be a lot to take in, but if she could get a little knowledge, at least she wouldn't be totally helpless on an op.

That was probably as good of a solution as any. Finding the victims they'd lost had become a full-time job. It was like they'd vanished into thin air. Half his efforts were also expended on hunting down Barnabas Drury. The man was as elusive as a wisp of smoke. Every lead had sent him to a place Drury had just left. He wouldn't give up, though. Drury would pay for what had happened to Myron. This time, he'd make sure he never saw the light of day again.

Liam stood. He didn't like the scenario Ash had painted, but his boss was right. If Aubrey Starr had intel, knowingly or unknowingly, that could lead them to a well-funded trafficking organization, then he'd do what he had to do. Putting up with a filmmaker for a few days would be worth it if it yielded those results.

"I'll talk to Jazz and Serena," Ash said. "Get them on a plane to Florida. They'll keep Starr safe and get what intel they can."

"All right."

He was at the door, about to open it, when Ash added, "And, Stryker, maybe this time you'll actually get to talk to her."

Liam let out a huff of a laugh as he walked out. There wasn't a soul at OZ who didn't know about his humiliating experience. The man known for his glib and smooth tongue had been rendered mute. They'd called him Froggy for months after that.

He'd thought about her from time to time. The woman had captured his attention in a way no one else had in years. Once or twice he'd considered getting her number and giving her a call but had never followed through. Until he found Cat, one way or the other, he didn't want the distraction. Besides, what woman would want to date a guy who was hung up on someone else?

Once he found Cat—or learned what happened to her— he might be able to rest. But not yet…not yet.

CHAPTER SIXTEEN

St. Augustine, Florida

The instant she entered her house, Aubrey knew someone had been there. The locks weren't damaged, the security system was still working, and there were no obvious signs of a break-in. But she knew.

After her abduction, she had been determined that nothing remotely similar would ever happen to her again. There had been times—more than a few times—that she'd felt as though someone was watching her. Her therapist had told her that hypervigilance after such a traumatic experience was a common response. And while that might well be true, it didn't stop her from taking precautions. Some would call it paranoia. She called it normal.

She had taken multiple self-defense classes and learned how to handle a handgun as well as a knife. She was prepared physically. In her home, she had a standard security system, but skilled intruders could bypass a security system in seconds. So she'd gone a step further and set subtle, obscure traps to alert her if her space had been violated.

Each time she went out, she left at least a half-dozen insignificant-looking items sitting around. Anyone else wouldn't give them another thought, but the instant she walked into her foyer, she noticed the first sign. On the entry table, a magazine she had left slightly askew had been straightened. As she went further into the house, she saw other signs. The pen sitting on her desk was no longer pointed toward the window. The paper clip that held a few printed pages of a script had been straightened. Before she'd left she had memorized each item and its exact position.

Going to the lockbox hidden beneath her entryway table, she entered a code and retrieved her Kimber pistol. Double-checking the clip to ensure she was ready for any threat, she went from room to room to make sure she was alone. Assuring herself that the intruder was gone, she went back to her bedroom and opened her closet. The secret panel behind her shoe shelf had been one of the few additions she'd made to the house. It held a treasure trove of research, some of which would make a lot of people very nervous if they knew about it.

Relieved that nothing had been disturbed, Aubrey closed the safe and replaced the panel. Closing the closet door, she took a deep breath. Had that been what they were searching for? Did someone know about her suspicions?

That had to be it, and if so, how had they found out?

She hadn't known what she would uncover when she'd started her research. She'd told no one what she'd found. And she still didn't know exactly what she had, but her gut told her to keep on going.

Still not feeling a hundred percent comfortable, Aubrey roamed through her house as she worked through the theory in her mind. It had started with an interview of a former trafficked victim. Thirteen-year-old Emma Griffin had been abducted during a camping trip with a school friend and her family. For two years, she had been held captive and raped repeatedly by dozens of strangers. To keep her docile and subservient, she had been given heroin every day. The drug had almost killed her, but in an odd way, it had also saved her life.

One day, she had been given too much and had over-dosed. Thinking she was dead, or would be soon, her captors had dumped her in an abandoned hut in the woods in upstate New York. But she hadn't died. Emma had managed to crawl her way out of the hut and onto a trail frequented by hikers. When she'd been found, they hadn't expected her to survive but she had surprised everyone.

Though Emma had been in and out of consciousness for weeks, when she'd finally woken, she could remember only bits and pieces of her ordeal. That had been over three years ago. She had been reunited with her family and had recov-ered her health. Her memory was still spotty about many things, but she had confessed to Aubrey that she still suffered from nightmares. Though the nightmares varied in many ways, one thing remained consistent. An image of a golden eagle swooping down to catch its prey was in each of the nightmares. The image was one she couldn't seem to shake.

Hoping to get the image out of her head, Emma had made numerous sketches of the eagle. When Aubrey had asked, she had eagerly given them up, saying she wanted them away from her.

When Aubrey had returned home from the interview, she had been typing up her notes while watching the raw footage of her talk with Emma. The pain in the young woman's voice when she'd described the image of that eagle was something that wouldn't let go.

Curious, she had started some digging and had found something quite interesting. Several years ago, a well-known artist, Francis Steinman, had been interviewed by a style magazine. He had become famous for his carvings of various wild animals. Some of his works had been highlighted in the magazine. One he was especially proud of was a carving of a golden eagle catching its prey. The piece had been commissioned by the wealthy and influential Marc Antony Ferante, who liked the carving so much, he had one made for every one of his homes. It became his insignia, so to speak. He was so enamored of it, he had insisted on buying the rights to the work, and Steinman had agreed never to carve the same image for anyone else.

An image of that carved eagle was the exact one that Emma had sketched.

From there, Aubrey started a deep dive into Ferante. The man was hugely influential and featured in tons of articles, hours of interviews, and at least a dozen books. She had only gone through a tenth of what she needed to, but she'd already spotted several red flags.

Connecting the nightmares of a young, traumatized woman to the wealthy Ferante was more than a stretch. Something told Aubrey not to let it go. There was something there.

And now that her house had been broken into, she knew she was likely on the right track. Problem was, where would it lead her? And whom could she trust?

Having someone break into her home and leave no trace of their intrusion told her one thing—they hadn't wanted her to know they were there. Had it been a fishing expedition? Maybe someone only suspected she knew something. Since nothing had been found, perhaps they would assume she had no information.

But she couldn't assume they wouldn't be back.

Her phone rang, and Aubrey jumped. Her nerves were ragged, and she was definitely freaked out.

Grabbing the phone from her purse, she checked the

display, recognizing the number immediately. "Hello, Kate. I didn't expect to hear from you again so soon."

"I have good news for you. I spoke with the leader of the organization I told you about. He is willing to allow you to do a ride-along on their next rescue."

"That's wonderful. Thank you for that. Should I—"

"One of their operatives, either Serena or Jazz, will contact you. You'll get more information from them on the where and the how."

"Thank you, Kate. I sincerely appreciate your help."

"You're very welcome. I enjoyed our meeting and look forward to talking with you again soon. The funds are ready when you are."

A wave of gratitude brought a lump to Aubrey's throat. Focusing on so much of the horrors, she sometimes lost sight of the good in the world. There were kindhearted, giving people who wanted to end human trafficking as much as she did.

Should she tell Kate about this? Who she was investigating and why? Not all wealthy people knew each other, but Kate Walker was a savvy, intelligent businesswoman and a former FBI agent. She might have insight Aubrey hadn't considered.

"Aubrey, everything okay?"

She shook herself. She was exhausted and running on fumes, barely had a grasp on reality right now. After a good night's sleep, she'd be better able to decide whom she could trust.

"Everything's fine. Just a little weary from traveling."

"Completely understandable. Get some rest, and we'll talk soon."

"I will. And thank you again."

"My pleasure."

A wave of exhaustion hitting her, Aubrey went through

her nightly ritual in record time. She double-checked the security system and all her locks. Then, placing her pistol on the nightstand, within easy reach, she slipped into bed. Even though fatigue weighed heavily on her, she stared into the darkness for a long while. Every noise she heard, her body went tense. Finally, just before dawn, she dropped into a restless, uneasy sleep.

THE MAN WATCHING the camera feed of Aubrey Starr's bedroom gave a giant yawn. The girl was in over her head. That was clear. Yeah, she knew her home had been broken into, and he was impressed that she'd been able to determine that intruders had entered. His people were the best at what they did, leaving absolutely no trace of an intrusion. For her to suspect a break-in was impressive. She was no dummy, but she was naïve. She assumed nothing had been compromised since her safe hadn't been found. She never considered that though nothing had been taken, something had been left. Cameras and mics covered her entire house, and they had already paid off. Tomorrow, whether she was there or not, he'd be checking out that little hidey-hole in her closet. He was willing to bet there were some interesting tidbits his employer would be very anxious to know more about.

CHAPTER SEVENTEEN

Northeast Florida Regional Airport
St. Augustine, Florida

"You want to make the call, or you want me to?"

Jazz sent a sideways look at Serena Donavan. "You're better with words. I'm too blunt. I'll just freak her out."

"That's not true. You're just honest to a fault."

Jazz added a grin. "That's a nice way of saying I'm rude and abrupt."

Serena laughed and then shrugged. "Maybe that's what she needs. Sounds like she might be in over her head."

"Yeah. Problem is, we can't tell her until we find out more about her. Ash isn't ready to trust her. And if he's not, then I'm not either."

Asher Drake had a sixth sense when it came to reading people.

Serena gazed out the window of the rental car. "It's beautiful here. Wish we had time to explore."

"Maybe you and Sean can come back here sometime. You know, when you finally decide to take some time off."

"Hey, we had a honeymoon."

Jazz snorted. "Three days in Bali. That's barely time to get a tan."

A pretty blush turned Serena's face pink. "We weren't there for the tans."

Jazz laughed, genuinely happy for her friends. No two people were more made for each other than Sean and Serena Donavan. Some people did find their happy ever after. Most didn't.

Ash and Jules had found theirs, too. A few months ago, they'd said their vows beneath the setting sun at their home in Montana. It had been beautiful and romantic. And just last week, they'd shared the happy news that Jules was pregnant. After all they'd been through, they deserved this happiness.

Jazz knew she wasn't destined for a happy ending—not like her friends. She had made her peace with that. She was luckier than most. She had found a family in OZ. She enjoyed her job, loved its purpose. She had a fulfilling life, and considering her life before OZ, every day she had breath was a miracle.

Her mind returned to their purpose for being here. "Kate told her we were going to get in touch with her, right?"

Serena nodded. "Yes. She's expecting to hear from us."

"Then I say we surprise her, just show up at her door. Nothing like a little unexpected company to throw you off your game."

AUBREY PULLED herself from the pool and stretched, working out any remaining kinks. Even though she hadn't slept well,

RELENTLESS

with all sorts of weird dreams haunting her, there was nothing like a good, strong swim to get the body in gear.

Wrapping the towel around her energized body, she grabbed her phone from the patio table. One of the reasons she'd tossed and turned was her uncertainty about what she should do with the information she had on Ferante. She needed to make a decision and soon. Someone else needed to know about her suspicions. What if something happened to her, and her findings died with her? Even though she had no real proof, only speculation and theories, someone else should be made aware of what she'd learned.

She'd woken still undecided, but the invigorating exercise had given her the answer she sought. She would call Uncle Syd and tell him. Even though she didn't want him to help her financially, she trusted his judgment. He'd always been there for her. Plus, he knew a lot more people than she did. He probably even knew Ferante. His insight would be invaluable.

She hadn't called the police about the break-in. There had been no point. Not only were the small signs she'd detected not provable, nothing had been taken. Her research was safe. But someone had been here—who they were and what they knew was still a mystery.

Still dabbing at her sopping hair, she dropped into a chair and pulled up her contact screen. Her finger hovered over her uncle's number. Would she be putting him in danger? That was the last thing she wanted. Was there any danger? She didn't know.

Indecisiveness wasn't her norm, and it was frustrating not to know the right answer.

The doorbell rang, giving her a reprieve. Wrapping the towel tighter around her body, Aubrey went inside and through the house to the front door. She wasn't expecting anyone and though her neighbors sometimes stopped by

119

with baked goods or a friendly chat, it was just past seven in the morning, and few were out and about at this hour.

She peered out the window, surprised to see two strangers at her door. One was a petite young woman, maybe mid-twenties, with short, ink-black hair, and dark eyes. The other woman was in her early thirties, medium height, with brownish-blond hair and light green eyes. They were both dressed casually in jeans, but there was nothing casual about their demeanor. Their expressions were set with confidence and determination.

Already suspecting their identities, Aubrey opened the door. "Can I help you?"

"We're friends of Kate's."

Kate had told her she would be contacted. Having them show up at her house was a surprise.

"Mind if I see some ID?"

"No problem," the dark-haired woman answered.

They both whipped out driver's licenses with their photos and names—the dark-haired one was Jasmine McAlister, or Jazz, as Kate had called her. The brown-haired woman was Serena Donavan.

Opening the door wider, she waved them in. "Sorry to be underdressed. I thought I'd get a phone call, not a home visit."

"After we chat, you'll understand why," Serena Donavan said.

Intrigued, Aubrey led them into her living room. "Would you like some coffee?"

"Yes, please," Serena answered.

Her eyes roaming the room, Jasmine only nodded.

Aubrey turned too quickly, causing her towel to slip. Wrapping it more securely around her body, she sent the women an awkward smile. "While the coffee's brewing, I'll throw on some clothes. Be right back."

Preparing the coffee by rote, she watched the two women from the corner of her eye. Though they both seemed pleasant enough, she sensed a surprising hypervigilance, as if they anticipated trouble.

She quickly finished and then went to her bedroom. Pulling off her damp suit, she dried herself thoroughly and then threw on a pair of jeans and a white button-down shirt. Since her naturally wavy hair was almost dry, she finger-combed it and decided that would have to do.

Five minutes later, she was back in the kitchen pouring coffee into mugs. Using a tray, she carried three cups of the steaming brew, along with creamer and sugar, and set it on the coffee table.

As they helped themselves, Aubrey settled back into a chair and did her own observing. Ever since they'd arrived, she'd felt as if she were being put to some kind of test.

The scrutiny was understandable to a point. After all, she was asking to be included in a covert human trafficking rescue. They didn't know her, didn't know if they could trust her. They could. She would never reveal anything they didn't want her to make known. She didn't make films about human trafficking to exploit the victims or their rescuers. She did it to try to save lives.

"I'm assuming you have questions for me?"

"Not at this time," Serena answered. "We've seen your films. You're very talented. And Kate has vouched for you. Anything else we need to learn from you, I'm sure we will as we go along."

Okay, this was going to be easier than she'd anticipated. She had been ready for an inquisition.

"That's great. When is your next one and where do I—"

"You're getting a little ahead of yourself," Jasmine said.

"How so?"

"The number one rule of all our ops is that the people

121

we're saving are our priority. The last thing we need is some untrained neophyte dragging us down and putting people in danger."

"I would never get in the way of—"

Serena held up a hand. "What Jazz is saying is that we need to make sure you're ready for any kind of threat that might come your way. Once you're with us, you're our responsibility. If something happens to you, it's on us."

"I would be happy to sign a document releasing your organization from all liability."

"It's not the liability we're worried about. We go in to save lives. Our plan is for every person to come out alive. We take that responsibility seriously."

"Bottom line," Jasmine added, "we need to make sure you're an asset and not a liability."

It was becoming clear why they'd shown up in person. While she could certainly understand their reasoning, she was also happy to be able to tell them it wasn't necessary. "You want me to go through some kind of training course. I'll do what I need to do, but I'm not completely helpless. I have weapons training and have gone through several self-defense courses."

"Excellent," Serena said. "We can give you half an hour to pack. Will that be enough time?"

"Pack? For what?"

"Our training facility."

More than a little surprised, Aubrey considered her options, which weren't many. If she didn't go, she wouldn't be allowed to go on the rescue. Not only did the film need this kind of in-depth look at a real-life rescue, she needed the experience for herself.

"How long will I need to be gone?"

For the first time, she saw surprise in both their faces. She didn't know if it was because of her quick acquiescence, or if they just weren't prepared for the question.

"Possibly a couple of weeks, maybe more."

"That's a long time to be away."

"Our people go through months of training. You'll only get the basics in that amount of time."

"Okay...all right. I'll go pack."

She showered quickly and was dressed in a matter of minutes. Gathering her clothes and toiletries together didn't take long either. Traveling extensively, she knew how to pack with both speed and efficiency. She used the rest of that time to gather the notes and research from her safe. Even though the lockbox was hidden, and she had felt comfortable leaving it here before, she knew the information was no longer secure. Wherever she went, her findings would go with her.

Bags packed, she went out of the bedroom to the kitchen, and was surprised to find both women taking care of the few dishes they'd used for the coffee.

"Hope you don't mind," Serena sent her a bright smile. "My mom was a stickler for leaving the kitchen in pristine condition before we left the house."

"Not at all. I appreciate it. I'm ready to go when you all are."

Hanging the kitchen towel on its peg, Jazz said, "We're ready, too."

They were almost at the door when Serena said, "Mind if I use the restroom before we go?" She scrunched her nose. "I hate those tiny bathrooms on the plane."

"Not at all. Down the hall, second door on the right."

"Great. I'll lock up for you and hit the alarm on the way out."

Following Jasmine, Aubrey went to their sporty SUV and loaded her suitcase in the back. She got into the backseat, unsurprised to see Jasmine slide in behind the wheel. She got the impression that the woman might be a bit of a control freak. Being one herself, Aubrey recognized like kind.

After a strained silence, Jasmine said, "You live here long?"

Aubrey hid a sympathetic smile. *Awkward* wasn't a term she would have originally applied to Jasmine McAlister, but there was no doubt of it now. She had a feeling the young woman wasn't much for small talk.

"Only a couple of years. I love the history here, the old buildings, gorgeous trees. I've filmed a couple of my documentaries here, for background mostly, but it makes a beautiful setting."

Jazz nodded and then was silent.

Aubrey cleared her throat. She usually had no issues carrying on a conversation but had to admit to some awkwardness herself. "Both Kate and Serena call you Jazz. Is that what you prefer?"

"Yes."

"All right."

The instant Serena came out of the house, she heard a relieved heartfelt sigh from the woman behind the wheel. Yes, definitely not a small-talker.

"Let's go. Just got a text. Plane's ready to go." Buckling her seat belt, Serena sent a small smile toward Aubrey. "Better buckle up. It might get bumpy."

Jazz drove through the streets as if she'd lived in St. Augustine all her life. In a surprisingly short period of time, they arrived at the airport. The SUV turned down a small access road and Jazz drove through the gate with a casual wave toward the man at the gatehouse. They traveled several more yards toward a large private jet.

Aubrey didn't know if she should feel honored or worried. Transporting her to an unknown location in a private jet seemed a bit extreme. Why go to so much trouble for someone who'd just asked to tag along on a rescue?

Leaning on an elbow, Serena turned to the backseat. "You're looking anxious and you shouldn't be. We don't have any ops going this week, so we scored the jet. Any other time, we'd probably be traveling commercial."

"When will I get to learn about who 'we' are?"

"When we learn who you are," Jazz answered.

They got out of the SUV and headed to the plane. Duffel bag in one hand and laptop satchel in the other, Aubrey stepped up onto the plane. The instant she entered, the atmosphere seemed to shift. Now unsmiling, Serena held out her hand. "I need your phone and laptop."

"Why?"

"In case anyone is tracking you. I'll disable any trackers and return them to you, good as new. You'll want to notify any family and friends that you'll be out of pocket for the next couple of weeks. That way, they won't worry."

Questioning why anyone would want to track her seemed pointless. It was becoming obvious that these people had an agenda beyond her seemingly simple request to do a ride-along.

After she relinquished the items, she settled into a seat. She hadn't been nervous but now she was rethinking her trust in the whole situation.

Holding Aubrey's laptop and phone, Serena spoke to Jazz in a low tone. Seconds later, Jazz headed to the cockpit. It wouldn't surprise her if the woman was also the pilot. Every time she turned around, something unusual happened.

Aubrey took in a few calming breaths. She had been in dangerous situations before. Even though her nerves jumped with adrenaline, this didn't feel exactly dangerous. Just very covert and unsettling. There were undercurrents at play here that she knew nothing about.

To calm herself, she took in her surroundings. The plane was decorated for both comfort and efficiency in cream and light green. Ten seats and two small sofas filled the space. The multicolored carpeting was short but thick and plush beneath her feet.

Whoever these people were, they were incredibly well funded. After the success of her first documentary, she had priced small private jets in the hopes of being able to buy one to make traveling easier for future films. It hadn't taken her long to realize she could barely afford the fuel, much less the actual airplane.

As if they'd coordinated their timing, Serena came through a door from the back as Jazz exited the cockpit.

With one of those small smiles Aubrey was beginning to learn meant nothing, Serena returned both her phone and laptop, and said, "Thanks. We're good."

Aubrey held the phone and laptop close to her. The comfortable and familiar items helped settle her nerves.

"Why don't you go ahead and text your people."

"I don't understand. Will I not be able to communicate with anyone while I'm gone?"

"It'll be best if you don't."

"Why?"

Serena gave her a reassuring smile. "You're getting worried again and you really shouldn't. It's just that we are very private."

Though the nervousness had returned, Aubrey did as she was asked and texted her mother, Becca, and her production assistant the same message.

I'm out of town for the next couple of weeks on research. Will get in touch when I return. Text me if you need me.

Not surprising, Jazz stood over her shoulder and read her text.

Aubrey tilted her head to look up at her. "You approve?"

Without a hint of guilt or embarrassment for her nosiness, Jazz nodded. "Yeah, that'll work."

The pilot's voice came into the cabin. "Seat belts on. We're cleared for takeoff."

In less than two minutes, they were traveling down the runway and lifting into the air.

Hoping to bring some normalcy back to her surroundings, she glanced over at Jazz who sat across from Aubrey. "How long is the flight to your training facility?"

Serena answered instead of Jazz, "There's been a change of plans."

"What kind of change?"

"The training will have to wait. We're going to our headquarters."

"Why? What happened?"

Unbuckling her seat belt, Serena stood and walked a few feet to an alcove. She returned with a handful of gadgets, some as small as a dime. Dropping them on the table in front of Aubrey, she gave her a speculative look. "This happened. These are the bugs and cameras I was able to find in your house in just a few moments. I had someone else go through after we left. He called and said he found two more."

She paused for a second and then said softly, "Looks like you have an enemy, Aubrey."

CHAPTER EIGHTEEN

Shock, outrage, and the overwhelming sense of being completely out of her element, swamped her. She'd had this feeling once before, when she'd been abducted. It was as if her brain traveled at warp speed, while the entire world moved around her in slow motion. Voices, soft and urgent called her name. Firm hands pushed her head to her knees.

Seconds later, everything stopped whirling and she heard Serena say in a calming voice, "That's it. Deep, even breaths. You're fine."

Now she was shocked for a different reason. She'd almost passed out. Normally the last one to panic in a stressful situation, she just didn't do things like that.

"I'm fine. I'm fine." Repeating the words over and over probably didn't sound like she was fine, but those were the only words her brain could form right now.

"Yes you are," Serena said.

A glass of water appeared in her peripheral vision.

"Sit up slowly and take a few sips," Jazz said.

Aubrey raised her head and then straightened her body. Gratefully accepting the water Jazz held out for her, she took small sips and with each one she felt her body returning to normal.

"Well, I guess the question of whether you knew your house was bugged has been answered."

Aubrey sent Serena an indignant look. "Of course I didn't know."

"Question remains," Jazz said. "Who would be so invested in knowing what's going on in your home?"

"I don't know."

Both women sat across from her but instead of looking directly at them, Aubrey gazed over their heads. Yes, she knew it was a telltale sign of lying, but she had to get her thoughts together before she could begin to answer their questions.

"That's not going to fly," Jazz answered. "You know exactly who's watching you."

"We think you're in over your head, Aubrey," Serena added.

"And who are "we"?"

"You answer our questions, we'll answer yours. Fair enough?"

She had a decision to make, because Serena was right. She was in over her head. What she'd thought was just a thread of information that might lead to something bigger had instead become much more complicated and dangerous than she'd anticipated. If Ferante was responsible for the cameras and bugs in her house, then he might well do whatever it took to prevent her from revealing what she knew. He had the money and the power to make her disappear forever.

She eyed both Serena and Jazz. Oddly enough, they were silent, as if aware she needed to figure out if she could trust them. Could she? Kate Walker had given her approval of them. And though she didn't know Kate all that well, the time she'd spent with her had been telling. She trusted the woman. Therefore, she should trust these women.

"Look." Serena's voice broke the tense silence. "I know you're scared, don't know who to trust. Telling you to trust us without giving you any real reason isn't fair. But until we know you better, we can't risk anything."

Aubrey took a breath. As much as she didn't like it, Serena had a point. The organization Serena worked for had a lot more to lose than Aubrey did.

"All right. What can I do to speed up the process?"

"Answer some questions, and let's see where we are."

"Okay, shoot." She winced at the words. She had a feeling neither of these women would hesitate to do just that if they deemed it necessary.

If she thought they would be easier on her because of the near fainting spell earlier, she was mistaken. The questions came quick, so fast and furious that she had little time to think. They asked, she answered.

Why do you do what you do?

Who backed your other films?

Who do you share your research with?

What do you hope to gain by going on a rescue?

Who is involved in the making of your film? Has everyone been vetted? How were they vetted? By whom? What do they know?

Both women asked questions, but Serena took the lead, and Jazz often followed up with additional ones. It was a good routine and Aubrey got the idea they did this a lot.

Though the questions were exhaustingly thorough, she had no problem answering. Most of her team had been with her for years. She trusted them with her life. They were as dedicated as she was to shining the light on the dark vileness of human trafficking. However, they had no idea what she had uncovered about Ferante. She was the only one who knew, or at least she'd thought she was.

By the time the initial questions had been asked and answered, Aubrey had consumed two full glasses of water and felt as if she'd been drained of all energy.

"Okay, let's take a break for a while. Jazz, why don't you see if Pippa has lunch ready yet? And Aubrey, why don't you go freshen up?"

Aubrey wasn't going to argue. Not only did she need time to herself, she needed to rid herself of all the water she'd consumed. Relieved to have some privacy, Aubrey gratefully headed to the bathroom. When she looked in the mirror, she had to grimace. Not her best look. Shock and stress had bleached her face of color.

She splashed her face with water, pinched her cheeks and took a breath. Whether they knew it or not, she was through with their questions. She had some of her own and she wasn't going to respond to any more of theirs until hers were answered.

She returned to the main cabin in time to see a flight attendant placing plates filled with sandwiches and salad on a pullout table.

Serena gave her a searching look. "Feel better?"

"Yes, but I have some—"

"Come eat. That'll make you feel even better."

Though her stomach knotted at the thought of putting food in it, Aubrey knew Serena was right. She hadn't had anything to eat since lunch yesterday afternoon. Without nourishment, she couldn't think straight.

As if an invisible barrier had been broken, Jazz gave her a genuine smile. "I think we've all worked up an appetite."

They sat around the table and were silent for a few moments. The chicken salad sandwich was delicious, and Aubrey felt her normal appetite return. Within minutes, she was feeling calmer and more in control. These people weren't out to hurt her, and if she were honest with herself, she could use their help and advice.

Munching on a carrot stick, Jazz asked, "Your bio says that you studied acting. Why did you change to documentaries? You were in a couple of movies and TV shows, weren't you?"

"Yes. Though the movies were just bit parts. And I liked acting well enough, but it lost its magic early on."

"How's that?" Serena asked.

"Nothing ever felt authentic. An entertainer has to be on 24/7. Always in the public eye, always being watched. That wasn't the kind of life I wanted. I thought about directing movies, but dealing with all the egos didn't appeal to me either. Filming documentaries didn't interest me until I started reading up on human trafficking. It's everywhere, in areas people could never fathom. I wanted to reveal those lies and truths."

That wasn't the biggest reason she'd chosen human trafficking as her first film and main focus. However, talking about her abduction and assault, as well as her near miss of being trafficked? No. Not with everything else going on. It would be just too much.

"I saw your first documentary," Serena said. "It was excellent."

"Thank you."

"This new one you're going to do—Kate said it's a follow-up?" Jazz said.

"Yes. Some of the victims I featured in the first film will give updates on their lives, where they are now. We still won't reveal their identities, but I think people will be interested in seeing what kind of impact their trauma has had on them and the people they love.

"But I also want to go into more depth, not only about the

rescuers, but the traffickers themselves. How each got into their line of work, why they do what they do."

"You know you won't be able to identify us either. Right?" Jazz said.

"That's not a problem. I just want to get into the mind-set of a rescuer. What makes him or her tick."

"We can definitely help you with that. But we still need some answers."

Aubrey shook her head. "I've answered your questions. I think it's time I get to ask my own questions."

"One more, and then we'll move on."

"All right."

"Who is so interested in you that they would put thousands of dollars' worth of equipment in your house to watch you?" Jazz raised her hand to stop Aubrey's automatic response. "And don't say you don't know, because we know you do."

"How do you know I do?"

"Because no one would go to this much expense and trouble unless they were afraid of being outed. Maybe you don't know a name yet, but you know something."

"How do I know I can trust you? I know nothing about you and your organization. You spirit me away from my house. You search it without my permission. You keep me here, grilling me for hours. How the hell am I to trust you when you've given me nothing other than more questions?"

Jazz and Serena exchanged a look, and they both nodded simultaneously.

"Fair enough," Serena said. "What do you want to know?"

"Who are you people?"

"We'll tell you what we can. If our boss feels like we can share more, we will."

"That's a start."

"We're an off-the-books organization that gets involved

in a variety of international and domestic incidents. We often prevent bad things from happening."

"For instance?"

"Terrorism, assassinations, wars."

"Human trafficking?"

"Yes. That too."

"Where do you get your funding?"

"That's not something you need to know."

Serena was right, but it had been worth a shot.

"Where are you taking me?"

"We're going to our headquarters. Our boss trusts you enough to have you stay there. We think you're in danger. Our plan is to protect you and help you. Will you let us?"

There didn't seem to be much choice in the matter. Not only was she about forty thousand feet up in the air, she had nowhere else to turn. Telling her uncle what she'd found was now out of the question. Putting him in danger was the last thing she wanted.

Bottom line was she trusted Kate Walker. Kate Walker trusted these people. And despite their heavy-handed questioning, she was beginning to trust both Serena and Jazz.

"All right. I can do that."

CHAPTER NINETEEN

Lake Tahoe, California

"My sources are telling me that she still plans to make the film."

Dread made his heart drop like lead. Even though he was alone, he unconsciously shook his head. "That's not true. Your sources are mistaken."

"Oh?"

The sound of that one word was so arrogant he wanted nothing more than to reach through the phone and strangle the caller.

His mind scrambled for an answer that would satisfy. "Medford's death destroyed her chances of getting it made. She doesn't have enough capital on her own. And there's no one else in the industry who will back her. The film will never get made."

"My sources have told me she's found someone outside the industry."

"Who? I haven't heard of such a thing."

"I don't believe it's my job to give you information."

"Perhaps not, but as we're on the same side, why wouldn't you?"

"Are we on the same side?"

He closed his eyes. No. They weren't on the same side. Hadn't been for years, if ever. If he could, he would destroy this bastard and everything he stood for. But that was the problem—he couldn't destroy him. He had no choice but to comply.

"I've done everything that's been asked of me."

"Do we really need to examine the blatant lies in that one statement?"

"That was a mistake…it won't happen again. It hasn't. I've complied with all requests since then."

"Oh, we'll make sure it doesn't happen again. We know where you sleep at night. More importantly, we know where the ones you love sleep."

The man waited for a response, but breathlessness kept him from giving one.

Completely uncaring that the words had stabbed him in the chest, the man continued, "I'm sure you'll hear the news about her new backer soon. You'll know what to do. Correct?"

Everything within him froze. *Know what to do?* Was he serious?

"Remember, we gave you fair warning."

Panic zoomed through him. "I'll find a way to stop her. I promise."

"We shall see. If not, then…"

The man left it at that. There was no need to finish the sentence. He knew full well what could happen. He had witnessed it firsthand. He carried that guilt around with him every second of every single day.

"Goodbye. Enjoy your vacation."

Enjoy his vacation? As if there was anything in his life

that he could actually enjoy. That dream had ended
years ago.

The call had ended, but the voice remained in his head.
That same voice, or one just like it, had been calling the shots
in his life for as long as he could remember.

When would it end? When would it ever end?

CHAPTER TWENTY

The touchdown was light, and as the plane taxied down the runway, Serena gave Aubrey a reassuring smile. "You've been a trouper, and we really appreciate your cooperation, but there's just one more thing."

"What's that?"

Jazz handed her a blindfold. "We're not that far from the airport, so you won't have to wear it for long."

Telling herself she'd come too far to cry foul now, Aubrey quietly took the blindfold and covered her eyes.

As she walked down the stairs of the plane with Serena beside her, telling her when to step, she tried to use her other senses to determine where she might be. The air was chilly, almost icy, at least twenty degrees cooler than Florida. It also felt thinner and drier. She wasn't given much time outside, but was urged into a vehicle, and then they were off. The drive to their destination didn't take long. Maybe fifteen minutes.

The instant they parked, she said, "Okay if I remove the blindfold?"

"Yes," Serena said.

Relieved, Aubrey jerked the cloth from her face and looked around. They were in a deeply wooded area. Some of the trees were types she didn't recognize, and many of them had either lost their leaves or had turned the dark, deep colors of autumn. The door opened, and she stepped onto a paved parking lot.

Drawing in a breath, she looked behind her and got her first glimpse of a large house that was at least five thousand square feet of rock, timber, and stone. Behind it, past the giant trees were majestic snow-covered mountains. Based on the mountains and considering the length of the flight, she surmised that they were in Wyoming or Montana.

Without being invited, Aubrey walked toward the house and stepped up onto the front porch. It looked like a typical oversized ranch house from the outside. She opened the front door, expecting that the house had been converted into an office building. She was wrong. A warm, welcoming entryway greeted her.

Aubrey gazed around, still confused about how a secret organization with obviously well-trained operatives worked out of a house that looked as though it belonged on the cover of a country-living magazine.

"Welcome to OZ."

She whirled around, surprised to hear the deep, masculine voice. A tall, blond stranger stood before her.

"OZ?"

"Option Zero." The man stepped forward and held out his hand. "I'm Asher Drake. And you must be Aubrey Starr."

"Hello, yes. I'm Aubrey."

"Kate's told me a lot about you."

She had the oddest urge to laugh. She truly did feel as though she were in Oz—completely out of her element, no real idea where she was, and three strangers were smiling at her. For just a split second, a sense of peace swept over her, and she had the strangest feeling that this was where her life had been leading her all along.

ASH WAITED a second to let her get her bearings. The expression on her face was one of both bewilderment and exhaustion. Serena and Jazz had been hammering questions at her since they'd met. He'd read their notes. She had to be feeling overwhelmed. Ordinarily, he might have suggested she take a moment for herself, but he knew to strike when the iron was hot. She would be less likely to prevaricate if the questions continued.

"Come. We can talk in my office."

He didn't look to see if she followed him. He had no doubt she would. The questions in her eyes told him she wouldn't wait much longer to learn the real reason she was here.

If she was honest with him, he would return the favor.

He opened the door to his office and smiled at Jules on the sofa. He'd asked her to sit in on the interview. Not only did she often see things from a different perspective, she would provide a calming presence.

"Jules, I'd like you to meet Aubrey Starr. Aubrey, this is my wife, Jules."

As the women exchanged greetings, Ash went behind his desk and stood, waiting. Nothing like a little intimidation tactic to get the ball rolling.

"I'm a big fan of your work, Aubrey," Jules said. "Your films always leave me in tears and feeling the need to do more."

"Thank you. That's the highest of compliments."

As Jules sat back down on the sofa, Ash nodded toward the chair in front of his desk. "Have a seat."

He noticed her eyes were on the window behind him.

Couldn't blame her. "Phenomenal, isn't it? I would've bought the house for the view alone."

"I've always loved the mountains."

"Yet you live in Florida."

She shrugged. "Sometimes, what you want and what you decide upon are contrary to one another."

"Guess that's true." He nodded toward the chair again.

As soon as she was seated, Aubrey said, "First of all, Mr. Drake, I want to thank you for allowing me inside your organization. Kate told me, and Serena and Jazz drilled it into my brain on the flight here, that this is an unacknowledged organization. I want you to know that I would never reveal anything that you didn't approve of first."

"Call me Ash. And you wouldn't be here if I wasn't sure of your trustworthiness. And while I believe what you say is true, I hope you'll understand that we'll want to see the finished film before anyone else."

"We can definitely arrange that. I have several other sources who can't be identified and have asked for the same consideration. Understand, of course, that I won't be open to changing the content of the film, but I will work with any concerns you have about anything that you think could identify your organization or its operatives."

"Good enough. Now, seems to me you've gotten on the bad side of someone."

"It's not the first time."

"Probably not. People who risk showing the underbelly of humanity often end up with enemies. This one seems particularly determined."

"I'll admit the cameras and bugs in my house were a shock."

"Serena described finding some of the most expensive gadgets on the market, including a couple that are still in the testing stage. Someone is determined to find out what you know."

Only by the tightening of her jaw did Aubrey give any indication that she was disturbed.

He hadn't intended to spring their theory of Lawrence Medford's death yet. This woman had endured several shocks today. One more might shut her down completely. But from her reaction, she wasn't getting it yet. These people would go far beyond bugging a house to stop her. Should he tell her how far?

Wanting Jules's take, he sent her a subtle, questioning look. She nodded, telling him she thought he should proceed.

"There's more."

"More?" Aubrey asked.

"Lawrence Medford."

"What about Lawrence?"

"His death wasn't an accident."

"I don't understand."

Time for bluntness. "He was murdered."

If she had been pale before, she was almost translucent now. He'd had his own experience with hearing bad news. Best thing to do was get it out as quickly as possible to begin processing.

"We've obtained video feed of someone going into Medford's house and letting those snakes loose."

"Snakes? I thought there was just one."

"There were at least four, maybe more."

She stared into space several seconds. Ash waited her out. Shock was like that. While your mind was numb, every reasonable explanation came knocking at you, trying to change your mind about the truth. Eventually, you allowed them in, but first you had to deal.

"I don't understand. Why would anyone want to kill Lawrence? That's just…" Her eyes widened, and her head shook in rapid jerks of denial. "You think he was murdered because he was going to produce and fund my film?"

"Yes."

"But that's ludicrous. Taking him out of the picture only delayed me. It didn't stop the project. If someone wants to stop the film, why not just kill me?"

"We don't know the answer to that."

"Then isn't it possible he was killed because he angered someone completely unrelated to my film? Medford wasn't the easiest person to get along with. I'm sure he had his share of enemies."

"That's true and we're checking into those. But Medford being murdered the day before you were scheduled to meet with him for a second time about your film seems too coincidental. Add that to the bugs and cameras in your home…" He trailed off, allowing her to absorb his inference.

She blew out a shaky sigh. "All right, I agree those things do seem odd, but odd coincidences happen all the time."

Ash saw no other way than to lay it on the table. "I've been at this a long time, Aubrey. My gut is telling me you've found something, maybe something you don't even know you've found. But there is someone who's willing to do whatever it takes to stop you. We need to identify him and find a way to stop him before he does something more."

"Ferante. Marc Antony Ferante."

Surprised at not only the name but the ease with which Aubrey had shared the information, Ash said carefully, "Why do you think it's Ferante?"

"A few years back, a young girl was kidnapped. She was trafficked all over the world. When she was finally rescued, she had blocked out most of her memories of her time in captivity. Most of the things she remembered were vague bits of information that didn't help the authorities. She remembered being called No. 7, blue water like the ocean, and very tall trees. None of that information helped to narrow down who took her or where she'd been. However, she has a recurring nightmare that both her parents and her therapists have dismissed as symbolism. I disagree."

"What was it?" Jules asked.

As Aubrey relayed the information about the eagle and her efforts to hunt down that image, Ash couldn't help but be impressed. She was a thorough researcher. He was also concerned. Ferante was an extremely powerful adversary. If he knew she was on to him—and it was looking as though he did—then she was in extreme danger.

"If Ferante is behind this, how do you think he found out about you?" Ash asked.

"I don't know, unless someone has been watching me all along. I would imagine my research has made more than a few people nervous."

"And there could be alarms set up," Jules added. "If you searched a site linked to Ferante, an alert might have been sounded. It's easy enough to trace the IP back to the searcher."

Aubrey nodded. "I'm careful about how I search, but that doesn't mean he doesn't have safeguards I haven't considered."

"What about the young victim who was rescued? Is it possible he's had her watched?"

"Her family changed their names, moved across the country. They've taken every precaution."

"What are you planning to do with this information?"

"I hadn't gotten that far. I just zeroed in on Ferante a week or so ago, before I went to California. When I returned home yesterday, I realized someone had been in my house, but my research wasn't found. Serena and Jazz showed up at my house today, and here I am."

"I know you're here for a rescue ride-along, but would

you be willing to work with our researchers on Ferante? Share what you have, if we do the same?"

"I'm willing to do anything necessary to bring down any human trafficker, no matter who he or she is. And if he is responsible for Lawrence's death, that's even more incentive."

"Excellent." Ash stood. "If you like, Jules will take you to your room. Come back in an hour, and I'll have someone show you around OZ."

The relief on Aubrey's face was telling. She needed time to herself, and he needed to do a couple more things before he allowed her access to OZ. Letting outsiders inside Option Zero wasn't something he did lightly. He would never be stupid enough to put his people at risk of exposure without making absolutely sure the outsider could be trusted.

He pressed a key on his phone for Serena. "What's up, boss?"

"How deeply have you dug into Aubrey Starr?"

"I've done a level three."

Three was the same level of background check that government agencies conducted for their employees. It was the level OZ used for informants and off-site contractors.

"Start a four. Let me know if anything pops up within the next half hour."

"That's not a lot of time."

"No, but it'll give us a deeper layer than we have now."

"We'll get on it."

"Jules took her to one of the guest rooms. She'll be back in an hour for a tour."

"I'll see you then."

With anyone else he'd worry he hadn't give her enough time, but Serena ran her research unit with utmost precision. The chances of her having everything, including Aubrey

Starr's favorite brand of toothpaste in half an hour were good.

Jules walked back into his office, and his heartbeat did a skip. A normal thing when she appeared. Hard to believe how his life had changed in such a short period of time. She had brought sunshine when there had once been only darkness.

Standing, he walked around his desk and held out his hand. "What do you think?"

"I like her. Anyone who can make the films she makes is good in my book. But she's more than just her talent. She cares."

"I agree. You think she's trustworthy?"

"Yes."

"You don't think it was too soon to tell her of our suspicions about Medford?"

"No. She's strong. Strong women don't want to be protected from the truth. She deserves to know everything."

"She's had quite a few shocks in the last couple of days."

"True, but she'll deal."

"Agreed." Wrapping his arms around her, he asked, "When's the last time I told you I love you?"

She snuggled into his arms. "Oh, I think it was about six fifteen this morning, right after my morning hurling session."

He kissed her forehead. "How are you feeling now?"

"Famished, of course."

"Then why don't we go grab an early dinner?"

"You don't want to be here when Aubrey gets the tour?"

"Serena and Jazz have this. She'll feel more comfortable with them anyway."

"You don't usually invite strangers here."

"I never invite strangers here."

"Then why Aubrey Starr? Most secret organizations like

OZ would see what she does for a living as a threat to their anonymity. You don't. Why?"

"Couple of reasons. Kate vetted her, and as we both know, Kate doesn't vet many."

"No argument there. What else?"

"She's gone through something, some kind of trauma. My gut's telling me she has personal experience with human trafficking."

"Why do you think that?"

He told her about the scars that both Serena and Jazz had spotted when Aubrey's towel had slipped after they'd arrived at her home. "Jazz said she saw a half dozen or more. She might have secrets but I don't think they're a threat to OZ."

"You think Medford's death and the bugs in her house could be related to what she went through?"

"Maybe. Who knows? She needs help, and that's what she's going to get."

Jules smiled up at him. "Now it's my turn to ask when's the last time I told you I love you?"

He chuckled. "From what I recall, it wasn't at six fifteen this morning."

She grimaced. "Yeah, probably not. Sorry. I think I might've called you a few bad names."

"You're entitled."

"Well, now that I'm not wanting to throw you off a bridge, let me tell you that I adore you, Asher Drake. You're everything I've ever wanted."

His heart filled with love for this amazing woman, Ash covered her smiling mouth with his own. How he'd gotten so lucky he would never know. He was just grateful and humbled that he had.

Pulling away, breathless, Jules beamed up at him. "Let's get out of here. I've got a hankering for more than an early dinner."

Holding hands, they walked out the door together. Yeah, damn lucky.

$\sim$

THE INSTANT the bedroom door shut behind Aubrey, she wrapped her arms around herself and closed her eyes. Was Lawrence Medford dead because of her? The awful thought drilled like a carpenter bee into her brain. What had she started?

Pacing back and forth, Aubrey reviewed her actions. What could have tipped Ferante off that she was investigating him?

She had been so careful. She had used incognito mode and a VPN for all her research. All searches had been scrubbed from her computer. No one could trace them back to her. She had told no one about her suspicions regarding Ferante, not even her team.

As much as she wanted to deny the possibility, Asher Drake was right. Medford's murder and the bugs and cameras found in her home were likely related.

When she'd first begun filming documentaries, the idea that she could be putting herself in danger had been nebulous. She was one little filmmaker. No one would care what she had to say. All that had changed after her first film. Not only had it received critical acclaim, she had gotten attention from people who wanted her to shut up. She had received numerous threats, all anonymous. She had taken them seriously, even going to the police. Nothing had been found. The police file was still open, and she would occasionally send the detective a copy of a threatening email or social media post. Like so many things these days, people could make all sorts of anonymous comments and be confident their identity would never be found out. She had been told to get used to it.

And so she had. But she'd still been cautious.

Not cautious enough, apparently. And Lawrence Medford might have paid the price.

Dropping onto the bed, Aubrey faced a harsh possibility. Should she scrap the film? The last thing she wanted was to put anyone in danger. Her films were made to save lives, not put them in jeopardy.

She would hold off on making that decision. For now, she would take the opportunity that Asher Drake and his OZ organization were offering her. Participating in the rescue of trafficking victims had been a goal of hers for years. Seeing it firsthand would give her the insight she would never get just by talking to the victims or the rescuers. Even if she ended up scrapping the project, she desperately needed to witness this event.

Wanting to get her mind off her sorrow, Aubrey unpacked her bags and then took a quick shower. Someone would be by soon to give her a tour, and since she didn't want to make anyone wait, she rushed through the shower. As she hadn't had the chance before she'd left home, she did take the time to wash her hair, though, as it still smelled of chlorine from this morning's swim.

Had that only been this morning? She felt as though she'd lived three lifetimes since then.

As she stepped out of the stall, she realized she had not even taken the time to appreciate her accommodations. She could be staying in a luxury ski resort. From the claw-foot porcelain tub to the marble double vanity with its array of top-of-the line personal care products to the extra-large shower stall, everything was designed for the comfort and delight of the guest.

Rubbing down her wet hair with a soft, fluffy towel, Aubrey returned to the bedroom and took in what she'd missed before. Hardwood the color of soft teak covered the floor. In the center was a queen-sized bed with a bedspread of muted green and pink. One wall was brick and stone with a gorgeous fireplace in the middle. Another wall was painted a light moss green. Between those two walls was a huge window with another breathtaking view. Two chairs had been placed before the window, a table between them. She could imagine waking up and sipping coffee while drinking in the beauty of the morning.

Knowing she was running out of time, she blow-dried her hair and applied a minimal amount of make-up. A little blush, mascara, and lip gloss went miles in making a girl feel better. Grabbing a pair of jeans and an olive-green sweater from the drawer, she hurriedly pulled them on. As she dressed, her eyes kept darting to the window numerous times. Amazing what peace she could get from just those few glimpses of the view.

The knock on her door came just as she finished dressing. She took one last glance back at the view and then straightened her shoulders.

She opened the door to a smiling Serena. "Ready for your tour?"

"Absolutely."

CHAPTER TWENTY-ONE

A size-fourteen shoe zoomed toward his face. Liam pivoted, whirled, and came back with a double kick to his opponent's sternum. The surprise on Sean Donavan's face would have been comical if he'd had a chance to enjoy it. Donavan recovered in an instant and came back full force, socking Liam in the gut. Though he wore protective padding, the force of the blow knocked him on his ass. He was back on his feet in seconds, coming hard at Donavan.

Muscles sang and adrenaline surged. This felt good. The first thing he'd enjoyed in months. He needed this to balance the frustration and fury bubbling inside him. Every single time he thought he was close to finding those victims in Colombia, they vanished. He wanted to find them. He needed to find Drury. So far, he'd come up empty on both.

Time was running out. He felt it in his gut. Something was going to happen. What, he didn't know. Death? Or were the victims going to be split up, and he'd be able to save only a few? What if one of them was Cat? He had to find them soon. Or else.

A thump on his jaw had him flying back onto the mat

again. A good reminder that he was sparring with one of the most gifted fighters he'd ever faced. Losing his focus was not a good idea.

Jumping back to his feet, Liam went at his opponent even harder and faster. Donavan moved at the last second, and the uppercut to his jaw glanced off his chin, but the double punch to his belly took the man's breath. Liam seized the opportunity to shut him down completely.

With stealthy precision, Liam punched, jabbed, whirled, and kicked. Since this was a training session, he didn't use full force. Still, he went for maximum enjoyment of getting the best of Sean Donavan. In hand-to-hand, no one at OZ was Donavan's equal. For the first time ever, Liam knew he had him. The other man had no defense other than to keep his forearms up to protect himself.

Feeling triumph, Liam was set up to send a final blow that would send his friend to the mat. Out of the corner of his eye, he saw someone watching. For a millisecond, he looked. The thought flashed in his mind that she had changed little in the four years since he'd first seen her. Her skin still glowed with a translucent light that he found mesmerizing. Her wavy golden-blond hair might be a little longer. She—

Liam flew backward as Donavan clipped him hard on the chin. Landing with a hard thud, flat on his back, he fought to catch his breath.

It didn't help that Donavan stood over him with a smug grin. "Thought you had me, didn't you, mate?"

Instead of answering, he shifted his eyes to the glassed area where he'd spotted Aubrey Starr. She was gone.

GUILTILY, Aubrey turned away from the sparring session. She'd distracted the dark-haired man, and he'd gotten clocked. She'd been frozen in shock, as she'd recognized him as the man she'd met years ago in Kosovo. She hadn't known the name of the organization that had rescued the trafficking victims. She had asked and was told they preferred to remain anonymous. Now she knew it had been Option Zero.

And she would be going on a rescue mission with them. This was surreal.

"Who was that?" Aubrey asked.

"The one grinning like an idiot is my husband, Sean," Serena answered with a laugh. "The one on the mat is Liam Stryker."

Liam.

She mentally shook her head. This wasn't the time or place to become enamored of someone.

"Come on," Serena said. "We'll show you around for a few minutes and then let you have some time to yourself. You've had a long day."

Solitude sounded heavenly to her. The day had brought an enormous amount of shocks and surprises. She'd had hardly any time to absorb even one of them.

Her unusual reaction to Liam Stryker was pushed to the back of her mind as she walked through the underground headquarters of Option Zero. She'd never heard of such an organization and couldn't help but wonder how many such entities existed that the public would never know about.

The place was massive. A maze of corridors led to rooms of varying sizes, some were empty, while others had chairs, conference tables, and desks.

"It's amazing that all of this is underground, but it's not dark or dreary like a basement or underground bunker."

"We've worked hard to make it that way. Our people spend many long, sometimes grueling, hours here. Working in a bright, sunny atmosphere, even if it's all illusion, makes the job a lot more pleasant."

Serena stopped at a door and pressed a keypad on the

wall. The door slid open, revealing a large area filled not only with computers and giant monitors, but also a half-dozen people.

"Here's where we gather the majority of our intel."

"Incredibly impressive." Since she wasn't one to beat around the bush, she asked, "Why are you allowing me to see these things?"

"You've answered all our questions. You've been vetted by both Ash and Kate. Besides, Jazz and I are good judges of character. We put in a good word for you. Come on." Serena grabbed her arm and led her toward the exit. "Let's grab some dinner. I think it's Eve and Gideon's turn in the kitchen, and they usually make something incredible. Then you can have the night to yourself to absorb everything."

As they walked back down the corridor, Aubrey couldn't resist a glance at the training area where she'd seen Liam Stryker. Her heart inexplicably dropped when she saw that the room was empty.

Jazz was waiting for them at the entrance to the main house. Aubrey followed the two operatives down a long hallway. The enticing scent of something spicy twitched at her nose, and her stomach growled in response. With her stomach still tied up in knots, she was surprised at how hungry she was suddenly. Along the walk to the kitchen, she kept spotting spectacular views, reminding her of her location. Maybe the mountain air had increased her appetite.

Two phones buzzed simultaneously. Aubrey watched as both Serena and Jazz pulled their phones from their pockets. They read whatever was on their phone screens and then raised their heads to look at each other in some kind of odd, silent language.

"Something wrong?" Aubrey asked.

"Looks like dinner's going to have to wait," Serena said. She sent an inquisitive look over her shoulder. "That rescue operation you were wanting has arrived quicker than we anticipated. Think you're up for it?"

"Yes."

"Then let's go."

∼

ADRENALINE SURGED through Liam's veins. Just when he was close to giving up hope…and now this. A more-than-credible lead, proof positive that those victims were still in Bogota, not five miles from the original house.

Liam stalked into the conference room. He had texted the team to meet him. They would need everyone for this op. Nothing could go wrong this time.

He was in the middle of the room before he noticed that they had an extra person, someone he definitely hadn't anticipated. The filmmaker was here. He swallowed a curse. This op was too important to have a neophyte tagging along. Catching Ash's eye, he jerked his head over to a corner for a private talk.

"When did we start allowing outsiders into OZ?"

Though Ash raised a brow at the confrontational tone, he said calmly, "You agreed to let her go on a rescue. Have you changed your mind?"

"No, she's welcome to go on another one, but this op's too important. I've already let those victims down once. I can't risk anything going wrong this time."

"What makes you think she would jeopardize the operation?"

"She's not an operative. She's not trained. If she can't help in the rescue then she's a liability. She can go on the next one, after she's had some training."

"Both Serena and Jazz have indicated she's calm and competent, not one to panic. Serena verified her assertion that she's weapons-trained and has good self-defense skills. I don't believe she'll be a hindrance. And we did agree to allow her access on our next rescue op."

Seeing that Ash wasn't going to back down, Liam clenched his jaw and nodded. "All right, but I want Jazz with her at all times."

"I don't think you'll get an argument from either of them."

With a jerk of his head for assent, Liam went to the front of the room. He still wasn't happy with an untrained newcomer tagging along, but he also knew that Ash would not allow someone on the op that he didn't trust. He'd have to let it go at that. He had bigger fish to fry.

Liam gave a blanket nod of acknowledgment to everyone in the room. "Thanks for coming on short notice. I thought we'd lost these victims for good, but looks like we've been given another chance. We're going to need to move fast, though. We can't allow what happened last time to happen again. If they get a breath of an idea that we've found them, they'll disappear again." His eyes veered to the woman in the corner. "We have an additional person tagging along on the op. Everyone, say hello to Aubrey Starr."

Instead of acknowledging his introduction, she seemed to shrink into the chair. What the hell? When he'd walked in the door, she had sat calmly and confidently in her seat as if she belonged there. Now she had grown pale and looked like she was going to slide onto the floor.

So much for the not-one-to-panic persona she'd supposedly shown Jazz and Serena. Tough shit. She was going to have to get over that. OZ was no place for the timid.

"Our target is a house five miles from the original location. My intel is credible enough that I don't see the need for long-term surveillance. The house belongs to a shell corporation. Serena's people are working to tie the ownership to a real person, but it's going to be slow-going. My guess is that it's Gomez's property, like the other one. It's likely he owns several such houses. I figure the group moves every few weeks to stay ahead of authorities.

"I'll go through assignments on the plane. Anyone have questions before we head out?"

THAT VOICE.

She had dreamed of that voice, heard it in her head a million times. Could this man with the grim countenance and disapproving glare really be her Lion?

She had been all eager to hear the specifics of a rescue and how it was planned. The moment she'd heard Liam Stryker's voice, she'd lost all concentration. Instead of listening to the content of his words, she had listened to the intonation, the accent, the sound. She had examined everything, anything she could that would confirm her belief that this was the man she'd connected with in a filthy, icy-cold prison in Syria.

How was that even possible?

Even though she had prayed and prayed that Lion had somehow survived, in her heart of hearts she had not believed that he had.

She mentally shook her head. No. It just wasn't possible. Plenty of people sounded like other people. It had been over twelve years. Her memory could be faulty. She was tired, had had an exhausting day. There were a dozen reasons why her brain could be malfunctioning. Out of the billions of people in the world, what were the chances of her finding the one man she'd longed for? It was impossible.

Maybe her subconscious, recognizing that she was attracted to Liam Stryker, had decided to assign the absurd notion that he could be the man she'd been obsessed with for so long.

Vaguely aware that people had gotten up and were milling around, Aubrey realized that she needed to do the same. But somehow, all she could do was sit there and stare at the dark haired-stranger with the voice of her Lion.

"Aubrey, you okay?"

She glanced up at Jazz, who was standing before her with a concerned expression on her face.

Her mouth was so dry she couldn't get a word out. She managed a nod and a grimace of a smile.

A bottle of water appeared in her vision. "Take a few sips, you'll be fine."

Doing what she was told, Aubrey drank from the bottle. She needed to get herself together. These people didn't know her. Behaving like a frightened mouse who'd run at the first sign of trouble would not instill confidence.

She drew in a few breaths, and peace followed. Whatever the answers to her questions were, she would find them. For right now, these people had a mission to accomplish. And she had a job to do, too. She intended to absorb every nuance of the rescue so she could one day put the experience into words. Focusing on what she had to do had gotten her through difficult times. This was no different.

"Better?"

"Yes. Sorry. Guess the excitement got to me."

Jazz grinned. "The first time I went on an op, I barfed." She looked over her shoulder and then turned back to Aubrey and whispered, "All over Xavier."

Despite the circumstances, Aubrey laughed, just as Jazz had intended. She could not imagine this überconfident young woman ever having an ounce of uncertainty about anything, much less throwing up from nervousness. However, she appreciated her attempt to make her feel better.

She took another couple of swallows of water and then stood. "Thank you. That helps. What now?"

"We all grab our go bags and head to the airport. We'll get something to eat on the plane. I'll—"

"Jazz, can I talk with you a sec?"

Aubrey froze in place. Liam Stryker stood before her. Though his words had been for Jazz, his eyes were on her. And they weren't friendly. She could easily guess his thoughts. She hadn't made the best first impression.

Reminding herself that she was made of grit and determination, Aubrey cleared her throat and said, "Thank you, Mr. Stryker, for allowing me to go along."

"You going to be able to stay out of our way?"

Even though she hadn't expected him to be thrilled with an outsider's presence, the unfriendly question told her he was the exact opposite of happy that she was here.

"I promise you won't even know I'm there."

Though his brows rose in obvious doubt, he just gave her a nod before turning to Jazz. "I need to talk with you."

Trying not to be hurt at his abruptness, Aubrey backed away. "I'll go grab my bag and meet you outside, Jazz."

Jazz gave her a quick smile. "Sounds good."

She got out of the room as quickly as possible. How ridiculous for her to think the extremely rude Liam Stryker could possibly be Lion. Other than the voice similarity, the two had nothing in common.

"DID you have to be so rude to Aubrey? You know we're all on the same side, don't you?"

He was genuinely surprised at Jazz's accusation. "I was rude?"

"Very."

Okay, maybe he'd been a little short with her, but seeing

her look as though she could pass out at any moment hadn't exactly filled him with good vibes.

"I'll apologize later. I just want to make sure you stick with her. She looks as though a loud sneeze would scare her off."

"Then you need to take a second look. She's one gutsy lady."

Jazz was known for her protectiveness of her OZ team-mates. Apparently Aubrey had been added as an honorary member of that exclusive club.

Ash appeared at his side. "Everything okay here?"

"Fine. I was just assigning Jazz the job of looking out for our guest."

"Then she's in good hands. I'll be ready to roll in about ten minutes. I just want to go up to the house and check on Jules."

"How's she feeling?" Jazz asked.

"Her morning sickness is easing, but we both agreed it'd be a good idea for her to stay close to home for a while."

"I'll go grab my bag. See you in a few minutes." Jazz gave Liam one last telling look and walked away.

"What was that about?"

Liam shrugged. He didn't have time to argue about Aubrey Starr and why he didn't want her on this op.

"Nothing. We're good. Tell Jules to feel better. I'll see you on the plane."

Ash looked like he was going to say something else, but then stopped himself.

"What?" Liam asked.

"Something going on with you? I mean, besides this op and your disapproval of an outsider?"

Yeah, he couldn't deny that his attitude was less than stel-lar. He should be pumped that they'd found the victims and would soon rescue them. It's what they'd been working on for weeks. Instead, he was suddenly just the opposite.

"Talk to me, Liam," Ash said. "Let me help."

How could he explain what had been hammering at his brain on and off for the last few days? How could he explain giving up? It wasn't in his DNA. Wasn't in the DNA of anyone at OZ. The idea was barely one he'd allow himself to consider, but it was simmering in his gut, and he couldn't squelch it the way he normally would. He was beginning to believe he would never find Cat. He had lived on hope for so long, but he had been lying to himself. He'd seen the eyes of the victims he'd rescued. The hopelessness, the absolute emptiness. The acceptance that she was dead was slowly seeping into his bones, and though he fought it, he couldn't bring himself back to a place of hope.

He shook his head. This wasn't the time nor the place for these thoughts or this discussion. The people they were going to rescue deserved his whole attention. He refused to give anything but his best.

"I'm fine. Just focused on getting it right this time."

Eyes narrowed, Ash gave him a hard, assessing stare and then nodded. "Then let's get going."

CHAPTER TWENTY-TWO

Being in the presence of eight highly trained operatives was a bit like sitting amongst a pride of lions. Even though they were sitting, they had an air of power and alertness about them. Aubrey got the feeling that if anything moved even the slightest, not one of them would miss seeing it.

She was seated across from Eve Wells and Gideon Wright. She could not imagine two more sophisticated and dangerous-looking people. Though Eve was a lovely woman, with midnight-black hair, a creamy camellia complexion, and intense blue eyes, Aubrey didn't doubt for a moment that she could be lethal when necessary. And her partner, Gideon, with summer-streaked blond hair and an easygoing grin, reminded her of a taller and beefier Brad Pitt. Except he had an edge to him no Hollywood actor could authentically emulate. He was the real deal.

It had been years since she'd felt out of her element, but there was no doubt about it—these people were a different breed.

Her gaze shifted to the man in the front row. His long

legs sprawled out in front of him, Liam Stryker had the slouch of a man at leisure, but like the others, it was all an act. A dangerous air surrounded him as if he could leap and devour prey within seconds.

Aubrey tried to observe him objectively, without the haze of uncertainty clouding her mind. He was tall, maybe about six-two. He had dark brown hair that was slightly shaggy, as if he'd gotten out of the shower, run his fingers through the dampness, and called it done. On anyone else it might have looked sloppy. On Liam Stryker, it worked. His dark brown eyes could sear with the briefest of glances. He had a sharp blade of a nose that leaned slightly to the left, as if it had been broken and set to rights by the owner of said nose. His mouth was nice, with a slightly thin upper lip and fuller lower one. And even though she'd only seen him frown, there were slight lines on either side of his mouth that made her think he wasn't always so grim.

The broad set of his shoulders told her he'd probably played sports in high school, maybe college, too. His hands were large, almost twice the size of hers, with long fingers and neatly trimmed nails. She could envision those hands being lethal when necessary. She could also imagine them being passionate, even tender.

A shiver swept up her spine as a slight flush of heat zoomed through her body. Just because he had a voice similar to the man she'd known as Lion didn't mean she should be attracted to him. He'd been nothing but gruff, bordering on rude, since they'd met. She liked friendly, easy-going men. Not grumpy jerks.

There were many things she'd forgotten about her ordeal in Syria. Some of them she'd forgotten naturally; others she had forced into a tight, small corner of her mind, never to be exposed to her thoughts again. But that time with Lion? She remembered every word, every breath, every nuance. Even as sick as she'd been, his gruff laughter had made her smile, his voice had soothed her like nothing else.

He had been kind, funny, and incredibly caring. Within minutes of hearing his voice, she had known he was a man she could trust with her secrets. He had been a man she could imagine spending the rest of her life with, growing old together.

This man with his grim countenance and tough demeanor had nothing in common with Lion. The voice? An anomaly, nothing more. Lots of people sounded like other people. How many could mimic other people's voices? It had been over twelve years since she'd heard Lion speak. Even though she'd told herself she would never forget his voice, perhaps that had been only wishful thinking.

Her mind shied away from that thought. She couldn't bear to think that the one thing she had left of him—his voice in her mind—was merely a product of her longing and nothing more.

Aubrey gave Liam Stryker another assessing stare. Even though she rejected the idea that this was Lion, she had to admit that the description of himself that he had given her fit this man very well. Dark brown hair, brown eyes, around six foot two, weight around two-ten. Lots of men fit that description, though.

As if aware of her scrutiny, he turned to look at her. The flush of heat in her body went hotter. Those dark eyes seared, and she felt as though he were looking deep within her soul, searching…and asking. What? What did he want to know? Should she go talk to him? Should she just ask the question that was pounding at her brain? Were you in Syria twelve years ago? Did you meet a desolate young woman in a dark, dank prison and give her hope and a reason to survive? Are you my Lion?

Was she afraid to know the truth? Did she already know it and refused to accept it?

No, it couldn't be him. He would have recognized her. Something about her would have triggered his memory. Based on his attitude he had no recollection of her, which meant he wasn't Lion. He just happened to have a similar voice and that was it. She was being fanciful and that wasn't like her.

Their eyes broke contact, and Aubrey mentally shook herself. She was here for one reason only, to experience as much as she could about rescuing human trafficking victims. Since she wouldn't be allowed to do any filming, she would need to absorb every nuance and emotion to be able to relay the experience in words.

Determined to put aside the emotions rioting through her, Aubrey took out pen and paper and did just that.

The rescue team is headed to Colombia. Even though I'm not allowed to film the event, the sheer enormity of what is about to happen could never be captured on film. These people with hearts of lions are putting their lives on the line to save others.

The excitement is palpable but tempered with a steely determination. Every face has a similar expression of intent. Their eyes fiercely convey their mission. They will save these victims and bring down their perpetrators. Why do they do what they do? What brought them to this time, this moment?

I hope to be allowed to learn that from each of them.

The group consists of eight men and women, all in their twenties and mid to late thirties. Physically fit, yes, but there's more than that. There's strength, there's compassion, there's purpose.

What made these people into warriors? Who are they? Why them?

"All right. Listen up."

Startled, she glanced up to see Liam Stryker standing at the front of the plane. A large monitor had lowered from the ceiling and the blueprints of a house appeared on the screen. The exterior, red brick and modern looking, gave no indication at all of the evil that went on inside.

"The schematics are on your tablets. As before, we have the approval of the Colombian government, but this time we're going in without local authorities knowing."

"Why's that?" Jazz asked.

"Turns out a clerk in the constable's office is related to one of the traffickers. He's the one that informed the traffickers we were coming and when."

"But Myron…" Jazz began.

"Wasn't needed. And knowing him, he didn't give up anything."

"That was a message for you." Gideon's grim tone matched his fierce demeanor.

"Yes."

There were nuances behind that word that held a world of bleakness. If she'd thought Liam Stryker looked intense before, that was nothing compared to the fury burning in his eyes now. Someone had crossed him. And that someone would pay.

"That's for me to worry about at another time. For now, let's talk about how we're going to get these people out. We can't let them down again."

He turned toward the screen. "There's a hill behind the house. We'll set up camp there and do reconnaissance. We'll go in an hour before dawn. Jazz, you and Ms. Starr will stay at the camp and coordinate with the aid workers."

No. She hadn't come on this trip to stay behind. Aubrey opened her mouth to object but stopped when she caught Asher Drake's eye. He gave a quick, subtle shake of his head. She immediately understood his meaning. Now was not the time to state her case. The OZ leader had promised that she would be allowed on this raid. She believed he would keep that promise. He would speak with Liam Stryker on her behalf.

She returned her attention to the other assignments Stryker made, impressed with his thoroughness and the confidence he exuded. This man had given this operation careful thought and would do everything within his power to make sure it was successful.

For the first time, Aubrey allowed herself to think about the victims who were about to be rescued. Normally when she was in the middle of a project, she focused on the work. She had a deep empathy for each victim but allowing herself to be drawn into their sadness wasn't helpful in getting their story told. She had to maintain distance, not only for the story, but also for herself. But for a few moments she gave thought to who they were, what they'd experienced. Would they recover? Could they?

Though her time with her captors had been limited, she had experienced pain, degradation, and a violation no human being should ever have to endure. Her memories of that time were crystal clear. Even after years of therapy and self-care, she fought against them daily.

She had interviewed numerous trafficking victims. All ethnicities, genders, and ages had been touched and ravaged by the evil industry of selling and using human beings for profit. Recovery was possible, but there would always be the memory of horror. That never went away.

"Any questions?" Stryker asked.

"Do we know how many victims yet?" Jazz asked.

"Latest intel says between eight and fifteen. All women, no children."

"That's a small blessing," Aubrey said.

Every eye turned to her. It was the first time she'd spoken to the group as a whole, and her words had captured everyone's attention. Several operatives nodded their agreement.

"Yes," Stryker said.

She had only ever seen the aftermath of child trafficking. The loss of innocence in a child's eyes was one of the hardest things she'd ever witnessed.

"Here's the plan."

As Stryker gave out assignments, Aubrey studied each person's demeanor on learning their place in the rescue. They got it. No one was here for the glory or for the adrenaline rush. They were here to save lives. There were no egos here.

The rest of the flight, Aubrey made notes, trying, without success, to think about something other than the similarities between Liam Stryker and the man who had saved her life. The man she'd loved for so long.

Could this be Lion? Could he have forgotten her? Could it have been that easy for him? If so, everything that she thought she knew about him had all been a lie. Had she been obsessed for twelve years with a man who had never really existed?

CHAPTER TWENTY-THREE

Bogota, Colombia

Camp setup took less than an hour to accomplish. Thick gray clouds and a light mist of rain gave a welcome relief from the smothering heat. They were two miles from the target house. The hill was high enough to give them an excellent view of the entire estate. Despite the rain, visibility was excellent. The trees surrounding them were thick and full of foliage, giving plenty of cover. Even a drone hovering right above would not spot them.

Things were ahead of schedule. The plan was to breach the estate at three thirty-five a.m. local time. That gave them two hours to observe before heading down.

Two telescopes were aimed at the house. Each of the eight operatives took turns manning them. Due to the terrain an underground escape should not be possible this time. Though Liam didn't discount anything, he was confident that there would be no escape-way for them.

The telescope had revealed no activity within the last hour. He'd watched two men exit earlier. Both appeared to be in their mid-forties. Based on the luxury car they drove away in and their clothing, they were affluent. Rich scumbags, poor scumbags. Didn't matter. If they thought to return for a repeat visit, they would be disappointed.

"Got a minute?" Ash spoke behind him.

"Sure." He glanced over at Sean. "Take this, will you?"

When he and Ash headed away from camp, he knew what was coming. Couldn't say he hadn't expected it, but that didn't mean the discussion would be any less irritating.

"Rain's a blessing," Ash said.

"Yeah. Last time I was here, thought I would melt."

"Mosquitoes don't seem as bad either."

"There's that."

"You know she needs to go along with you."

Liam sighed loudly. "She'll hear the audio. She can't film anything anyway. She can view from a telescope and catch almost everything going on. This is too important to risk a screw-up, Ash."

"We'll make sure she doesn't."

"Why is this so important to you?"

"I believe what she does is important. The more people see the ravages of human trafficking, the more they'll be aware of the danger. We see the horror every day. We know it exists. The average person has no real idea. If her work can prevent one child or one adult from being taken, then we need to do what we can to help her."

Arguing against Ash's reasoning was pointless. Mostly because he didn't disagree. The more people were aware of the dangers, the better the chances of fewer people being abducted.

"My question is," Ash continued, "why are you so opposed? You got something against her?"

"I don't even know her."

"Everyone else has made a point of talking to her,

welcoming her to the group. You're the only one who hasn't bothered. Is it because of what happened in Kosovo?"

"This has nothing to do with Kosovo. This has to do with the fact that not only is she not a trained operative, she looked like she was going to slide out of her chair back at headquarters. She might make good documentaries about the ravages of human trafficking, but she's not ready to see it up close and personal."

"She's had quite a few shocks over the last couple of days. Had a lot of things thrown at her in a short time span. I think we can give her some slack, don't you?"

He stared hard at Ash. The man was the leader of OZ but this was Liam's op. If he said no, Ash wouldn't like it, but he'd accept it. However, he also knew that Ash would never suggest something that would put a mission in jeopardy.

He blew out a frustrated breath. "Fine. Fine. She can go, but I still want Jazz to stick to her like glue."

"That shouldn't be a problem. Both Jazz and Serena seem protective of her."

Liam stared out past the trees, past the canyons, into the gray mist. "Yeah, she seems like a nice person."

"What's wrong, Stryker? It's not just the filmmaker. You blew me off before, but I know there's something else. What is it?"

"I think this might be the last one, Ash. If I don't find Cat this time, I'm done."

"What do you mean, you're done?"

"I can't keep doing this."

"You're going to stop rescuing trafficking victims?" Ash snorted loudly. "You won't stop…you can't. Rescuing is in your blood."

Ash was right. He couldn't stop rescuing, didn't want to stop. But he would stop putting his heart and soul on the line. Every single time he'd gone into a rescue, there had been that chance he would find her. If he didn't this time, he had to let her go. There was no choice in the matter.

"No, I won't stop, but Xavier said something not too long ago that got me to thinking. I have no life, not really. Seeing you and Jules together, Sean and Serena, I'm glad for you guys—you deserve all good things—but it just makes me realize how much I've put my life on hold." Shaking his head, he sent Ash a grimace of a smile. "Sorry. Don't know why I'm all the sudden philosophical."

"You have every right to a life, Liam. And I'd say Cat would be the first one to tell you that."

"Yeah, she would." He glanced down at his watch. "Almost go time."

Giving him a slap on the back, Ash grinned. "Let's go put some assholes out of business."

"Sounds good."

Getting that off his chest had helped. He would focus on the op, save the victims, and take down some human scum. And then, if Cat wasn't there? Well then, he'd get on with the rest of his life. Hollowed out? Yeah, maybe. But Ash was right. Cat would be the first person to tell him he needed to get on with his life. It was time to do just that.

THE NIGHT WAS thick with darkness, obscuring all light. If not for the occasional streetlight, she would have had no idea if they were on the road or in the middle of a rock quarry. The Jeep bounced over the rough terrain, increasing the nervousness in the pit of her stomach. Aubrey sat in the back, gripping the seat. She wasn't frightened, but she did feel anxiety. This wasn't anything she'd ever experienced before. In film school, she'd been taught to embrace the moment, become the moment, to be able to reveal its authenticity. She was definitely doing that. This was as real as it got.

"Don't worry," Jazz said softly beside her. "The adrenaline rushing through you will subside. Just take even breaths."

"Thank you." She owed both Jazz and Serena so much. They had talked with her about what would happen. Even though she had been in the meetings when duties were assigned, she couldn't say she had understood everything. The two women had explained in detail what to look for, what she would see, and what might happen.

She wore what was apparently standard uniform for OZ —camo pants, black T-shirt, and a Kevlar vest. She had asked about carrying a weapon but both Jazz and Serena had shaken their heads at the request. She couldn't blame them— they had no real idea of the extent of her training. But she wouldn't be defenseless. She knew plenty of ways to defend herself if it became necessary. She didn't expect to have to do that but she was going into an unknown and dangerous situation. Not being prepared for any contingency would be foolish. She didn't do foolish anymore.

"When we get there," Jazz said, "just stick with me no matter what. We'll go through the back, along with Gideon and Xavier."

She nodded. They'd gone over the drill several times with her. She didn't resent the repetition. Everything they did, everything they said, was meant for one purpose—a successful mission.

They turned all lights off as the vehicles approached the house.

"All looks quiet," Ash said from the front seat of the Jeep.

"Yeah," Xavier answered. "Maybe too quiet."

"Listen up," Liam said. "Xavier's right. It does seem too quiet, but we go in as planned."

Hearing the voice in her ear that sounded so much like

the voice in her dreams was surreal. How many times had she woken with *that* voice in her head? That had to be Lion's voice. It had to be. *Didn't it?*

"You ready?" Jazz asked.

Aubrey nodded, refocusing. Whether Liam was Lion or not didn't matter right now. What mattered was that he, along with the rest of these operatives, was about to rescue a dozen women, thereby giving them another chance at life. She had dreamed about seeing an operation like this first-hand one day, and that time was now. She was more than ready.

They'd parked on an access road about three hundred yards from the property. Tall hedges surrounded the property, obscuring much of the structure, but as they approached the yard, she could see glimpses of the house through the greenery. All looked peaceful.

Staying close to Jazz, Aubrey lowered her head and moved forward with the group. They were ten feet from entering the property when the first shot rang out.

"Take cover!" someone shouted.

Aubrey had barely realized what was happening when she found herself flying through the air. She landed with a thud, and then a large body fell on top of her.

"Stay down," Liam Stryker growled into her ear.

Since she couldn't move and could barely breathe, that wouldn't be a problem.

Shots fired rapidly for several breath-holding seconds, and then all was quiet.

"Eve, you see him?" Liam asked.

"Yeah. Give me a sec." And then, "Found him."

There was the sound of glass breaking and then complete silence.

No one moved for what seemed like forever. Aubrey,

needing to breathe, whispered softly, "Mr. Stryker? Do you think you could get off me now?"

"Shh."

She took that to mean *no he could not.*

They waited several more seconds and then he lifted himself slightly off her and said, "Jazz, you copy?"

"Yes."

"Where are you located?"

"About ten feet to your right."

"Crawl this way. Then take Starr and hide behind those bushes until this is done."

"On my way."

"But I want to see the—"

The body on top of her covered her again, and he whispered fiercely in her ear, "Nobody gets killed on my watch. Got that?"

"Yes...okay."

It probably was only a couple of minutes, but it felt like an eternity before Jazz said behind them, "I'm here."

Liam rolled off her and Aubrey was finally able to breathe.

Jazz grabbed her arm and said, "Belly-crawl with me over to the bushes."

Following Jazz's lead, Aubrey wiggled on her belly to the tall hedges.

"We'll stay here until we get the all clear," Jazz said.

"What happened?"

"We missed a lookout. He was up in the attic, so we didn't see him."

"Why did he stop shooting?"

"Eve took him out."

She hadn't known where Eve had gone, only that she hadn't been in the two vehicles with the rest of them. Apparently, she had been a distance away.

She raised her head slightly and looked at the house. Lights were on in several rooms, but she heard no sounds of violence like she'd expected.

"Why is it so quiet?"

"Your earbud probably got dislodged when Liam tackled you."

She felt a hand at her ear and then a slight pressure. Voices and noises exploded. In awe, Aubrey listened as the rescue went down.

CHAPTER TWENTY-FOUR

Easing the door open, Liam peered inside the room. He jerked back a half second before a bullet would've hit him head on. They'd experienced little resistance but this guy in the attic was apparently intent on staying the course. Eve had handled one of the attic shooters quite handily. Now it was Liam's job to convince this other guy that he didn't want to go the same route.

"Habla English?"

"Yeah," a man answered in a distinctly Midwestern accent.

"There's no way out for you. The house is surrounded."

"Then I guess we negotiate."

"Not sure what you've got to negotiate with. Looks like we've got all the cards."

"Oh yeah? What about this?"

"Please help me. I don't want to die."

Cursing under his breath, Liam took a step back to regroup. The voice had been a woman's, quivering with terror.

"Okay, you do have some cards. How do you want to play

this?"

"Me and the girl walk out of here. Once I'm safe, I'll let her go."

Yeah, right.

"What happens if I say no?"

"Easy. I kill the girl."

"And then I kill you."

"Maybe so, but you got a dead girl on your hands. I'm assuming that's not in your plans."

The guy had a point.

Liam stepped a few feet from the attic entrance and said softly, "Hey, Ash. You close?"

"On the second floor. Did I hear right? He's got a hostage?"

"Yeah. Can you come up here and keep him busy? I've got an idea."

"On my way."

Should've expected this. The op had gone too smoothly. With the exception of the lookout that Eve had taken care of, they'd experienced almost no resistance. Yeah, a shot here and there but nothing they couldn't handle. In his experience when something was too easy, there's trouble brewing. He'd never lost a victim, and he wasn't about to start now.

Ash came up behind him. "What's the plan?"

"You keep him talking. I'm going to go at him from the outside."

"How's that?"

"There's a balcony and a window."

"You do realize that's not really a window, right? And that balcony? It's for decoration only. It's not built to hold a gnat's ass, much less a two-hundred-pound man."

"Yeah, but it is a way inside. Just keep him busy. I'll do the rest."

"Hey," the guy shouted, "what's going on out there? We

got a deal or not?"

"Hold on," Liam yelled back. "I'm conferring with my boss."

"Well, hurry up. I don't have all day."

"Be right with you," Liam assured him. "I can't authorize squat without talking to the boss man."

"Well then, let me talk to him instead."

"Yeah…okay. That's a good idea." Liam sent a grin to Ash. "Keep him talking. I'll let you know when I'm ready."

Liam headed downstairs, hearing Ash's authoritative warnings of what happens in most hostage situations. Sounded dire, but Liam knew this asshole's kind. He wasn't going to give up without concessions. OZ didn't do concessions.

Sean and Xavier met him in the foyer. "What's the plan?"

"Follow me around back. I may need a boost."

He had to give them credit. Instead of telling him it was a boneheaded idea, they followed him.

Double-timing it, he was at the back in seconds. Daylight had broken, giving him a good view of the railing he needed to get to. There was only one opening on this side of the house. His best bet was to go straight up.

Hearing a noise, he turned to see Xavier holding a rope with a grappling hook. "Sean's looking for a ladder in the garage. If this holds, I figured it might get you there faster."

When they weren't working, he and most of his OZ teammates spent hours climbing the Bitterroot Mountains. Scaling a house should be a lot easier. Hopefully, he'd find a foothold or two to help him on his way.

Taking the coiled rope, Liam took aim and hoisted it up at one of the balcony posts. He missed the first time around, grunted in frustration, and gave it another go. Second time, he snagged the post and gave it a good, hard yank.

"This'll do." Thankful for the gloves he'd remembered to

stuff in his jacket, Liam was gloved up and walking up the wall in seconds. Ash continued to talk to the guy, delaying him by assuring him that he wanted to work out some kind of a deal. Ash was good, but the tone in the man's voice said he was getting impatient. Liam needed to get up there ASAP.

Fifteen feet from the balcony, the steel post creaked audibly. That wasn't good. Liam climbed faster, hoping he could make it before the thing completely broke. Nine feet from his destination, the rail bent and then snapped. In a flash, he was plummeting to the ground.

Grabbing hold of a protruding brick, Liam stopped the free fall. He plastered his body to the wall and assessed the situation. A thirty-foot fall might not kill him, but it would lay him up for a while. He didn't intend to fall.

Doubly thankful for his gloves, Liam found invisible little crevices in the brick and started the climb again.

"Stryker, you on your way?" Ash said in his ear. "This guy's getting antsy."

"Couple more minutes."

Thunder rumbled overhead. A storm was brewing, and the sweltering humidity covered him in a sheen of wet, hot heat. Sweat dripped into his eyes, and he fought the sting. Stretching with all his might, he reached the bottom of the decorative balcony and hung on for several seconds to gather his strength before swinging himself over the railing. He landed with a soft thud and held still for a moment to ensure the thing would hold him. When nothing moved, Liam took an easier breath.

Peering into the small window, he noted a few concerning things. The guy had his gun pointed toward the door where Ash stood. He was burning up, his clothes, soaked in sweat, were stuck to his body, and his face was tomato red. Definitely agitated. But most concerning of all, Liam could not see his captive.

"Ash, you see the woman anywhere?"

"I spotted her once. I think she's in the corner to the right of the window. Looked like her hands are tied."

"I'll grab his attention. You get the woman."

"Copy that."

Liam took another quick look inside and inwardly cursed. Taking a clean shot was out. The guy had moved, and now most of his body was hidden behind a stack of boxes. Liam considered his options. If he tried to wing an arm or shoulder and missed, the man could easily swing around and take out his captive.

He took a step back and quickly considered his best plan for entry. Ash had been right. The window was barely a window and was for decorative purposes only. There was no latch, no way to slide the thing open. The only way in was to go through it. The glass was thin, not double-paned. It was going to hurt, but with no other options available, this was his best bet.

Grabbing hold of the window frame, Liam told Ash, "I'm coming in." Slamming his feet into the window, he crashed through.

~

AUBREY STOOD LOOKING up at the small shattered window where Liam had been. Her heart in her throat, she had seen him climb up the wall and then almost fall to his death. She had been sitting with some of the rescued women, offering comfort where she could.

Without realizing it, she'd jumped up and started running toward him. Just when she was sure there was no way for him to save himself, he'd grabbed hold of something and halted his descent.

Knees weak, she'd then watched as he climbed back up

toward the balcony, grabbing hold of what were apparently crevices in the bricks to help him move upward. It soon became apparent that he was an expert climber.

She had finally been able to breathe when he'd climbed onto the small, rickety balcony. She, along with several of the operatives, stared up at him. She hadn't had any idea what he planned. She certainly hadn't expected to see him hang from the window's edge and then slam through the glass.

Multiple shots rang out and then there was silence.

Her earbud gave her an idea of what was going on.

"Thought you were going to distract him," Ash said.

"He was out of my line of sight. Couldn't take the chance."

"You're bleeding."

"Yeah, I figured. Check on the girl. I'll be fine."

"Gideon, we need a medic up here," Ash said.

"Already on my way," Gideon answered.

Feeling helpless, Aubrey glanced over at Jazz, who stood beside her. "What can I do to help?"

Her face showing her concern, Jazz shook her head. "Nothing. Gideon has medical training. He'll take care of them."

Aubrey followed Jazz back to the tents that the aid workers had set up. The young women ranged in ages from late teens to mid-twenties. Those waiting to be treated sat quietly, sipping coffee or soft drinks.

"What's the protocol now?"

"We stand by and assist where needed. Our part is mostly over. Liam and Ash will check with Tessa, the head of the aid group, to see if any of them are willing to talk to them."

"That's not mandatory?"

"No. Our main goal is making sure they get what they need. If Tessa believes any of them are willing to answer questions, she'll let us know."

"Do you ever follow up, check to see what happens to them?"

"Liam keeps tab through the various aid organizations."

"Ash is in charge of OZ but Liam is in charge of rescues?"

"Not all of them, just the ones involving human trafficking. And speaking of the devil, look who's here."

Aubrey glanced around and spotted Liam walking toward them. He had more than a few cuts and scratches on his face and arms, along with two bandages, one on his left wrist and another on his neck. Other than that, he looked none the worse for wear.

She watched, secretly fascinated, as he headed directly to the first tent and stuck in his head. Several seconds later, he retreated. Each time, she saw something odd change in his demeanor. His gait when he'd walked toward the tents had been confident and determined. His shoulders had been straight and proud but with each tent he checked, his shoulders seemed to slump.

He turned away from the last one, and his eyes searched the remaining women waiting their turn in the tents. He shook his head slightly, and Ash, who stood beside him, laid a hand on his shoulder and murmured something in his ear.

Whatever he said must not have set well with Liam, as he pulled away and stalked off.

Jazz sighed and shook her head as if she knew what was happening and it had saddened her.

Curious, Aubrey said, "Why is he upset?"

Shrugging, she said, "It's a Liam thing."

Before she could inquire what that meant, Serena came up behind them. "Everyone's in custody."

"What about the guy in the attic?"

"They're taking him to the hospital. He should be well enough to go to jail soon."

"Liam looks rough," Jazz said. "How badly is he hurt?"

"I asked, but you know the answer."

Jazz gave a laugh. "Of course. The one we always get."

Both Jazz and Serena said in unison, "It's not Syria."

Her knees like jelly, Aubrey sat down abruptly in a chair. There was a strange buzzing in her head.

"Hey, you okay?" Jazz asked.

"Yes," she answered weakly. "Just a lot to take in."

"Need some water?"

"No, I'm fine." She gave both women what she felt was her very best fake smile. Jazz seemed to buy it but Serena looked both concerned and puzzled.

"What..." Aubrey cleared her throat of the sudden dryness and started again, "What does that mean, 'It's not Syria'?"

"They were on a mission together there," Serena said. "All of them were injured. Liam, too."

"So whenever any of them are hurt," Jazz continued the story for Serena, "the answer we usually get when we ask about their injuries is—it's not Syria."

Syria.

Before she could parse the implications of that information, Jazz asked, "Do you want to try to talk to any of the women?"

Refocusing, Aubrey said, "If possible. I don't want to cause more harm."

"I'll double-check with Tessa. See what she thinks. In the meantime, you want to go through the house. See the aftermath?"

Her eyes tracked to where Liam had gone. She definitely wanted to go inside the house, but her instincts told her to follow him.

Reading her intent, Jazz took her arm and tugged her toward the house. "I know you want to get his take, but it's not a good time right now. You can talk to him on the way back home."

CHAPTER TWENTY-FIVE

L iam stared into the night. The face reflected in the airplane window showed the grim countenance of a beaten man. Dark thoughts swirled in his head. He was done. He couldn't do this anymore. Looking for Cat had consumed him for years. She was his first thought in the morning and his last one before he dropped off to sleep at night. When he wasn't working on an OZ op, he was digging for intel, hoping to find some kernel of information he'd missed.

Giving up was not his way, but in this he had no choice. If he was going to have any kind of life—any peace at all—he had to let her go. She was likely dead. After twelve years of captivity and torture, how could she not be? It defied all odds that she could have survived even a few years, much less twelve.

So why did he feel as though he was abandoning her all over again? The darkness he'd felt the day he'd left the prison without her was once more washing over him. Once again his soul was ripped to shreds, and he had no clue how to stop the bleeding this time.

He saw the reflection of Aubrey Starr before he felt her sit beside him. Turning, he looked at her, really looked at her. She was attractive, there was no denying that. Soft golden hair, gray-blue, intelligent eyes, and a natural upward curve to her full lips as if she smiled often.

She hadn't been a burden, not like he'd feared. She had, in fact, even made him smile a couple of times. There was just something refreshing and pure about her interest in their operation. Not self-serving but empathetic and caring.

Realizing he hadn't been exactly friendly to her, he did his best to give her a welcoming look.

"You look angry," she said.

So much for the effort.

"Been a long day."

"The operation was successful. Twelve women rescued. No one died."

"Yes."

"And yet?"

He shrugged. "There are a lot more out there."

"But for today, you can't be happy for those you rescued? For the families that will be reunited? For the bad people who will be punished?"

If only it was that simple. Or maybe that's the way it should be.

"Yeah, I guess I can." He took a breath and said, "Sorry you didn't get to see what you came to see. Things didn't turn out as we'd planned."

"I saw more than I'd ever seen before. The house…" She shook her head. "I don't think it should be called a house, more like a torture chamber. I cannot fathom the hell those women endured."

"Did you get enough for your project?"

"I'm not sure. I need to put my thoughts together, get everything down. Once I do that, I may have questions."

"I'm sure any of us can help you with that."

"Serena said you're the go-to person for human trafficking."

"I've had my share of experience."

"Is there any reason you're so interested in it? Do you know someone who was trafficked?"

No way would he tell her about Cat. The last thing he wanted was their story to end up being discussed in a film. That was private and none of anyone's business.

"It's a multibillion-dollar business. The idea that people sell human beings to make money is repugnant. I want to do my part to stop it."

He could tell she was disappointed in his answer. Her eyes darkened, lost a bit of their sparkle.

"Whatever the reason, I'm sure the people you've rescued are extremely grateful."

"What about you? Why do you do what you do? Seems the whole focus of your films is on informing people about human trafficking. Did you know someone who was trafficked?"

"No. But I'm of the same mind as you. The evil of selling a human being for profit is a disgusting act that needs to be stopped."

"I've seen your films. They're good."

"Thank you."

"This new one you're making. It's a follow-up to your first one?"

"Yes, but I want to go more in-depth. I felt like I just barely scratched the surface in the first one."

"I understand you've created some enemies."

"That's not uncommon. I can protect myself."

There was a wide divide between being able to personally protect herself from an assailant and protecting herself from an assassin.

"You'll be safe at OZ."

She shook her head. "I can't stay at OZ. I have to get home, get to work."

"We can arrange protection for you."

"I can afford my own protection. I'll be fine."

The thought of her in harm's way bothered him immensely. Okay, yeah, he was attracted to her. Had been the moment he'd spotted her in Kosovo. He told himself his protectiveness was normal. That was his job. Had been since the day he'd popped Bobby Bishop in the mouth for saying something off-color in front of his sister.

Aubrey Starr was stubborn, independent, passionate about her work, and beautiful to boot. The fact that he was attracted to her doubled his need to protect her.

He'd talk to Ash, get her the protection she needed. Did she know that that producer's death was no accident? He hadn't asked Ash if he'd told her and was frustrated that he didn't know. She would need the best protection out there. OZ knew some of the finest bodyguards in the world. They would make sure she stayed safe.

"I understand you were once in Syria."

The question came out of the blue, and he was definitely not in the frame of mind to talk about Syria. "Yeah." His voice was hard, hopefully deterring any further questions.

"I wanted—"

"Syria is in the past. It's not something I want to relive or revisit."

"But I—"

He gave her the hardest look he could give to a non-enemy. "Forget about Syria. Understand?"

"Yes…okay. Sorry."

Hell, maybe he was the one who should be sorry. She looked as though she'd been slapped.

He couldn't talk about his missions in Syria. Any of them. They were all still classified. And the one that had changed his life? No way in hell. He could only imagine what a film-maker would want to do with that story.

Thankfully, giving them both a break, Serena appeared beside them. "Hey, Aubrey, mind if I pick your brain a minute?"

"Sure." She stood and then turned to Liam. "Thank you for letting me go on this op with your team."

"Not a problem. Hope you got something out of it."

She didn't move for several seconds, just continued to stare at him. Her eyes bore into his, and he could swear she was trying to communicate something to him. What, he had no clue. Finally, she gave a little nod of her head, straightened her shoulders, and walked away.

Serena gave him a disapproving frown and then moved away, too. Yeah, he was batting a thousand today.

Liam turned back to the window and looked out into the darkness again, his thoughts grim once more. Maybe he needed to take some time off. Go see his family back home in Missouri. Go fishing. Climb a mountain. Anything to get away from this gaping hole that used to be his heart.

AUBREY MADE it back to her seat with as much dignity as possible. Everything within her felt numb. While she answered Serena's surprisingly simple questions about where she grew up and her family, her eyes kept veering toward the man in the front row of the plane.

He'd told her to forget about Syria.

Should she have forced the issue? Just come out and asked him? Why hadn't she? It was either a yes-or-no answer. How hard was that? *Impossibly hard*, her mind whispered. Because if she asked and he denied it, then he would be lying. Or would he?

Exhaustion weighed on her like a lead blanket. She was

running on fumes and those were almost gone too. Her brain felt like mush, and more than anything she wanted to find a private place to cry her eyes out.

"Your bio said you went to the University of Connecticut."

She shook herself out of her brain fog. "Yes. It's where I got my undergraduate degree."

"I'm surprised you didn't go to New York University. They have an excellent visual and performing arts program."

"I actually did go there for a short time."

"Really?"

"Yes...I..." No, she would not go down that road. "It just didn't work out, so I stayed out a semester and then enrolled at UConn."

She sent another glance toward Liam, then returned her attention to Serena. "Why the interest in where I attended college?"

"Just part of our records. We have a file on everyone associated with OZ."

In her blurred, stressed-out mind, it made sense, so she continued to answer the seemingly innocuous questions never once considering there was another reason for them.

Her eyes shifted to the man in the front row again. Why didn't she just go up to him and blurt it out? What was wrong with her?

"Hey." Serena snapped her fingers in front of Aubrey's face. "You okay?"

"Yes...sorry. Did you say something?"

Serena glanced to where Aubrey's eyes kept straying. "You seem very interested in Liam. Is there a reason?"

"No, I just..." She gave herself a mental kick. "The rescue was a success but he acts as though it wasn't."

"He's not generally an ass. He's just going through a rough time right now."

"Why's that?"

Serena stared at her for several seconds before giving her the oddest answer she could imagine. "He gave up on a dream today."

Before Aubrey could explore further, Serena stood. "I'd better go check and make sure Sean hasn't eaten his weight in peanuts. Get some rest."

Leaning back in the seat, Aubrey tried to do just that. But her eyes wouldn't leave the man in the front row. What dream had he given up?

Unable to keep her eyes open any longer, she closed them and felt herself drifting. A part of her brain told her not to sleep. It wanted to stay awake and dwell on the man only a few yards away.

Exhaustion won. As she entered into the twilight phase of sleep, Liam's voice echoed in her mind, *Forget about Syria.*

Her soul whimpered, *No.*

CHAPTER TWENTY-SIX

St. Augustine, Florida

Aubrey sat in the backseat of the rental car as they drove through the quiet streets. No surprise they were deserted, as it was just after four in the morning. Eve had told her going in at this time would give her a better opportunity to not be seen. And apparently for the foreseeable future, that's what needed to happen.

She was being taken to a safe house. How they'd managed to find one in such a short time frame wasn't something she was going to ask. Probably just as well since she doubted either Eve or Gideon would tell her anyway.

She was grateful for the protection—really she was. If Lawrence Medford had been murdered because of his involvement in her project, then she definitely needed help. However, she had the distinct feeling that Eve and Gideon weren't all too thrilled to be in charge of protecting her.

They had been professional and polite, but not especially friendly. She was being treated as a job and that was exactly what she was.

Silly, really, but she missed the warm companionship of Serena and Jazz. They'd both hugged her when she'd left OZ and told her they hoped to see her again soon. She hadn't had the heart to tell them that that wasn't likely. If she decided to scrap the project, there was no reason for any further contact.

No further contact. Was that really how she was going to leave it? Why hadn't she just come right out and asked Liam Stryker if he was Lion? Even if he'd said no, at least she could know for sure. Instead, she was stuck in limbo, not knowing and hating herself for not having the courage to ask. She had always, *always*, prided herself on being the kind of person to take the bull by the horns and not back down. It was how she'd lived her life since returning from her ordeal in Syria. So why when it came to the most important moment in her life had she chickened out?

The car turned onto her street and Aubrey roused herself from her self-castigation. She was exhausted and even though she'd be sleeping in another strange bed for a while, she looked forward to being able to do that. In the past three days, she'd had minimal sleep and multiple shocks. Those fumes she'd been running on earlier no longer existed.

Gideon pulled into the drive and glanced over his shoulder. "Can you get what you need in half an hour?"

"Yes. It won't take long. I just need some more clothes and a few personal items."

"Okay. Hang back while we check things out."

She looked at her house, which looked the same to her. She saw nothing to indicate any trouble. The two-story white clapboard house was almost twenty years old and a little outdated, but she'd fallen in love with its giant porch, black shutters, and large overhanging eaves. The pool in the back had been another selling point. It was the first home she'd ever owned. She'd spent half her savings updating the interior and making it a peaceful retreat. Her heart was sad that she might have to move out and find something new. But this trouble wasn't going to go away overnight.

If the people who'd bugged her house had been watching, they knew she had taken her research with her. There was no reason for them to search again. But if they had killed Lawrence Medford, then someone could be waiting for her to come home.

Both OZ operatives stepped out of the car, and though they were discreet, she noted they'd both pulled their guns. Tension zipping up her spine, she held her breath as they went up onto the porch.

Eve peered through the window of her front door and said something to Gideon. He nodded, and then they held their guns up at the ready. Something was definitely happening.

Opening the door, she whispered, "What's wrong?"

"Stay there," Eve said.

Gideon turned the doorknob, and she was about to call out and tell him she had the key when she realized the door easily swung open. Someone had broken into her house again.

Her heart pounding, Aubrey ran forward. There were no sounds, nothing to indicate danger. Using her phone's flashlight to brighten the darkness, she went up the steps. Her foot had barely touched the front porch when she noted that whoever had broken in this time had left her a message. An unmistakable one.

Stunned, she stopped at the front door and took in the devastation. Everything was destroyed. Sofa and chairs were upside down, ripped to shreds. The legs of her chairs had been broken and sawed off. Even her throw pillows were in tiny pieces, with foam and feathers floating in the air from the breeze of the open door.

Eve appeared at the entryway of the living room. "I told you to stay in the car."

Ignoring Eve's ire, Aubrey said, "Is every room like this?"

"Yes. Your clothes have been shredded, too."

She told herself these were material things that could be replaced, but she did have a few sentimental items she never wanted to lose. Even without asking, she knew they'd been destroyed, too. Why would the photos of her parents and her beloved doll collection escape the wrath?

Gideon appeared beside Eve. "All clear." He sent a sympathetic glance toward Aubrey. "I'm sorry. I don't think you're going to find anything to save."

"She'll deal," Eve said. She sent Aubrey a telling look. "Won't you?"

The words and look were exactly what she needed. Anger replaced shock and sorrow. "Yes, I'll deal."

They didn't stop her as she went from room to room. Nothing had been spared. Even the hand towels in the guest bathroom had been shredded. Whoever had come through here had one agenda—total destruction. They had succeeded.

She saved her bedroom for last. What had once been a place of solace and comfort was now a garbage dump. Sheets, pillowcases, curtains were all shredded and piled on top of a ripped-open mattress. The four-poster bed that she'd purchased right after she'd gotten her first paycheck from the one and only TV show she'd gotten a part in, had been sawed in two.

She turned and noted that her clothes from both the closet and her drawers were all in a pile in the middle of the floor. They were torn and ripped, and on top of that pile were her dolls. Her dad had given her one each year for her birthday. He'd gifted her the last one the week before he died. All twenty-one of them had been decapitated, their body parts broken and cracked.

Refusing to give in to the grief of that one sight, Aubrey straightened her shoulders. In an instant she reversed any indecision about continuing the project. No way were they going to stop her. Nothing and no one was going to defeat her. The perverted bastards would not win.

If they thought they could keep her from making her film, they were wrong.

Gideon stood at the bedroom door. "Your car…" he said.

She didn't even wince. "I'm assuming it's totaled?"

"That'd be my guess. Bastards took a sledgehammer to it."

If she didn't cry about her dolls, she refused to shed a tear over her ten-year-old Mazda RX-7. Yes she'd loved it but so what? Everything else she'd loved was gone, too.

"We'll get someone in here to clean this mess up. Doubt they left fingerprints but you never know."

"What about my gun?"

"What gun?"

She went back to the foyer. The table with the hidden compartment was turned over, but didn't look broken. Stooping down, she turned it around, and was relieved to see the wood was intact. She pressed the hidden release button, and the compartment opened, revealing her handgun.

"That's handy," Eve said.

Standing, she held the gun steady in her hand, oddly comforted. Was it a coincidence that the only item undisturbed was a weapon? She didn't think so.

She took one last look at the destruction. "I'll need to call my insurance agent."

"You can do that tomorrow."

"All right." Aubrey turned toward the front door. "Thank you."

Without a backward glance, she went down the steps and back to the car. The contents of the duffle bag she'd carried to Montana and the gun in her hand were all she had left.

That didn't matter. She would replace what she needed. For now, she wanted to get someplace alone and lick her wounds.

And then, dammit, then she would get back up and go at these people full force. They thought they had defeated her. Little did they know they'd only made her more determined.

CHAPTER TWENTY-SEVEN

Montana
OZ Headquarters

Sitting in Ash's office, Serena chewed on her bottom lip as they waited for Liam to arrive. She had come to Ash yesterday and presented her findings. He had been full of questions, and she had managed to answer most of them. Yes, there were still holes. And no, she wasn't completely sure of her theory but there were way too many coincidences to ignore.

The conversation she'd had with Aubrey on the plane had given her the insight she'd needed to probe deeper. There'd been only small clues before, but that fifteen-minute discussion had created a framework for the puzzle. She had spent the last two days filling in those pieces. She wasn't there yet, but it had been enough to come to Ash and tell him her theory.

He'd been surprised and more than a little intrigued.

Ash had placed a call to Kate and had gotten more infor-

mation. That, with what she had, almost sealed the deal.
Now, to present the information to Liam and let him decide
what he wanted to do with it.

It infuriated her that she hadn't picked up on this from
the beginning. Years ago, when Liam had asked for her help
in identifying the woman he'd known only as Cat, she had
done her best. There hadn't been much to work with. She
had taken all the information he'd given her, optimistic that
she would find her. She took pride in her ability to dig up
intel no one else could find. She had been a star at her
previous job. If there was a secret to be found, Serena was
the one given the task. No one was her equal.

Leaving the State Department had been a little scary for
her. There, she had been comfortable and secure in her value.
But when Sean had told her about OZ and invited her to
come over, she hadn't hesitated. Not only would she be
working with the man she loved, she would be given carte
blanche to delve deeper into secrets than she ever had before.
She hadn't regretted her decision one moment. OZ's funding
was phenomenal, her intel team was second to none, and she
actively participated in the missions. Instead of handing over
intel to someone else who would use it to save a life or stop
an atrocity, she got to do that herself.

Then Liam had asked her to find Cat. Serena had taken
on the task with her normal confidence. She knew her stuff.
But every clue and lead he'd provided had fizzled out and
died, going nowhere.

Was she seeing things that weren't there simply because
she wanted them to be true? For years, she had watched
Liam grow grimmer and grimmer. With each rescue, lives
were saved, but the one that Liam wanted to save the most
was never there.

She hated seeing the disappointment on his face, the

despair. Sean had told her she took too much on herself, and though she knew he was right, she couldn't stop feeling guilty. This was what she did. How could she not find this one person?

This time the clues were too numerous to ignore. Not just the facts she now knew, but also the less obvious ones she had witnessed and ignored until they'd practically slapped her in the face.

"You're nervous." Ash made the statement as if surprised.

"I am. If I'm not right…"

"But if you are right…"

The smile he gave her was all she needed. She took a breath. Yes, if she was right, then she would have given peace to the man who'd saved her husband's life.

Other than the basic details, the guys rarely talked about their time in Syria, which was understandable. Pain that deep could be shared with those who'd experienced the same thing, but to an outsider, even a beloved spouse, there were some things never mentioned. It was only by chance that she'd learned that Liam had stepped in front of a bullet meant for Sean. If he hadn't been there at that exact moment, her husband, the love of her life, would be dead. How could she not want to give him peace?

"Before Liam gets here, there's another matter we need to discuss," Ash said.

Just one look at her boss's face told her what he meant, and though she wanted to deny its existence, she couldn't. She had known this day was coming.

"Is it time?" she asked.

"Soon. I got the word yesterday. We need to be prepared for the fall-out."

Prepared? How could she prepare for the tsunami that would happen? She could only hold on for dear life and pray that it didn't destroy them.

"Just let me know what you need me to do."

Compassion glimmering in his eyes, Ash nodded. He knew exactly what she feared. She knew he feared it, too.

Hearing a noise coming from the front part of the house, Serena returned her focus to the here and now. If there was one thing she'd learned in her life, it was to celebrate the victories. Giving Liam what he wanted most in the world definitely counted as one.

He stomped through the door of Ash's office, a scowl on his face. "This better be good, Ash. I was ten minutes away from getting on a plane to Canada."

"I think you'll be glad you stayed." Giving her a nod, Ash said, "All yours."

Serena watched Liam turn in surprise. He hadn't seen her sitting on the sofa.

Taking a breath, she came forward and sat in a chair in front of Ash's desk. "I need you to hear me out before you say anything. Okay?"

His brow furrowed in confusion, Liam dropped into the chair across from her. "You know I'll always listen to you. What's up?"

"There are a few things about Aubrey Starr I think you should know."

Still looking puzzled, Liam shrugged. "Okay. Like what?"

She laid out the facts. "She's thirty-one. When she was nineteen, she attended New York University, where she studied drama and acting. But she was only there for one semester. She didn't go anywhere the next semester. Then, the next year, she enrolled in and eventually graduated from the University of Connecticut."

"I don't get where you're going with this."

"You promised to hear me out."

"Okay...okay. Keep going."

Serena continued, "When I asked her why she didn't

continue her education at NYU, she brushed it off and said it just didn't work out. I could tell there was more, but I didn't push. When Jazz and I went to her house, she had just come in from a swim. We both noticed multiple scars on her body that looked like the result of knife wounds."

She had to give Liam credit. Even though his expression had turned to a dark frown, he continued to listen without interrupting.

"I came to Ash with my findings. He called Kate to see if she could give more insight. She said that Aubrey admitted to her that the reason her films focused on human trafficking was because several years ago, she was abducted. She said a ransom was paid to her captor before she was sold into human trafficking."

He stared at her for several long seconds. Doubt, disbelief, and maybe a tinge of hope shimmered in his dark eyes.

"Liam, you know me. I don't rely on conjecture or supposition. I check and recheck. I can't say I am one hundred percent sure of this."

"But you're sure enough to tell me. That's pretty damn sure."

"Yes."

He surged to his feet and headed to the door.

"Liam, wait. There's more."

He stopped but didn't turn. "Say what you've got to say then."

"Aubrey's full name is Katarina Aubrey Starr." She watched his shoulders slump and forced herself to add the last item on her list. One, that in her mind, was proof positive. "The name of her production company is Lion's Legacy."

She went silent, waiting for either his acceptance or denial. She didn't expect his anger.

Whirling around, he glared at her accusingly. "Are you

telling me that the woman I've been searching for going on thirteen years just happened to come into our lives without us knowing it?"

"Looks like."

LIAM SHOOK HIS HEAD. How was this even possible? Aubrey Starr was Cat? The girl he'd met in a filthy prison was the beautiful, talented woman he'd been snarling and growling at from the moment he'd met her?

"Something else," Serena said. "When you started talking in the meeting, before the op, did you see her reaction? She was sitting quietly, attentively, but the moment you began to speak, it was like she'd been knocked for a loop. She got pale and still."

Because she had recognized his voice. It wasn't hard to believe that after all this time she would still know his voice. They had talked incessantly. Actually, he had talked much more than she had. Her voice had often been so hoarse, she'd had laryngitis much of the time. Which was why he hadn't recognized her voice.

"When we were in Colombia," Serena continued, "I mentioned Syria, and I thought she was going to pass out. She made light of it, said it was all the excitement, but the more I thought about it—along with all the other clues—I couldn't stop thinking that we might have completely missed the obvious."

His eyes closed in regret. "That's why she asked me about Syria."

"When was that?" Serena asked.

"On the plane, when we were headed home. She brought up Syria. I shut her down. Told her to forget about Syria. That it wasn't a topic up for discussion."

"You didn't know."

No, but he should have. How could he not know? Okay, yes, her voice had been hoarse when they'd been in prison. She'd had an awful upper respiratory illness that had sometimes taken her voice completely away. But still, why hadn't he known? How could he not know? And what had she thought when he hadn't recognized her? Or had she thought he did and didn't want to acknowledge her?

She had known, that much was obvious. Or at least suspected. Why hadn't she told him? Why couldn't she have just blurted it out? *I'm Cat.*

Was that why she'd come to talk to him? Had she been about to tell him, and he'd told her to forget about Syria? Hell, had she thought he knew who she was and didn't want to acknowledge her? The pain in her eyes when she'd gotten up from her seat told him in retrospect that was likely the case.

"Where is she now?"

"St. Augustine," Ash said.

His heart thudded with dread. "Alone?"

"No. Gideon and Eve are with her. Which is a good thing. When they arrived, they found her house had been ransacked. Everything was destroyed."

Liam closed his eyes. He should've been there with her. He could've if he'd taken his head out of his ass for a moment and realized what was going on.

All this time, he'd been looking for a victim. But Aubrey Starr was no victim. She was a warrior on a crusade to inform the world to help put a stop to human trafficking.

"She's at a safe house now. Eve and Gideon will stay with her until we can get her full-time security."

"I'll take care of that. I'll head there now."

"I figured. Plane's tied up, but I went ahead and chartered one for you."

Not for the first time did he thank God for Asher Drake. And Serena…

Turning to her, he grabbed her into a hard hug. "Thank you. You are the absolute best."

Her eyes sparkling with tears, she beamed up at him. "It was my pleasure. Now go get your Cat."

CHAPTER TWENTY-EIGHT

St. Augustine, Florida

She stood in a kitchen that wasn't hers, washing dishes in a sink that wasn't hers, looking out a window at a backyard that wasn't hers.

Ever since she'd returned to Florida, she felt as though she moved in slow motion. Thoughts whirled through her brain, but she felt slow, awkward. Shock, Eve had told her, could do that. While the world went on around her, she was in a cocoon of numbness.

Thankfully, even though she was moving at a snail's pace, other people were not. Things were already in place to protect her loved ones, thanks to Eve and Gideon. She wouldn't tell her family what had happened. They would only worry.

The people assigned to watch over them would be discreet. No one needed to know what was going on. The less they knew, the safer they'd be.

Once her family was protected, she sent a mass text to her entire team and told them the project was on hold indefinitely. She had thanked them, assuring them she would send their pay for their hard work, but had encouraged them to take new jobs. She hated losing them, but not only did she want them free of danger, she knew word would spread throughout the industry that the project had been canned. Ferante and his people would assume they'd won.

They hadn't.

If she stopped the project, evil won. A child rapist would get away with his crimes. If she had the means to put him away where he could never hurt a child again, how could she not?

She had done her first documentary on a shoestring budget with almost no help until it was time to distribute. She had rented her equipment and spent every waking hour for two years creating *The Lost Ones*. She would do that again. It would take her longer, but at least this way she wouldn't put anyone's safety on the line but hers.

Silly, really, but she found herself excited for the challenge. She needed the resulting insane schedule. If she didn't keep busy, she would lose her mind.

Maybe if this insanity hadn't been going on, she would have talked to Liam Stryker in a mature, calm manner. She would have told him about Syria and asked him if he was the man she knew as Lion. It should have been as simple as that. But because of the shock, the bubbling emotions, she'd let nervousness and fear stand in the way. With just a few words she could have known, once and for all, if the man she'd dreamed about for years was alive and well.

Instead, she had lost her nerve. Part of her had wanted to know, another part had feared the truth. What if it was him? What if he remembered her, but the things they'd shared had meant nothing to him?

That would mean she had based her life on lies. Her career, who she was, and what she did were all influenced by those few days in a prison with Lion. If he wasn't who she thought he was, what then? Was she going to start questioning her whole life?

A slight noise in the living room refocused her thoughts, reminding her she was not alone in the house. Gideon Wright and Eve Wells were two of the most confident and competent people she could imagine. An air of danger and sophistication surrounded them both. Having been with them for two days now, she had gotten to know them a little. Gideon had a wry and disarming charm. Eve, on the other hand, was a take-no-prisoners, no-nonsense person. She asked direct questions and gave Aubrey the impression that getting beneath her serious façade would take some work.

Gideon had no problem with his partner's serious side, though. More than once she'd heard Eve break into peals of laughter at something Gideon said. The sound was a burst of joyous noise as if delighted to have been set free.

Despite Eve's standoffishness, Aubrey knew that she could talk to her about Liam. She would listen, and she would care. And she would offer counsel.

Why didn't she do that? Instead of standing here, staring at nothing, worrying about the should-haves and might-have-beens, why not go to a woman who knew him well and voice her suspicions? Eve might even know something about Liam's time in Syria. Even though that subject seemed to be taboo, she could at least try.

Feeling immensely better, Aubrey finished the dishes in the sink. She would take some coffee into the sitting room and ask Eve to join her.

She opened the cabinet, about to reach for the coffee tin, when an achingly familiar voice behind her said, "Cat."

Her heart stopped. She carefully shut the cabinet door. Turning slowly, Aubrey faced him. Lion, the man she had dreamed of for years, the man who'd saved her life, was Liam Stryker.

"It is you," she whispered.

"Why didn't you tell me?"

"I didn't know what to say, how to say it. I wasn't completely sure. Your voice sounded so much like Lion but I couldn't be sure. And it was so long ago. I thought you might have recognized me and just didn't want to say anything. I was so afraid it hadn't meant as much to you as it did to me."

He shook his head. "I've been looking for you for twelve years."

"I never really believed I'd ever see you. I thought you were dead."

They stared at each other with new eyes. He was so strong, so handsome. Everything she'd always dreamed he would be. And he was standing only a few feet away from her. Aubrey's heart beat so hard that she knew he had to hear it. What now? What would they say to each other? How did they go forward? Or did they?

Liam apparently had no such doubts. Striding forward, he was in front of her within seconds. About a half foot away, he stopped and held his arms open. Overflowing with emotions, a sob of joy breaking free, she ran into them. Breathing in his masculine scent, embraced in his warmth, Aubrey knew she had found her home, her heart.

His voice gruff and filled with emotion, he said, "I never thought I'd get to hold you."

"I dreamed of you so much. Of those days together. Of your voice. If you hadn't been there with me, I would have died. I know I would have."

A noise at the kitchen door caught their attention. They both turned to see Eve and Gideon standing there. Gideon had a huge grin on his face, and Eve's eyes were suspiciously bright.

"We're going to take off now," Gideon said.

Giving them a grateful smile, Aubrey said, "Thank you both."

"Our pleasure." Gideon's gaze went to Liam. "Call us."

"Will do and thanks."

She didn't hear them leave. As she burrowed her face against Liam's chest, emotions overwhelmed her. He was here. He was actually here.

He breathed into her ear, "You okay?"

"Yes, but could you just hold me for a little longer?"

I'll hold you forever if you want.

He didn't say the words aloud. She might not want that. There were a million things they didn't know about each other. But in the most basic way possible he knew everything he needed to know.

Holding her soft, fragrant body against his, Liam decided it just couldn't get better than this. After twelve long years of searching, of agonizing over what had happened to her, of not knowing if she was dead or alive and suffering, to be holding her, knowing she was alive and healthy. It was almost more than he could fathom.

A shudder went through her and into him. She was just as overwhelmed as he was.

"Let's go sit down."

"Okay."

His arm around her shoulders, he steered her into the living room. The moment they were seated on the sofa, she went back into his arms.

How long they sat there, he didn't know. Didn't matter. They both needed this.

She shuddered out another breath and said, "I thought

you were dead. The prison was decimated, and I thought the blast had killed you."

"No. That happened a day after our escape."

"How did you get out?"

"My team rescued us."

"But you were injured, weren't you?"

"Yeah, we all were. How'd you know that?"

"When we were in Colombia, Jazz asked Serena about your injuries. She replied with what she said was the standard answer: It's not Syria."

He snorted a dry laugh. He hadn't realized how predictable they'd become.

"Our helicopter was hit by mortar fire. We went down in the middle of the desert. Six of us survived."

"Six?"

"Yeah. Ash, Xavier, Sean, Gideon, Hawke, and me. We were all pretty banged up."

"I haven't met Hawke."

"No." He blew out a breath. Getting caught up in those dark memories wasn't something he wanted to do. This day was all about them.

"We lost him a few years back."

"I'm sorry."

He squeezed her shoulder in appreciation.

"Is that why you didn't keep our date? Because of the crash?"

"Yeah. I was in a hospital in Jordan. But you were there? You went to the library?"

"Yes." She said it on a breath of air and he felt the hurt to his soul.

"I'm sorry I couldn't make it. First time I've ever stood up a date."

And it had been the most important one of his life.

"My mom tried to convince me you were a figment of my

imagination. She said I needed a hero and conjured you in my mind."

"Can you talk about what happened? How you escaped?"

"I didn't escape. My uncle paid my ransom."

"I thought you said your family didn't have the money."

"My mom and dad couldn't, but my uncle came through for them. He's Syd Green."

"The movie director?"

"Yes. I didn't even consider that he might help. He and my parents had a bit of a riff years ago. His daughter Becca is my best friend, but the families hadn't been close in a while. Uncle Syd didn't hesitate when my dad called him. He stepped up in a big way."

He wanted to ask her what happened to her that day, but not if it brought back bad memories. There was plenty of time to talk about that. But he would need to know soon. He had vowed to find the people who'd abducted her and make them pay. He had failed and was no closer to finding them than he had been the day he'd made that promise. She might have clues and insight to help.

Her cries and screams were still in his head—they always would be. But to have her in his arms, safe at last… Never had he witnessed a miracle, but not only had he done just that, he was the recipient of that miracle.

"Isn't it weird? We actually met each other a few years ago."

Yes, the infamous smoke bomb that had taken his voice. If he had been able to speak, what might have happened?

"If I had been able to speak then, and you recognized me, would you have told me?"

She laughed softly. "I hope so. I can't believe I didn't blurt it out the moment I heard you a few days ago. I was stupid."

"You were in shock. There's a big difference."

She tilted her head and smiled up at him. "Still my defender."

He wanted to kiss her...oh hell, he wanted to kiss her. Not yet. Way too soon.

"Okay, Aubrey Starr, tell me about yourself."

When she started talking, he couldn't believe he hadn't recognized her from the beginning. Didn't matter that her voice was unrecognizable. The way she told a story, her syntax and expressions, were exactly as he remembered.

Settling back, he listened as she described her life. She told him about her mother and how she'd lost her father only a year after her return. She told him about her decision to change from acting to filmmaking, how her experience had inspired her.

Her courage and grit amazed him. Her experience might have destroyed another person, but she was made of sterner stuff. She had taken a traumatic event and turned it into a mission.

When she yawned, he noted the time. Well after three in the morning. They'd been talking for hours. After the harrowing ordeal she'd had, she needed rest. Problem was, he didn't want to let her go.

"It's late." He hugged her against him. "You need sleep."

She snuggled into his arms. "I'm afraid if I let you go, I'll find it was all a dream."

"I promise I'll be here when you wake up. I'm not going anywhere."

As much as he wanted to stay like this, he had a responsibility to take care of her. She was at a safe house for a reason. Someone wanted to stop her from making her film.

"Why don't you get ready for bed? I'll lock up and come in and say good night."

"Okay."

. . .

LETTING GO of him was hard but it was made easier by knowing he was actually here. All she had to do was say his name, and he'd be there. Having dreamed of this for years, the reality was more surreal than she'd ever imagined.

She went to the bedroom she'd been using and then winced as she realized something. She had nothing remotely attractive to wear. A few days ago, when she'd packed for her trip, she had thrown in a couple pairs of her oldest, most comfortable pajamas. They were fine when she was alone, but now that they were the only nightwear she owned, she wished she'd packed newer, prettier ones.

Yesterday, at Eve's urging, she'd gone online and ordered some clothes. The OZ operative had insisted that she use Eve's name and credit card so the purchases couldn't be traced back to Aubrey. She needed everything, including the most basic things like underwear and nightwear. She'd found some lovely things, but they weren't due to be delivered until tomorrow. She had nothing remotely pretty to wear tonight.

Shaking her head at the silliness of her thoughts, Aubrey went about getting ready for bed. In the middle of washing her face, she looked in the mirror and thought about what Liam saw when he looked at her. Did she look like he'd pictured her? Did he think she was pretty? Or was he disappointed?

The thoughts were shallow and not exactly the norm for her, but she couldn't help herself. Whenever she had pictured Lion, she had thought of him as tall, rugged, and handsome. He had lived up to that fantasy and then some. The arms that had held her were rock hard, and his whole body had felt like solid steel.

A knock on the bathroom door told her she'd been spending way too much time daydreaming.

"Be out in a minute."

Hurriedly she brushed her teeth and threw on the newest

of her pajamas. The light blue color went nicely with her skin tone, but the pattern of pink pigs with wings was a little embarrassing. The pj's had been a gift from Becca, a nod to one of Aubrey's favorite sayings, *When pigs fly.*

Since she could do nothing about them, she shrugged and opened the door. Liam stood in the middle of the bedroom. He had changed into a pair of sweats, a T-shirt, and he had taken his shoes off.

"I thought, unless you object, we could both sleep here." He added with a charming smile no woman in her right mind could resist, "No monkey business, I promise."

Gladness soared through her heart. "I would like that."

They got into bed as if they'd been sleeping together for years. If anyone on the outside had seen them, they'd likely think that this was beyond strange, but this felt as perfect and right as anything she'd ever done.

She settled against him and he pulled her even closer.

"No nightmares tonight."

She looked up at him. "You have them, too?"

"Oh, yeah. About every night. You?"

"Yes."

"Those days are over."

"Yes, they are."

"Can I ask you a question?"

She snuggled deeper into his arms. "You can ask me anything."

"Do you need to be in a specific place or use special equipment to work on your film?"

"Just my laptop, for the time being. I have a lot of work to do on the script. Once I start editing, I'll need some additional equipment. Why?"

"Come home with me?"

She didn't even have to think about it. *Home* would be wherever this man was. "Yes."

He kissed her then. Just a small caress of his mouth on hers but it was wonderful, magical. Perfect.

Settling into his arms, she whispered, "Tell me a story."

"My pleasure."

She fell asleep with his voice in her ear and knew she had never felt more safe and secure than she did at that moment.

CHAPTER TWENTY-NINE

Cyprus

M arc Antony Ferante was bored. He had everything he wanted, everything he needed. It wasn't enough…would never be enough. He was a consumer, a user of all things. Whatever came to mind that he desired, it was his within seconds of having the thought.

He didn't consider himself better than anyone else. Truth was, he didn't consider anyone else at all. They were here for his use, entertainment, enjoyment—whatever he desired—he had people to supply that need night and day.

He had wealth—in the bank, in stocks, the choicest properties. There was literally nothing in this world that either he didn't already have or couldn't get with one command.

Still he wanted more. A dissatisfaction loomed within him, and he couldn't put his finger on what that something was. It amused him in a way, because he knew once he decided on what that something was, he would have no trouble obtaining it. He was just that good.

The phone beside him intoned a delightful tune, one he'd had created just for him. If there was one thing he wanted above all others it was to have what no one else could get.

Reaching over, he slid a slender finger across the answer icon. "Yes?"

"The girl dropped the film."

A self-satisfied smirk lifted his mouth. "Of course she did." The little message he'd sent to her house had no doubt scared her silly. People were just so predictable, especially women.

"You won this round. Doesn't mean it won't come back in the future and bite you. You need to be more careful."

Ferante rolled his eyes at the overdramatic tone. "You worry too much. She was just some nobody trying to make a name for herself. I knew that once I set my dogs on her, she wouldn't last. They never do."

"Maybe so, but you're on her radar now. She may talk."

"Then we should have disposed of her. That was my suggestion, if you remember."

The man sighed. "Yes, I know that, and while it was a good suggestion, I have to weigh many variables before commissioning such things. You only have yourself to be concerned with. I have a responsibility to many."

"Of course you do." Ferante mentally shrugged. Soothing the beast never hurt his cause. Little did the beast know that he was as disposable as everyone else. He was, however, infinitely more useful than most.

"If she starts talking, we won't have a choice, though, will we?"

Another sigh. "No, we won't."

Knowing it was a foregone conclusion at some point, Ferante said, "Let me know when you want that to happen. My man is still in play. His methods are quite unique—he's the artistic sort and a bit eccentric. However, he does know how to get the job done."

"I would like to avoid that, if possible."

Understanding his reasoning but not agreeing with him, Ferante made noises he thought sounded sympathetic. It was tiresome, but sometimes one had to pretend to care. An amusement in its own way, because people were just too stupid to accept that he did not care at all, about anyone but himself. He held regard for no one, not even for this man who'd started him in the business.

"I'll call you if anything changes. In the meantime, if you could keep a lower profile, that would be helpful."

"I do what I do. People who don't like it shouldn't exist."

There was the expected shocked silence. He didn't really understand why there was shock, though. It wasn't as if he made a secret of how he felt. He prided himself on his openness. He was actually the only authentic person he knew.

"There are people watching your actions."

Ah, yes, the all-powerful people who believed they made the world turn. He didn't mind doing for them what he did. It was often an entertaining and mutually beneficial arrangement.

"Rudy, Rudy, Rudy," Ferante mocked. "Don't worry so much. I'm not."

There was a long pause. Yes, he knew the man hated the shortened name. And that's exactly why he used it.

Finally, frustration obvious in his voice, the man said, "Goodbye."

Not bothering to end the call—it would end on its own— Ferante drew in a breath of fresh air. The blue of the ocean before him competed for beauty with the crystal-clear sky. It was picture perfect.

Maybe that was the problem. It was too perfect. He

needed to think on that. What could he do to mar perfection? What would be the challenge?

The solution came like a flash, and he knew exactly what he needed to do.

CHAPTER THIRTY

Montana
OZ Headquarters

L iam pulled into the drive of OZ and was pleased to see all the cars and SUVs. The gang was all here. He'd asked all operatives to show up for a brief meeting. Every one of them deserved to meet Aubrey again. They had been with him on every mission to find her. They needed a new introduction.

Aubrey was a little apprehensive, but he knew that would pass. Whether she was ready to accept it or not, they were now her family. No matter what happened between the two of them, OZ would always be there for her.

What would happen between them was up in the air. Not for him. He had known for years that what he felt for her was more than a need to rescue a woman. In those few days, he had fallen hard. And each time he looked at her now, he fell a little bit further.

He hadn't sprung any of that on her. Scaring her off was

the last thing he wanted. After all the things that had happened over the last few days she was still feeling a little overwhelmed. They had finally found each other. The other stuff could wait.

"They're really all here for me?"

He grinned at her. She looked as though she were getting ready to face a firing squad.

"They're not as scary as they look."

"Actually, the only scary one was you."

"Really?"

"Yes. That first day, you glared at me."

"Yeah…sorry. That was a bad day. I was finally accepting I'd never find you."

She shook her head. "I still can't believe you looked for so long."

"I swore to you that I would never give up on you. Can't believe I almost did."

She grabbed his hand from the steering wheel and held it to her face. "Thank you for that. I don't think even my family would have spent so many years looking. They would have just accepted I was gone."

Liam almost groaned at the silken smooth skin against his hand. She was soft and sweet, and he wanted her with a passion he'd only ever read about. Yeah, he'd felt desire. He was human. This went eons beyond desire.

"You know," she said conversationally, "if you keep looking at me like that, I'm going to have to kiss you."

"Don't let me stop you."

She glanced over at the OZ house. "Think anyone's looking?"

"Does it matter?"

Instead of answering, she unbuckled her seat belt and reached for him. He met her halfway. Sharing their first real kiss in front of OZ seemed right.

She tasted like springtime, fresh and sweet. He wanted to linger, to savor, but he let her set the pace. The fact that she instigated it meant everything.

Breathless, she pulled away and smiled. "You taste the way I dreamed you would."

"You dreamed of kissing me?"

"Yes. Is that surprising?"

"No, since I dreamed of it, too."

"Really? You dreamed of kissing you? That's a little egotistical, isn't it?"

He pulled her in for a quick, hard kiss. "You're a smartass. I like it."

She looked at the OZ house again. "I guess we'd better go in."

"We don't have to stay long. We'll go in and visit. I want to get to my house before it gets too dark."

"I can't wait to see it."

Liam smiled to himself. He couldn't wait either.

THE MINUTE LIAM and Aubrey stepped up on the porch, Serena opened the door and then yelled out, "She's here, guys!"

Surprised, Aubrey halted. Liam gently nudged her forward. Before she could take a step, Serena grabbed her arm and pulled her into a hug. "I'm so glad it's you!"

She whispered a soft thank-you in Serena's ear and got another hug in return. "It was my pleasure." She stepped back and said, "Come on in. Everyone's been dying to see you."

She walked into the house and was greeted like a long-lost sister, with shouts of welcome and a big hug from Jazz and Xavier.

Grinning, Jazz said, "Don't look so surprised. We feel like we've known you for years."

Apparently sensing that she was feeling a little overwhelmed, Liam threw an arm around her shoulders, and said to the group, "We can't stay long. Just wanted to say—"

"But we have champagne!"

A beautiful older woman rolled a trolley out of the kitchen filled with glasses, ice buckets, and two large bottles of champagne. Though Aubrey had not met Rose Wilson, she instantly recognized her as the woman Liam had told her was the one person OZ could not function without.

Rose stopped in the middle of the room and put her hands on her hips. "Oh, Liam, she's just as pretty as you described her." Walking around the cart, she came toward Aubrey with outstretched arms. "Welcome home, my dear."

More than a little emotional at the enthusiastic and warm welcome, Aubrey accepted the hug from Rose. The moment she stepped back from the hug, Liam tugged her back against his chest and whispered in her ear, "We don't have to stay if you don't want to."

She glanced around at all the smiling faces, and moisture blurred her vision. These people had risked their lives to find her. They had been there for Liam in his darkest moments. Supporting him, loving him. They were his family. There was no way she could brush this off as if it meant nothing.

Instead of answering him, she swung her gaze around to take in everyone and said, "Thank you so much for what you did, for what you do."

A champagne glass appeared in her hand. The room went quiet and Aubrey looked up to see Asher Drake standing in the middle of the room. "You'll have to forgive our enthusiasm, Aubrey. We don't get many days like this." He raised his champagne glass. "Here's to Aubrey, a woman of courage and grace. And to Liam, the man who refused to give up on her."

. . .

LIAM FOLLOWED ASH. Before he could take a second sip of champagne, Ash had caught his eye and nodded toward his office. He'd left Aubrey in the capable hands of Rose. Thankfully, she'd gotten over her initial uncertainty and seemed to be enjoying herself. He would spend a few moments getting Ash caught up, and then he was taking Aubrey home.

Ash closed the door and headed to his desk. "Have a seat."

"Something going on?"

"Yeah...maybe. I may have a location on Drury for you soon. You still interested?"

The thought of leaving Aubrey so soon after finding her created a hollow feeling in his chest. But he owed this to Myron.

"Where's your intel coming from?"

"Our old friend Omar Schrader."

A former weapons broker, Omar Schrader had become a CI for OZ. After the initial shock of realizing his previous job had ended and that if he went back to it, he'd end up in prison, Omar had accepted his new role with amazing aplomb.

"Don't tell me Drury's involved in weapons trafficking, too?"

"Apparently he's in dire need of cash."

That wasn't surprising. The bastard enjoyed a lavish lifestyle, and few things were off the table for him. Drury had no ethics. Mix that with a need for fast cash, and he was the devil incarnate.

"What intel do you have?"

"Omar thinks he's still in Colombia. Seems a group of militia have hired him to find them a cache of assault rifles. He contacted Omar."

"They set up a meet?"

"Not yet. Omar's been communicating with a middleman. Ronnie Wiggins."

Liam huffed a humorless laugh. "Yeah, he's been an on-again, off-again sidekick of Drury's for years. I kept hoping they'd end up killing each other, but no such luck."

"I'd like to keep Omar away from the fray. Word gets around he ratted out Drury, he's a dead man."

"Just get me a location for Wiggins, I'll handle the rest."

"Good enough." His mouth went from his normal businesslike grim to a slight smile. "How's it feel to have found her?"

"Like a thousand-pound weight is off my shoulders. Truth is, I'm still reeling."

"Yeah, modern-day miracles are rare, but I'd say this comes as close as I've seen. You guys been able to talk about what happened to her?"

"Not yet. I want to give her some time before I start with the questions."

"I'd like her to spend some time with Serena. Share any other intel she's got on Ferante. She might feel more comfortable talking to a woman about Syria, too."

Liam nodded. "Good point." He stood and headed to the door. "You need me for anything, you know where I am."

"Yeah," Ash said. "And, Liam?"

He stopped at the door and looked over his shoulder. "Yeah?"

"You're going to have to let go of the guilt."

He didn't need to ask Ash what he was talking about. The same guilt had been eating at him for years. Aubrey had been tortured because of him. The sounds of her pain and terror were ingrained in his memory like the foulest of smells. It reeked within his insides, and nothing and no one was going to be able to lessen the stench. Yes, they had found each other, and yes he would spend the rest of his life making it up to her for what she had endured, but no way in hell would he ever overcome the guilt of not being able to prevent her pain.

Unable to give Ash the answer he wanted, Liam turned and walked out the door.

CHAPTER THIRTY-ONE

Speechless, Aubrey stepped out of Liam's SUV and stared at the log home in front of her. She was beyond stunned. It was her house…her dream house.

Now she knew why she had detected a hint of nervousness from him when they'd left OZ headquarters. Liam had built this for her. She had described to him in detail the mountain home she dreamed of owning someday. And this was exactly what she had envisioned.

This told her all she needed to know. Doubts and fears subsided. During those long days in darkness, she had found her light, and so had Liam.

"It's perfect," she breathed softly.

"My memory might have been faulty on a few things, but I think I was able to get the gist of it. I had to fill in a few gaps with things I thought worked, but if there's something you don't like, we can change it."

"It's perfect. Just as I pictured it." Turning away from the house, she faced him. "Why, Liam? Why did you do this?"

She knew…at least she thought she knew, but she wanted, needed, to hear the words. She had created a film company in Lion's honor and, inspired by him, had dedicated her life to making films that made a difference. And Liam had dedicated his life to finding her, and he had built this beautiful home with her in mind. Yes, she knew the answer, but she needed to hear the words from him.

His dark eyes swam with emotion. Emotions she recognized in her own heart.

Realizing she couldn't wait to give him the words herself, she said, "I've been waiting a long time for this moment," she whispered. "To tell you I—"

Before she could say them, he pressed a finger to her lips. "We need to talk first, though. Okay?"

"Okay."

"Come on. Let me show you around. Then we'll sit on the deck and talk."

She followed him into the house, commenting on various aspects that pleased her the most. From the wraparound porch, to the heavy oak double-door entrance, to the wide-open living space, to the exposed beams of the ceiling, everything was exactly as she'd dreamed. The décor was comfortable and easy. The colors were muted earth tones with the occasional splash of color in a throw pillow or painting.

"I haven't done a lot of decorating. I thought about getting a decorator to come in, but…" He shrugged. "I figured you'd have an idea or two about that, so I waited."

If he didn't stop, she was going to break down into a mess of emotional tears. This man had done so much for her already.

"Come on. Let me show you the view."

She stepped out onto the deck and caught her breath at the beauty.

"Those are the Bitterroot mountains. We climb them occasionally."

He pulled out a chair for her and then sat beside her. For

long moments, they drank in the view. The sheer majesty of the snow-capped mountains brought peace and lessened her nerves. He wanted to talk to her. And she needed to share some things with him. They both needed to face that last day in prison before they could move on.

She settled herself and began, "The day they took me away." She drew in a breath. "Let me start from the beginning. Okay?"

She had only ever told her therapist everything that had happened while she was in prison. Her mother and Becca knew some aspects of it, but she hadn't been able to share all of them. But with Liam, she could. He was the one man, the one person who would understand.

"Any way you want to do it."

"My cousin Becca and I were supposed to travel to Paris together. She caught a bad cold a couple of days before we were supposed to leave. She has asthma and her doctor recommended that she not go. She was disappointed, but I was devastated. Nothing and no one could talk me out of going by myself."

She paused for a few minutes, contemplating how that one decision had cost her so very much. Naïve and clueless, full of youthful arrogance, she'd believed she had the whole world in her hands and nothing could touch her. Certainly nothing was going to stop her from doing what she wanted to do.

Yet, if she hadn't gone, she never would have met Liam.

"I was in an open-air market when they took me. I don't remember a lot. They injected me with some kind of sedative. When I woke up, I was in a room. My hands were tied, and I had a hood over my head. I couldn't see anything. I could hear them, though. There were three of them."

She paused again, gearing up for the next part. Apparently knowing what was coming, Liam took her hand from the arm of her chair and entwined his fingers with hers. He squeezed gently.

Taking strength from the tender gesture, she continued, "While two of the men held me down, one of them raped me. I fought, screamed, cried. They hit me to shut me up. I remember their vile words and their laughter the most."

She paused again. Liam didn't say anything, giving her the time she needed to regroup.

"When he finished, one of the men carried me to a large cell and chained me to the wall. When he walked away, I was able to pull the hood from my head. That's when I saw the other women.

"There were eight of them in there with me. They didn't speak and I was in too much pain to say anything. I don't know how long I was there. Maybe a day or two, I'm not sure. I think a couple of the women tried to talk to me but I was in shock. Then I got sick. When I started coughing continuously, they moved me to a cell by myself.

"I don't know how long I was there before you came. Maybe a couple more days. No one would talk to me, tell me why I was there. One of the men would just shove food into my cell once a day and then leave. I thought I would die there.

"I was in the midst of crying and praying for a miracle when I heard the most beautiful voice I'd ever heard say, 'Hello.'"

Tears filling her eyes, she turned to him. "You were the answer to my prayers, Liam. I never told you that and so regretted not telling you before they took me away that day. You saved my life. Without you talking to me, encouraging me, giving me hope, I wouldn't have survived."

"And yet I almost got you killed."

"What do you mean?"

. . .

Now it was his turn to tell her what he knew about her last day. The guilt he'd carried with him would never go away, but she deserved to know everything.

"I knew they would use you against me. I shouldn't have made a connection with you. I should've kept my distance."

The hurt on her face was painful to see, but he had to make her understand that what she went through that last day was his fault.

"When they took you, I could only imagine the horror of what you were going through. A few hours later, one of the men—the British guy—came back. He had a recording. It played for two days straight."

"A recording?"

"Of your…assault. I heard you screaming and crying. You were calling out for me, and I couldn't do a damn thing but listen as they tortured you. All because of me."

"No."

"Yes. If I hadn't gotten close to you, you would've been spared. I fell into their trap. I knew what they wanted, to use you against me, and I let them get away with it. What you went through was my fault."

"Listen to me, Liam, it wasn't." She held up her free hand to stop him from talking. "They never asked me anything about you."

"Don't try to make me feel better, Aubrey. I heard what they did. For two damn days, I listened to it. Even after the batteries ran out, I could hear you in my mind. I know what they did."

"No, you don't, Liam. They probably wanted you to think that, but that's not what happened."

His frown darker than any she'd ever seen from him, he said, "What do you mean?"

"They put a hood over my head and took me to that same room as before. I know it was the same, because it smelled like garlic, like the first time. I think that's where they must've eaten their meals. Anyway, they threw me around. Mostly to scare me, I think. I cried and screamed. They laughed and called me names. And yes, I'm sure I did scream your name. I couldn't help myself. You were my only anchor, so I called for Lion numerous times, I'm sure.

"Finally, one of them pushed me so hard against a wall, the blow knocked me out. When I came to, I was on the floor. They were a few feet away from me, talking about what they should do with me. Two of them wanted to sell me to some man in Austria. But the British one thought they should take the ransom that was offered.

"I was dazed, in pain, so it never really hit me that someone was going to pay my ransom. They argued for a while, and finally the British guy convinced the other two that the man in Austria would likely be disappointed that I wasn't a virgin. He said he wouldn't pay as much for me, so the ransom money was a safer bet."

"Are you sure they didn't ask what you knew about me, what I told you?"

"I promise you, Liam. They never mentioned you. At all."

"The recording was explicit, Aubrey. I heard them." Even now, after all these years, he could close his eyes and hear her pleading, crying for them to stop. Hear her screams of pain and terror as she called out for him.

"Could it be they recorded what they did to me that first day?"

"I don't know. You called out my name. Maybe the recording was from both the first and last days."

Hell, the bastard had even given him a clue, and he hadn't caught on. He'd said the recording was his little Cat's greatest hits, implying it was more than one event. How had he missed that?

What had they wanted with her if it wasn't to get intel from him?

"There's more."

He jerked back to the present. "What?"

"Once they agreed to take the ransom, the British guy said something I'll never forget."

"What did he say?"

"He said they were to send me home with a message. Seconds after that, they pulled me out of the corner, and the British guy started stabbing me."

Liam closed his eyes. The scars Serena had mentioned.

"He didn't intend to kill me, even the doctors said that. The cuts were deep, but he apparently knew enough about human anatomy to make sure he didn't hit any major arteries. I passed out from the pain and blood loss. When I woke up, I was in a hospital in Connecticut."

Send her home with a message.

A message to whom and for what reason?

She had been taken for a completely different reason than what he'd thought. Selling her had likely been one of the reasons, but not the main one. Why could an NYU college student, a young woman from a small town in Connecticut, be targeted in Paris and taken to Syria? What was the real purpose of her abduction?

That was something he intended to find out.

Was that why he'd never been able to find out anything about her? Everything had been covered up. It was like she had never existed. Serena Donavan was the best in the business when it came to finding people, and she had not been able to confirm that Cat even existed.

"When you came back home, did they do any kind of investigation?"

"Yes. I talked to someone from the FBI and the State Department. I was out of it for a few days, but when I woke, I told my parents about you, about the other women. Several people came in and got details from me.

"I didn't hear anything for several days, but when I demanded to know what was happening, I learned that the prison had been decimated. They had no information on who had taken me or why. It was just assumed it was for the money."

And yet there had been no official record of her abduction anywhere. If that wasn't the definition of a coverup, he didn't know what was. They'd given her minimal information, counting on her being too damaged and unknowledgeable about how investigations worked. Showing her the destroyed prison had been their final proof to her. *It's been destroyed, those people are dead, now get on with your life.*

He'd learned long ago that if something smelled like a dead rat then it damn well was a dead rat.

"Liam? What's wrong?"

He'd get to work on that later. For now, he needed to concentrate on Aubrey. She had just shared the most painful, agonizing moments of her life. She needed him to be fully present. And he needed to hold her and reassure himself that she was here, safe and secure.

"Come here." He tugged on the hand he was still holding and pulled her up and onto his lap. He held her for several long moments, breathing her in and cherishing the strength and fortitude of this one precious woman.

She was shaking a little, revealing that the story had completely drained her.

"I don't know why that happened to you, and I wish I could have been there for you."

"You were there. If I didn't have your voice in my head, telling me to be strong, be brave, I wouldn't have survived."

Holding her tight, Liam closed his eyes as he envisioned the pain and terror she'd experienced.

"What about you? You said your team rescued you. Were you in the military?"

"Yeah. Special Ops. I was a SEAL. So was Xavier. We got moved from our team and put on special assignment. We were in Syria to help a small faction that was trying to infiltrate a terrorist group. Somebody ratted us out. We got nabbed to give up the names of those people."

"Did you ever find out who ratted you out?"

"No, not really. We got some intel pointing to certain people, but nothing we could hang our hat on."

"So you're like Jason Bourne or maybe Ethan Hunt?"

He snorted with laughter. "Not hardly. Those guys get shot, beat to a pulp, and blown up, then show up the next day with a bruise on their chins. When I get hurt, it shows."

"Were you injured when you escaped the prison?"

"No, not then. Although I was close to the point of insanity, thinking about finding you. I had decided to lure them into my cell and overpower them. Don't know if that would've worked, but I realized they weren't going to bring you back. My only option was to escape. Then I didn't have to. The team came and let me out. I went looking for you. No one was there."

"The other women were gone too?"

"Yeah. Everyone was gone except for the three men my team took down. None was ever identified."

"It was hard for you, leaving without knowing what happened to me."

Hard was the mildest word he would use to describe how he'd felt. "I knew you weren't there, but I couldn't get it out of my head that I was leaving you behind."

She gave him the saddest of smiles. "When we made that date to meet in New York, a big part of me knew it would never happen. But I held on to the hope."

"We'll do that someday soon. Go to New York, the library. Just like we planned."

"I'd like that."

Arms around each other, her head on his shoulder, they took in the beauty around them and the peace within them. There were still things to say, things to share. He had an investigation to launch. But for now, for just this little while, Liam soaked in the calm. His world was in his arms. What more could a man want?

CHAPTER THIRTY-TWO

Aubrey watched Liam devour the meal she had prepared, delighted that he seemed to be enjoying it so much. She hadn't had much to work with—the man's pantry and fridge were in dire need of a grocery trip. Not only that, he wasn't exactly into health food.

"Did you know you have eight boxes of mac and cheese?"

"It was on sale." He took another giant bite of the pasta with tomato sauce, chewed, and then grinned. "This is good. First home-cooked meal I've had in a while. I'm usually home a couple nights a week at the most. When I am here, I pop a couple of frozen dinners in the microwave."

She wasn't the most domestic person in the world, and definitely not the best cook, but she needed fresh fruits and vegetables daily.

He swirled up another massive forkful of pasta and carried it to his mouth, but stopped halfway. "This is a lame, first-date question, but what do you like to eat? What's your favorite food?"

Before she could answer, his eyes wide with mock horror,

he added, "You're not a tofu-omelet-and-kale-milkshake kind of girl, are you?"

"What if I am?"

He shoveled the pasta into his mouth and shrugged. "Then I'll build another pantry just for you."

Her heart melted. Not because he said he would build her another pantry, but because to him it was a foregone conclusion that she would be staying with him indefinitely.

"You can relax. I'm an all-American cheeseburger kind of girl, but I do like fresh fruits and vegetables."

"I can handle that."

"Maybe after Serena leaves, we can go to the grocery store."

Serena was coming over to review the information she had given them on Ferante. What she had wouldn't hold up in court—most of it was conjecture and theory. But she had gladly given all she had to OZ and would offer any aid they needed. The man needed to be stopped. For Emma and for all the others he'd destroyed over the years, she would do whatever was needed to help bring him to justice.

"We can do that. I'll—"

He stopped and frowned down at his phone.

"What's wrong?"

"Looks like I'll have to leave for a couple of days."

"What's going on?"

"Just got a text from Ash. A guy we've been looking for has been located. I need to go have a chat with him."

A "chat" with Liam was likely not a little conversation like it was for most people. Guns, knives, blood, and guts were often involved.

"This is crazy, but it suddenly occurred to me that what you do is very dangerous."

"You going to be able to handle that?"

"Will I worry? Absolutely. But this is who you are. You

save lives, and I can't think of a more worthy thing to do. I would never want to change you."

He took a swallow of his drink and then grabbed her hand, his fingers entwining with hers. "We haven't talked about where we're going with this. But I need to know. Are you with me?"

Her heart soared with happiness. "I'm one hundred percent with you. I fell in love with a strong, honorable, golden-voiced man named Lion. My love hasn't changed just because his real name is Liam."

His chair scooted back, and he was up in an instant, pulling her up with him. Cupping her face, he roamed his eyes over her. "And I fell in love with a sweet, spirited, courageous woman named Cat. Nothing's changed to make me feel any differently."

"Are we crazy?" she whispered. "Other people would say we don't really know each other."

"Other people don't matter. We know each other in the most basic way possible. The other stuff we'll learn along the way."

He kissed her then, the way she'd been longing for him to kiss her from the beginning. His mouth moved over hers tenderly, persistently. His tongue entwining with hers promised delicious delights and pleasure untold.

She moaned against him, wanting more. Wanting everything.

The ringing doorbell reminded her that not only did they have company coming, Liam had to leave.

They pulled away, breathless. The heat in Liam's eyes matched the fire burning in her body.

"When I get home, we're going to spend days and nights together, exploring all those things we don't know about each other. Okay?"

"It's a date."

CHAPTER THIRTY-THREE

Cartagena, Colombia

Sweat poured down Liam's body. The air was so thick and wet, one could almost imagine rain poured from the sky, except that bright blue sky held a blazing sun that baked everything within seconds of exposure. He'd honestly never been this hot, and if hell was hotter than this, he was going to do his dead-level best not to end up there.

"I swear, Stryker. I ain't got no notion where Drury could be."

Tightening his grip on the creep's shirt collar, Liam couldn't prevent a laugh. When scared, Ronnie Wiggins lost his fake Spanish accent in a hurry. Hailing from somewhere in the southern US, Ronnie did his best to bring an international flair to his criminal activities. But when he figured he was seconds from losing his life, the Southern came out.

Liam much preferred him this way.

Pulling Ronnie closer, he spoke softly. "You used to be

partners. Even though you parted ways, I'm willing to wager you keep tabs on each other."

"Then you gotta know if I give him up, he'll come after me."

"Not if I take him out of circulation. He won't be around to bother you, Ronnie. Just think, you won't have to compete with him anymore."

A gleam entered Ronnie's bloodshot eyes. Yeah, he liked the idea of having to compete with one less slimeball. But fear overcame greed, and Ronnie shook his head. "He'd find out. He always finds out stuff. Even if he's not around, he'll get somebody to do the deed for him."

"I can protect you."

"I can't risk it, Stryker."

"You're risking more if you don't."

"What's that mean?"

"It means I've got a network of people who'd be glad to send out some information. Maybe spill that Ronnie Wiggins was behind the leak that got Drury locked up last year."

"But that ain't true!" Ronnie whined.

"Don't you keep up with the news? Truth is in the eye of the beholder these days. Drury trusts you about as far as he can throw that tree over there. When he hears that news, no way he won't believe it. That'll tip him over the edge, and he'll be after you for the rest of your life. You won't be able to rest, won't be able to sleep. You'll be looking over your shoulder forever. You really want to live like that?"

"But...but..."

"Up to you, man."

Worrying his teeth over his dry lips, Ronnie looked everywhere but at Liam. Any other time, he might've felt a tinge of guilt for leaning so heavily on the lowlife, but he couldn't afford that feeling. Drury was directly responsible for Myron's death. Catching the slug was one last thing he could do for him.

Plus, getting him out of circulation meant one less human trafficker. It would be a good day for all when he took the maggot down.

"I'm running out of patience, Ronnie."

"How'd you even find me? I've been lying low. Hadn't seen or talked to nobody but Drury." His eyes narrowed. "You ain't in cahoots with that arms-dealing guy, are you?"

"Arms? You selling illegal weapons, Ronnie? Maybe I should just take you in, let somebody else find Drury and tell him how you ratted him out. You'll be locked up in prison, nowhere to go. I bet Drury's got lots of friends there, just looking to do him a solid."

"No, no," Ronnie said rapidly. "It ain't nothing like that. I'm just a go-between. I don't do the bad, not like Drury."

"Yeah, you keep thinking that, Ronnie. And now your time is up. You've got five seconds to tell me where he is or life is going to get pretty damn bleak for you."

"You said you can protect me, right?"

"I keep my word. Now spill."

"He's in Bogota. I'm supposed to hook him up with the broker."

"That right? Guess that's not gonna happen. Where in Bogota?"

Eyes darting left then right as if he expected Drury to appear before him, Ronnie swallowed hard and said, "He's got a woman he stays with there."

"Her name?"

"Lucretia. Lou for short. She's a bartender at Las Casa Mi. She's a nice woman. I met her a couple of years ago. I don't know what she sees in the man."

Liam had to give the guy credit. Once Ronnie made up his mind to spill, he did that and more.

"You know," Ronnie went on conversationally, "he's only been in the trafficking business a few months, but he's making tons of money. I told him for years he should. He's got the gift for it."

"And you don't?"

"Ain't my style. Too much work. People are real sensitive about that shit these days."

"Imagine that."

The sarcasm went right over Ronnie's head. "Yeah, I know. Weird. Anyways, to each his own, I always say. Live and let live."

"Yeah, you're a real philosopher."

"How much you gonna give me?"

"I beg your pardon?"

"I gave you some good info. It's gotta be worth something."

"It is. It's worth your life. I told you I'd protect you. That's your payment."

"That ain't right."

"No. What's not right is that people are being sold all around the world, and the only reason you don't do it yourself is because it's too much trouble. Now, take the protection, or get out of my sight."

"Okay, okay. Whatever. Can you at least send me somewhere nice?"

"Oh, it'll be nice all right." Liam spoke into the mic on his lapel. "Come on in. He's ready."

Liam nodded at the two local men who'd come along to take Ronnie to his new digs. Who knew? Ronnie might turn out to be a changed man. The sisters of Perpetual Blessings had arrived in Uganda last week and had sent out an urgent plea for help. Ronnie might not appreciate the irony but Liam definitely did. No way would Drury think to look for Ronnie at a humanitarian rescue site in Uganda.

To save his own life, Ronnie Wiggins would be helping to save the lives of others.

If that wasn't irony he didn't know what was.

He headed back to his SUV and on the way pressed the call icon for Ash. "Hey, I got the intel."

"How many of us do you need with you?"

"Not sure yet. I'll do a check and see where we are."

"Sounds good."

"Anything on the other?"

He'd met with Ash before leaving and told him what Aubrey had revealed about her last day in Syria. There was something altogether hinky about her abduction, torture, and release. Without her knowledge, he'd asked Ash to do a deep dive into her family. The stabbings she'd endured had been meant to send a message. To whom and for what reason? Had she been taken as a punishment or a warning for someone?

"Not yet. Serena dug up some things but nothing that would raise more than a brow or two. We'll get there, though."

"Yeah, I know. Thanks for doing this. I know that—"

"Stop right there. What's important to an OZ operative is important to us all."

"Thanks, man. I'll call you as soon as I find Drury."

"Sounds good. Stay safe."

Liam pocketed his phone and climbed into his SUV. He wanted this over and done with. For the first time ever, he had someone waiting at home for him. Her name was Katarina Aubrey Starr, and he could not wait to return to her.

CHAPTER THIRTY-FOUR

Cyprus

The tedious boredom would soon be over. He had put a plan into place that would keep him entertained for weeks, if not months. It had been so easy. With one phone call, life was grand again.

When the girl he'd known as No. 7 had died, he had been outraged. Giving the young ones drugs rarely worked out well. It had always been his policy to gain compliance through bribes and coercion. Mix in a little fear, and you get a perfect and well-behaved girl.

This one had been special. He had enjoyed her on numerous occasions and even considered bringing her into his stable full time. She was young and malleable. Once she had aged beyond his preference, he could have sold her for a nice profit. Instead, she had OD'd in one of his houses, which was infuriating.

Maybe if he hadn't been so upset, he would have ensured that the girl was actually dead. When he'd told his people to dump her body, he had assumed they would make sure she was no longer breathing, like any fool would. Instead, the morons had taken her to the woods and left her. Not only had the girl still been alive, she had dragged herself to civilization.

Good thing he had a bevy of spies. Even though the story had been quickly covered up, the enticing tidbit that a young girl had been found on a hiking trail in upstate New York had caught the attention of one of his people. The woman had put two and two together and made an inquiry. Wasn't long before she'd pieced together the mystery and contacted him.

No. 7 was still alive.

By the time his people had tracked her down again, she'd been too old to bother with. The girl had no clue of his identity, and he'd been prepared to look at her as the one that got away. And then he'd learned something exciting.

She had a younger sister.

Still a little younger than he preferred, so he had been willing to wait. He'd kept a watch on the family. And now… now, she was almost just right.

The family had changed their names, moved across the country to Iowa of all places. They thought they were safe, thought they'd hidden themselves. They were wrong.

When he'd learned that Aubrey Starr, that little busybody filmmaker, had visited the family, he'd known something was up. Had she found out something?

She was making a new documentary—like the one she'd done a few years back. That one hadn't stepped on his toes. But if she was talking to No. 7, the new film might point toward him. He couldn't allow that to happen.

His plan had been to silence her permanently. Problem was, she had some protection. Wasn't that a kick in the ass?

The girl who was trying to uncover dirty deeds had her own dirty little secret.

Maybe she didn't even know—didn't matter to him. But it did present some problems. He'd been told that taking out that producer, the money man, would fix things, that she wouldn't be able to do the film without his money and backing.

To be sure, Ferante had sent someone to her house to snoop. And what had he found? Not only did she have a secret hiding place, she had disappeared, taking whatever she'd been hiding with her.

He'd told his people to make a statement. They'd sent a few photos to show him they'd done just that. He approved. That didn't mean she was safe, though. He had eyes and ears everywhere. He'd find the little bitch and have her put down for good. He didn't care who her contacts were.

But for now he had other fish to fry. He wanted No. 7's sister. Now. Immediately. What if the parents got antsy and disappeared? He couldn't afford to lose the girl. She was still a little young, but he could wait her out. Wouldn't hurt to do a bit of training while he waited.

In just a few days, she would belong to him. Who knew, he might actually keep this one for himself.

Happy for the first time in a long while, he picked up the phone and made a call. "Have my yacht readied. I want to leave in two hours."

Not bothering to wait to hear that his command would be obeyed, he ended the call. Leaning back in his chair, Ferante smiled. There was nothing that made him feel more like a king than being at the helm of *The Jewel*. All 199 feet of her was his, and she obeyed his every command.

In fact, that's where he'd have his newest acquisition brought. Being surrounded by a mile of ocean with no place to run would encourage compliance in record time. And if it didn't, he had other ways.

~

The other side of the world

RUDOLPH ULRICH SAT at the large oval table, surrounded by people he didn't trust. They had been together for years, brought together for one purpose. He knew them better than he knew anyone else, including his own son.

But today, because of that son, he was facing them as adversaries.

The meeting hadn't been called for him to argue his son's case. Those kinds of meetings didn't exist for this group. No, they were here for one reason only. They were going to render judgment. And though he already knew what had been decided, he couldn't resist trying to change their minds.

"I'll speak to Marc Antony. Let him know in no uncertain terms that he has gone too far. I can make him stop."

"If you could make him stop, why haven't you done so before now?"

They were all at the same level, but the man who'd asked the question had a tendency to pretend to be the leader. He wasn't, but people rarely challenged him.

Appealing to his or anyone's humanity would do no good. They had taken an oath years ago, and that was the only code by which they lived. Eschewing any kind of personal life for the greater cause, they were of one mind. He was the only one who'd dared defy his oath to have a family.

All right, not really a family. He hadn't even known he had a child until a woman he barely remembered contacted him and told him he was a father. He had thought about having them both killed—he didn't need the hassle—but had changed his mind when he'd seen the boy. Instead, he'd had only the boy's mother taken out of the picture. He didn't want her interfering. Then he'd given the child over to a couple he knew to raise him. Thanks to him, the boy had never wanted for anything. Problem was, the more he got, the more he wanted.

When Rudolph had brought his son, Marc Antony, into the organization, he had believed he would be an asset. And he had been. Unfortunately his unusual tastes had often interfered with his responsibilities. Rudolph had warned him numerous times, but to no avail. Marc Antony wanted what he wanted. And now it could cost him everything.

"I do believe your silence tells the tale."

He inwardly sighed. There was no need to argue. They wouldn't change their minds. It wasn't like he had any kind of affection for the boy. But Rudolph didn't take failure well. Failing at fatherhood wasn't really failure, though. Not really.

"I will take care of the details," Rudolph said.

"That's not necessary. It's being handled."

Showing weakness and subservience was not in his best interest. These people would chew him to pieces given the right incentive. He refused to give it to them. Rudolph Ulrich was a wealthy, powerful man in his own right. He bowed to no one, especially this man with his arrogant condescension.

"I said I would handle the situation and I will."

They stared at each other for several long seconds. No one spoke and the room was filled with an explosive tension. Finally, the other man gave a nod of his head and said, "Then do it."

And that was that.

He watched the men and women stand, and without the socializing one might see after an ordinary business meeting, they dispersed without speaking to one another.

He stood and wasn't surprised to feel lighter than he had when he had arrived. Within a few hours or a few days, the biggest mistake of his life would be no more. There were advantages to having no emotions. This was one of those times.

CHAPTER THIRTY-FIVE

Iowa City, Iowa

The night was dark and peaceful. A distant train and the closer noise of a howling coyote were the only sounds to compete in the stillness. Houses lined up in rows, filled with sleeping families who were unaware that danger had arrived in their city, on their street. A danger no one would see until it was too late.

Blueprints of the house had been easy to obtain. They had been studied and memorized. There would be no escape, no way out. The family consisted of parents and three children —an older teen girl, a boy of about fourteen, and the youngest, a girl of about eleven. The youngest was their target.

The team was set. Two women would enter the house. The goal was to take the girl without anyone knowing. If they were discovered, two men waited on the outside. They would come in and handle the situation. Killing them all was an option that had been given to them, but he hoped it wasn't necessary. Making it more complicated often caused issues. Simple was best.

Get the girl, get out. That was the goal.

The man spoke into his mic: "A and B, are you set?"

A female voice answered: "A and B ready."

"Go."

He watched from a safe distance. He wouldn't participate unless things went awry. They shouldn't. He had trained these people. They knew what to do.

Two barely discernible shadows slipped in through the garage door. Surveillance had revealed that the family, though apparently safety conscious enough to have a security system—which his people had easily dismantled—the lock on the garage door leading inside the house was a standard one. His people could quietly break that lock within seconds.

Confirming his thoughts, B whispered, "We're in."

That should be the end of communication until they had the girl wrapped up and brought outside. He would drive past the front of the house and stop, open the cargo door of his van, and the girl would be deposited inside. The same routine had been accomplished over a dozen times with no difficulties. He expected nothing different this time.

Two minutes later, he heard a slight but unmistakable pop, pop. Apparently someone in the family had woken and the threat had been handled. Now the whole family, with the exception of the youngest girl, would die.

"C and D," he said into his mic. "Go in."

"Copy," D answered.

Two more shadows, bigger and bulkier than their predecessors, ran across the yard and through the open side-door of the garage. Tense now, he waited.

Another pop, pop sound in his earbud told him all he needed to know. Four family members, four pops.

"Get the girl and get out," he said softly.

"I don't think so," an unfamiliar voice said beside him. He barely had the chance to turn, and his mind had no chance to register another 'pop' before excruciating agony went through his head.

A big hand reached into the van and grabbed the man's head before it could fall onto the steering wheel and possibly sound the horn. No need to disturb this quiet, peaceful neighborhood with the obnoxious blare of a car horn.

Pushing the dead man over into the passenger side, the shooter got into the driver's seat and started the engine. Pressing his mic, he said, "We ready to roll?"

"Yes," a voice answered. "We've got them loaded up, and the house is locked down."

"Let's go."

Two dark vans, one filled with four dead bodies and the other with one dead body, drove silently down the quiet, peaceful street, waking no one. The house they'd left behind would tell no secrets. No one was home. In an unexpected windfall, the family who lived there had won an all-expenses-paid trip to Disney World. In two days, they would return home, refreshed, tanned, and happy, never knowing that death had struck inside their home. They would go on with their lives, completely unaware that danger had been only a breath away.

∾

Cyprus

THE GENTLY SWAYING yacht sat upon water so smooth and calm barely a ripple moved. Skies, clear and cerulean blue, looked down upon the serene setting.

Dressed in swim trunks and glistening with tanning oil,

Marc Antony Ferante stood at the helm of his boat. This was just what he'd needed. The sea air invigorated him like nothing else. He would take a few days for himself. Get the sun he needed, the rest he required. Then he would have his newest acquisition brought here. She was being retrieved at this very moment. And soon, very soon, she would be his.

Ferante smiled. Yes, he was no longer bored. Life was once again interesting.

The massive explosion came without warning, shooting from the boat toward the sky. Only the squawking seabirds witnessed the giant eruption that flung fiery pieces of wood, iron, and steel a mile into the air.

Barely a minute later, the sea was calm once more. Remnants of what had once been a grand yacht floated along the peaceful waters. The rest of the wreckage, including Marc Antony Ferante, sank to the bottom of the sea.

CHAPTER THIRTY-SIX

Montana

Breaking News: *A yacht belonging to billionaire businessman Marc Antony Ferante exploded off the island of Cyprus this morning. It is believed that Mr. Ferante and three crew members were on board. There were no survivors.*

This is a developing story. Stay tuned for updates as we learn more about the explosion.

Aubrey stared openmouthed at her laptop screen. She had been working for hours and had just stopped for a quick break when the breaking news had popped up on the screen.

Ferante was dead? Had he been murdered? Had his evil deeds finally caught up with him?

Standing, Aubrey paced around the room as she considered the consequences. Emma would no longer have to be afraid of him. Her family no longer had to hide. Dozens of children, perhaps hundreds, were no longer in peril of being sold and abused by the vile monster.

She didn't discount the relief she felt for her safety. She didn't have to hide from him now. She would be able to complete her film without fear that he could hurt someone she loved.

How she wished she could call Liam and discuss this with him. He or someone at OZ might have intel on what happened. Not for a moment did she consider they were involved in Ferante's death. Even though they didn't hesitate to stop evil people, Option Zero didn't assassinate them. They might, however, know who had.

She couldn't call Liam though. Since he'd left, he had sent her several texts. He'd told her in his last one this morning that he would be out of touch for the next few hours.

She couldn't even call Serena or Ash and talk to them. The entire OZ team was on a mission. Liam had told her if she needed anything, she could contact Rose at OZ. And though Rose was a lovely person, she doubted that she would want to discuss Aubrey's conjectures on Ferante's death.

Sighing, she walked out onto the deck and was immediately at peace. The majesty before her put everything in perspective. When Liam returned, they'd figure things out.

What did this mean for their future? Being out of danger meant she didn't need to stay here for her safety. She had things she needed to do at home. Liam had told her that her house had been cleaned out, but she wanted to see to things herself. She'd talked to her insurance agent, and he'd mentioned it would be helpful if she came in person to discuss all the items she'd lost.

So many things had been handled for her, and while she appreciated the help, she was independent-minded enough to want to take care of matters herself.

Maybe Liam could take a few days off, and they could go to Florida together. St. Augustine was one of the most beautiful cities in the country. She could deal with her personal business, and they could have time to explore and have fun. Just like a normal couple.

The thought sent a shiver of delight through her. They had kissed, talked of the future a little, but not much more than that. She wanted days of being alone with him, exploring all the delightful feelings he brought out in her. Never had she felt so happy, so free. She had found the love of her life. Now she wanted to start enjoying that life with him.

The distant ringing of her cellphone had her running back into the room. Liam! Maybe he had heard about Ferante's death and was calling to tell her. Maybe he was calling to say he was headed back home.

After a quick glance at the display screen, she blew out a disappointed sigh. Not Liam. Her cousin Becca. Taking a second to settle her disappointment, she answered the phone with a cheery, "Hey sweetie, what's up?"

A sobbing Becca responded, "I got fired!"

"What? What are you talking about?"

"They canned me, Aubrey."

"Who canned you? Why?"

"That's just it. I don't know," she wailed. "Two days ago, the director, Samuel Mann, told me he was incredibly pleased with my performance. He said I was the perfect Maya. He said he was thrilled that he had cast me in the role, that no one could have been Maya but me. Then this morning, he called me into his office and said he changed his mind. Some of the producers saw the dailies and didn't like me as Maya at all. They're going to put the film on hold for a few months and then start again with a different actress. My career is ruined!"

"No, it's not. You're a brilliant actress. No one will be able to play Maya the way you did. They'll realize that, I'm sure."

"I don't think so. They've already removed my name from all the promotional material. My agent said she doesn't know what happened."

"But you have a contract. They can't just fire you without cause."

"That's what I told my agent. She said she's working from that standpoint, but not to get my hopes up. She said they've made it clear I'm out, no matter what."

"But that makes no sense. Did you talk to your dad? Maybe he can help."

"Yes, I called him. He said he'll fix things. I don't think he can, but I'm hoping he can at least find out what I did wrong. He's in London, but is going to catch the first flight back. They've got a big snowstorm, so he isn't sure when he can get here. Can you come, Aubrey?"

"Of course I'll come. I'll catch the first flight out and text you my arrival time. Okay?"

"Thank you."

"And don't you worry. We'll figure this thing out. There's got to be some kind of mistake."

"I don't think so, but having you here will make things so much better."

After reassuring her cousin she'd be there as soon as possible, Aubrey ended the call and immediately clicked on a travel site. She booked a flight leaving in an hour and a half. She went to the bedroom to pack, thinking about all she needed to do. Liam had already told her he likely wouldn't be home until after the weekend. It was only Tuesday. She could fly to LA, settle Becca down, and be back before he returned home.

Thankfully, he'd left her the keys to his SUV, so she didn't have to depend on a taxi. Packed and ready in fifteen minutes, she quickly texted Liam to let him know what was going on. And since she knew he would worry, she added that the threat they were concerned about no longer existed. He would know what she meant.

Five minutes later she was out the door. As she drove

away, her heart ached a little, almost as though she were leaving for good. That was silly. She would be back in a few days, and then she and Liam would make good on all those delicious promises they'd made to each other.

~

Bogota, Colombia

ASSESSING THE THREAT BEFORE HIM, Liam considered his chances of coming out of this without serious injury. They weren't great. Two against one was almost a fair fight. Three against one was a little much. He figured he'd faced worse odds, but he'd usually had some backup. Unfortunately, he was on his own for this gig. His fault and no one else's. When he'd spotted Drury going into the bar the day before, he had decided to do this alone. Bringing the whole crew here to bring down only one man had seemed excessive.

He'd called Ash and told him he was doing this solo. Ash had been relieved. They'd gotten a call about a possible assassination attempt in Hamburg, Germany. Ash and the team were on their way there now.

He and Drury had fought hand-to-hand before, and Liam had always come out the victor. Problem was, Drury traveled with a posse these days. Liam should have done more surveillance. That's what he got for half-assing an op. The excuse that he wanted to get back to Aubrey wasn't a good one. Not when there was a possibility he wouldn't return home at all.

Cocky was helpful only when it was mixed with intelligence. The dumbass move of not looking to see if anyone had followed Drury was going to cost him.

The back alleyway of a bar was not going to be the place he died. Not when he had Aubrey waiting at home for him.

No way, after searching all these years and finally finding her, was he going to let a low-life, scumbag take that away.

The alley was filth-ridden, even by alley standards. Liam assessed his chances of finding a weapon. Liam's gun was now beneath a dumpster. The big guy standing behind him had been the one to relieve him of his weapon. He'd make sure to retrieve it as soon as he handled this situation.

The knife in his boot was insurance. It was well hidden and he'd pull it out at an opportune moment. Revealing it too soon could cost him. For now, Liam preferred to improvise.

One man was behind him, another was to his left. Drury stood in front of him. Though the smirk on his face was infuriating, Liam had to give the man credit. It was well deserved.

"Well, well, well. It finally happened. Liam Stryker is going to get the ass-kicking I've been dying to give him since we had our first dustup in Mexico."

"'Dustup' is such a mild word for the bloodied mess I made of you, Barney. I should've let you bleed to death instead of calling for help. I won't make that mistake again."

"And neither will I. My friends and I will ensure you never get out of Colombia."

"I'm still surprised you have friends. How much do you have to pay them?"

"Insulting me is only going to make your pain worse."

"I'm going to do much more than insult you, Barney. I'm going to put you away for good. What you did to Myron was unconscionable."

"He ratted me out."

"He was trying to save lives, slimebag. You were selling human beings."

Drury shrugged. "We all got to make a living. He chose his path, I chose mine." He grinned and added, "Mine pays better."

If he was trying to piss Liam off, he was doing a good job. There was nothing Liam wanted more than to shove this bastard's teeth down his throat. First he had to get rid of the two Neanderthals before he'd even get a chance at Drury.

Out of the corner of his eye, he spotted his first break. A plank sticking out of a garbage bin. Liam took a step back.

"Retreating, Stryker? Not surprised. You've always been more talk than action. I—"

Not giving Drury time to finish his sentence, Liam grabbed hold of the wood and, whirling around, slammed it into the closest guy's head. The man dropped like a rock. Taking advantage of their surprise, Liam surged forward and rammed the plank into the other man's gut. Unfortunately, that seemed to only piss the guy off. His fist swung upward, clipping Liam's jaw and sending him a couple of feet back and onto his ass.

Scooping a fistful of dirt on the way back up, Liam was on his feet in seconds. He took a running start at the man who held out his arms and planted himself, waiting, almost like he thought Liam might throw his body at him like a ballroom dancer. If he had a second to think about it, he'd laugh. A foot from his target, Liam threw the dirt into the guy's face. Snarling a curse, the man clawed at his eyes. Liam struck hard. Fist to chin, fist to gut, double kick to the groin. One last punch to the face and the man fell like a giant oak.

Liam turned in time to see Drury draw his gun. Sliding the knife from his boot, he threw it, hitting Drury in the shoulder. Drury's shot went wild, missing Liam's head by a few inches. Drury grabbed for the knife, and Liam was on him in an instant. The knife wound wouldn't kill him. The bastard didn't deserve an easy death. That was too good for him. Rotting away in a prison was the goal.

Pushing him facedown on the ground, he pulled Drury's hands behind his back and zip-tied them. Leaving him for a minute, he went over to Drury's still unconscious cohorts and tied them up as well. Both men were coming around, but the glazed look in their eyes told him it'd be a couple of hours before they were all there. By that time, they'd be locked up tight.

Returning to Drury and just for the fun of it, he zip-tied the man's ankles.

Drury's body jerked with rage. "You're not going to win, Stryker. I'll hunt you down, and when you least expect it, I'll kill you. Just you wait."

"Oh, give it a rest, Barney. The only place you're going is a six-by-six jail cell. You'll be lucky to see daylight before your hundredth birthday."

"Stop calling me Barney!"

Feeling generous, Liam said, "You prefer Bernie?"

Roaring, Drury reared up and tried to buck him off. Wasn't going to work. Leaning over, Liam whispered in his ear, "You've killed your last innocent man, asshole."

"Nobody's innocent, not even a sanctimonious asshole like you."

"Maybe not," Liam said cheerfully, "but at least my name isn't Barney."

Before Drury could throw out another insult, Liam heard a shout. "Hey, Stryker. You around here somewhere?"

"Back here!"

When he'd spotted Drury, he'd called Charlie Hudson, a local bounty hunter he'd worked with in the past. The guy was decent, occasionally providing intel to OZ. Liam gladly threw him business when he could. Three different countries had bounties on Drury's head. Charlie would get a nice chunk of change, and the world had one less creep running around in it.

A win-win in Liam's book.

Charlie came around the corner with another man. They

made an interesting pair as Charlie was close to seven feet tall and probably weighed twice as much as Liam. The other guy was shorter than average and thin as a whip. They both were holding their Glock 45's at the ready and had the expressions of junkyard dogs at feeding time.

"Good timing, Hudson."

"We aim to please. This here's Trey." His eyes bloodshot, likely from an all-nighter, Charlie took in the three tied-up men. "Look's like you made a nice catch."

"Just make sure they stay caught."

"No worries on that," Charlie assured him.

Enjoying himself, Liam watched Charlie haul Drury over his shoulder like a bag of flour. Upside down and furious, his face blood red, the man cocked his head and sneered, "You'll get yours, Stryker."

Deciding he'd give the guy a break, Liam didn't respond.

Drury bounced against Charlie's broad shoulder as he was carried away. Charlie's partner rounded up the other two men, who thanks to the hard knocks on their heads, were subdued.

"Might want get them checked out," Liam called after them.

Charlie lifted a hand in acknowledgment seconds before he rounded the corner and disappeared from view.

Satisfied at the day's work, Liam picked up his knife, wiped it against his leg and returned it to the sheath.

He spotted his gun lying beneath a dumpster where one of the goons had thrown it when they jumped him. Took a few minutes to fish it out. He wiped it down as best he could. He'd had the SIG since he'd started working for OZ and was a stickler about keeping it in pristine condition.

On the way back to his car, he checked his messages. He'd turned his notifications to silent and hadn't checked them since he'd texted Aubrey this morning.

Frowning at the display, he was more than a little concerned to see that he had several missed calls, a couple of texts, plus a voice mail from Aubrey. He clicked on the message.

Hey, it's me. So listen, I'm on a flight to LA. My cousin got fired from her job and needs a shoulder to cry on. Don't worry about me. That...uh guy...he's not a threat anymore. He was killed a few hours ago. Sorry, I know this is a weird message, but I don't know what I can say in a voice mail. You're going to need to teach me some covert words or something. Anyway, I'll call you as soon as I can. And...well, I love you, in case you didn't know it. See you soon.

Liam took off running to his car. Ferante was dead and Aubrey was going back to LA unprotected? No way in hell this was a coincidence.

CHAPTER THIRTY-SEVEN

LAX
Los Angeles, California

The two-hour-and-twenty-minute flight from Missoula to LA had given Aubrey plenty of time to think. By the time she arrived at the airport, she was sure she had made one of the biggest mistakes of her life. What if this was all a ruse to get her out in the open?

Her rational mind told her she was being ridiculous. Ferante's death had absolutely nothing to do with Becca being fired from the film. The man was dead, so there would be no threat from him anymore. It was just one of those odd coincidences that happened from time to time. She was silly for even imagining the two were related.

The more intuitive part of her brain told her to beware. The fine hairs on the nape of her neck added to her concern. Paranoia wasn't altogether a bad thing. Not when it came to staying alive. It was something she'd gotten used to, but somehow with Liam, she'd let her guard down. She had been safe and secure and felt no danger. That feeling had disappeared.

If she'd had more time to think about things, perhaps she wouldn't have rushed to LA. That couldn't be helped now. The plane was landing, and she was here whether she should be or not.

Becca was to meet her in baggage claim, and as the plane was barely five minutes late, she was likely already there waiting.

Grabbing her carry-on from the overhead compartment, Aubrey followed the rest of the passengers off the plane and into the airport. She gave herself a stern lecture as she made her way to baggage claim. She was surrounded by hundreds of people. No one was going to try anything here. And why would they? Ferante had been the only threat. He had known she would expose him, so he had threatened her. Now that he was out of the picture, she was safe.

But why didn't she feel safe?

She spotted Becca standing in the middle of baggage claim. Even though people passed by her, she seemed to be in another world, her expression dulled by sorrow. She looked lost and forsaken. Aubrey's heart broke for her. Her cousin had worked hard for this chance. Being the daughter of a famous director could only take you so far. To advance further and get the big, life-changing roles, talent and hard work were the most important components. Becca was a gifted actress, dedicated to her craft. Why on earth had she been fired from a part that seemed tailor-made for her?

"Becca!" Aubrey called out.

Startled, Becca lifted her head and gave her a brilliant smile. She ran toward Aubrey, and the closer she got, the more fragile the smile became. By the time she was hugging Aubrey, the smile was completely gone, and tears were streaming down her face.

"Oh Becca, don't cry, sweetie. We'll figure this out, I promise."

"I know…I know," she sobbed. "I just wish I knew what I did wrong. No one will tell me anything. It's like it's some big secret. But it shouldn't be if it involves me. I should be told why."

"Did you talk to someone else?"

Becca pulled away, wiped her eyes and delicately blew her nose with a tissue. "No…not really. I tried to discuss it with Jensen, but he blew me off. Apparently since I'm no longer the star of the movie, he doesn't want to have anything to do with me."

Aubrey swallowed a groan. No only had her cousin been fired from her dream role, Jensen Riggs, an up-and-coming actor and Becca's co-star in the movie, had broken up with her. Even though they'd only had a few dates, and getting her heart bruised was nothing new for Becca, coming on the same day she was fired from her dream role would be a bit much for anyone.

"I knew it wouldn't last," Becca was saying. "We'd only been out a few times, and he wasn't all that much fun to be around, but to have him treat me like I wasn't important to him anymore because I'd lost the role…" She shook her head, and the tears increased to a steady flow. "It was just too much."

"I know. But don't you worry. We'll get this straightened out, and you can tell Jensen Riggs to get lost when he comes crawling back to you. Which he will."

"My career is over, Aubrey. I just know it is."

Aubrey snorted. "When pigs fly."

Her cousin didn't laugh as she'd hoped. The despair in her eyes broke Aubrey's heart. Ignoring the people milling around them, she held Becca's shoulders firmly and said,

"Listen to me. Remember when we were five years old? Remember the promise we made to each other?"

Sniffling, Becca nodded. "We promised we'd never lie to each other."

"Exactly. So believe me when I tell you this. You are one of the most gifted actors I've ever known. There is no way your career is over. This is just a little bump in the road, nothing more." Aubrey shook her slightly. "I promise you, Becca."

"You really believe that, don't you?"

"With all my heart."

Smiling once again, she linked arms with Aubrey. "Thank you for coming. You always make me feel so much better." She turned to the exit. "Come on. I managed to park out front, but if I don't move soon, I'll get a ticket."

The minute they stepped outside, Aubrey had that uneasy feeling again. Unable to explain the oddity to Becca, who knew nothing about the issues she'd been dealing with, Aubrey did her best to act normal as she carefully examined their surroundings. There were dozens of people around. Families hauled their luggage into vans, business people stood in line, waiting for cabs, couples stood around chatting. No one looked the least bit interested in them.

She settled into the passenger seat of the Audi Q5 and buckled up. As Becca slowly steered out of the parking space and into the stream of traffic, Aubrey continued to keep her eyes out for any hint of a threat.

Just as Becca turned onto Century Boulevard, Aubrey's phone rang. She glanced at the readout and felt a wave of calm wash over her. Liam might be thousands of miles away, but just knowing she was about to talk to him lessened her stress level.

"Hey," she said softly.

"Aubrey, where are you?"

The tension in his voice told her what she had suspected. This could be a trap.

"I'm in LA. Becca just picked me up at the airport." And then, before he could tell her himself, she said softly, "I screwed up, didn't I?"

"I don't know. What I do know is I don't want you to take any chances. Tell Becca to drive to the nearest police station. I can be there in a few hours."

"Okay. I—"

"The man that's been watching over Becca just texted me. He's about five cars behind you. He's going to follow you to the police station."

Relieved to know they weren't completely alone, she said, "Thank you, Liam. I'll tell—"

A black SUV cut in front of the Audi. Becca managed to avoid rear-ending it. Traffic was heavy, as usual, and aggressive drivers were the norm, but that had been a little too close for comfort.

"What's that guy's problem?" Becca muttered.

Her heart beating faster, Aubrey kept an eye on the vehicle as she said softly to Liam, "Hold on."

"What's going on?"

"An SUV almost drove us off the road. It's dark so I can't see what kind of—"

"Find a police station," Liam barked. "Now!"

"Okay. Okay." She glanced at her cousin. "Becca, I know this is going to sound weird, but we need to—"

She didn't get to finish her sentence. The SUV came back over into their lane. Becca jerked the steering wheel to the left. The SUV rammed into the side of the Audi. Becca screamed as their car left the road and flew over the railing. Airborne, Aubrey saw tops of trees and flashing lights in a massive whirl of colors and sounds. She heard Liam's voice in her ear but couldn't comprehend the words.

Metal scraped and squealed against metal, bent and broke. The world went upside down and then ended on an earth-shattering thud as tortured, mangled steel landed with a hard, definitive crash.

She heard herself scream Liam's name and then knew nothing more.

CHAPTER THIRTY-EIGHT

Ronald Reagan UCLA Medical Center
Los Angeles, California

Pulling into the hospital parking lot, Liam slid into a visitors spot, and for the first time since the crash, took a moment to himself. For twelve hours, he had done nothing but concentrate on getting to Aubrey. He had bribed, coerced, threatened, and shouted until he'd figured someone at some point was going to lock him up. Thankfully, Ash and OZ came through for him.

The call to Aubrey had gone dead seconds after the wreck. He had pictured every terrifying frame in his head. They'd been run off the road, hit a guardrail, and then plummeted into a ravine.

Getting a private jet readied and able to fly straight to Los Angeles from Bogota should have been impossible. And though he'd had to wait over an hour for the plane to arrive and be readied, he'd been in the air much sooner than should have been possible. Miracles were like that, and since meeting Aubrey, he realized they happened much more frequently than he'd ever recognized.

On the flight, he'd learned multiple things. Becca had been life-flighted, her injuries serious and life-threatening. Aubrey's were comparatively minor, and she had been transported by ambulance to the same hospital.

When she'd arrived at the hospital, he'd been able to talk with her briefly. A doctor was checking her over, and though she was in shock and had said only a few words to reassure him she was fine, she was gloriously alive, and that had been an answered prayer.

Becca, however, hadn't been as lucky. She had multiple fractures, head trauma, and severe blood loss. They'd been able to stabilize her, but her condition was critical.

After talking with Aubrey, reassuring her he was on the way, and telling her to stay with the bodyguard, he'd called Malcolm Pitts, the man who had been assigned to watch over Becca. Giving the man a piece of his mind had done nothing for the situation. Pitts hadn't offered much more information than Liam already knew. A dark colored SUV had slammed into Becca's Audi, running her off the road. It hadn't stopped, and no one had been able to get a license plate number or description of the driver.

It was a dead end for now.

After talking to Pitts, he'd put in a call to Serena. Though she was in Germany with the team, she had been able to give him a brief update, which had been both frustrating and eye-opening.

"I still don't have a lot, Liam. I saw nothing in Aubrey's parents' background that looks the least bit shady. Her dad, Matthew Starr, was a well-respected English professor at a local community college. Her mom was a high school biology teacher. Their standard of living was commensurate with their income. No arrests, not even a parking ticket. Aubrey was a typical only child. A little spoiled but basically a good kid. She got good grades, was never in trouble. She was on the swim team and was the star of several school plays."

As much as he wanted to know these things about the woman he loved, they weren't pertinent. On top of that, he had some massive guilt for having her family investigated without telling her what he was doing. It had made sense at the time, but maybe all of this could have been prevented if he'd told her what he suspected. Serena's next words had confirmed his fears.

"Her uncle, on the other hand, there's something off about him."

She hadn't had much, but it was enough to prompt a deeper dive, and it gave Liam something to focus on during the long flight to LA.

Syd Green would be arriving in LA soon. He'd been informed he would receive a police escort from the airport, having been told it was a courtesy because of his celebrity status. Whether Syd believed that was the truth, Liam didn't care. He had only two priorities right now. Making sure Aubrey stayed safe and having a very candid talk with her uncle Syd.

Exiting his vehicle, Liam stayed aware of his surroundings. No one should know he had any connection to Aubrey, but he was discounting nothing at this point. It was obvious that this was bigger than just Ferante and his sick perversions. How far it went and who was involved, he didn't yet know. But he would keep digging.

Twelve years ago, Aubrey had been targeted. Not a chance abduction, but a well-planned, well-coordinated event. But why? He was going to find out.

The elevator rang, announcing the third floor ICU unit, and the door slid open. Aubrey was there, looking both devastated and heartbroken. She had a bruise on her chin, a small bandage on her forehead, and her right wrist was wrapped in gauze. Her eyes were red from crying and filled with tears the moment their gazes met. He stepped out of the elevator, and she was in his arms in an instant.

"Thank God you're here," she whispered against his chest.

Liam closed his eyes as the magnitude of his feelings for this woman overwhelmed him. He had loved her from that first moment in a dark, damp prison cell. He would love her forever.

Pressing a kiss to her head, he asked, "How's Becca?"

She shook her head and let loose a sobbing sigh. "I think she's just holding on till Uncle Syd gets here."

"Come on. Let's go sit down."

He gave a nod of dismissal to Malcolm Pitts who'd been standing a few feet from Aubrey. Thankfully the man didn't seem to want to stay around and offer more excuses. Liam was in no mood to hear them. He waited until Pitts had disappeared before leading her to a private corner of the waiting room.

As soon as they were seated, Liam said quietly, "Tell me."

"I messed up so badly, Liam. It's my fault. All of it. If I had taken the time to think, I never would have come here. On the same day Ferante is killed, Becca gets fired. Whoever's responsible knew she would call me, and I would come running. I put her in danger."

She was in no way responsible, but telling her that would sound like platitudes and empty words. Once her uncle arrived, they would get to the truth. Until then, he would steer around the responsibility factor and get the facts.

"When did you know you were being followed?"

"I didn't. I was on alert, though. The two-hour plane trip gave me time to think. By the time we landed, I knew I'd made a mistake."

"Did you say anything to Becca?"

"No. Maybe I should have. She was just so upset. She'd gotten fired, and then the guy she'd been dating dumped her. I didn't know how to tell her that all of it might have been just a ruse to get me out in the open."

"Telling her wouldn't have prevented anything. No one could have predicted this."

"I just don't understand. I didn't have anything concrete on Ferante. Not really. And now that he's dead, the threat against me should be gone. Shouldn't it?"

He didn't understand all of it either, but now wasn't the time to tell her that her uncle was knee-deep in some kind of coverup. He needed something concrete before completely destroying the image she had of the man she'd loved and trusted all her life.

"Tell me about the accident."

"We were on Century Boulevard. It was raining, just a steady drizzle, but enough to make the streets shiny and visibility a little difficult. Becca wasn't driving fast. Everything seemed normal. She was in the middle lane, and this dark SUV veered into our lane. I couldn't tell much about it. It was dark and rainy, making it hard to see.

"Becca managed to avoid him...I think she blew her horn. She just thought he was a reckless driver, I guess. Anyway, it veered over again, but this time he hit the front fender of Becca's car. She lost control and hit a guardrail. I think the car rolled a couple of times before it landed at the bottom of a big ditch.

"I don't remember much after that. When I woke up, I heard Becca moaning. I somehow ended up in the backseat. I managed to climb over and Becca..." She swallowed hard twice before she continued, her voice thick with emotion. "She was upside down. I couldn't see her face. She was saying something."

"What was she saying?"

"She said Jensen."

"Who's Jensen?"

"The guy she's been seeing. The one who broke up with her." Tears filled her eyes. "He must have meant more to her than I realized."

"Aubrey?"

Liam turned to see a disheveled-looking middle-aged man striding toward them. If he hadn't expected Syd Green to show up, he wouldn't have recognized the man. The few times Liam had seen him on television and in photos, Syd Green had looked both elegant and supremely confident. This wild-eyed man with mussed hair and a ravaged expression bore no resemblance to the famed director.

"Uncle Syd!" Aubrey jumped from her chair and ran into her uncle's arms. "I'm so sorry."

They held each other, and while he was one hundred percent sure that Syd Green was involved in whatever this shit was, there was no doubt in Liam's mind that the man was grieving.

After several moments, Green backed away and asked thickly, "Where is she?"

"In ICU. They asked me to step out for a few minutes. They said they'll let me know when I can go back in." She glanced behind her and said, "This is Liam Stryker."

Liam met Green's eyes, and while there was no indication the man knew about his suspicions, his gaze went guarded and wary.

Before either man could speak, a nurse appeared in front of them. "Are you Becca Green's father?" she asked.

"Yes," Green said huskily.

"You'll want to go in now."

The urgency in her tone, along with her words, left no one in doubt that time was running out on Becca's life.

Green quickly followed the nurse while Aubrey turned in to Liam's arms with an agonized sob.

CHAPTER THIRTY-NINE

They sat in the Bereavement Room, which was basically a small alcove off of the rest of the ICU waiting room. Aubrey's entire body ached with grief. Every single molecule felt the pain of loss. Becca, her best friend since they were barely able to walk, was gone. She hadn't woken from her coma, and though the nurses assured them she knew her loved ones were there, Aubrey didn't believe it. Becca had been gone only moments after the wreck, her body just hadn't known it.

Her uncle had been stoic up until she took her last breath, and then he had lost it. They had held each other, comforting one another in their shared grief.

How was she going to tell her uncle that it was all her fault? How could she explain that if she had never come back to LA, Becca would still be alive? She had put a target on Becca and would have to live with the horror of knowing she'd caused her death.

"Here, drink this."

She opened her swollen eyes to see a large hand holding a cup of steaming tea in front of her. The hand belonged to

Liam. How could she have gotten through the last hour without him? He was her rock.

Taking the tea, she whispered her thanks and then took a sip. Sugar exploded on her tongue.

"I know it's sweet, but it's good for shock. Just sip slowly."

Nodding, she did what she was told. She couldn't think past the next second. She should probably be doing something, helping her uncle with the arrangements, calling her mother. Yes, she needed to call her mother.

"I need to call my mom and let her know."

"Would you like me to do it?"

She looked at him then, really looked at him. Unshaven, slightly scruffy, and absolutely beautiful. His bloodshot eyes were filled with sadness, but she also detected a simmering anger. She was angry, too. Somewhere deep inside her, a burning, bubbling anger was brewing. The sadness and grief were weighing it down, but it would soon erupt and spew.

"Thank you, but I can do it." She glanced around. "There's really not a lot of privacy here, is there?"

"Come on, we'll find you a place."

And he did. While her muddled brain worked on getting her phone out of her purse and then trying to remember what time it was in Florence, Italy, Liam found her an empty hospital room.

"Take your time. I'll be right outside."

She entered the stark, sterile room, and the door closed behind her. It was the first real privacy she'd had since the accident, and as much as she wanted this moment to sit down and sob, she couldn't. She had responsibilities, duties. Her uncle was depending on her. She had betrayed him in the worst way possible. The least she could do was take care of this and whatever else he needed from her.

She pressed the call icon for her mother.

·　·　·

LIAM STOOD OUTSIDE THE DOOR. Hearing the sobs inside, he wanted to go in and comfort her but knew she needed this time. As he waited, he kept a watchful eye on the door Syd Green was behind. He was signing papers, making arrangements. When he was done, there would be a conversation.

Verbally attacking a grieving father on the worst moment of his life didn't sit well with him. The soul-wrenching grief was real. He believed Syd Green genuinely loved his daughter and had not planned for this to happen to her. But that didn't mean he hadn't planned for it to happen to Aubrey. She'd been the target, Becca had simply gotten in the way.

It could have been Aubrey. The thought kept whirling in his mind. If the killer had gotten his intended target, Aubrey would be in that hospital room with a sheet covering her mangled body. A part of him wanted to drop to his knees in thanksgiving that she'd been spared. The other part wanted vengeance.

A door opened, and Syd Green shuffled out. His expression was the living definition of defeat and despair. While Liam's conscience told him how wrong it was to go after a broken man, his rational brain reminded him that you struck when your opponent was the most vulnerable.

"Do you know who did this?" Liam asked.

"What?" Green looked more confused than guilty. "They haven't found the vehicle that hit them. Witnesses said it was a dark SUV, just like Aubrey described. That's all they have to go on."

"But you know, don't you, Green?"

"Why would you think I know?"

Liam stared at him then, his eyes knowing, accusing.

Acknowledgment and then something like fear swept over his face. "What do you know about any of this?"

"Enough to know that Aubrey was the intended target.

That she got on the wrong side of some very bad people and they want her dead. And I know you're in neck-deep with them."

"That's not true. I only know…" He shook his head and his eyes filled with tears. "They've taken everything from me. Everything."

"Then they need to be exposed."

Liam saw a change wash over Green, a resolve. His spine went straight, shoulders no longer slumped, and a glint appeared in his eyes.

"You're right, they do. But who are you? For all I know, you're one of them."

"If I was one of them, Aubrey would be dead, wouldn't she?"

He saw the knowledge in his eyes before he nodded. All sympathy ceased to exist. This man had known that his niece was in danger, that powerful people wanted her dead, and he had done nothing to warn or protect her.

"You bastard."

"You don't understand. I couldn't stop them—I don't even know who to trust."

"You know enough to let Aubrey know that she's in danger, and yet you did nothing." He was in front of the man before Green could move, inches from his face. "You're going to tell me everything, and I mean everything."

"You can't stop them. Nobody can stop them. They're too big. They're everywhere."

"We'll see about that. I—"

"What's going on?"

Aubrey's alarmed voice stopped him cold. Turning, he faced her. His desire to protect her from the truth had almost gotten her killed. Even though he knew he was going to break her heart all over again, he couldn't keep this from her.

"Your uncle has some things he needs to confess."

"What? What's he talking about, Uncle Syd?"

"It's complicated, Aubrey," her uncle began.

"Let's go back into the room and uncomplicate it, shall we?" Pushing Aubrey gently forward, he sent Green a hard look of warning.

Green followed them into the room, and Liam shut the door. "All right, Green. Talk."

"Liam, wait. What's this about?"

Taking her hand, he sat on the edge of the bed and pulled her down beside him. "Your uncle knows who did this."

Her eyes wide, she jerked her gaze up to her uncle. "What? How do you know? What's going on?"

"It's…" Green shoved his fingers through his already wild hair. "I'll have to start from the beginning."

He stared at the wall for several seconds. Liam couldn't tell if he was working on a convincing lie or just gearing himself up to unload what he had been living with.

With a loud, shaky sigh, Green began, "When I was seven, my parents' lives changed drastically. We'd never had a lot of money, but one day it was like Christmas morning. We moved to a nicer house, we had better food and clothing… everything was better. It wasn't until I began second grade that I realized how different things really were. I was sent to a private school, which wasn't anything like where I went for first grade. And while I learned normal things, I also learned about obedience to the cause."

"And what cause was that?" Liam asked.

"I don't know."

"Don't give me that bullshit."

"It's the truth. That's the beauty of the whole thing. Don't you get it? The right hand doesn't know who's controlling the left hand. There are hundreds, perhaps thousands, of us out there. We live our lives, but we know at some point we'll be called on to do certain things."

"You don't obey a cause without knowing who or why."

"Maybe you don't, but I did. I was just a kid. It wasn't until later that I saw their power, what they were capable of. I learned that I could have a successful career and a normal life, but when I was asked to do something, I had to obey or else."

"What things were you asked to do?"

"Mostly innocuous things, harming no one. I steered people toward certain projects and away from others. I hired certain people. I added scenes to movies to soften the stance on various issues or removed them if they were deemed too negative.

"None of those things was difficult. I became famous. I had a good life, with a wonderful family. I was content. Too content. I became complacent, believing that nothing more would be asked of me."

"And then something changed?"

"Yes. They asked me to do something I didn't want to do, and I refused."

"What did they ask?"

"They wanted my daughter."

"What did they want with Becca?"

It was the first time Aubrey had spoken since Green had begun his story. Liam winced at her hoarse, ravaged voice. She sounded so much like the lost young woman he'd met twelve years ago.

"They wanted to bring her into the organization so they could control her the way they controlled me. They asked me to recruit her. I said no."

"What happened?"

Green's gaze met Aubrey's. "It was twelve years ago."

And the mystery of Aubrey's abduction in Paris was becoming clear. "They were supposed to abduct Becca, but they took Aubrey instead?"

"No. They were going to take both. When I learned of it, I thought I could stop it." He returned his gaze to his niece, his expression one of sorrow and guilt. "I knew I couldn't explain why I didn't want you two to go to Paris, so I gave Becca something to make her ill."

"You gave Becca a cold?"

"It was a small virus, nothing serious, but it made her sick enough to keep her at home. I assumed you wouldn't go without her. I didn't know until after you were taken that you went to Paris alone."

"That's why I could never find any information on her abduction," Liam said grimly. "There were no police records. No FBI or State Department files. The authorities were never notified of her abduction, were they?"

"No. It was handled...internally."

"But I talked to people from the State Department and the FBI," Aubrey said. "My parents talked to them. They were kind, supportive. They told me about the prison being destroyed."

"They were actors I hired. I gave them some talking points. Their biggest assignment was to ease everyone's minds. I knew Matthew and Elizabeth wouldn't let go until they were sure everything had been done that could be done. It was an elaborate scheme, but I had no choice in the matter. If I had told anyone what really happened, it would have put my family in even more danger."

"So they were going to sell both of us into human trafficking? Becca and me?"

"No. I believe it was a scare tactic—to get me to comply. But when they realized Becca wasn't with you, they were going to cut you loose and let those men..." He swallowed hard, and then continued, "I convinced them I would recruit Becca if they returned you. They agreed. I paid a ransom, but they were still angry."

"That's why that…that man said they were to send me home with a message," Aubrey whispered. "Those stab wounds were a message to you."

"Yes, I'm afraid so. I'm so sorry."

Aubrey shook her head. Liam could only imagine the pain and betrayal she was feeling. In the span of a few hours, her entire world had fallen apart. Again.

"I thought you were such a hero," she whispered. "For paying my ransom. Handling things with the authorities. But you were a traitor…to me, to my parents. To Becca."

"I tried to make it right. Once I paid the ransom and you came home, I hoped it was over. I hoped they would reconsider." He closed his eyes and a lone tear rolled down his pale, lined face. "But of course they wouldn't. They still wanted my compliance—still wanted Becca. I refused again. So they—"

"They what?"

"They punished me."

"How?" Liam asked.

"They took my wife away instead."

"Aunt Jenny?" Aubrey whispered.

"Yes."

"What…what did they do?"

"Gave her some kind of drug that caused a massive stroke. I didn't know about it until the police came to my office and told me. By the time I got to the hospital, the damage was done."

Aubrey sprang to her feet. "Excuse me." Covering her mouth, she ran toward the bathroom.

Liam gave Green a hard look. "Stay put." Striding to the bathroom, he held Aubrey's hair and rubbed her back as she vomited and gagged.

When she stopped and leaned against him, he asked, "Better?"

"No, not really." She glanced up at him through the hair that had fallen in her face. "Is this really happening?"

He brushed the hair from her face. "I'm afraid so, sweetheart. I'm sorry."

"What do we do now? They're not going to stop."

"We're going to find out who these bastards are and stop them."

She nodded wearily. "Better go check on Syd. I need a few minutes alone."

He dropped a kiss on top of her head. "I'll be right outside if you need me."

Liam returned to the room, relieved to see Green still there. Going after him and hauling him back inside would've been a pain. The man didn't look as though he had the energy or the will to do anything more. He was sitting in a chair, sipping from a cup as if he barely had enough life in him to lift it to his mouth.

"One of the nurses brought tea. It might help Aubrey to drink some, too."

The only thing that would to help Aubrey was if her uncle weren't such a lowlife. Because he'd made a deal with the devil, his entire family had been destroyed.

Something hammered at his brain and he wanted to address it before Aubrey returned. "Who were they?"

"I've already told you. I don't know. Why won't—"

"I'm not talking about this organization or entity or whatever you call it. I'm talking about the men who abducted Aubrey. The men who beat and terrorized her. I want the name of the bastard who raped her, stabbed her. He's British. You know who he is."

Green blew out an explosive sigh. "He's dead. They're all dead."

"How do you know?"

"Because I made sure of it. Think what you want about

me Stryker, but I never intended anything like that to happen to Aubrey. When I found out what they'd done to her, I arranged for the monsters to be dealt with."

"How did you find them?"

"I traced the money. They never left Syria. They were dead within days of Aubrey's return."

Liam tried to be glad about that, to be at peace that the promise he'd made to himself—finding and punishing Aubrey's attackers—had been done already. Didn't diminish the fury. He had wanted to be the one to make them pay. But he did console himself with one thing. They hadn't been alive these last twelve years. That would have to be enough.

Green took another sip of tea, then looked up at him. "You knew this was about me all along. How?"

"Not at first. And I didn't know much. When Aubrey told me what her abductors said about sending her home with a message, I knew it likely had something to do with her family. Her parents were squeaky clean. You, not so much."

Green's smile was sad. "The gambling debts."

"You owe a lot of people a lot of money, including Marc Antony Ferante."

"He was one of their pawns, too."

"Did you hire someone to kill Ferante?"

"No. I imagine that was the organization meting out their own brand of justice. They don't tolerate disobedience very well."

"What about Lawrence Medford? Did you arrange for his death?"

"No. That was Ferante. I just…"

"You what?"

"I persuaded him that if Aubrey's funds for her project were taken away, she wouldn't be able to continue with the documentary. He knew she had something on him that might expose him. He agreed, for a price, to take out Medford and leave Aubrey alone."

Liam could barely get his brain around all the lies and conspiracies. Did any of these people even have a conscience?

"What did Ferante do for the organization?"

"Blackmail is one of the ways they keep people in line. Ferante was a master at gathering secrets. Whenever someone was stubborn about following their orders, they'd often call Ferante for help. He provided them intel to coerce their obedience."

"He apparently wasn't too valuable to eliminate."

"None of us are. We're all expendable. They've eliminated many. Others just take their place."

"Who have they eliminated?"

When he began to name names, Liam pulled out his phone and recorded them. He recognized a few, mostly prominent and wealthy people. One name that caught his attention was Nora Turner.

"The senator from Ohio?"

"Yes. You knew her?"

Everyone at OZ knew Nora Turner. She had almost destroyed Ash, multiple times.

"Her death was ruled a suicide. I saw the coroner's report myself."

"Yes. And the explosion on Ferante's yacht will be blamed on faulty wiring or a gas leak. It happens all the time."

A knock on the outside door told him their time was up. The nurse who'd lent them the room stuck her head inside. "Sorry to disturb you, but we need this room."

"Not a problem," Liam said. "Thanks for letting us use it."

Aubrey stepped out of the bathroom. Though she was still ghostly pale, making the bruise on her chin even darker, her eyes were clear and determined.

"Where to now?" she asked.

"There's a safe house about an hour outside LA. We'll head there for more debriefing. My SUV is parked to the left of the hospital's entrance. I'll bring it around."

He had expected at least some semblance of an argument from Green but apparently the man was too defeated to fight anymore.

"Let's go."

No one spoke as they walked out of the room and into the elevator. He did notice that Aubrey sent a tortured look toward the room where Becca had died. Grief surrounded her like an invisible barrier. At some point, the anger would penetrate. When it did, he wanted her as far from danger as possible.

They reached the exit, and Liam said, "Stay here. I'll be right back. You see any kind of threat, scream as loud as you can."

He walked out onto the drive and evaluated. The parking lot was filled with cars, but he saw only a few people. To the left of him, about ten yards away, a couple got into their car. To his right, a man and woman with two toddlers entered their vehicle. Straight ahead, an elderly man shuffled toward his car. Nothing was out of place, everything seemed calm.

Clicking the key fob to unlock the door, he strode to the SUV, jumped inside, and started the engine. He was driving toward the building when he saw Green walking alone in the parking lot.

Sliding his window down, he shouted, "Green, where are you going? Get in here! It's not safe!"

As if he hadn't heard him, Green continued to stride through the parking lot. He didn't appear to have a specific destination or purpose. His steps were slow and awkward, almost shuffling.

From the doorway of the hospital, Aubrey shouted, "Uncle Syd!"

"Aubrey!" Liam yelled. "Get back inside. I'll get your uncle."

He shoved the SUV into park, jumped out, and ran toward the man. "Green, what the hell are you doing? Where do you think you're going?"

Finally acknowledging him, Green stopped suddenly and glared at Liam. "I have nothing else to tell you. I've given you all I know."

"All right, fine. But you need protection. You think they're going to let you live?"

"Do you think I care?" Looking up at the sky, he raised his hands, and walking in circles, shouted, "Come and get me, you bastards! I'm ready! You've taken everything from me! I have nothing left."

"Uncle Syd, please!"

Liam turned to see Aubrey running toward them. "Get in the car," Liam snapped. "I'll take care of your uncle." Turning back, he growled, "Green, get in the car!"

"No!" Looking back up at the sky, he shouted again, "They can't hurt me anymore!"

Liam took a running leap, preparing to tackle the man. One way or the other, he was getting inside the car. He stopped short when an expression of horror crossed Green's face. He clutched his chest, and Liam caught him before he could drop to the ground.

"No! Uncle Syd!" Leaving the safety of the SUV, Aubrey ran to her uncle, falling to her knees beside him.

Liam gently laid Green on the pavement. He was gasping for breath, his entire body twitching and writhing, his face deathly pale.

"Go get some help, Liam. I'll stay with him."

"I'm not leaving you alone." He looked around and saw a couple standing a few feet away. "Get a doctor out here!"

They nodded and ran inside the hospital. Less than a minute later, two people in hospital garb ran toward them.

Aubrey was leaning over her uncle, urging him to stay alive. When help arrived, Liam pulled her away to allow them to attend him.

Aware that she was in danger, but knowing there was no way she would leave her uncle, Liam stayed as close to her as possible. His eyes continually roamed the parking lot, looking for a threat.

For several long moments, they watched as CPR was performed. Liam already knew it was a hopeless cause, but he had to give the medical people credit. They worked tirelessly to try to save him. It was no use. When a nurse stood and looked over at them, he knew the words before she said them.

"I'm sorry. There's nothing more we can do."

CHAPTER FORTY

Three Days Later
OZ Headquarters
Montana

"Looks like we have more questions than answers." Liam's eyes roamed the room, taking in the perplexed expressions of his fellow operatives. Returning his gaze to Jazz, who'd made the statement, he nodded. "That about sums it up."

"Who are these people?" Gideon asked. "And how many are out there?"

"According to Green, more than we can fathom."

"Perhaps so," Ash said, "but I don't think it's as dire or as hopeless as it looks."

"How's that?" Gideon asked.

"Green was a pawn. As was Ferante. Looks like Senator Nora Turner was, too. Their relationship with this entity or organization was the ultimate quid pro quo. For status, wealth, and even the price of staying alive, keeping their families safe, they did certain things to aid this group."

"That's a good thing, how?" Xavier asked.

"We focus on finding who is in control. Once they're exposed, the others will lose their power."

"Cut off the head of the snake," Eve said.

"Exactly."

"Okay, but how are we going to find the snake head?" Xavier asked. "Everyone we know who was involved is dead."

"We start from the beginning," Liam said. He hadn't slept much in the last few days, trying to come up with an answer. "Go through every name Green gave me. Find connections. There have to be some. We work it until we find the one thing that connects them all."

"I've already been looking into this school that Green claimed he attended," Serena said. "His bio only reveals what university he went to, which was UCLA. There's nothing about his formative education. Looks like a lot of his early years have been erased. It's got to be somewhere, though." She shrugged. "We'll dig until we find something."

"And in the meantime, how much danger is Aubrey in?" Jazz asked.

The other thing that had kept him from sleeping. "I don't know. The only players she knew about—Ferante and her uncle—are dead."

"Is she still going ahead with her documentary?"

Since that was one of the many items they'd yet to talk about, he just shook his head. "Hard to say."

"How's she doing?" Sean asked. "Sorry I couldn't be there to help at the memorial. Serena said she looked like death." He winced and added, "Sorry. Poor choice of words."

He couldn't argue with the assessment. The light had gone from her eyes, and he feared he'd never see it again. Her entire world had been upended. She had barely talked to him since their return from LA. It was like she'd gone inside herself to hide.

"Becca was like a sister to her; her uncle a second father. Having him die in front of her, on top of all the things she just learned from him, that he had something to do with her abduction, and all the abuse she endured…" He shrugged. "That's a lot to deal with in one lifetime. She got all this in the span of an hour."

"Just one of those things would destroy many people," Jules said. "But your Aubrey is made of sterner stuff. The ordeal she survived in Syria might've broken a weaker person. She just needs time."

"I can't believe her mother didn't even come to the memorial," Serena said.

He couldn't either. Though he'd yet to meet her, he wasn't much of a fan of Elizabeth Starr. She had left it up to her daughter to take care of all the arrangements for the double memorial, saying she wanted to remember Becca and Syd in good times.

And since Aubrey's safety was Liam's primary concern, they'd had their first argument. Having her front and center at a memorial for two well-known celebrities had nightmare written all over it. He wasn't sure which had infuriated her more—the bulletproof vest she'd had to wear beneath her elegant black dress, or having several OZ team members covering her every step.

The paparazzi had been in a frenzy. The tragic story of two deaths, father and daughter, both famous, had caught their imagination and they couldn't get enough. The memorial had been limited to invited guests only, but hundreds of people had parked themselves outside the large cathedral, clamoring for any kind of news or photo op.

As the only family member in attendance, Aubrey had received the brunt of attention. That attention was the last thing he'd wanted for her, but he couldn't ask her not to attend. Not that it would have done any good. He was learning that Aubrey Starr was an independent, very stubborn woman. And as he loved that independent, stubborn woman with every fiber of his being, he'd been determined that she stay safe.

Having protection twenty-four seven, giving her almost no privacy, had been smothering. Though she had handled herself with grace and dignity, he knew she'd been hanging by a thread.

They'd all flown back to Montana together on the OZ plane. She had sat silently in her seat with only minimal interaction with anyone. Other than the empty look she'd given him each time he tried to talk to her, they'd had no communication. He was giving her space and time. She was hurting, and he was hurting for her. He had to believe she would come around. She had to.

"Will Green's cause of death just remain a mystery?" Xavier asked.

And that was one of the most infuriating things that had happened. The heart attack had been too coincidental. Had something been in the tea he'd seen Green drinking? Which nurse had brought it to him? When questioned, no one had admitted to delivering it to him. The paper cup, which could have provided evidence about what might have been in the tea, had mysteriously disappeared from the room.

At his urging, Aubrey had insisted on an autopsy. When Liam had called for the results, he'd learned that paperwork had suddenly appeared, ordering an immediate cremation. The autopsy had been canceled, and Syd Green's body had been cremated, destroying any evidence that could have explained his death.

Liam had lived with the need for secrecy most of his adult life. He understood the need for them. Having been a SEAL, then a covert agent, and now an OZ operative, almost everything he did was undercover and hidden from the world. But at least his secrecy usually resulted in saving lives. From what he could tell, the secrets these people kept revolved around destroying and taking lives.

"Where do we go from here?" Jazz asked.

"We start digging even deeper," Serena answered. "My team is working overtime."

"There's another link that we hadn't considered," Ash said. "Aubrey was taken to the same prison that I was. A prison that somehow Syd Green and Nora Turner apparently knew about, or this organization has some connection to."

"It's like a gigantic spiderweb that's intricately tied together," Eve said.

"True." Ash sent a smile over to Serena. "But we've got one of the best teams for untangling spiderwebs."

"Yes, we do," Serena said. "We'll find them. It's just going to take some time."

Liam checked his phone to ensure he had no messages from Aubrey. He'd been away for several hours. He didn't like being away from her this long. The grief would come out one way or the other. He intended to be there for her when it came.

Standing, he looked around the room. "Thank you guys for being there. Don't know what I'd do without any one of you."

"That's what we're here for, brother," Gideon said.

"Unless something comes up," Ash said, "Liam's going to take a few days off."

"Give Aubrey a hug for me," Jazz said.

"Tell her I'll call her soon," Serena added.

"Will do. And thanks again."

He walked out of the conference room and headed to the front door. Eve called his name, stopping his progress.

"What's up?" he asked.

"I know Aubrey's hurting, and you're at a loss on how to make it better for her."

"Yeah…exactly."

"I have some news that might help. That thing we talked about."

"It's done?"

"Yes. They're being shipped to you. Should arrive sometime next week."

Liam grabbed her in a quick hug. "Thank you."

"You're welcome. Just make sure she knows that no matter what, we're here for her. She's one of us."

CHAPTER FORTY-ONE

The blinking cursor mocked her. Her eyes dry, her body numb, Aubrey sat in front of a blank screen and felt just as empty as the file before her. She had nothing left. Writing had always been a panacea, her release and escape. But now she couldn't write a word. Her entire life felt like a lie. How could she write about truth when she didn't even know what it was anymore?

Losing Becca hurt more than she could have fathomed. As children, they'd played with each other every day. And even when her parents had moved from California to Connecticut, they'd talked almost daily on the phone. Their holidays and school breaks had been spent in each other's homes. She had told Becca about her first kiss and had consoled Becca each time a boyfriend had broken her heart.

The last few years, they'd seen less of each other because of their careers, but they had still talked several times a week. And now her sweet, precious cousin was gone and it was all so senseless.

And Uncle Syd.

Unable to stare at the blank screen any longer, Aubrey

stood and began to pace. She always did her best thinking this way. However, she doubted a hundred miles of pacing would help her to understand why her uncle had done what he'd done.

The man she'd believed was one of the kindest, most generous people in the world had been a fraud and a murderer. Aunt Jenny's death had been nothing less than murder. Her uncle might not have initiated it, but he had done nothing to prevent it, nor had he gone to the authorities with what he had known.

Lawrence Medford's death was on him, too. It didn't matter that he had diverted Ferante's attention to keep her safe. A man was dead all the same.

The fact that he had been indirectly responsible for her abduction was another mind-blowing, nauseating truth. She had thought him such a hero for paying her ransom. When he'd made sure there had been no media exposure, she had been in awe of his influence and thought he was so very kind. His protection of her privacy had helped ease the trauma she'd endured.

Instead, he had paid actors to make her and her parents believe his lies.

She had a thousand questions she wanted to ask him and a million tears she wanted to shed. She could do neither. Syd was dead, and her questions might never be answered. The tears had dried up, too. Not since Becca's death had she been able to cry.

Liam was most likely disgusted with her. While he was so incredibly supportive and brave, she was like a frozen lump on a log. She couldn't talk to him. No matter how loving and tender he was, the words simply would not come. Since they'd returned home, she had stayed in the guest room. Not because she didn't want to be with him. It was as if she had nothing left inside her. She was a shell of a person.

The entire OZ team had been amazingly supportive. Liam had told her they were her family now, and while she very much appreciated that sentiment, she still felt alone.

Even her mother had abandoned her, although she couldn't say she was all that surprised. She and her mother had lost their connection after her father passed away. Tragedy either brought people closer together or tore them apart. In this case, it had definitely been the latter.

Though it hurt at the time, not having her mother attend the memorial was really a blessing in disguise. Acting normal would have been impossible, and there was no way she could tell her mother all the things she had learned. Telling her that Aunt Jenny had been murdered was impossible. Elizabeth Starr had loved her younger sister. There was nothing to gain in letting her know the truth. Especially when the details were so blurred and sketchy. Who, what, and why were as clear as mud.

Wrapping her sweater tighter around her body, Aubrey looked out at the glorious view. It had been snowing most of the day, and the scenery was incredible. How could she see the beauty before her but feel only the ugliness within?

"Aubrey!"

She turned at the sound of Liam's voice. He had left this morning before she'd emerged from her room. The text he'd sent her had simply said he had a meeting at OZ and would be back as soon as possible. It was now late afternoon, and the relief she felt was tangible. She was sick of her own company.

Catching a glimpse of herself in the mirror, she grimaced. No way was she going to meet him looking like something a cat had spit up.

"I'll be down in a minute," she called.

Hurriedly, she combed her hair into some semblance of order, washed her face, and brushed her teeth. She had actually dressed in something besides sweats this morning so when she stepped back and gave herself a once-over in the mirror, she wasn't totally bummed out. Yes, she was still pale and looked like she'd lost her best friend—which she had—but at least she didn't have the appearance of a wraith, as she had the last few days.

She walked out of the bedroom to find Liam heading down the hallway toward her room. "You okay?"

"I'm fine. Just needed to tidy up a bit."

"You had anything to eat?"

Of course she hadn't. Her appetite had been off since the wreck. She couldn't eat, couldn't sleep. This morning she'd gotten dressed and gone straight to her laptop where she'd done absolutely nothing but stare at the thing all day.

"No."

"I brought dinner." He held his hand out. "Let's go."

She got the distinct impression that saying no wouldn't be a good idea. He had a glint in his eyes that she'd learned meant business.

The instant she reached the kitchen door, her nose began to twitch. "Something smells incredible."

"I went to my favorite deli in Missoula. Homemade chicken noodle soup and ham and cheese on croissants."

Suddenly ravenous, Aubrey grabbed bowls and plates from the cabinet while Liam pulled a couple of sodas from the fridge.

Within minutes, they were sitting at the table, consuming what had to be the best meal she'd ever eaten in her life.

"Good?"

She mumbled something incoherent and kept eating. Several moments passed before she finally looked up to see Liam grinning like a loon.

"What?"

"I was about to ask if you wanted the rest of mine."

She laughed, and oh, did it feel good. This man, this wonderful, beautiful, giving man could make her laugh when she'd thought she never would again.

"I don't think I've ever tasted anything this good."

"Aw, that's because you haven't seen what I brought for dessert."

His stretched his arm out and snagged the bag from the counter. Placing it in front of her, he said softly, "Enjoy."

Expecting some sort of spectacular sight, she peered inside the bag at the ugliest cookie she had ever seen. Of all the things she'd thought it could be, a homely cookie hadn't been it.

"What is it?"

"Taste it."

Curious at the mischievous glint in his eyes, she pulled the cookie out and took a small nibble. Myriad tastes, textures, and flavors exploded in her mouth. Humming her approval, she took a bigger bite and then another.

"Oh my gosh," she said with her mouth still full, "what in the world is this?"

"The bakery calls it their miracle cookie."

Miracle was the perfect name for it. She tasted chocolate, coconut, possibly cherry or raspberry, cinnamon, and a couple of other spices she couldn't identify. Combined, they created the most delectable taste she'd ever experienced.

She looked at the empty bag. "Where's your cookie?"

"I just brought one."

"You didn't want one?"

"I wanted you to have a miracle." He gave her a sweet, sexy smile. "I already found mine."

The lump in her throat grew without warning. She swallowed hard and said huskily, "You've been my miracle for twelve years."

He took her hand and kissed it softly. "I've missed you."

CHRISTY REECE

She knew he wasn't talking about being away from her for twelve years, but her absence over the last few days.

"I'm sorry. I—"

"No. You have nothing to apologize for. What you're dealing with is unimaginable. I just want to help in any way I can."

"You are helping. I just—" She paused for a moment. "Have you ever had something hurt you so much that you couldn't even articulate how bad the pain was?"

"Yeah." The look he gave her told her what that pain had been. The day they'd taken her out of that cell, and he'd believed she'd been tortured because of him. Yes, he definitely understood her pain.

Standing, he held out his hand. "Let's go somewhere more comfortable."

He took her to the family room with its deep sofas and retro game machines. Flipping a switch, he turned on the gas logs of the fire, and then they settled onto a sofa.

She put her head on his shoulder and for the first time in days, felt her body relax.

"Ready to talk about it?"

"Not yet," she said. "Soon. Just not yet."

Instead of pressing the issue, he squeezed her gently and said, "Okay."

He settled them deeper into the sofa. "My dad," he began quietly, "was the greatest storyteller I've ever known. This was one of the first stories he told me."

Aubrey listened intently. His dad had passed away when Liam was a young teen and from the few stories he'd shared about him, Aubrey knew he had been his hero.

"A long time ago, there was this family of angry squirrels."

"I didn't know squirrels could get angry."

"Well, most of them are pacifists. You know, gathering nuts, climbing trees, doing squirrely things and living their

304

lives like proper squirrels should. But there are a few, a very few, angry squirrels. And this family. They were the angriest of them all."

Aubrey relished the timbre of his voice, the thud of his heart, the warmth of his body against hers, and felt perfect peace.

LIAM FIGURED she fell asleep around the time the youngest of the angry squirrels met the youngest of the happy squirrel family.

He remembered his dad's story like he'd heard it yesterday. He'd realized years later that the tale was his father and mother's story. His dad's family had been the angry family, bitter and mean. He'd said he figured he would have ended up like the rest of them if he hadn't met Mary Sue Murphy, who had changed his life.

Just as Aubrey had changed his. The day he'd met her, his life had become infinitely more meaningful. And even though it had taken twelve years to find her again, everything in his life had led him to her.

Their problems were far from over. This organization or whatever the hell it was wanted to kill her or stop her from making the documentary. He would fight to his death to keep her alive. And if something happened and he wasn't around, the OZ team would always protect her. It was what families did.

Aubrey thought she'd lost hers, but she had gained a stronger, more powerful one that would do whatever was necessary to keep her safe.

Holding her close, Liam closed his eyes with the comforting knowledge that no matter who or what came after them, she would be safe.

CHAPTER FORTY-TWO

She woke to the most delicious sensation. Liam's mouth was moving softly on her neck, nibbling at hidden erogenous zones she'd had no idea existed.

Moaning softly, she languidly wrapped her arms around his shoulders and pulled him closer. She existed in a sensual twilight state for several more moments, unaware of anything but Liam's warm, hard body lying next to her. She didn't think she'd ever been this relaxed or content. Nothing was real except for this moment in his arms.

Cool air skimmed her body, and she realized that her blouse was halfway off her shoulders. She blinked her heavy lids, trying to discern where she was.

Finally opening her eyes, she realized she was in his bedroom, on his bed.

"How did I get here?" she murmured.

"I brought you here a while ago. You've been asleep for hours."

Sleeping had been almost as difficult as eating the last few days. And now, because of Liam, she had eaten a nutritious meal and had taken the longest nap of her life.

"How do you feel?" he asked.

"Better. Much better. Thank you."

He raised his head and smiled down at her. "My pleasure."

Cupping his jaw, she caressed it softly, relishing the sting of beard stubble against her palm. "What did I do to deserve you?"

"And I was just thinking the same thing."

"Seriously. You're like a dream come to life."

"Ask my sisters when you meet them. They'll tell you I'm more of a nightmare."

"I'll bet they adore you."

"They do now, I guess. They didn't when we were living in the same house."

"Were you overprotective?"

"After my dad was gone, I decided it was my responsibility to be the man of the house and interrogate every guy my sisters brought home."

"Aren't you younger than two of them?"

"Yeah." He grinned as he added, "I learned early to never let age override arrogance."

Knowing what she would have done in the same situation, she winced. "How bad was it?"

"Let's just say when three sisters gang up on you, no matter how big or arrogant you try to be, they can bloody your nose pretty good."

"Did you learn your lesson?"

"I tried to tone it down a bit. But I still checked the guys out." He shrugged. "They're my sisters."

"And you're a good guy."

"Sometimes." He lowered his mouth over hers. "Sometimes not."

With a groan, she gave herself up to the incredible taste and texture of his kiss. How many times had she dreamed of this? Fantasized about how he would taste, how he would feel? The fantasy had nothing on reality.

She wanted to feel his body against hers, she wanted him inside her, loving her. She wanted to love him the way she'd always dreamed.

He raised his head. "I need to go lock up. Be back in a few minutes."

The second he disappeared through the door, she was out of bed and stripping off her clothes as she headed to the bathroom. She hadn't showered today, hadn't washed her hair in days. Could she do all of that and be back in bed before he returned? She didn't know, but she was going to try.

She quickly brushed her teeth and then jumped into the shower. Hot water sluiced down her body as she reached for the shampoo bottle. A noise behind her had her turning. Liam stood in the doorway of the shower. Completely nude, his eyes gleaming with heat, and a sexy smile on his face, he said, "Mind if I join you?"

Breathless, her heartbeat double-timing, she held out her hand in invitation. He was beautiful. With broad shoulders, a slight sprinkling of dark hair on his chest, hard abs, and long muscular legs, Liam Stryker exuded male perfection.

Aubrey was suddenly self-conscious. She was far from perfect. She rarely thought about her scars. They had been part of her for so long, and she had survived the ordeal. But now, with Liam, she wanted to be beautiful for him, to be as perfect to him as he was to her.

As if unaware of her hesitancy, Liam walked purposely toward her. Cupping her face, he set his mouth on hers and gently, thoroughly devoured her lips. Moaning her approval, Aubrey gave him everything in that kiss—her love, desire, need, and devotion.

He lifted his mouth from hers and spoke softly, emphatically, "You are, without a doubt, the most beautiful creature in the universe."

Tears filled her eyes at the complete adoration in his expression. He believed that—he really believed that. Fear and anxiety evaporated into wisps of nothingness. This was the man she had loved for twelve years. Liam Stryker, her Lion, was her soul mate. They had become one long before this intimacy they were about to experience. He was hers, she was his.

Fully confident in her beauty and his love, she forgot everything but how very much she adored this man. And how long she had been waiting for this moment.

LIAM GENTLY TURNED AUBREY AROUND. "I'll take care of your hair." He grabbed her shampoo and squirted a quarter-sized amount of liquid onto his palm. Inhaling deeply, he smiled at the scent. The mystery of why her hair always smelled like peaches was solved. Lathering the mass of thick, golden strands in his hands, he rubbed her scalp, careful of the sore spot on the side of her head from the car crash. When she moaned her delight and leaned against him, he figured he was doing it right.

When he finished, he pulled them both under the pulsing water. Rinsing her hair thoroughly, he then added a dab of conditioner. She turned and looked up at him in wonder. "You're very good at that."

He grinned down at her. "I worked in my mom's salon after school until I joined the Navy. Shampooing and floor sweeping were my specialties."

"I would imagine you were very popular with her clientele."

"Let's just say I probably made more money there in tips than I did my first couple years in the Navy."

He turned the water off and opened the shower door. Stepping out, he snagged a towel from the warming bar and held it out for her. Yeah, he knew she was hesitant. Not only was this new to her, the uncertainty in her expression was easy to read. She thought the scars would bother him. They did, but not in the way she feared. He wished once again that he'd been the one to find the man who'd done this to her and do the very same thing to him. But in no way did her scars do anything but make him love her all the more.

Enveloping her within the warmth of the towel, he thoroughly dried her, and then brought her close, murmuring against her ear, "I love you, Katarina Aubrey Starr."

With that, he picked her up, towel and all, and carried her to the bedroom. Laying her on the bed, he took a few seconds to drink her in. She was lovely, curvy, and luscious.

She held out her arms to him, and he joined her on the bed. Kissing and caressing up and down her body, he paid particular attention to her scars. He refused to pretend they didn't exist. There were eight of them—one on each extremity, two on her abdomen, one on her shoulder, and the last one, possibly the deepest one, was on her left breast.

After he'd kissed each one, he returned to her breast and paid special attention to the scar.

"I know the scars are ugly. I thought about getting plastic surgery, but going back under the knife wasn't something I wanted."

"You see scars, I see badges of courage. What you endured, what you survived….you're one of the strongest, most courageous people I've ever known. Do not, for one moment, think otherwise."

Tears glistened in her eyes. "I love you, Liam. With everything that I am, everything that we are together, I love you."

Lowering his mouth to hers again, he delighted in every sigh, every gasp. He wanted to take away her nightmares, erase all memories of every horror she had endured. When they were both at the shattering peak, Liam rose above her and held still for a moment. He watched her face, looking for any signs of fear or hesitancy. What he saw made his heart turn over. Love, like he'd never known, shone in her eyes.

"You're my everything," he whispered, and with that, Liam slid inside her, making her his own in the most elemental way possible.

She had been his from the beginning. She would be his until his last breath. Together, they were one.

CHAPTER FORTY-THREE

New Port Beach, California
Rudolph Ulrich's Estate

Bringing a killer inside one of his homes wasn't something Rudolph took lightly. However, things were getting dire and he needed the privacy. No one here would talk, as his servants were eternally loyal. Tying him to any murder would never happen. Conducting the meeting here would ensure complete privacy and anonymity. That didn't negate the fact that the man before him had killed dozens of people. He had to tread carefully, but he also wanted to get his point across.

Rudolph put as much anger as he dared into his accusation. "I don't have to tell you how disappointing the outcome of your last job was."

"Disappointing?" The killer raised an arrogant brow. "I made the kill. That's what you hired me to do."

"You were hired to take both of them out. You failed."

"Hey, it's not my fault Starr survived the wreck. The other one died. It was a good, clean kill."

"How is it a good kill if your target is still alive?"

A dangerous light entered the man's eyes, and Rudolph swallowed hard. Perhaps he was being a little unfair. The other man was right. One of them had been killed.

"I still don't understand why you couldn't take out Syd Green. My solution worked perfectly."

"You know that's not my type of kill. It had no creativity, no panache." He shrugged and added, "Poison is so blasé."

Hard to believe this man could say those words with a straight face, but he knew the guy actually believed them. He had known from the beginning that retaining the acclaimed killer Promethean might cause problems. He was proficient in his kills, and that was what was needed. Unfortunately, he liked to be creative. When Ferante had told him the snakes in Lawrence Medford's house had been Promethean's idea, Rudolph had been intrigued. It had definitely worked out well. No one had suspected murder.

He'd contacted Promethean with a couple of job offers. The undetectable bomb on Ferante's yacht had been successful. Authorities had already closed the case, blaming faulty wiring that had likely started a fire that had reached the fuel tank.

If he had learned anything in his life, it was to clean up any mess he made. As he had made Ferante, Rudolph had taken care of him. Problem solved.

Hiring the team to take out the men Ferante had hired to kidnap the child in Iowa had been handled with one easy phone call. Ferante and his twisted perversions were now merely a bad memory.

But there had still been the residuals. When he'd told Promethean he wanted Syd Green dead, too, and offered the way, one would've thought he'd been asked to walk barefoot through glass. The man had looked horrified and had refused point blank.

If ever there was a diva in the assassin world, it was this man.

Syd Green had had to go for many reasons. He had defied orders on numerous occasions, and everyone was tired of his defiance. Taking out his daughter Becca had been Green's final punishment before his death.

Not that it had been difficult to find another killer to do away with Green. Rudolph had plenty of people from which to choose. But still, it had been one more thing about the whole ordeal that he'd wanted over quick and fast. And it had worked perfectly. He'd even had the same man deliver the fake request for Green's immediate cremation. He would definitely put the other killer on top of the list for next time. There had been no dramatics, no excuses. He'd done the job, received payment, and that was that.

There was one last piece of business to handle. Aubrey Starr had to go—there was no choice in the matter. The infuriating filmmaker was one last loose end and then the whole debacle could at last be put to rest. The hit-and-run had been the perfect solution, taking out both Green and Starr. Yet, Starr still lived.

"I still need you to take care of the filmmaker."

"She's in hiding."

"I'll lure her out. You just need to make sure you succeed this time."

The killer glared at him and while Rudolph tried to maintain a hard expression, he was sure fear showed in his eyes. Getting his hands dirty this way turned his stomach. He was in the highest tier, much higher than Green or even Ferante. He should not have to be involved in this kind of low-level planning.

They were punishing him because of Ferante. That much was obvious. And the level of their punishment would only increase if he didn't get this right. For the first time in his long career, he realized how expendable he really was. He'd come too far, done too much, to allow this bump in the road to be his end.

"I'll make the arrangements to bring her back to LA, and I'll let you know where and when. How you get it done is your problem."

Promethean smiled. "It's not a problem...it's my pleasure."

CHAPTER FORTY-FOUR

Montana

Days passed in sublime delight. Aubrey managed to bury the grief and sadness and instead concentrate on the joy in front of her eyes. The miracle she'd been given. The man she'd loved for so long was here with her. With each day that passed, she fell a little deeper in love, and had come to the conclusion that their chance meeting had not been chance at all. They had been brought together for a reason, and though separated for a long while, their reunion was made all the sweeter and stronger for the pain they'd endured.

She delighted in learning the little, everyday things about Liam, and each day she learned something new. He had a penchant for mountain climbing on his days off, liked westerns, both movies and books, hated what he called artsy-fartsy films, preferred his coffee black, his wine red, and his beer ice-cold. He sang in the shower, badly, and he had an addiction to Peanut M&M's. Something she had discovered on their first grocery trip together.

He also had a need to protect the weak and vulnerable. That had been revealed to her when they'd been walking in the snow, and he'd found a half-frozen pygmy owl floundering on the ground. He'd scooped it up in his gloved hands, wrapped it in a warm towel, and called a wildlife expert, who came within the hour and took the bird away with the promise of a full report on its health as soon as possible.

She'd told him about the one and only TV show she'd been in and its short-lived success. Explaining how her shift in focus from acting to creating documentaries had occurred had been easy. If there was anyone who understood why, it was Liam.

When she'd told him about going to the NYC library that day and how heartbroken she'd been until she had somehow inhaled the scent of roses, he'd held her close in comfort. They had lost twelve years of being together, which made their days here and now even more poignant and precious.

They talked endlessly about the silly and the serious, watched movies, tried out their favorite recipes on each other, and made love. She reveled in his seemingly endless passion for her. All her earlier insecurities had disappeared.

She knew Liam would have to return to work soon. While they had enjoyed idyllic days of wonder and nights of passionate delight, the rest of the OZ team were still working. And one of the things they were working hardest on was finding out more about this mysterious organization.

The end of the beautiful days came much sooner than she had anticipated. The morning started perfectly with Liam waking her with a kiss and making slow, sweet love to her. They showered and had just finished breakfast, looking forward to a day of playing in the snow, when the call came.

Her phone lay on the counter a few feet away. Liam grabbed it and handed it to her. "LA number," he said quietly.

Her shoulders went tense, and her heart thudded with

dread. "I'll put it on speaker." Sliding her finger over the answer icon and then the speaker, she said, "Hello?"

"Is this Aubrey?"

"Yes, this is Aubrey. Who's this?"

"Hello, Aubrey. It's Norman Hartley. As you know I was your uncle Syd's attorney. Becca was also my client." He cleared his throat and added, "I'm sorry for your loss."

"Thank you."

"Both Syd and Becca left you a substantial amount of money and property. I was wondering if it would be possible for you to come to LA within the next few days. There are papers to sign and items to review. It would be best to do those things in person."

Aubrey sent Liam a questioning look, and though his face was grim, he nodded.

"I'll see if I can work that into my schedule. Where would I go?"

"I'll text you the details. If you'll let me know what day you'll be here, I'll be sure to set aside a couple of hours to go over the details of their individual estates."

"All right. Thank you."

Her hand shaking, Aubrey ended the call and dropped the phone on the table. She had known this day was coming. Before they'd agreed to the moratorium on talking about what had happened, Liam had told her that at some point they would again try to draw her out.

"This is a ruse, isn't it?"

"Could be legitimate, but I don't doubt for a moment that they'll know the moment you notify Hartley you're coming."

"You think he's in on it?"

"Not necessarily. But who knows? He might be one of their many pawns."

"What now?"

The dangerous glint in his eyes sent a shiver through her. "We take the fight to them."

"How?"

"We'll set a trap. Don't worry. We'll work that out with the OZ team. You don't have to be involved."

"What do you mean?"

"One of the female operatives can take your place."

"That won't work."

"Of course it will. We'll make it work. Eve is about your size and height. We have a makeup artist on retainer who can—"

Aubrey shook her head. "You don't understand. I know Norman Hartley quite well. He was a frequent guest of Uncle Syd's for various get-togethers. He knows exactly what I look like."

She paused a beat and then said, "I'll have to go to the meeting, Liam. I'll need to be the bait."

CHAPTER FORTY-FIVE

Los Angeles, California
Law Offices of Hartley, Sharp, Weeks, and Franklin

Her legs only slightly shaky, Aubrey stood at the reception desk and said in a clear, no-nonsense voice, "I'm here to see Mr. Hartley."

The well-dressed, serious young woman looked up at her. "Your name?"

"Aubrey Starr."

"He's on a conference call at the moment, Ms. Starr. Have a seat, and he'll be with you soon."

"All right. Thank you." Turning, she and her companions made their way to the small, elegant reception area.

"So far," Liam murmured beside her, "typical law office layout and atmosphere. Nothing out of the ordinary."

She knew he was trying to calm her with those low tones that sent warmth and comfort through her bloodstream. He didn't want her here and had made sure anyone within hearing distance knew his opinion. Aubrey had been adamant. If they wanted this to work, she had to be the bait.

Norman Hartley was no dummy. She'd played chess with the man and had even talked to him once about investing in a project. He wouldn't be easily fooled and would know in an instant if a decoy showed up in her place.

She had thought she knew the elderly attorney. She never talked to a potential investor without making sure there were no skeletons in their closet. He had looked squeaky clean to her. But OZ had ways of getting intel that were realms out of her league.

Serena had conducted a deep dive into both Hartley and the law firm. It was one of the top firms in the country and one of the world's leading for wills and mergers and acquisitions.

On paper, Hartley, the senior partner, was about as staid and conventional as the stereotypical attorney could get. He was also enormously wealthy, with a few questionable business interests. Nothing glaringly illegal, Serena had said, but a few unethical practices here and there that could get him disbarred if anyone chose to push the point.

The rest of the law firm, all forty-seven of them, including paralegals, secretaries, and assistants raised no red flags. Liam wasn't buying it, though, and said until they knew different, every one of them was a suspect.

She glanced over at him, and her heart melted. Dressed in a dark blue Armani suit, stark white button-down shirt, and blue silk tie, he was certainly dressed for the part as a successful, well-to-do attorney. However, if that granite jaw of his got any harder, it would shatter. No one looking at him would see him as anything but a threat.

She said softly, "You might want to tone down the glare. You're making the receptionist nervous."

"We're not here to put anyone at ease."

She glanced over at Gideon who sat opposite them, and sighed. Gideon had the same expression on his face. No wonder the receptionist kept switching her gaze between the two of them. It could, however, have to do with the fact that both men were exceedingly handsome.

Tense moments followed as they waited to see what would happen. No one believed this would be what it appeared to be, a review of her uncle's and Becca's wills. There would be an attempt on her life today. How and when were the big questions.

Finally, a lovely young woman appeared in her vision. "Ms. Starr? Mr. Hartley can see you now. Please follow me."

Every muscle strained with tension, Aubrey held her breath as she followed the woman.

This was it.

HATING EVERY PART OF THIS, Liam sat a few feet away from Aubrey as they waited to be called into Hartley's office. Gideon was within easy reach of her. When the threat came, in whatever form, he wanted to meet it head on. Gideon would see to Aubrey. The moment he realized all the arguing in the world was not going to prevent this from happening, he'd pulled Gideon aside, and made it clear that Aubrey was to be the man's number one concern. No matter what happened, she was to be protected at all costs. Liam would handle the rest.

Gideon had just given him one of his mild looks and walked away. He knew he was probably lucky his friend hadn't clocked him. Gideon Wright was one of the most capable, ruthless men he'd ever known. Telling him what needed doing was a little like advising a cobra how to bite.

Everyone at OZ knew what the priority was and didn't need the reminder. He'd done it anyway. By the time this op was over, his fellow OZ operatives would likely want to skin him alive.

When the woman called for Aubrey to follow her, Liam and Gideon were right there with her.

After taking a few steps forward, the woman turned and gave both men a wary look. "Umm. I believe Mr. Hartley is expecting only Ms. Starr."

"These gentlemen are my legal advisors," Aubrey said calmly.

"Of course."

With each step they took down the hallway, Liam watched for threats. Having a killer pop out from behind a door seemed a bit too obvious, but he was putting nothing past these people.

They stopped at a double door and the woman knocked. Hearing a man say, "Enter," she opened it and walked inside.

Liam went in first, followed by Aubrey, then Gideon.

Three anomalies caught Liam's eye. The room was large, holding a conference table that would seat at least twenty-five. No way a senior partner didn't have his own private conference room. Why use this large one?

Secondly, and he thought it might explain the reason for choosing this room, several large windows covered one wall. A couple of them had old-fashioned push-out openings. Call him paranoid, but how easy would it be to shove an unsuspecting person through the window? They were on the twelfth floor—instantaneous death.

The third oddity he observed was Hartley himself. In the photographs Liam had seen, the man was a healthy seventy-year-old with a head full of iron-gray hair. He played golf twice a week and was on a tennis team at his club. Research had also revealed that just over a week ago, he'd spent two weeks in Tahiti. Unless it had rained fourteen days straight, the man should have a tan. But Hartley was sickly pale, and when he stood to greet them, his hands were visibly shaking.

Yeah, the guy knew something was about to go down.

Aubrey and Hartley exchanged friendly pleasantries and then both sat at the table. Gideon sat to Aubrey's right. Liam took a chair a couple of seats away from her. He wanted room to observe and be ready to pounce when needed.

Aubrey seemingly listened intently to every word Hartley spouted. Liam's heart hurt for her. Hearing what her uncle and cousin had left her couldn't be easy. Considering what Green had left her, she would have some decisions to make regarding his many homes and properties.

He wanted this over for her, for them. They had waited twelve years to be together, and since they'd found each other again, danger had stalked her every move. Waking in the morning with Aubrey in his arms and knowing she was completely safe forever was his dream.

"That takes care of the houses and properties," Hartley said. "There are several personal items as well."

"Do we need to review each one?" Aubrey asked.

"Just a few." He sent a quick glance to the cellphone in front of him and added, "I've ordered refreshments."

Hearing the quiver in the man's voice, Liam felt every nerve ending in his body go on alert. He exchanged a quick glance with Gideon and saw the acknowledgment in his eyes. Refreshments meant that another person would be entering the room.

And that person would enter with the intent to kill Aubrey.

THE CART JANGLED with fine china and crystal as it made its way down the hallway toward the conference room. Though his heartbeat rarely rose when he was on a job, he felt a little extra blip for this one. He took pride in every kill. There was no point in doing them if you weren't going to enjoy yourself. Sure, the money was nice, but it was the thrill that caused his adrenaline to surge.

This would be the most elaborate undertaking he'd ever endeavored. Dozens of people would be unknowing pawns in the biggest scene of his life.

As an actor, he loved stretching his creative muscles, and nothing got his blood zooming faster than when he could combine his two passions—role-playing and killing. What a challenge!

The disguise was elaborate and one he wouldn't want to use on a regular basis. Not only was the costume horribly uncomfortable, he didn't want to get the reputation that he would go to these lengths for any old job. This was a special hit, and when he pulled it off, there would be no doubt in anyone's mind that he, Promethean, was the greatest ever.

Now to get the party started.

AUBREY'S MIND buzzed with facts and figures. Her uncle had been a wealthy man, and because his daughter was gone, the bulk of his estate was going to his closest living relative, his niece. She wanted nothing from him. Everything he owned was tainted by the betrayal of his family and his country.

Becca's will had been simple, straightforward, and absolutely heartbreaking. When Hartley had read that Becca had left all her jewelry and clothes to Aubrey, she had wanted to break into hysterical laughter. That sounded like something Becca would do as a prank. Their tastes had been totally different, and she thought her cousin was most likely grinning down from heaven at the joke.

She would donate what she could, and the other things, like Becca's collection of classic old movies and rare first-edition books, she would keep and treasure.

All those things would have to wait until she could think without the veil of sorrow and fear blurring her mind.

At the mention of refreshments, Aubrey went tense, and the entire atmosphere of the room shifted to a crackling awareness. Hartley swallowed nervously several times and shuffled pages in front of him as if he was looking for something. It was as if everyone was holding their breath for the killer to strike.

She heard dishes rattling outside the door, and when a young woman entered the room, Aubrey was a little surprised. This woman didn't look like a threat. She was the same person who'd led them to the conference room. Dressed in a body-skimming dress of royal blue and stiletto heels, she looked as though she should be on a runway in Milan, not in a staid law firm serving tea and cookies.

"Thank you, Angelina," Hartley was saying.

"I'll pour the tea if you like," Angelina said.

"That's not necessary. We can serve ourselves."

Giving everyone a blanket smile, Angelina backed out of the room and shut the door.

Aubrey glanced at the lovely tea set. Was the tea poisoned? Liam suspected her uncle had been killed that way. Maybe the cream or sugar? Or the cookies.

"Tea, Aubrey?" Hartley asked.

"No, thank you," Aubrey said. "I really would like to proceed and get this over with."

"Of course, of course." The lawyer glanced over at Liam and Gideon. "Mr. Thorndike, Mr. Sims, would either of you like refreshments?"

Both Gideon and Liam shook their heads. If Norman Hartley thought it strange that neither of her legal advisors had spoken a word beyond hello since entering the room, he was too polite to say so.

Which was likely why he spilled the tea on the way to his mouth when Liam growled, "You really shouldn't drink that."

Setting the cup back onto the saucer, Hartley frowned at him. "Why is that?"

"Either you really don't know, or the tea isn't poisoned."

"You think I would knowingly drink poisoned tea?"

"You're not going to ask why I would think the tea is poisoned?"

"I'm assuming you believe someone means your client harm." His eyes went hard as diamonds. "Is that right?"

Fascinated, Aubrey watched Norman Hartley transform from the pleasant, slightly boring man to someone she didn't recognize.

He turned to her and said, "You're doomed, my dear."

Shooting up from his chair, Liam strode toward Hartley, and snapped at Gideon, "Get Aubrey out of here." Grabbing hold of Hartley's tie, he jerked him up and snarled, "What do you know, asshole?"

"Only what I'm allowed to know." His smile went sly. "That's how they work, you know. No one knows whom to trust. The tea, as you say, could be poisoned. I stopped worrying about that long ago. Life is entirely too short to wonder if today will be the day they're through with you. When they're ready for you to go, there's no stopping them."

Still holding Hartley by the tie, Liam turned and snarled, "Get her out of here. Now."

Gideon already had a hand on her arm, pulling her up. Aubrey grabbed her purse and took one step toward the door. She jerked in surprise as an ear-piercing alarm split the air.

"It's the fire alarm," Hartley shouted.

Shoving Hartley back into his chair, Liam ran toward Aubrey, who was already being hustled toward the door by Gideon.

"Let's go!"

∾

THE KILLER WAITED. Going in too early would be detrimental to his plan. With doors blocked, people would be running frantically around like crazed ants.

Smoke billowed through the air, and screams bounced against the walls as people ran through the hallways looking for a way out. But there wasn't one. He had taken care of that.

∾

WHILE GIDEON HELD on to Aubrey's hand, Liam led the way down the hallway. The stairway was right around the corner and—

He halted. A large crowd had gathered in front of the stairway door. Several people pounded on it. The door was either locked or blocked. Terror on their faces, a dozen or so turned around and headed the opposite direction in search of another outlet.

Liam pressed his earbud. "Ash, can you hear me?"

"Yeah," Ash answered. "What the hell's going on?"

"We've got a fire up here. Doors are blocked."

"Must be confined to your floor. No alarms have gone off anywhere else. I hear firetruck sirens screaming. We're headed your way."

Liam glanced back at Aubrey, who looked more outraged than scared. He read her perfectly, and he felt the same fury himself. This maniacal killer was willing to take out dozens of people to kill just one.

That wasn't going to happen, not on his watch.

"Hey, the door's open," someone shouted.

The crowd turned as one and began running back to the stairway door. Liam saw Aubrey slip from Gideon's grasp and fall to the floor.

"Aubrey!" he shouted.

A fireman appeared in the middle of the crowd and grabbed Aubrey up. A rush of relief flooded through him. Shoving people out of the way, Liam ran toward her.

As he got closer, something clicked in his mind. Where had the fireman come from? Why was there only one? How had he suddenly appeared within the crowd?

"Gideon? You copy?"

"Yeah. I got pushed back."

"The fireman. He's got Aubrey. I think he's the killer."

"I'm coming, man." He heard Gideon roar, "Move!"

Feeling as though he was fighting upstream against a herd of terrified buffalo, Liam continued to push people aside. A hallway door pushed open, and the fireman stepped inside, Aubrey still in his arms.

Liam surged forward, practically leaping over the heads of two people. He grabbed the fireman before the door could close.

"Not so fast."

A knife slashed toward him. Aubrey screamed and grabbed the man's hand. In a nightmare scene, Liam saw blood bloom on her arm as the knife sliced through her jacket.

Roaring with fury, Liam leaped onto the man and took him to the floor. Grappling the knife from his hand, he managed to spare a glance at the door. Gideon appeared, and Liam yelled, "Get her out of here! I've got this."

He locked eyes with Gideon, and he knew the man understood. They'd had this conversation already, and now the possibility was a reality.

Liam turned back to the man who'd gotten to his feet and

had taken off his breathing helmet. A grin covered the man's face, a face that looked vaguely familiar, though Liam couldn't recall why.

"Guess I'll just have to get the girl another time. But you, I'll take care of now."

Liam dropped his suit jacket to the floor. Yeah, he was more than ready for this.

"Bring it," Liam growled.

CHAPTER FORTY-SIX

Lights, sirens, and people shouting surrounded Aubrey. She sat on a chair someone had pushed her into. While a paramedic cleaned and bandaged her arm, she stared frantically up at the twelfth floor. Where was Liam? They'd left him there to handle the killer on his own. How could they do that? The man had killed so many. How could Liam handle a trained killer?

Tears blurring her vision, she glanced wildly around and spotted Serena running toward her. Aubrey jumped up and then sat back down when the paramedic snapped, "Sit still."

She did as she was told but yelled at Serena as soon as she thought she could hear. "Liam's still in there. We have to get him out. He's in there with a killer."

"He'll be fine."

"No, you don't understand. He's got a knife."

"Have faith," Serena said. "He—"

A loud blast brought their attention back to the building. Fire exploded from the windows of the twelfth floor.

Ignoring the warnings, Aubrey was back on her feet and running toward the building. They'd just left him in there.

He was going to die, and no one was going to save him. She couldn't let that happen. She would not lose him again. She couldn't.

"Aubrey!"

At the entrance of the building, she turned to see who had called her name. Ash was waving a hand toward her. She looked to where he was pointing and saw a man carrying another man over his shoulders. The closer he got, the clearer he became. It was Liam, carrying a man in a fireman's uniform.

Seeming to move in slow motion, Aubrey ran as hard as she could. Two firemen pulled the man off Liam's shoulders. The instant he was free, Aubrey hurled herself at him. He wrapped his arms around her and buried his face against her neck. "I thought I'd lost you."

"And I thought I'd lost you," she sobbed.

"I—"

He wobbled on his feet, and Aubrey pulled away. "Liam?" She glanced at his shirt and realized it was soaked with blood. He had lost all color, and the strangest expression crossed his face a second before he collapsed at her feet.

Ronald Reagan UCLA Medical Center

Surrounded by seven OZ operatives, Aubrey sat in the hospital's small waiting room. How could it be that just over a week ago she'd been in this same place, watching Becca take her last breath and then, only an hour later, seeing Uncle Syd take his?

And now this.

This couldn't be happening. Not now. Not to Liam.

He was in surgery. The knife had nicked his liver, possibly

his intestine. He'd lost a lot of blood. Doctors couldn't believe that he'd walked out of the building on his own, much less that he'd carried a man on his back.

That man was now in the morgue. He'd died on the way to the hospital. Aubrey didn't care about him. His intention had been to kill her. Instead, he might've killed Liam.

No! Her mind silently screamed the word. She had lost almost everyone she loved. She couldn't lose him. *Please God, please.* She couldn't lose him.

"Here, drink this."

Dry-eyed, she looked up at Eve, who for the first time since she'd known her, looked exhausted and worn out.

"I don't think I can drink any more caffeine."

"It's green tea. Decaf. I carry it with me wherever I go. It's good. Will give you some energy. Try it."

Taking the cup, Aubrey sipped and felt the warmth permeate her being. It was good, but nothing was going to make her feel better. Not until the surgeon walked through those doors and told her that Liam was going to be okay. That was the only way she was ever going to be able to function again. Liam had to live.

"Hey."

She looked up to see Serena coming toward her. All the other operatives had been in the waiting room with her, but Serena had been somewhere else.

She dropped down into a chair beside Aubrey. "How you holding up?"

Unable to articulate the agony she was experiencing, she just shook her head.

Wrapping an arm around Aubrey's shoulders, Serena hugged her. "Have faith. You and Liam were brought back together again for a reason. It wasn't for this."

A tendril of hope unfurled within her. Serena was right. There was no logical reason that they should have found each other again. But they had. She had to believe it wasn't just so she could watch him die. They were meant for more than this.

"Thank you."

"I know you're hurting and you're exhausted, but I need you to do me a favor."

"What?"

"I need you to look at the guy who tried to kill you."

"Why?"

Serena held her phone up in front of Aubrey's face. "Because I think you might know him."

Surprised, Aubrey blinked her tired eyes to focus better and stared hard at the photo of a dead man. A man she most definitely recognized.

"Jensen Riggs."

"He's an actor, isn't he?" Serena said.

"Yes. He and Becca dated a few times, but he broke it off when..." Realization came quickly. "That's why she said what she said."

"Who said what?" Eve asked.

"After the accident, before Becca passed out, she said his name. I just assumed it was because she was thinking of him. They had just broken up, and although she said he hadn't meant that much to her, her pride was hurt. She'd just been canned from the movie and—"

Realizing she was rambling, she gave herself a mental shake and refocused. "But maybe she recognized him as the driver of the SUV who ran us off the road. What if she was trying to tell me it was Jensen?"

"Makes sense," Eve said. "The guy was definitely trying to kill you today. And we know you were lured out of hiding. He could've been keeping close to your cousin the whole time just to find out where you were. I'd say he's the likely culprit for all the killings."

"An actor who's also a contract killer?" Serena shook her head. "Nothing about these people should surprise us anymore."

The thought that Becca had been used by a killer hurt her heart. Her cousin hadn't deserved any of this.

Eve and Serena continued to discuss the who and why. Jules and Jazz threw in their own theories. Words surrounded Aubrey, but she zoned out of the conversation. Her entire focus was on Liam.

Was he in pain? She remembered how much a knife stabbing into flesh hurt. That first moment of shock and then the deep, penetrating agony that followed. How had he negotiated twelve floors with a deep knife wound and a man on his back?

It defied reality, but then again, almost everything to do with Liam Stryker defied reasonable explanation. She had once thought that meeting him in that prison in Syria had been pure chance, but she had long since decided that chance had had nothing to do with it. Then seeing him in Kosovo and having no idea who he was because he couldn't speak. It was as if their souls had been given a brief reprieve, but someone had said, *Not yet*.

And then bringing them together one last time through their work?

No, things like that just didn't happen without a reason. Divine intervention was the only explanation. Faith had been a hit-or-miss thing for her over the last few years, but as she looked around her, at the people who knew and loved Liam Stryker the best, she realized they were as mortal as she was. She had no strength to fight an unseen battle, and as strong and mighty as they were, neither did they.

She could only pray and have faith that the one who'd brought them together would see them through. Liam had once told her that she existed for a purpose, and she wouldn't die in that prison. He had been right. But Liam existed for a purpose, too. And it wasn't to die by the hands of an assassin or an evil shadow organization. He had so many things to accomplish. They both did, and they would do them together.

Feeling much more peaceful, Aubrey gathered her remaining strength and prayed as hard as she knew how. Liam was her miracle, and he desperately needed his own miracle.

She wasn't sure how long she sat there, alone and praying, but when she heard the doors to the surgery unit swing open, she was on her feet.

Liam's surgeon walked toward them. Dressed in scrubs, the man had a weary but triumphant look on his face. "He's going to be fine. He'll need to take it easy for a few weeks, but he's in good physical health, so there should be no complications."

"EVERYBODY GOT OUT OF THE BUILDING?" Liam asked. He was lying on the bed, a numb ache in his side that he knew would worsen once the painkiller wore off. He wanted to get as much information as possible before that happened.

"Yes," Ash said. "All accounted for. The fire was contained to the twelfth floor. The only injuries sustained were the normal bumps and bruises of people getting shoved out of the way."

"What about Norman Hartley? Anybody talk to him?"

"Oh yeah, we had an interesting conversation with the man. Said he had no idea what we were talking about. Denied every word."

He wasn't surprised. Plausible deniability seemed to be

the group's favorite way out of trouble. "We have a recording, though. Right?"

"Yes. After hearing it, he finally conceded it was his voice but claimed he was on some kind of medication that made him talk out of his head. Claims to know nothing about this secret organization or the plot to kill Aubrey."

"What about this Jensen Riggs guy? What do you have on him?"

"Not much. He's been an actor a half-dozen years or so. He say anything to you?"

"Oh yeah," Liam grinned. "Quite a lot, in fact." He switched his gaze to Aubrey, who was sitting quietly at his left. Beyond kissing his cheek when she'd first arrived, she hadn't said a word. He needed to give Ash all the intel he had and then concentrate on her. She had been through hell the last few hours.

Turning his attention to Ash again, he said, "The guy knew he was dying. Lost too much blood not to know, but he wanted to make sure he was remembered. His ego wouldn't just let him die without bragging about what he'd done. Walking down twelve flights of stairs gave him plenty of time to spill. He lost consciousness around the third floor, but he was amazingly chatty before he passed out. Remember when Jules said Medford's death sounded like something a killer named Promethean would do?"

"Yes. She said he prided himself on being unique."

"Well, she was right. He was Promethean. He claimed to be responsible for twenty-nine kills."

"Were they all related to this organization?"

"Apparently not. Said his first one for them was Lawrence Medford. Said Ferante hired him for that."

Ash frowned. "So he didn't kill Ferante?"

"Actually, he did. Another man hired him. Apparently,

Ferante bragged about the man's skills. Stupid of him, since Promethean had no loyalty to anyone. When he was contracted to kill Ferante, it was no skin off his nose. It was a job."

"Did he cause the wreck with Becca and Aubrey?" Ash asked.

For the first time, he saw a small glint of interest in Aubrey's eyes. Liam felt a bit of relief. At least he knew she was listening. He'd feared she was in too much shock to be aware of what was going on.

"Yes. He got hired for the movie Becca was working on, and they started dating. He figured she would eventually reveal where Aubrey was. When nothing was working, they arranged for Becca to be fired. Evidently, Riggs knew that Aubrey would be the first person Becca would call."

Aubrey's body jerked at that news. She was still blaming herself for Becca's death, and he was going to make sure she knew she wasn't responsible.

"His plan was to kill both Aubrey and Becca. That's what he'd been contracted to do."

Aubrey raised her head. "Why would the organization want to kill Becca?"

"To punish your uncle. He hadn't been delivering on his promises. They had likely already decided to kill him, too, but killing his daughter beforehand was his punishment."

"And so they killed Syd Green, too?"

Liam shrugged and then winced. Yeah, pain meds were wearing off. He needed to get this done. "Yes. Promethean didn't do it, though. Said it was too common for him. Said someone else was contracted to take out Green."

"Did this Promethean guy or…Riggs, tell you who hired him to kill Ferante and Aubrey?"

"Yes. Rudolph Ulrich."

"Damn." Ash's expletive held both shock and not a little concern. Something Liam thoroughly understood. This was much bigger than a meager senator like Nora Turner or even a famous movie director. The group was not only international; the reason for their existence was even murkier than before.

"Who's Rudolph Ulrich?" Aubrey asked.

"He's the owner of about forty different businesses, all under the umbrella name of Warco." Liam said.

"I've heard of Warco," Aubrey said. "They're huge."

"Yes," Liam said. "And incredibly influential."

"Doesn't Ulrich live in Switzerland?" Ash asked.

"Yeah. Zurich, I think. We've been looking at this group as being only in the US. Even though Ferante lived in Europe, he was a US citizen. Ulrich isn't."

"Just how big is this organization?" Aubrey asked.

"That's the question we'll be asking Ulrich," Ash said as he headed to the door. "I'll get the plane ready for a trip to Switzerland." Before walking out, he sent both of them a searing look. "Get some rest, both of you."

The instant the door shut, Liam scooted over to make space on the bed. "Come over here."

"I don't want to hurt you."

"The only thing that will hurt me is if you don't come over here and let me take that sadness off your face."

She joined him then, lying gingerly next to him. Liam wrapped both arms around her and let his body relax. She was here with him, and she was safe. Right now, nothing else mattered but that.

"Promise you'll never leave me like that again," she whispered.

"I promise," he whispered back.

CHAPTER FORTY-SEVEN

Zurich, Switzerland

Rudolph tried to ignore his shaking hands as he zipped up his last suitcase. They wouldn't touch him, he assured himself. He was one of the most influential men in the world. Just because things hadn't worked out the way they'd requested meant nothing. He had done wondrous things for them. Their agendas were vast and multifaceted. He had accomplished the impossible.

Just in case, he had a plan. A wise man always had a contingency plan, and his wisdom was hard fought, earned through adversity. People looked at him and thought he had it easy. They were wrong. Wealth didn't mean one didn't have problems. It meant only that the problems were bigger.

"Your plane is ready, sir. Would you like me to load your luggage in the car?"

"Yes, Geoffrey. Thank you."

Rudolph Ulrich took one last look at his home. He had several, but this one was his favorite. He would likely never see it again. Just because he didn't think they'd come after him didn't mean they would allow him to continue his current lifestyle. Things would have to change. He told himself that was fine. He had his own island. Had loyal servants who would see to his every need.

Millions of people would envy him. He need never lift a finger again. He was through kowtowing to people who only used him for what they could get out of him.

He was free!

Rudolph stepped out of his bedroom suite and into the hallway. He felt the slightest rush of wind and had barely a second to wonder about its source before massively large hands lifted him from the floor and flung him over the railing of the landing.

As he was on the third floor of his mansion, he saw many of his favorite possessions on his way down. The statue of Venus perfectly positioned in an alcove so when the sun hit the stained-glass window a certain way, Venus appeared to be smiling. A few feet lower, he spotted the Van Gogh hanging not far from the west wing stairway. And just before he reached the bottom, he saw the enormously expensive crystal figurine of an angel. Three people had bid eighteen million euros for the piece, but he'd made the winning bid at twenty and had been enormously proud.

He had no time for regrets, no time to curse the ones responsible. No time to wish he had lived a different life.

With a resounding thud, his body landed on the cold marble tile.

CHAPTER FORTY-EIGHT

Two Weeks Later
Montana

Wearing soft gray sweats, one of Liam's chambray shirts with the sleeves rolled up, and thick wool socks, Aubrey sipped delicious French roast coffee as she gazed out the giant window of their bedroom. Snow-capped mountains, majestic and ancient, as far as the eye could see looked down upon her.

She had to be the most blessed person alive. Liam Stryker, a man of honor, who was gentle, kind, gorgeous, and incredibly courageous, loved her. So much had happened over the last few weeks, her mind had barely been able to grapple with the consequences of one thing when something else had arisen. She had been exhausted in both body and mind.

They had returned to Montana ten days ago. Liam's stay in the hospital had been blessedly uneventful and brief. Upon their return to his home, they'd stayed secluded, cocooned by a white, snowy world on the outside and warmth and contentment within. Liam continued to heal and their love continued to grow deeper and stronger.

The only event to mar their idyllic world was the news that Rudolph Ulrich had been found dead in his home in Zurich. According to news media, Rudolph had tripped over a rug in the hallway and lost his balance. He had somehow tumbled over the railing of his balcony and fallen three floors. He had died instantly.

The world mourned a great business leader, innovator, and philanthropist. A monument was being discussed in Ulrich's hometown. Flags were lowered to half-mast in three different countries to honor the man who had done so much for so many.

And while the world believed Ulrich had died tragically from a common household accident, a select group of people knew the truth. Rudolph Ulrich, while hugely influential and wealthy, had failed to live up to expectations.

Everyone was apparently expendable.

What the man had done and to whom he had answered were still mysteries. Liam had included her in all the research and numerous OZ meetings regarding who the members of this group were. So far, every lead had led to a dead end. It didn't help that all the players they'd known about were now deceased.

How many members were there? No one knew. What was their purpose? What did they want? Power and money, obviously. But what else? What was their end game? Did they have one? No one knew any of those answers, but they were out there, manipulating lives, corporations, and governments.

Liam had told her that OZ would find the answers. Though he was optimistic that the mystery would be solved, he was realistic that it would take time. One thing he assured her was that OZ never gave up.

Today was Liam's first day back at OZ. He didn't antici-pate needing to leave on an op anytime soon, but it could come at any time. And he would need to be ready to roll.

The fact that she had almost lost him and that he was back to putting his life on the line was an issue she tried not to think about. Never would she want him to change, but that didn't take away the worry or concern. Liam Stryker was born to rescue. He had definitely rescued her.

She glanced behind her at the shelf he'd had installed. When they returned from LA, she had been mentally exhausted. Losing two of the people she'd loved most in the world, learning that one had betrayed her, and had almost gotten her killed more than once, and then almost losing Liam had put her in an odd state of numbness.

When he'd opened the door to their bedroom that first night back, a smile had lit up his face. "They're here."

Wondering what he was talking about, she'd peeked inside the room and had been surprised to see a stack of boxes in the corner.

"What's that?" she'd asked.

Liam had dropped onto the bed. His face had been pale and she'd known the trip had exhausted him more than he wanted to admit.

"Grab one of the boxes, bring it over here, and let me watch you open it."

Puzzled, she'd done exactly what he'd asked. She'd grabbed one of the boxes, and as he reclined against a stack of pillows, she'd opened up that first box.

In it had been a doll. A doll just like her father had given her.

"How did you know?" she'd breathed.

"Eve told me that out of everything that was destroyed at your house, losing the dolls hit you the hardest. She knew of a man and woman who restores dolls."

"You mean these are the originals? This is the doll—"
She'd glanced over her shoulder at the stack of boxes, swiftly
noting there were twenty-one of them. The exact number of
dolls her dad had given her. "All of these are the originals?"

"Of course."

She hadn't been able to speak for several seconds. The
fact that he had gone to such lengths for her went well
beyond her ability to express her appreciation. Liam had
understood. Instead of waiting for her to recover, he'd settled
deeper into the pillows and said, "Tell me their stories."

So while he'd rested, she had opened each box and shared
the memory of what year she'd received the doll and what
she remembered about the event. It had been one of the
sweetest moments of her life.

After that, their days and nights had been filled with
laughter, passion, and the sheer joy of being together.

They hadn't talked about the future. Her career was in
limbo. Until she could figure out a way to make her documentaries without putting anyone in danger, she would
work on them by herself.

She had thought she was doing fine. Even her nightmares
had disappeared. But then Liam had done something that
had brought everything to a head.

They'd just come downstairs to prepare breakfast when,
instead of heading to the kitchen, Liam had led her to a
window at the far east corner of the house.

Standing behind her, he'd put his hands on her shoulders
and said, "I think that's a good place for the pool, don't you?"

"Pool?"

"You had one at your home in Florida, and I know you
were on the swim team in high school. We'll figure out a way
to enclose it during the coldest months so you can swim all
year."

Somehow, inexplicably, that had been her breaking point.

Tears had filled her eyes, and she had turned into his arms with an anguished sob.

He hadn't asked why. He had known. She hadn't yet cried over Becca or her uncle. She hadn't yet cried after almost losing Liam. Except for the dolls Liam had had restored for her, she had lost all her possessions and possibly her career. None of those events had broken down her defenses.

Until then.

Tears she had needed to shed for weeks had come forth like a flood from heaven. Even now, when she thought about that day, her eyes grew misty. This time though, the tears weren't from sorrow but from the memory of Liam's tenderness. He had understood where they'd come from, and he had just gently held her and let her cry.

After that, she'd felt a cleansing and freedom she hadn't expected. Whatever happened in the future, she had her Lion, and that was all she needed.

The doorbell rang, bringing her out of her reverie. Wiping the dampness from her face, she went to the door and peered out. She saw footsteps in the snow, but no one was around.

Cautious, she opened the door and found two boxes waiting for her. Since they were addressed to Cat, she knew they were from Liam. Only a select few—her OZ family—knew about that name.

Picking them up, she carried them inside and placed them on the coffee table. The rectangular box was taller and much heavier than the square, flat one.

It didn't occur to her to call Liam. He had sent these to her and obviously intended that she open them without him being here. She opened the card attached to one of the boxes and read it.

I will be twelve years, seven months, and five hours late for our date. See you at six. PS: Open the heavy box first.

Giddy with excitement, she opened the heavy box and pulled out a statue of a lion. It was a replica of Fortitude, one of the lions in front of the New York City Public Library, where they had planned to meet.

A lump the size of Montana in her throat, she turned to the other box, already knowing what it contained. Removing the lid, she peeled away the tissue paper and sighed with delight at the navy blue dress with yellow and white daisies. Just like the one she had described to him that she would be wearing when they met for their date.

Taking the dress from the box, she held it against her body and looked into the mirror on the wall in front of her. Reflected was a pink-cheeked woman with stars in her eyes and a beatific smile on her face. A woman who had a date with the man of her dreams.

MORE NERVOUS THAN he'd been in his life, Liam knocked on his own front door. The boxes were gone, so he knew she'd found them. And since he hadn't heard from her, he figured she'd definitely opened them. What he didn't know was how she had reacted. Or what her response would be for the next part.

The door swung open, and there she stood, dressed in the blue dress with the daisies. Much the way he had imagined her over the years. She'd left her hair down, letting it lie on her shoulders in soft, golden waves. Her face glowed with an inner light, and her lips, the color of the pink roses he held in his hand, were tilted up in a delighted smile.

He took one step inside and then halted in panic.

"What's wrong?" she asked.

He nodded at the floor. "I forgot to send shoes to go with your dress."

Her laughter both joyous and sultry, she took his hand and pulled him inside. "Thick wool socks have become my favorite footwear."

Handing her the bouquet, he said with all truthfulness, "You look beautiful."

"Thank you. I feel beautiful. And you look quite handsome, too."

That was good to know. No one had bought him clothes since he was a teenager, but since he hadn't wanted Aubrey to know what he was going to do, he hadn't been able to take any clothes with him to change into. Rose, bless her, had taken care of that for him. The dark gray suit and light blue shirt were a perfect fit, and the blue tie with tiny yellow and white daisies a whimsical nod to Aubrey's dress.

He glanced over his shoulder and noted she'd placed the lion statue in a prominent place on the mantel. "I see Fortitude arrived safely."

"He certainly did."

His heart thudding with anticipation, he took her hand. "I can't wait any longer." Pulling her with him, they stood in front of the statue together. Removing the ring from his pocket, he held it out to her.

Her fingers shaking slightly, she gingerly touched the antique princess-cut diamond ring. His mother had sent it to him a few days ago with the demand that he bring Aubrey to meet the family as soon as possible. Since he always did what his mama told him to do, he'd already booked a flight for them to Missouri next week.

"It was my grandmother's."

"It's perfect." Raising her head, tears sparkling like diamonds in her eyes, she whispered, "You're perfect."

Liam shook his head. "I'm far from perfect, but I do have a perfect love for you. Aubrey Starr, my beloved Cat, would you do me the great honor of being my wife?"

Her voice husky, she answered, "Liam Stryker, my handsome, courageous Lion, I would be honored to be your wife."

Slipping the ring onto her finger, he pulled her into his arms and kissed her with all the love and deep passion he felt for this precious, wonderful woman.

Although it had taken twelve years to get to this point, all of that was behind them now. His Cat and her Lion were together at last.

∼

THANK YOU

Dear Reader,

Thank you so much for reading Relentless. I sincerely hope you enjoyed Liam and Aubrey's love story. I fell in love with both of them and hope you did, too. If you would be so kind as to leave a review at your favorite review site to help other readers find this book, I would sincerely appreciate it.

Next up in the OZ series is Heartless. I'm only a few pages into the story, but I'm loving all the surprises already!

To learn about my other books and what I'm currently writing, please visit my website at *www.christyreece.com*.

Last Chance, A Last Chance Rescue Novel

Sweet Justice, A Last Chance Rescue Novel

Sweet Revenge, A Last Chance Rescue Novel

Sweet Reward, A Last Chance Rescue Novel

Chances Are, A Last Chance Rescue Novel

WILDEFIRE Series writing as Ella Grace

Midnight Secrets, A Wildefire Novel

Midnight Lies, A Wildefire Novel

Midnight Shadows, A Wildefire Novel

ACKNOWLEDGMENTS

I am beyond blessed to have so many wonderful and supportive people in my life. Writing can be a lonely, solitary endeavor, and I could not do what I do without the following people:

My husband, Jim, who loves and encourages me in ways too numerous to mention. Thank you for the laughter, for bringing me goodies to keep me going, and for handling a million things that I take for granted. You are, and will always be, my one and only beloved.

My beautiful mom, who inspires me everyday.

My incredible and precious fur-babies who bring me smiles and more love than I ever thought possible. I would mention all their names but I would run out of room!

The amazing Joyce Lamb whose copyediting and fabulous advice are always on-point.

Kelly Mann of KAM Designs for your gorgeous cover art.

The Reece's Readers Facebook group, for all your support, encouragement, and wonderful sense of humor.

Anne, my first reader, who always goes above and beyond

in her advice and encouragement, and knows just what to say to keep me going.

My beta readers, Crystal, Hope, Julie, Alison, and Kris, who always offer great suggestions and much-needed encouragement.

To Kara, my last reader, who always finds those things I missed even after reading it a thousand times.

Linda Clarkson of Black Opal Editing, who, as always, did an amazing job of finding those superfluous words that seem to sneak into my writing without me knowing it. So appreciate your eagle eye, Linda.

Special thanks to Hope for your help and assistance in a multitude of things. Thank you for your generous heart and for keeping me on track.

To my all readers, your support means so much to me. I thank you for your patience and encouragement as I continue to learn my way around a new series and brand new characters. I hope you love them as much as I do!

ABOUT THE AUTHOR

Christy Reece is the award winning, NYT Bestselling Author of dark romantic suspense. She lives in Alabama with her husband and a menagerie of pets.

Christy loves hearing from readers and can be contacted at *Christy@ChristyReece.com*.

DISCOVER THE ACTION-FILLED
WORLD OF OPTION ZERO

Beneath a barrage of bullets and destruction, six men defied death and betrayal to form an unbreakable bond of friendship and loyalty. Though the people responsible sought to destroy them, in the end, they only made them stronger.

And like a Phoenix rising from those ashes of destruction, Option Zero was born.

Both hated and respected, OZ works under the cover of anonymity. They have free rein—as long as they don't get caught. If that ever happens, they'll be tried and convicted without help from any government.

Receiving intel from multiple sources throughout the world enables OZ to do things ordinary citizens could never accomplish. But they're living on borrowed time. Many have tried to take them down, and at some point, someone will succeed. It's a price they're willing pay.

The warriors of OZ will stop at nothing to achieve their objectives.

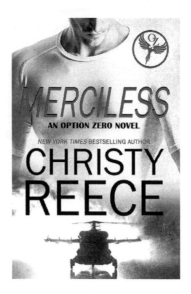

Merciless
Option Zero
Book One

Somewhere between darkness and the dawn lies a truth that could get them killed.

Years ago, Asher Drake lost everything he loved. He had followed the rules, done the right thing, and was repaid with betrayal. Now, as leader of Option Zero, he plays by his own rules and handles things a different way. Ash knows he might not live to see another day, but one thing is certain, he will fight till his last breath for what's right.

Out of dark desperation, Jules Stone became someone else. Having experienced the worst of humanity, she battles her demons by fighting for those who can't fight for themselves. But the shadows linger. When an opportunity arises to pay a debt, Jules accepts the offer, hopeful that the shadows will disappear forever.

Secure in the knowledge that power is the ultimate weapon and truth is only a matter of perception, an enemy watches, waiting for the perfect moment to strike.

Putting aside the pain of the past, Ash and Jules must join forces and fight their demons together before the darkness becomes permanent and destroys them both.

DISCOVER THE MYSTERIOUS WORLD OF GREY JUSTICE

THE GREY JUSTICE GROUP

There's More Than One Path To Justice

Justice isn't always swift or fair, and only those who have felt the pain of denied justice can truly understand its bitter taste. But justice delayed doesn't have to be justice denied. Enter the Grey Justice Group, ordinary citizens swept up in extraordinary circumstances. Led by billionaire philanthropist Grey Justice, this small group of operatives gains justice for victims when other paths have failed.

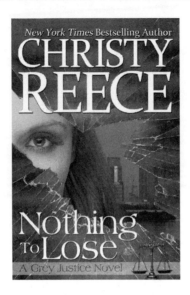

Nothing to Lose
A Grey Justice Novel
Book One

Choices Are Easy When You Have Nothing Left To Lose

Kennedy O'Connell had all the happiness she'd ever dreamed—until someone stole it away. Now on the run for her life, she has a choice to make—disappear forever or make those responsible pay. Her choice is easy.

Two men want to help her, each with their own agenda.

Detective Nick Gallagher is accustomed to pursuing killers within the law. Targeted for death, his life turned inside out, Nick vows to bring down those responsible, no matter the cost. But the beautiful and innocent Kennedy O'Connell brings out every protective instinct. Putting aside his own need for vengeance, he'll do whatever is necessary to keep her safe and help her achieve her goals.

Billionaire philanthropist Grey Justice has a mission, too.

Dubbed the 'White Knight' of those in need of a champion, few people are aware of his dark side. Having seen and experienced injustice—Grey knows its bitter taste. Gaining justice for those who have been wronged is a small price to pay for a man's humanity.

With the help of a surprising accomplice, the three embark on a dangerous game of cat and mouse. The stage is set, the players are ready...the game is on. But someone is playing with another set of rules and survivors are not an option.

DISCOVER THE THRILLING WORLD OF LCR ELITE

A Whole New Level Of Danger

With Last Chance Rescue's philosophy of rescuing the innocent, the Elite branch takes the stakes even higher. Infiltrating the most volatile locations in the world, LCR Elite Operatives risk everything to rescue high value targets. Unsanctioned. Off the grid. Every operation a secret, danger-filled mission. LCR Elite will stop at nothing, no matter the cost, to fulfill their promise.

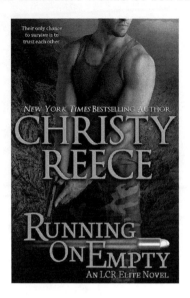

Running On Empty
An LCR Elite Novel
Book One

The Danger Has Only Begun

Having survived a brutal childhood, Sabrina Fox believed she could handle anything. That was before she watched the love of her life die before her very eyes. Brokenhearted, her emotions on lockdown, she finds purpose and hope as an LCR Elite Operative rescuing victims from some of the most volatile places in the world.

Covert ops agent Declan Steele is used to a life of danger and deceit, but when the one person he trusted and believed in above all others sets him up, he'll stop at nothing to make her pay. Finally rescued from his hellish prison, Declan has one priority—hunt down Sabrina Fox and exact his revenge.

Trusting no one is a lonely, perilous path. Sabrina swears she's innocent and Declan must make a decision--trust his heart or his head. As memories of their life together returns, he realizes just how treacherous his torture had been and the target of his revenge shifts. But when Sabrina is taken, retribution is the last thing on his mind. With the assistance of Last Chance Rescue Elite, Declan races to rescue the only woman he has ever loved before it's too late.

Made in the USA
Middletown, DE
04 January 2021

30667427R00224